Francis C. Armstrong

The Young Middy

The perilous adventures of a boy-officer

Francis C. Armstrong

The Young Middy
The perilous adventures of a boy-officer

ISBN/EAN: 9783337339852

Printed in Europe, USA, Canada, Australia, Japan

Cover: Foto ©Andreas Hilbeck / pixelio.de

More available books at **www.hansebooks.com**

BOSTON:

J. E. TILTON AND COMPANY.

1867.

THE YOUNG MIDDY.

CHAPTER I.

FEW who have ever visited Cornwall but must remember the beautiful and romantic bay of Penzance. At the western extremity of England, Penzance enjoys, in general, a mild and equal climate. The great severity of winter is rarely felt, and, if it is, its duration is very short indeed. About a mile from the town, towards the west, and on the gentle and verdant hill that rises from the shores of Mount's Bay, stood, in the year 179–, the handsome mansion of Captain Barlow, a distinguished naval officer. He was not at this period employed, though England had just then commenced her long and sanguinary war with revolutionary France. Captain Barlow's family consisted of his wife and child, his son at this time entering on his seventeenth year. He had already served five years as a midshipman aboard two or three ships; had sailed round the world; visited many lands; had seen and mingled in several actions with piratical craft in the West Indies and on the coast of America; and, during the last year of his service, had distinguished himself greatly, considering his years, in two or three frigate actions; but, returning to England, his father, who had succeeded to a very handsome property, wished him to remain at home, being an only son. Too dutiful to think of disobeying a father's wishes, Henry Barlow, who was a remarkably fine, high-spirited boy, handsome, well made, and powerful for his age, remained at home. He was regretted by all his naval companions, for he promised to be an honour to a service England may well be proud of.

That his son, who passionately loved the sea, might still enjoy excursions on his favorite element, Captain Barlow purchased a very handsome cutter yacht of some sixty tons burden, a very fast and beautiful boat, with handsome cabin, and every other accommodation.

An excursion was planned to the Scilly Islands, almost a *terra incognita* to Englishmen, who know a great deal more of the islands in the Pacific or the Archipelago than the Channel Islands.

Henry wrote for his cousin Alfred Hammond to join him in his excursion to the Scilly Islands. Henry Barlow was exceedingly attached to young Hammond. They were at school near Exeter for three years together.

At the same school Henry also formed a sincere friendship for a remarkably high-spirited lad, named Magnus O'More, also, like Henry, destined for the sea. The two boys wished that circumstances would permit their commencing their naval career in the same ship. This did not occur, but they wrote to each other, hoping that they yet might meet, and renew their early friendship. The events of this story will show how strangely that wish was accomplished. Alfred Hammond left school a year before Henry Barlow or Magnus O'More, the death of an uncle, an immensely wealthy West Indian planter, having bequeathed his whole fortune to young Hammond. The two cousins were both fine handsome boys, but widely different in characters, disposition, and habits. But our narrative of singular events will unfold their character, more particularly to our young readers than we, at this period of our story, could do. Myrtle Hill, the name of Captain Barlow's residence, was beautifully situated on the shores of Mount's Bay, within a mile of the town of Penzance. The views its windows commanded were strikingly picturesque and varied. On the west, Mousehole, Newlyn, and the bold promontory that shelters the bay from the western gales; to the eastward, the shores of Marazion, and the bold and romantic rock called St. Michael's Mount.

This singular and at times insulated mount, is crowned by the ruins of a once famous abbey, or place of religious worship.

The mount itself is a remarkably bold, precipitous succession of rocks, a most striking and picturesque object, whether seen from the sea or land; but grandest when its base is lashed by the stormy waves of the broad Atlantic, agitated by heavy south-westerly gales.

The town and harbour of Penzance could not, at the period of our story, boast of a very secure place of refuge for distressed shipping. Its quay, small, ill-built, and inconvenient, was a mere wall, that but indifferently protected the craft within from the fury of the waves without.

The *Ruby* yacht, Captain Barlow's pleasure vessel, was now ready for sea; he only waited for the arrival of a friend of his who was to accompany them, for Alfred Hammond had arrived some days previously.

" Well, cousin Alfred," said young Henry Barlow, entering a drawing-room where his cousin was listlessly reclining on a sofa reading a book, " I see you have nearly finished the story of the Castaways. Now, tell me candidly, how would you like to lead the kind of life described in that book, so prettily got up, and nicely bound ? In the first place," continued Henry, as Alfred leant back on the sofa, with a smile on his handsome, youthful countenance, " there is a most charming, delightful island, said to be abundant in fruits of all kinds, the scenery lovely, and of course the climate delicious. Then the birds of all kinds are so extremely amiable and accommodating in their natures, that they wait till you take them up. You can then feather, roast, and finely dine on them. The fish, in great variety, I find are equally anxious to be caught, in order to afford you a variety of food. In fact this island, like Ireland since the visit of worthy St. Patrick, exists entirely free from all poisonous animals, frogs, toads, &c. ; it's quite a Paradise."

" Well, Harry," returned Alfred, with a listless air, " that's just such a Paradise as I should not like to be an inhabitant of. Now, just fancy for a moment! In the morning I should have to proceed after some of those accommodating fowls ; having taken the innocent biped up, the next process is to kill it, then feather it, then light a fire, and finally sit down and roast it, smoked and burnt, and disagreeable to look at ; nevertheless I must eat it, and this most disagreeable process I should have to undergo every morning before my appetite could be appeased. Then, of course, comes the same interesting process for dinner, varied perhaps by depriving some of the finny tribe of their existence, and so on, day after day. Ah, defend me from such a delectable island! I am obliged to you, Harry ; but pray let me remain as I am. Not being the least romantic, I detest all kinds of adventures ; the very exertion would kill me."

" Upon my word it's almost absurd to hear you, my dear Alfred, talking about exertion killing you ; you appear to dislike all exercise of the body, and give way to, I will not call it idleness, but most certainly it is an inert habit that will grow upon you. Now, only think for a moment, if you were not heir to great wealth, and had positively to exert yourself, why, your life would become miserable."

"But my dear, eloquent, moralizing cousin," said Alfred with a smile, "you seem to forget how differently I would have grown up had such been the case. Now there is no need of bodily exertion, more than necessary for exercise; it's fatiguing and unpleasant. You, of course, do not feel it so, because the four or five years of your life passed as a midshipman, forced you to exert all your faculties of mind and body. You thus acquired a taste for exertion, violent exercise, and excitement; for I remember, in our early school-days, you and our dear light-hearted and spirited companion, Magnus O'More, dearly loved all kinds of wild sports and exploits, and were never easy; whilst even then I loved quietness and ease."

"But, my dear Alfred," returned Henry, laughing heartily, "you are too easy; to listen to you, a fine active lad going on seventeen years of age, talking of ease and quietness, one would fancy you some staid elderly gentleman, whose early days were passed in perpetual turmoil; really, I would wish something could occur to rouse you out of your supineness of disposition."

Alfred Hammond laughed good-humoredly, saying, "You amuse me, dear Harry. Now, I really do think you would like to see me forced to stir my stumps, as you style my legs. Perhaps you would like us to be cast on a desert rock during this voyage, or be taken prisoners by the French, and forced to work, or any other gentle method of rousing me into exertion; depend upon it, if any such catastrophe was to occur, it would kill me."

"Nonsense, Alfred, not a bit of it! it would do you good; it's sheer indolence, and it will, as you grow into years, get such a hold of you that it will poison your existence."

"Ah!" returned Alfred, very quietly stretching himself on a sofa near the bow-window, which commanded a glorious view over the sparkling waters of Mount's Bay, "you are turning fortune-teller, Harry. Now, sit down, and tell me the history of that adventure of yours with the pirates, and explain the device so beautifully executed on the piece of plate presented you by the owners of the *Eliza*—this is a very hot day, quite overpowering."

"I will do no such thing, Alfred; what, encourage your lazy way of spending a glorious day? Reading is very proper and very commendable at times and seasons, and a good book is instructive, and all persons should read; but to lie on a sofa, half asleep, reading stories, and confining yourself whole summer days, is unhealthy and unnatural, and will ruin your constitution."

"Upon my honor," laughed the really good-natured, but truly indolent Alfred Hammond, " you are now going to turn doctor, and prescribe for me. Do you see anything the matter with me, — just feel my pulse? You know my appetite is excellent, and I sleep well."

"Ah!" said Henry. "Yes, you do sleep eighteen hours out of the twenty-four. Ah! I should like to see you keep the Dog's Watch * aboard ship, and that for a month or two; you would then be right glad to pick out a soft plank for a snooze upon."

"What a barbarous, killing life you must have led, my poor Harry," returned Alfred. "Some of these days you must tell me your adventures at sea."

"That I will willingly; but rouse up, and let us go for a cruise in the cutter to St. Michael's Mount, and climb to the castle, sit in the saint's chair, and see the sun go down so gloriously in old ocean."

"St. Michael forbid!" ejaculated Alfred. "What, climb

---

* Four to eight in the morning.

a rock several hundred feet high, to sit upon an angle of a rock to see the sun set? You're mad, Hal! Just look at the thermometer, nearly 80 in the shade, and to talk of climbing a rock! Just sit down here, and I will read you two or three chapters out of this history of St. Michael's Mount. Why, one of my ancestors, a certain Colonel Hammond, in the time of Charles the First, besieged St. Michael's Castle, and reduced it after very hard fighting indeed."

"Which very clearly shows," said Henry Barlow, "that your ancestor, Colonel Hammond, at all events, was not infected with the *dolce far niente* disposition that you are troubled with."

Alfred laughed. "Wait awhile, Harry. We sail in a few days, in your father's beautiful yacht, for those out-of-the-way islands called the Scilly Islands. Now, it is to be hoped that these lumps of rock, which scarcely any one hears of till they come into Cornwall, will be somewhat cooler than this holy headland, now styled Penzance ; and, if so, I faithfully promise you to walk round a whole island. Now, will not that please you, and shew you what I can do when I am roused?

Henry Barlow smiled ; he thought for a moment, and then starting up, said, " Be it so ; you will be forced some of these days to throw off your indolent habits, and the sooner the better. I'm off for a cruise."

" Now, there is not a finer or handsomer lad in Great Britain than cousin Harry," soliloquized Alfred Hammond, looking after his cousin as he left the room ; " but he is infected with a feeling of perpetual motion. He is never easy unless he is out in a breeze of wind, climbing some precipitous rocks, or crossing the country on some man's unruly horse. Well, I am sure this is a much more comfortable mode of passing a hot day." So, opening his book, he continued reading till he fell asleep, which generally occurred with the indolent but kind-hearted Alfred Hammond.

On the 21st of July the *Ruby* yacht left the harbor of Penzance, with a fine steady breeze from the eastward.

The party aboard the yacht consisted of Captain Barlow, and his friend Mr. Pearson, and the two cousins, Henry and Alfred.

At this period the war had been commenced between France and England; but there was very little to be apprehended from French cruisers or privateers, during the short run of scarcely forty miles, from Mount's Bay to the Scilly Islands.

Young Henry Barlow was in his glory.

He was steering the *Ruby* himself, which, under her immense mainsail, and gaff-topsail, was running rapidly out from the land, so as to clear the bold point forming the western headland of the bay.

Alfred Hammond was comfortably reclining on a bench, with a soft cushion on it, which he had brought up from the cabin, and was amusing himself sketching Penzance, and the picturesque object that stretches out into the bay, called St. Michael's Mount, and passing it at the time was a British cruiser, under a cloud of snow-white canvas.

"You pretty and picturesque town of Penzance, Barlow," said Mr. Pearson, looking back at the pleasing scene they were leaving, "is a very ancient place. I believe, in fact, all Cornwall affords remnants, and striking ones, of the past."

"Yes," returned Captain Barlow, "Penzance is an old place," looking, as he spoke, over Alfred's sketch, which was well executed. "You are making the Mount much too high, Alfred," said the Captain. "Indeed, I remark that most artists do so."

"It's high enough as it is, uncle," returned Alfred, rubbing out part of the Mount. "Only fancy Harry wanting me to climb yesterday to the top of one of those towers."

"Yes," returned Captain Barlow, "and it would have done you a great deal of good if you had, Alfred; but mind, you must take no end of excursions when we get to the islands: you will have to exert your activity there, I assure you. But I beg pardon, dear sir," continued the Captain, "for not answering you; Penzance is a very old place."

"Leland describes it as a small place, about a mile from Mousehole; so that it must have been a very insignificant place then, at all events."

"Why, yes, so it must; for the little fishing town of Mousehole is insignificant enough now," put in Alfred, looking back at the busy little cove. "Is there not a legendary story about Penzance, uncle — a kind of prophecy?"

"Yes, there is an old rhyme in the Cornish language that runs thus, said Captain Barlow:

"'Some strangers would land on the rocks of Merlin,
  Who would burn Paul's Church, Penzance, and Newlyn.'"

"Did any thing of the kind happen, sir?" inquired Alfred.

"Well, a party of Spaniards did land near Mousehole in the year 1594 or 1595, and burned down some houses, and the Church of St. Paul's, and Mousehole itself. Starboard a little, Harry," continued Captain Barlow, addressing his son; "you are shaving the head rather close."

"Lot's of water, father: I was here last week fishing, and had nine fathoms of line out."

"Still, it's a bad system, that close shaving, especially when no object is to be gained."

"So it is, papa," returned the lad, putting the helm a starboard. "Young sailors are very fond of it."

"What do you call close shaving, Harry?" said Alfred, shutting up his sketch-book. "I'm beginning to get hungry already."

"Why, close shaving is going as close to an object as you can without touching it."

"Oh, that's it — is it?" returned Alfred; "how far do you count it from Penzance to the islands?"

"Something under forty miles," said Henry; "from the extremity of the land you see, away to the westward, it's about thirty miles."

"If you were standing upon the summit of Land's End, of a fine morning, you could clearly see the islands," said Captain Barlow, —

> "Where the great ocean mingles with the sky,
> Are seen the cloud-like islands gray in mist." *

Before dinner was announced, the yacht was abreast of Longships, a range of dangerous rocks off the Land's End. They all stopped to look upon the noble lighthouse Mr. Smith was then erecting on those dangerous rocks; this gentleman had obtained a grant from the Trinity-house, and his compensation was to be a certain rate on all ships passing the Land's End.

"That will be one of the most useful lighthouses on the coast of England," said Captain Barlow. "Some years ago, I passed a tremendous night off this coast in the *Minerva* frigate; the gale was awful, and the darkness intense. We were lying to under storm staysails; I knew I was not far off these rocks; but what a boon a light would have been that night, for with the dawn we made the rocks out, not two miles off, with a fearful sea foaming over them!"

"It's a terrible life that of a sailor!" said Alfred to Harry; "how did you bear it at all?"

"I gloried in it, Alfred; and I wish," he added in a low voice, "that I was in the navy again."

---

* Sir H. Davy.

"Well, every one to his taste," said Alfred; "I like this kind of sailing, and I never feel sick; but to be cooped up as you were, swinging every night in a horrid hammock, badly fed, and kicked about like a cur dog, and be mast-headed for hours for nothing, I could never have stood it!"

"What a mountain, Alfred, you are making out of a mole-hill! but come along to dinner. If this breeze lasts we shall take our tea in St. Mary's."

It wanted an hour of sunset as the *Ruby* came within a couple of miles of St. Mary's, the largest island of the group; the singular appearance of this strange cluster of islands, rising from the bosom of the deep, attracted the attention and roused the curiosity of all aboard.

"They are not all inhabited, of course," observed Mr. Pearson to Captain Barlow, "for I see some that look like barren rocks."

"Only five or six are inhabited," said the Captain; "the one we are making for, St. Mary's, is the largest; it's full three miles long and over two broad. That with the lofty lighthouse is St. Agnes, and there away to the south-west, where you see the ground-swell breaking on those sunken rocks — there Sir Cloudesly Shovel perished, and the crews of three noble vessels of war."

"Ah!" said Alfred Hammond to Henry, "these islands are very unlike the fanciful islands I was reading of yesterday. I think you would soon get tired of a Robinson Crusoe life on one of those barren-looking rocks. How on earth people live on them I can't think."

"There is," said Captain Barlow, turning to his nephew, "as hardy a race of pilots living here as any in Great Britain, and a very happy, contented, though simple community inhabiting St. Mary's. To be sure, they are shut out from the world; but that island constitutes their home, and I dare say they would not change it for another."

"There are great remains of antiquity, are there not," observed Mr. Pearson.

"Yes," returned the Captain; "the Druids had a temple here; and, besides, there are some very ancient sepulchres."

As they approached, and ran past some high rocks, thousands of sea-fowl rose into the air, actually darkening the sky, and uttering the most piercing and discordant cries. The sea is rarely calm on those rugged rocks, for a perpetual swell from the great Atlantic runs in on them, covering them with foam, and filling the ear with the dull heavy roar of the broken waves.

A gray mist was stealing over the waters as the sun went down in its ocean bed, gradually covering and embracing the whole cluster of islands. The next moment the yacht swung to her anchor in the snug harbor of St. Mary's.

CHAPTER II.

The party in the *Ruby* yacht were to spend eight or ten days in St. Mary's. The first three days were remarkably fine. Captain Barlow, and Mr. Pearson, and the curate of St. Mary's, spent the day in examining the antiquities, and other objects of curiosity.

Henry insisted on his cousin's keeping his promise in walking round the island, which he did, grumbling considerably at the difficulties they encountered. They visited several curious caves and singularly-shaped rocks.

The fourth day the two boys took the yacht's light gig and pulled to St. Agnes — ascended and viewed the lighthouse. Afterwards, leaving the two sailors ashore eating their dinner, Henry, by great persuasion, induced Alfred to pull with him to an island called the Parrot Rock, about a mile, as he thought, from St. Agnes, to have a shot at the sea-parrots.

" Just hail for the men," said Alfred, " it's too hot."

" Nonsense, the pull will do you all the good in the world," said Henry.

" Well, really Harry, I feel perfectly well as it is, without a pull of two miles ; however, he added good-humoredly, if you wish it — come along."

That day and the preceding one were unusually calm as to ground-swell, scarcely a motion disturbed the surface of the water. Still it was not a clear day ; a kind of heat-haze rendered the horizon on all sides indistinct ; the old pilots,

if consulted, would have said there was going to be a change
of weather. The two youths pulled for the rock, which was
much farther than they thought, and began shooting at the
numerous parrots, puffins, and divers, that flew in wheeling
flocks over their heads, or plunged beneath the glassy surface ; so intent were they that they paid no attention to the
haze that had crept up to them on all sides, and suddenly, to
their great surprise, they were enveloped in one of those dense
fogs, none but those who have witnessed them off the Scilly
Islands can have any idea of.

"Hillo! here's a fog in earnest," said Henry, laying
down his gun, and looking round him ; but so dense was the
vapor that they could barely see from one end of the boat
to the other.

"We are in a nice mess!" said Alfred, startled. "You
see how rash it was to leave the island without the sailors!"

"My dear Alfred, I confess it was wrong, because it will
subject you to perhaps a little more fatigue, but otherwise
the men could not save us from the fog. But take your oar,
and let us pull in this direction ; there is neither swell nor
ripple unfortunately, or we should be at no loss to guide ourselves ; but pull for ten minutes, and we will then fire our
guns ; if we are in the direction of St. Agnes they will answer our firing."

Alfred looked uneasy, but Henry, after carefully examining the water, said cheerfully, "Pull away in this direction."
They pulled for about twenty minutes, when a sudden motion in the water caused Henry to pause ; the next instant
the boat struck against a large rock just level with the water.
They were amongst a hundred of sunken rocks, some just peep-
ing above water, others a foot or two under ; as usual
where sunken rocks are, there was a good deal of agitation
on the water. "We are in the wrong direction," said

Harry, vexed; for he saw that Alfred was pale, tired, and frightened.

He fired the guns, and then listened, but no return was made.

"This is terrible, Harry!" said Alfred; "I am not accustomed to the sea, but I am afraid we shall have to pass the night in the boat. It is not far from sunset now, and yet there is no gleam through this horrid vapor."

"It is uncommonly thick," said Harry; "but depend on it, when they see this fog, they will send out boats, with a compass and fire guns; however, we may hit upon the island yet, so let us keep pulling."

Alfred, with a heavy heart, did so, but soon gave up. "I really cannot pull: I have never been used to so much exertion; let us wait till daylight, or some boat comes across us."

"We shall see St. Agnes' light in another hour or two, even in this fog, so close as we must be;" but by this time they had, unknown to themselves, pulled full three miles more away from St Agnes.

"Well, certainly, there is no great use in pulling," said Harry; "for we may be rowing away from our right direction."

He had scarcely said the words than a noise was heard in the air, and in a few minutes a strong breeze sprung up, driving the fog before it, but continuing as thick as ever.

To say which way the wind was was out of the question; Henry thought from the east, and in fact it was. Alfred now got fairly frightened, and had no power to pull an oar, but threw himself on the stern-sheets, upbraiding Harry for his folly and foolhardiness in going without the sailors.

Poor Harry confessed he was wrong — did all he could to console and re-assure his cousin. As to himself, he felt no fear whatever ; the boat was a good safe one, it was summer weather, and he knew, or at least supposed, that his father would put to sea in the yacht, and in the morning they would be overtaken.

But Alfred was inconsolable ; he lost his temper, got sullen and sulky, and refused to even keep the boat from drifting as little as possible.

"Perhaps," said Henry, "this wind may blow us upon one of the islands, no matter which, as long as we get ashore."

But the wind increased to a strong breeze, and the fog did not lessen, and it began to grow dark.

Poor Alfred, unaccustomed to the sea, though a sufficiently brave boy otherwise, lost nerve altogether, and cried bitterly that they would be drowned, for the sea was getting up rapidly. Presently Henry called out, "There! there! is St. Agnes' light!" and true enough, through the fog, was to be seen the lofty light, but in so dim and strange a fashion, that, did you not know there was such a light near, it would be impossible to say what it was.

"Now, Alfred, dear, try and row ; this is a light boat ; surely we can pull her to yonder light."

"I can never pull in this tumble of a sea ; I am not used to row in rough water."

"But try, Alfred ; if I had a pair of sculls, I am sure I could pull her ahead."

But Alfred could do nothing ; he threw himself on the bottom of the boat, and lay fretting himself to death.

Henry, to hinder the sea from wetting his companion, with an oar steered the boat right before the wind. It was now quite dark, and still the light of St. Agnes, dimly gleaming through the fog, was to be seen, when the loud boom of a cannon, in the direction of St. Agnes, pealed over the waters.

"A gun from the *Ruby!*" exclaimed Henry, with a shout of joy. "Cheer up, dear Alfred, I guessed my father would put to sea; just rouse up and let us keep the boat from driving so fast before the breeze; the yacht is sure to catch us, for she will naturally run before the wind and I will fire a gun; they will soon come within hearing."

"I can't row," said Alfred despondingly; "I am sick, and the boat rolls so."

The words were scarcely uttered before Henry cried out, "Holla!" a ship right upon us. The next instant, though he shouted at the top of his voice, the boat was struck violently by a vessel close-hauled. Alfred would undoubtedly have perished had not Henry, foreseeing the shock, seized his jacket with one hand, and, making a desperate effort, grasped the shrouds of the vessel, the boat disappearing under them, Alfred clinging in intense agony with his arms round Henry. Several of the crew of the stranger sprung into the shrouds, having heard Henry's shout, and seen the boat strike the side, and, grasping the boys by the body. hauled them in upon deck.

"Thank God! thank God!" said Henry fervently, as he regained his feet; and, throwing his arms round Alfred, he embraced him with the fondest affection, saying, "Oh, Alfred, how mercifully we have been spared!"

"Who in the world have we here, my lads?" exclaimed a gruff, harsh voice, the owner of it coming forward, several sailors holding up battle lanterns to examine the two boys. "Why, where do you come from, my hearties? did you swim aboard?"

Again the sound of a gun pealed through the air.

"There's a gun again!" said the skipper of the strange vessel; "keep her away a couple of points," he shouted to the helmsman, "and ease off the sheets, my lads."

"Please, sir," said Henry, addressing the speaker, "that gun is from my father's yacht; we have been blown off from St. Agnes' Island; if you will lie to, and fire a gun"——

"Lie to, and fire a gun!" exclaimed the skipper, with a brutal laugh and every second word an oath; "why, what do you take me for — is there any other trifle you would like? Well, if that ain't a cool request! Now, I just wanted a couple of powder monkeys, so hold your tongue you, and go forward, and make yourselves useful, for we want no skulkers aboard the *Fury*."

"And do you think, sir," said Henry indignantly, "that we are to submit to be treated in this manner? Do you know who we are? My father is Captain Barlow, of the Royal Navy."

The skipper of the *Fury* burst into a hoarse laugh. "What do I care for you and the Royal Navy?" said the brutal fellow. "Did I ask you aboard my craft? How am I to know whose are those guns just fired? They may come from a French privateer. No, no; you will not find Paul Driver, of the *Fury* privateer, such a ninny! So, hearken ye, once for all; whilst you are aooard my craft, and eat my grub, you shall work; I'll be hanged if you sha'n't! There, mate, take those youngsters forward, and let me hear no more of them." So saying, the skipper turned round on his heel, and walked aft. Henry Barlow's young blood boiled at this brutal language and treatment. He did not so much care for himself, but he saw Alfred trembling with rage and offended pride, and he knew how little calculated his cousin was to stand or submit to the hard life it was very evident he would be forced to bear, at least for some days. As he stood hesitating, one of the men caught him by the arm, saying, with a kind of blunt good-nature, "Come, come, my lad, don't be after making a tom-fool of yourself. Take an old salt's advice — never play with a tiger till you draw his teeth and cut his claws — it's never safe. Our skipper's an out-and-out real Bengal tiger when roused; better clap your paw on a hot gridiron than on him; wait till to-morrow. Our lieutenant is a good seaman, and a good-natured chap besides, and he has a good hold over our skipper at times. So you speak to him, and may be they will put you aboard some merchant craft or other; but if you stay, you will find our life a jolly sort of one, if you have only as much pluck in you as a calf; and, as I seed your eyes when you faced old Growler, I should say you have."

"But surely, my man," said Alfred, choking with vexation, and in fact almost stupefied at the idea of such treatment, "surely it appears incredible, that any captain of a ship should dare to treat the sons of gentleme " —

"Och, bother; *gintlemen!*" said an Irish sailor, standing near; "oh, be *aisy!* sure we're all *gintlemen* aboard this craft except our skipper, and faix he's the king here. An' sure we had two as fine lads as ever you clapped eyes upon the last trip we made to the coast of France; but a little pill, in the shape of a six-pound shot, took the head off one, and, whilst the other lad was staring with his mouth wide open, at seeing his comrade's head where it oughtn't to be, bedad a musket-ball went into his mouth, and choked him — you had better come below."

"I will stay on deck," said Alfred; the tears of wounded pride running down his cheeks. "I will never be made to herd with savages."

"Savages, do you call us?" said a sailor, with an oath. "Come forward, Bill, and throw the light of your lantern on this youngster, who calls himself a gentleman, and us savages — why, he takes us for niggers!"

The decks of the privateer were crowded with men; some

were laughing, some cutting their jokes upon the two unlucky lads, who had thus so strangely stumbled upon one of the
most brutal and vulgar privateer captains out of any port in
Great Britain.

"Come, my dear Alfred," said Henry soothingly, "we
nearly lost our lives, and God has spared them; a few days
of this rough life will not kill us. To-morrow this brute of
a skipper will be sober, for I am sure he is not so now; he
will repent of his conduct to us. At all events, we shall
have a chance with the lieutenant; let us sit down here to
windward."

"It is your fault," said Alfred, in a tone of bitter reproach, "that I am exposed to this insulting and cruel treatment; your fondness for wild exploits and mad adventures
is likely to be gratified at last; but, be satisfied, this will
kill me!"

Throwing his arm round his cousin's neck, Henry said in
his gentle, loving voice, "Yes, dear Alfred, it is my fault;
I acted thoughtlessly and heedlessly, but who could have for-
seen this result? Forgive me, my cousin, and do not let the
words of that brutal skipper take from me the love of my
early companion and cousin."

"God bless you, Harry!" sobbed the really kind-hearted,
but spoiled boy, touched at hearing Henry taking his harsh
words so calmly and affectionately; "I am very selfish and
weak, so forgive me; but indeed, indeed, I am not able to bear
such rough treatment!"

"Nevertheless, dear Alfred," said Henry Barlow seriously, and pressing his cousin's hand, "we must bear patiently
and meekly whatever it is the will of God to inflict on us;
you are nearly as strong and as tall as I am, you are healthy,
and active if you will; all you will have to do is, to exert
you body and mind, shake off your inertness, and show these

rude but still, I dare say, brave men, that gentlemen can act, and bear adversity like men, and show courage and firmness also; depend on it, they will respect you, I know sailors well."

"Ah! it's all very well for you, Henry; for you have been brought up a sailor, and I have heard you say a midshipman has to bear a great deal of rough usage; but as to me, who never experienced the slightest ill-treatment or ill-nature from any one, to bear the taunts and sneers of a set of privateer's men who are little better than pirates — why, I am no more fit than a girl."

"You underrate yourself and your powers, dear Alfred; I think I know you better than you do yourself. Sit down here; you will be sheltered from this cold wind under the lee of the bulwarks."

Alfred sat down beside a long brass gun, as wretched and miserable in mind and thought as could well be. Henry did not bestow a thought upon himself, his sole wish was to soothe and shelter Alfred; he blamed himself severely for his indiscretion in tempting his cousin into an excursion that had turned out so very unfortunately, and vowed, as he had done so, he would, if necessary, sacrifice himself to save his cousin from hardship and ill-usage. He did not, neither could he, foresee the consequences that were to follow this untoward meeting with the privateer; he suspected a few days' rough usage and that was all, but he fretted to think how much pain and agony their unaccountable disappearance would cause their parents.

None but the watch remained upon the deck of the *Fury*. The tipsy skipper had gone below, and all was silent aboard, save the rush of the strong breeze through the rigging, and the noise of the waves as the sharp bow of the schooner cut them asunder as she drove rapidly through the water.

Henry gazed around him with the eye of a sailor; it was a dark night and a foggy one, but he could perceive that the *Fury* was a very long and beautifully modelled craft on deck. She was remarkably neat and trim in her spars and riggings; he judged her to be about three hundred tons; she carried eight brass guns, eighteen-pounders, and a formidable pivot gun between her masts. The crew, as he afterwards learned, consisted of seventy-five men, including skipper and officers.

"It is lucky," sighed Alfred, "that the weather is warm, or what suffering" —

"But, my dear Alfred, we shall, I fear, be aboard this craft a few days; therefore it will be impossible for you to endure several nights this way, exposed to the weather. To me it is nothing, for I have been accustomed to it."

"Yes," said Alfred, "I shall feel it bitterly; but to go below, amongst those rough, swearing, privateer's men, ten times worse;" and the poor boy hung his head on his breast, tears forcing themselves from his eyes as he thought of his home, and the luxuries he had accustomed himself to. Naturally indolent and fastidious, and weakly indulged by his doating parents; Alfred had every prospect of becoming an indolent, luxurious, and utterly worthless individual. He looked upon the skipper of the *Fury* as a perfect unnatural savage. He made him shudder, and filled his mind with an indescribable terror. Added to this, Alfred was not naturally brave. He was not a coward, for he had, young as he was, a fine mind, and a strong sense of rectitude and principle; but he would at all times rather shun danger than face it.

Henry Barlow exerted himself during the remainder of that night to cheer and console his cousin; but it was in vain, for he gave himself up to complete despondency.

One or two of the men, less rough in their ways than their

comrades, came and spoke to the boys, told them not to make such a fuss about nothing, it was only a cruise of a month or two. It was summer weather, and they would soon come to like a seaman's life, especially aboard a privateer. At all events, to take their skipper quietly, for he was like a fiend when roused.

Henry answered them civilly and thankfully for their advice. He said the sea was nothing new to him, for he had served five years as a midshipman aboard vessels of war, and he liked a sailor's life; but that his cousin was differently reared, and was the only son of a gentleman of very large fortune; that their captain's conduct was perfectly unjustifiable; he had no manner of right to force them to become sailors against their will; still, he was perfectly willing to do the duties of a seaman, if his cousin was spared and civilly treated.

"I tell you what, my lad," said an old weather beaten sailor, "you speaks like a lawyer. I perfectly agree with you as how our skipper's conduct is, as you say, *unjustable*, or some such shore-going word, and it puzzles me. He's a rough one, we all knows; but his roughness to you in perticler is curious. But, take the world as it goes, we are a jolly lot, take us rough and smooth. We eats, drinks, and fights; and fights, drinks, and eats; and always, mind that, sleeps with one eye open. We're privateer's men, but not pirates. So, take an old salt's advice — rough it; it will do you good in the end, though you be gentlemen; and if a stray shot doesn't stop your log, why you will have your share of our prizes, and go ashore when ye likes. So, don't sit moping there! go down below — there's the two boys' berths vacant — and take a snooze when you can."

"Well, Bill," said an Irish seaman, "I never heard you spin sich a long yarn afore; faix, you'd make a fine mimber of Parliament intirely."

"You never knows what you'd make till you're tried," said the old tar. "Now, you may think what you please, but my father intended me to follow his own trade, and that was a pig-drover; but, somehow, the pigs and I could never agree, they went one way and I the other. What became of them I can't say, for I shipped myself as a lad aboard a craft bound to New York, and I never seed my father or the pigs since."

"A dutiful son you were, Bill," said the Irishman. "Now, faix, my ould father had a bit of pride in him, and says he to me, 'Thady, my jewel, I'll make a man of you — I'll make a priest of you.'"

"A priest!" echoed three or four of the crew gathered about the two lads, smoking and chewing tobacco at a furious rate, to the infinite horror and disgust of poor Alfred; for, in 179–, young gentlemen of seventeen did not encourage mustaches, and walk about with a cigar or a Dutch pipe and its appendages dangling from a button-hole.

There did not appear to be much discipline during the night-watch aboard the *Fury;* there were no lights at the mast-head, and only one officer walked the deck aft, also smoking; there appeared to be no precautions taken, notwithstanding the thick fog.

To get rid of the conversation, which seemed to annoy Alfred, Henry wished him to go below, and occupy the berths offered them.

"Better, dear Alfred, make a beginning."

"No!" returned his cousin sharply and bitterly, "I will never lie down in their filthy dens; when daylight comes, and this skipper becomes sober and knows who we are, he will not dare to detain us."

"I hope not," said Henry, "but these privateer skippers are oftentimes very rough customers, but there are exceptions.

I remember when aboard the *Menelaus*, falling in with a splendid yacht-like privateer, of over four hundred tons, and eighteen guns ; she was handsomer than any corvette in the service ; she was commanded by a perfect gentleman, was called the *Lily of Devon*,* and her owner and commander was called Gorman de Lacy ; no king's ship was ever better worked or handled."

Henry thus endeavored, by various little anecdotes of his seafaring life, to beguile the time, and chase from the thoughts of the dejected Alfred the recollection of their unpleasant situation.

---

* The exploits of the *Lily of Devon* will shortly appear before the public in a three-volume work.

CHAPTER III

Towards morning Alfred fell into an uneasy slumber, leaning his head against Henry's shoulder. As to Harry Barlow, he was a strong, hardy boy; he looked aloft, with a feeling of pleasure, upon the well-set sails and taper spars. As the gray dawn broke through the mist, which, as the sun rose, began to disperse, and as the breeze freshened, it vanished like the drawing up of a curtain; and then the bright and glorious sun fell unchecked upon the sparkling waters, and the schooner dashed so swiftly through the white-crested waves, tossing the foam from her sharp bows, that Harry forgot all in the pleasure he experienced, gazing upon a scene he so admired and loved. The watch was changed, men came tumbling up from below; some were washing and scouring the decks, others taking a pull at the braces, and the cook busy with his coppers. All became life and animation; the two boys were objects of considerable curiosity as they walked the deck, Alfred looking pale and dejected; their handsome persons and fine features, the fine materials of their garments, though consisting of a simple jacket and trousers of blue cloth, very plainly showed that their station in life ought to have insured them civility at least. Some of the men spoke civilly enough to them, and, as they were asleep when they came aboard, they were curious to know how they got there. Henry spoke to them cheerfully, and asked them the name of the schooner, and their captain, and where she hailed from.

They told him that she was named the *Fury*, was fitted out by some Liverpool speculators, and was commanded by Captain Driver; the lieutenant's name was Ross, and the mate's, Higgins; the skipper and mate were both desperate tyrants, and not to be contradicted, but Lieutenant Ross was a brave and good officer.

About eight o'clock in the morning, the skipper and the mate, two old cronies, who both drank hard, swore awfully, and who lived in a perpetual storm of oaths — every second word an imprecation, which we suppress — came upon deck. The skipper had a glass under his arm, with which he scanned the horizon; there were a good number of vessels in sight in all directions, two to the westward were evidently vessels of war.

"Where are those two boys we picked up last night, Higgins?" demanded the captain of the mate. Lieutenant Ross was confined to his berth by a sprained ancle.

"I see them for'ard," said the mate. "What will you do with them useless lumber?"

"I'll make use of them," said the captain, savagely. "I do not forget the name Barlow. One of them is a stout able youngster; put him into Jones's mess, let the other help the cook, he wants a boy."

"Send those boys aft," roared the skipper.

"Go aft, there, my lads," said the old man-of-war's man; "take my advice, do as you are bid, and be civil."

"I will not be ordered by that man," said Alfred, pale with intense vexation, and leaning against the caboose.

"Then, if you don't catch it, youngster," said the old sailor, filling his jaw with a plug of tobacco.

Henry gently begged Alfred to take things quietly. "What can we do, dear Alfred, against the will of this savage? do exert yourself for a few days; depend on it, we shall fall in with some man-of-war, and our case will receive redress at once."

- Seeing the two boys standing by the foremast, Captain Driver, with a flushed face, strode over to them. He was a short, powerful man, about forty; his face strongly pitted by the small-pox, immense dark bushy eyebrows, and a cold cruel gray eye.

"So you wouldn't obey orders?" said the skipper, pausing before Henry, and fixing his eyes savagely on him.

"I received no orders," returned Henry, calmly but firmly; "and, if I had, I can see no reason why I should obey you or any one here. I am quite willing"—

"Stop!" shouted the skipper, clinching his huge hand, "or I'll level you with the deck. Come here, three or four of you," calling to his crew; "take this fellow, and shove him up to the topgallant crosstrees, and lash him there; he shall have eight hours of it for his impudence."

"I can mount to the topgallant crosstrees as well as you, or any other one aboard," said Henry, with a flush of indignation on his handsome features; "but I tell you to your face, you're a cowardly ruffian, and if there's law or justice in England, you shall suffer for this. I'm an officer's son, and not to be insulted by vulgar abuse, such as your's."

Captain Driver clenched his hand, and was making a rush at Henry, who never stirred an inch; but Alfred rushed between them, saying —

"Indeed, indeed, captain, we will do what you bid us, only do not strike Henry;" but the captain would have struck, nevertheless, had not his hand been seized from behind by a tall, strong, well-looking man, who hobbled across the deck with a stick helping him.

The skipper turned round in a rage, and beheld his lieutenant. "Come, come, Captain Driver, don't give way to passion; you surely can't mean to strike the boy, let his tongue be ever so saucy."

" I think I'm master of this ship, Lieutenant Ross," said the skipper sulkily, still not attempting to renew his attack upon Henry, whether from shame, or a certain power the lieutenant possessed in the ship, and which latter was the case; for though the captain was ostensibly the commander, yet several of the owners insisted on putting a lieutenant in her, as a check to the well-known ferocity of the skipper, who, savage as he was, was extremely successful in privateering.

In answer to the captain's assertion, " I think I'm master of this ship," Lieutenant Ross said: " I would be the last man to dispute your authority, but recollect these two boys are not under your command."

" Command!" growled the captain. " What brought them here? If they eat my grub, sure they shall work."

" We are willing to work for the food we shall consume," said Henry, addressing the lieutenant. " All we want is common civility. You, sir, are a gentleman."

" Come, none of your palaver," interrupted the skipper; " gentlemen, indeed! we don't want gentlemen here."

" Allow me, Captain Driver," said Lieutenant Ross, " to settle this matter, and you will have no cause to grumble."

" Settle it, if you like," growled the skipper, turning away, and joining his mate Higgins, a great surly-looking seaman, about five or six and thirty.

" The sooner," whispered Higgins, " you get that spy Ross out of the ship, the better."

" Let me alone," said the captain; " I'll work them yet."

Lieutenant Ross, who had served in the navy several years, and was third lieutenant of a 32-gun frigate, but left the service from pique, being brought to a court-martial for some very trifling offence, for which he was very severely reprimanded. Seeing no chance of promotion after this, he left the service, and accepted the lieutenancy of the *Fury* privateer, with the promise of being her commander the next cruise. This Captain Driver secretly got information of, and he determined, some way or other, to git rid of his lieutenant, and then make Higgins lieutenant in his place.

Lieutenant Ross heard Henry's account of their being lost in the fog off the Scilly Islands, and then getting aboard the schooner. He stated also who they were, and that he himself had served five years as a midshipman; but that his companion and cousin, Alfred Hammond, was quite new to the sea, delicately reared, an only son, and heir to a large fortune.

" It's too bad," said the lieutenant, " the way you have been treated; but I tell you what I can and will do for you. I will take this young gentleman into my berth, and share my crib with him. You are fond of the sea, and accustomed to it. You shall be a kind of midshipman aboard, and sleep in the steward's berth, till we find an opportunity of restoring you to your parents, or putting you aboard a craft bound home."

Both Alfred and Henry were in raptures with Lieutenant Ross, and expressed their deep gratitude for his kindness, and hoping it would not embroil him with his commander.

" Oh, no," said Lieutenant Ross, " this is not a man-of-war. There are certain reasons why I must bear with Captain Driver, and he with me. We certainly do not pull well together, but we drag along in a kind of fashion."

Henry and Alfred were now in a measure reconciled to their situation; Alfred promising to bear his lot with patience. As to Henry, his activity, and his cheerfulness, and his evident knowledge of a sailor's life, rendered him a favorite with some of the men who were not exactly friends of the skipper or the mate Higgins.

The *Fury* was bound on a cruise to the French coast, off Belleisle ; the British fleet were off Brest, but cruisers were all along the coast of Brittany.

Lieutenant Ross was an extremely mild, gentlemanly man, about eight-and-thirty, rather serious in manner, never swore at the men, but carried on duty in a quiet orderly manner ; there were wild spirits aboard the *Fury*, but the lieutenant was, generally speaking, a favorite. He took a great fancy to Henry, would talk to him of his early life, and seemed to feel his position ; he frequently had both lads of an evening into his berth, and constantly read a chapter from the Bible before parting for the night ; this was a great consolation to the two boys, who were well and religiously trained.

Henry often wondered how Lieutenant Ross, so serious and quiet in manners, could bring himself to associate with such a person as Captain Driver.

" I will give you," said he one evening to the two boys, " as it's a calm and nothing to do, a short sketch of my life ; it will serve to pass away an hour."

Henry and Alfred thanked Lieutenant Ross, and expressed their delight in listening to him.

" My father," began Lieutenant Ross, " was a gentleman of small property, but still sufficient to insure independence and comfort. My mother was from an humble class of life..

" My brother and myself were their only children ; from my earliest years, I perceived I was no favorite with either father or mother, and, as I grew older, I could in no way account for this ; for I certainly showed them as much affection as my brother John, who was younger than I by eighteen months ; we went to a good school in Bridgewater, for my father's little property was in Somersetshire.

"We were about ten and twelve years of age, when we returned to spend the midsummer holidays at home. My brother John was a very wild, passionate boy, caring little what he did; but his mother doated on him; he was very, indeed remarkably handsome, and, though nearly two years younger than myself, fully as tall. One day — alas! it's a day I shall never forget — I was swinging John in a swing we had in the orchard, when I thought, as he urged me to send him higher, that the bough of the tree to which the rope was fast, gave a strange noise. 'It's not safe, John,' said I.

"'Stuff and nonsense!' he returned; 'you're afraid to go high yourself, and you won't swing me; give me a good high one.'

"'Well, indeed,' said I, 'this shall be the last, for the branch may be rotten.' Up went the swing to its height, and then, to my horror, the branch broke, and John, with a frightful cry, came to the ground with violence.

"Our mother heard the cry and ran out, she saw me pale as death bending over John, who was insensible. 'It is you that have done this!' screamed she, frantic with alarm; and thinking John dead, she snatched up a piece of the broken branch and beat me across the face; my father came out, and the servants; John did not move, and I was stupefied, bleeding from the face and eyes from the blows I had received; my father took a stick and beat me till I became insensible. God forgive them, as I do!" said Lieutenant Ross, sadly; "they are no more — father, mother, brother, all gone, and all died without either blessing or forgiving me of a deed I was perfectly innocent of intending.

"My brother recovered, but he became humpbacked and crippled.

"My life was now so utterly wretched, that one night I stole from my bed, dressed myself, put the savings of many

months into my pocket — about twenty-five shillings — and
got out of the window, and left my home forever. I walked
on without a thought of being pursued, for I knew that was
not likely ; I had too often been told to go, and wander over
the earth with the mark of Cain upon my forehead ; and
yet, God knows my heart, I would cheerfully have taken my
brother's deformity if it would have insured my parents'
blessing and love.

"My intention was to get to Bristol, and get a cabin-boy's
berth aboard some of the foreign-bound vessels. When day
broke I got over a hedge, and lay down under a haystack in
a farmyard, and slept two or three hours, and then resumed
my road. The first village I came to I inquired the distance
to Bristol, and was told thirty miles. I bought some bread
and cheese, drank some water from a spring, and then walked
ten more miles, and slept under another stack. It was the
month of June, and the weather was fine. I met one of
those great wagons with their eight huge horses going along
the road, and, feeling my feet sore, I asked the wagoner how
much he would charge for a lift of a few miles. 'Oh, my
boy, I will charge thee nothing ; my horses would no more
feel thee than a fly !' I got in, and lay down on some straw,
and slept four hours, for it was dark as the wagon entered
the great yard of a coach and wagon inn in ———. I
went up to the wagoner to thank him ; he patted me on the
head, saying, as he swung his great lantern round till the
light came on my face, 'Where be ye a-going, my poor boy?
ye be young to be all alone, and no a country lad neither.'

" 'I am going to Bristol,' said I. 'Well, then,' said the
good-natured fellow, ' so be I. You shall come into the
house with I and eat some supper, and ye shall then ride in
my wagon to Bristol.'

" I told the man he was very kind, and that I would go

with him and help him in any way, and that I had over a
pound, and would pay for my supper.

" ' Lord love 'ee, my poor boy, keep your little money ! I
have seven young things myself, and I love 'em all ; so ye
shall stay with I till we reach Bristol.'   And so I did, and
a kinder creature never breathed than that simple-hearted
wagoner.

" The day after arriving in Bristol I went along the quay,
looking at all the ships ; but I wanted to find a ship with
three masts going to foreign parts.   I soon learned to find
them, and aboard I went, and asked if they wanted a boy.
I tried them all ; but they only laughed at me, told me I was
a young runaway, and that my hands were too white and
small to work.

" I began to be afraid no one would have me, or that some
of the captains would take me before a magistrate ; for they
all said I was a runaway from school.   I was a strong,
hearty lad of thirteen, and I saw younger than myself aboard
several vessels.   Well, thought I, it's my clothes.   They
take me for a gentleman's son.   There was one ship I took
a great fancy to ; she was a barque called *The Brothers*.
The captain looked such a nice elderly man, and the mate
was so civil ; he patted me on the head, and took me into his
berth in the round-house on deck.   ' Now, tell the truth,'
said he ; ' you have run away from school, afraid to be
flogged, I supposed?'   ' No, indeed, sir,' said I.   ' Now,
tell me the truth,' said he, ' for I know you are a gentleman's
son ; and our skipper said yesterday that you were a runaway, and that some father or mother were fretting after
you, and that you ought to be taken up and sent home.'

" ' Well,' said I, ' I will tell you the truth,' and I burst
into tears.   I then told him.

" ' My poor little fellow,' said he, soothing me, ' I see it would be better for you to earn your bread honestly than return to your home. I tell you what I will do ; for even if our skipper knew your story, he would not take you, it would not be exactly right. We sail the day after to-morrow. Do you see this place?' showing me a kind of berth under his own, only having a slide to close it up. It was about six feet long, and the mate kept his shore traps in it.

" ' Well,' said he, ' do you think you could live there for a couple of days? To be sure, I can close my own berth up in the day, and then you can stretch your legs by coming out.'

" ' Oh yes !' said I, delighted, and kissing his great, rough, honest hand.

" ' Very good ; you buy three or four loaves and a piece of cheese — I'll give you a bottle of water — and come here to-morrow night, and watch me from the quay ; I will give you a sign when the coast is clear : then run up the plank, and stow yourself away. I'll give you the signal when we're clear of the land, and then you may come out. Don't be afraid of our skipper ; he's as nice an old fellow at sea, as ever lived, and he will give you a berth and something to do in the cabin, and so you will get on to be a sailor ; but it's a rough life at best, my boy.' ' Oh! I love the sea,' said I, delighted, ' I always delight in reading of shipwrecks, and ' —

" ' Avast there, my boy !' said the mate ; ' them 'ere kind of things do very well to read of for landsmen. We sailors never love to hear of wreck. The " Lord keep us from shipwreck " is the sailor's prayer.'

" Well, my young friends," continued Lieutenant Ross, " I did as the good-natured mate desired me, and stowed myself away nicely upon a mattress he put in for me to lie upon. I had bread and cheese, and the mate, Mr. Jenkins, slipped me in slices of beef now and then. He used to lock his door in the day, and I got out and stretched my legs. The ship was under weigh, and I knew by the motion when we got out of the river.

" There must have been a very strong breeze the second day; for I heard it roar through the rigging, and the ship heeled over a little. The third day the mate whispered me through the slide, ' you may come out as soon as you hear the bell give four. Don't be frightened, but walk up to the captain, and beg his pardon for hiding in the ship. Trust to me; I won't be far off.' "

" Now this was a trying scene for a boy of thirteen to go through; but I was not at all a timid or bashful boy. I was resolved to be a sailor; and, as they could not throw me overboard, why, I could stand scolding and abuse pretty well."

" Please to come up, sir," said one of the crew of the *Fury;* " there's a sail on the weather-bow, and she brings a breeze with her."

" Let us go on deck," said Lieutenant Ross. "Our skipper is drunk, I suppose; generally is, he and that fellow Higgins, when there's a calm of several hours."

Henry and Alfred took their caps, and hurried on deck.

CHAPTER IV.

Lieutenant Ross and the two cousins, on coming on deck, perceived that it was no longer calm; a fine breeze from the south-east had sprung up. The vessel seen on the weather-bow was soon made out to be an English bark, which passed within hail.

She was outward bound, and, carrying a press of canvas, was soon at a distance.

The French coast was in sight, so the *Fury* was hove to.

The next day was so perfectly calm that the *Fury* remained nearly stationary. In the evening, Lieutenant Ross resumed his story.

" I now prepared to come forth from my hiding-place. Pushing open the round-house door, I walked out on the deck. At first I was not noticed, till, passing the round-house towards the wheel, I came full before Captain Grantley, who was standing with a telescope in his hand, just before the binnacle."

" ' Hillo ! ' exclaimed Captain Grantley, starting back, and staring at me in utter astonishment. ' Why John, John Jenkins ! ' he called out to the mate, who was, apparently, quite busy coiling a stray rope, ' this is the identical boy that wanted me to take him to sea.'

" I walked up to the captain, and, in a very humble tone, said, ' I hope, sir, you will forgive me hiding aboard your ship; but indeed, indeed, I will work the worth of my food.'

" ' Where did the boy hide, Jenkins? He must have come out of your berth.'

" John Jenkins was inclined to laugh. 'Well,' said the mate, ' I'm glad it's flesh and blood, at all events; for the last two nights I thought, when I turned in, I heard some queer kind of noise, like a snore, and' —

" ' Come, come, John, this won't do,' said the captain, laughing. ' You're not going to get to windward of me in this kind of way. You smuggled him aboard yourself. I saw you had a fancy for the boy. Now, come here, my little fellow,' he continued good-humoredly. ' I'm not angry, for two reasons, — first, there would be no use in being so, and next, it would be cruel to a youngster like you. Now, tell me your name, and why you persist in going to sea.'

" I did so, and the captain seemed pleased. ' Well,' said he, ' I will take care of you; I see you do not leave any parents fretting after you, so my mind's easy, and I ,believe what you tell me. You shall attend on me in the cabin. You can write and cipher, I suppose?'

" ' Oh yes!' said I, joyfully, and thus my first step at sea was gained.

" No better man, as a man and an officer, ever existed than Captain Grantley. I then discovered that he had his wife and daughter aboard; we were bound to Malta, and then for Constantinople. He took his wife and daughter, the latter a very pretty nice child of nine years of age, for the good of their health. He was part owner of *The Brothers.*

" Mrs. Grantley was a very kind, amiable woman, and, when she heard my story, she wanted me merely to attend her, and write, and do other little things in the cabin; but I

was resolved to be a sailor, and the captain and mate thought
it better that I should learn every thing belonging to a sailor's
life.

"I was very happy aboard that ship. The work was
done without swearing or rough words. All seemed to pull
together, as if her name had an influence over her crew.
Captain Grantley kept the Sunday as properly as he could;
he was very particular. His men dressed decently on that
day; as little work was done as could be dispensed with,
and he read prayers to his family, and John Jenkins regu-
larly attended.

"We had a long but very pleasant voyage out; she was a
fine ship, and sailed well, but we had a perpetually foul wind.
We touched at Gibraltar, and I was permitted to go ashore
for a couple of days with Mrs. Grantley and her daughter
Mary.

"The little girl became very fond of me, and I of her.
We reached Malta in six days after leaving Gibraltar, and
then made sail for Constantinople. I felt an intense desire
to see Constantinople. I remembered all I had read about
it, and I fancied in my own mind I should see some of the
stories in the *Arabian Nights* realized.

"Certainly the sail through and from the Dardanelles to
the Golden Horn, can scarcely be surpassed in beauty.
Mrs. Grantley and Mary were in raptures. By this time I
had become very useful aboard. The captain, after leaving
Malta, hurt his right hand, and had to keep it in a sling for
nearly three weeks; I, therefore, kept his book and his
accounts for him; read books with Mary, and taught her
figures.

"Before I reached Malta I could go aloft and lie out on
the yards, and go and furl the topgallant sail. Active and

healthy, and always willing to learn, my dear young friends, soon brings the young hand in at sea.

" We had one or two heavy gales off the African shore before we made the Dardanelles, but suffered no loss ; and, as I said, anchored the 24th of September, before Constantinople. Our admiration of this beautiful and strange city was soon changed on landing at the Seraglio stairs — the heat also ashore was oppressive, and the filth and swarms of dogs was detestable.

" We were three weeks there, during which time Mrs. Grantley and Mary only went twice ashore.

" We discharged, took in our cargo, and, getting a favorable wind, the latter end of the fourth week sailed for England.

" Having cleared the Dardanelles, the prevalence of strong northerly gales kept us very much to the southward. We were, according to the captain's reckoning, some sixty miles from Cape Bona, on the coast of Africa.

" It was a Sunday evening. *The Brothers* was under single-reefed topsails, with topgallant-sails set now and then the last three preceding days, the heavy squalls forcing us constantly to reduce our canvas.

" Sunday evening it became stark calm, the sky dark and lowering, with a heavy, oppressive atmosphere ; a long and singularly quick heave of the sea set in from the African coast, and yet the little wind that rose as the sun went down was from the south-east.

" Captain Grantley said the glass had fallen rapidly ; and John Jenkins had all our light canvas in, the topgallant-mast struck and the boats well secured, for he said we were sure to have it before morning.

" We were very short-handed, for we had five hands in a low fever, and Mrs. Grantley also was poorly. About ten o'clock that night the darkness was positively appalling. I have never seen any thing like it since; you could not see a human figure within a yard of you.

"By midnight there was not a breath of wind: the sultriness terrible. We could not see the sky, for we stood on the deck of *The Brothers* as if a pall was suspended over the ship.

"The vessel rolled heavily too, for she was deep. 'I don't like it,' said John Jenkins to the second mate; 'there's not wind enough to blow a candle out, and there's a hurricane aloft. Rouse up the men to close-reef the topsails!'

"I went up with John Jenkins himself, for we had few hands, as I before remarked, and lay out on the main-yard, and commenced reefing the maintopsail; that done, and the men had gone down, I stopped for a moment, standing upon the main-top, listening to the strange sounds in the air, when the ship was suddenly struck by a whirlwind, of such extraordinary force that she reeled under it till her yards touched the water; a loud report followed, it was the foretop-sail split to ribbons; slap went the main shrouds — I thrust my arms through the netting and held on; the next moment the mainmast, sprung some few days before in a squall, went by the board, and the moment after I was plunged into the boiling and seething sea. My first sensation was that of smothering, but I was unhurt, and quite sensible of my situation; for I continued to keep myself above water on the mast-head, and standing on the immense tops the ship had to her mainmast, though the sea whirled over me in sheets so that I could scarcely breathe; then came a flash of lightning and a peal of thunder, simultaneously, so blinding and deafening that I was stupefied. The next flash, I saw the ship driving before the hurricane dismasted.

"How I retained my hold during the following four hours

of horror, I know not. Providence inspired me with hope
and the nerve to hold on ; to be sure I had myself lashed to
the upright side of the tops, and, except when the sea swept
over me, I stood quite clear of the water.

"Just before, the rain came down in a perfect deluge—
such rain as you never see in our temperate clime ; but wind
and sea fell like magic, and suddenly the sky became rent
asunder, dawn made, the rain ceased, and the rays of a win-
try sun broke through the vast masses of stormy clouds that
drifted away slowly to the south.

"I looked round me with a shudder, but nothing met my
sight but the spars and yards of the dismasted ship ; luckily
the rigging had given way, for had the mast remained fast,
and the ship dragging it through the water at the furious rate
she was driven along by the tempest, I must have perished.

"It was not cold, fortunately, and hope still lingered in my
heart ; but you will confess my fate looked dreary enough.

"It kept calm all the morning, and, the sky clearing from
the north-west, a light breeze sprung up from that quarter,
and I slowly drifted along towards the African coast. Could
I live till the mast reached that shore? No, impossible ; it
was sixty miles off, and I did not drift two miles an hour.

"I thought of good Captain Grantley, of Mrs. Grantley,
and, as my eyes closed in slumber towards sunset, I thought
little Mary Grantley was moistening my lips with water.

"I slept, and woke in the night shivering and thirsty ; I
did not feel hunger then, but, as the day wore on, I felt the
first pangs of want of food. Again the sun went down, and
the wind shifted into the east and south-east, and finally remained south, blowing stronger. I now began to fancy death
would be a relief ; my lips were parched, and I suffered cruel
pains. The next day's sun rose ; this I considered would be
my last. I looked round—oh, joy ! I beheld a sail ; my

head drooped on my breast, and, for the first time, I shed tears.

"The sail was coming up from the south-east, and I soon made her out to be a large ship, carrying royals and studding-sails alow and aloft. I watched her with an eagerness that blinded me; my lips were glued together. Would she pass near? I could make no signal, for I was too weak. Only I had lashed myself in the beginning, I should long before have ceased to exist.

"Presently I saw the great ship quite plainly; she was a vessel of war, under a cloud of canvas; and then, oh joy! I saw her studding-sails taken in; and presently she was so close that I saw numbers of heads over her bulwarks gazing at me.

"My senses then, with the re-action, left me. I recovered as the men in the man-of-war's boat lifted me to carry me into the ship.

"I was put into a berth, and the surgeon visited me; I had slight nourishment given me at first, but, judiciously treated, in three days I was well enough, but weak, and my limbs a little stiff, and subject to cramp. I was aboard the *Rattlesnake*, thirty-six gun frigate, commanded by Captain the Honorable Edward Gordon Ross.

"This coincidence of name was curious, and led to bettering my fortunes. When able, I was asked my name, the name of the ship I was aboard at the time of the accident, &c.

"When quite recovered, I was taken by one of the officers into the cabin, where Captain Ross was, lying on a sofa, having but just recovered from a severe attack of fever. He was a very handsome man, about forty-two or three, with a very sweet expression of countenance.

"'They tell me, my lad,' said he, 'that your name is Ross —Edward Ross?'"

"'Yes, sir,' I replied.

"'Pray,' said he, 'where do you come from?'

"I told him without any reserve who I was, my motives for leaving home, and the kindness I received from Captain Grantley. He seemed struck with my simple tale; and, after a moment, said, 'Are you still inclined, my boy, after this last mishap, to follow the sea?'

"'Oh yes, sir!' I replied, 'that does not alter my views.'

"'Would you like to serve aboard a King's ship?'"

"My face, I suppose, showed my delight, for Captain Ross smiled. 'Well,' said he, 'you are the son of a gentleman, have the same name as myself, and you may be a relation; you shall act as a midshipman aboard this ship, and when I reach England I will get you rated as such.'

"Captain Ross was as good as his word. We reached Plymouth in eleven days, and, finally, I became a midshipman. Captain Ross made inquiries concerning my parents; he learned that my father was dead, and had left his property to my brother John. He advised me to write to my mother, and beg a reconciliation. I did so, but I received a terrible letter of reproach and expressions of bitter hatred, for, as my mother unjustly said, destroying my brother; never to write to her again, or attempt to see her. I showed the letter to Captain Ross; he read it, and threw it in the fire. 'You are,' said he, 'I find, a distant relative of mine. You have done your duty; think no more of the neglect of your mother and brother; study when you can, and trust to your profession for name and fortune.' Two days afterwards I sailed in the *Rattlesnake* for the East Indies, but not with the kind and noble Captain Ross as commander; he retired from the service.

"Thus, my dear boys, ends the second epoch in my life; when we have time, I will tell you the third, and that will bring me lieutenant of this privateer.

"My star," he added, sadly, " has not been a bright one : it was ever clouded — how will it set? Now let us go on deck."

CHAPTER V.

THE crew of the *Fury* were now exceedingly anxious to commence capturing some of the enemy's merchant craft. One morning, when just abreast of Belleisle, they caught sight of a very fine brig standing in for the mouth of the Loire River. Chase was instantly given. The *Fury* was a splendid sailer, and came rapidly up with the supposed merchant brig, when she suddenly hove up in the wind, hoisted the privateer flag, and prepared to receive the *Fury*.

Now privateer against privateer was something like the meeting between King, the highwayman, and Turpin. "What," said King, "Dog bite dog?"

Nevertheless, Captain Driver shortened sail, and the men were called to their posts, and all became ready for a sharp action.

Henry and Alfred had watched the chase with widely different feelings : Henry, with a feeling of excitement — he had a post allotted him — was armed with a pistol and a cutlass.

Alfred's cheek blanched as they approached the French privateer. For the ordinary scenes of life the poor boy was perhaps brave enough, and very likely his courage in his position in life would never be tried. But here was a severe trial of his nerves altogether. Henry watched him with intense anxiety. Even Lieutenant Ross came over, and, touching him on the shoulder, said kindly, "Go below, my dear boy, there is no necessity, neither have we any right to compel you to witness or share in our contest. Pray, go below."

"No, sir!" said the poor boy, though his voice trembled, for his pride was roused. "If you please, I will stand by cousin Henry." A scornful laugh sounded near, and Henry saw the captain looking on with a savage scowl on his purple face.

"I could shoot that man," thought Henry; and then he said to himself, "No, I have allowed a wicked reflection to enter my mind, I will leave him to another hand to punish."

The French privateer first opened fire from her long twelve-pounders. One shot struck the bulwarks of the *Fury*, about four yards from where Henry and Alfred were standing. Alfred was pale as death; but when he observed the splinters knock down several of the men, and lacerate one terribly, he found it impossible to resist the impulse; he turned and rushed below, the mate Higgins shouting, "Come back, you coward!"

Henry stamped with rage as he heard several of the men laugh out loud; but there was no time for thought or reflection, for a furious fire ensued between the two vessels. The crew of the *Fury* worked their guns with skill and vigor; and Captain Driver, a bold and skilful sailor, watching his opportunity to run the *Fury* aboard the brig; and Lieutenant Ross, followed by the boarders, Henry with them, as eager as any, leaped aboard the enemy, and a furious hand-to-hand fight took place, in the midst of which, to Henry's amazement, he beheld Alfred with a cutlass in his hand, and bleeding from some cut near the face.

The privateer, *Heureux*, now surrendered, Captain Driver having rushed aboard with the remainder of the *Fury's* crew, the moment before Lieutenant Ross fell by a blow from a handspike, and one of the Frenchmen rushed at him to finish him, when Alfred raised the pistol he held and fired; as he did so, he dropped the pistol, and stood trembling as he saw the man fall, but he thus saved Lieutenant Ross's life.

"My dear, dear Alfred," said Henry, seizing his hand, with a feeling of delight, "I knew the power was with you to be brave, and that you would show it. Are you hurt?"

"No, no, Henry, there was no courage in my act — pride and shame — no, no, I am a great coward!"

"No, my boy," said Lieutenant Ross, wiping the blood from his face; "you have moral courage, which is worth all the brute valor in the world."

The *Fury* had three men killed, two severely wounded, and eight or nine slightly. The French privateer suffered more than double in killed and wounded. This turned out, after all, a fortunate capture, as the *Heureux* had a valuable booty aboard, besides a considerable sum in specie; but they were forced to abandon the brig, for, in working out from the mouth of the Loire, or rather the channel between Isle Normountiers and the rocks, she grounded, and became so leaky that Captain Driver abandoned her, and got rid of his prisoners by giving them the boats.

Lieutenant Ross was confined to his cabin for some days from a hurt in the leg. The two lads passed a good deal of their time with him. "I intended," said Lieutenant Ross, "if we had brought that brig off, to have sent you to England in her with the second mate, who is rather an inoffensive man and a good sailor. However, another prize or two will send us home."

The following evening he commenced the third epoch of his life, at the request of the two lads, as follows: —

"I shall pass over the six years of my life as a midshipman. On my return to England, I passed my examination with some credit, visited my patron, Captain Ross, who promised me an early appointment. Accordingly, three months afterwards, I received the appointment of third lieutenant to the *Kangaroo*, thirty-two gun frigate, to sail in a month for the West Indies.

" I now went to Bristol to inquire after the fate of *The Brothers*, and was rejoiced to hear that not only had she escaped that terrible night, but was shortly expected home from what was to be her last voyage. I heard Mrs. and Miss Grantley were residing at Clifton, and so I went immediately to see them.

" I cannot describe to you their joy and expressions of pleasure at seeing me, for they supposed I had perished. Miss Grantley quite won upon my heart; though scarcely sixteen she was already a charming young woman; and I confess, when I recollected her former fondness for me when a boy, I was inclined to hope that it would be continued now that I was become a man, and, before I left, I had every reason to hope, in another year or two, that she would not refuse my affection.

" From them I learned that *The Brothers*, when dismasted, drove before the gale for nearly five hours, and, when almost within five miles of the African coast, the storm lulled. The next day they rigged a jury-mast, and, with the change of wind, got off the coast; and finally, after four days' hard work, got into Malta, and then, under a proper jury rig, succeeded in reaching Bristol, after stopping a fortnight in Gibraltar. ' That Captain Grantley fretted terribly at my loss, and so did poor John Jenkins, and indeed,' added Mrs. Grantley, very kindly, ' I could scarcely pacify Mary, who wept incessantly.'

" Taking leave of Mrs. Grantley and Mary, and leaving many kind remembrances for Mr. Grantley and worthy John Jenkins, I set off to join the ship I was appointed to — she was in Portsmouth.

"The *Kangaroo* * was a remarkably handsome frigate of her class, and handsome frigates were rare in the British navy in the year 1782. She was commanded by Captain Henry Scot, an officer whose name was detested by all seamen who had any knowledge of his character; he was the greatest tyrant afloat; a cruel persecutor of both officers and men upon the most trifling occasions — woe betide the seaman who infringed upon the etiquette of the quarter-deck. Before we were a fortnight at sea, the crew were half-frantic with the discipline of the ship. The first lieutenant was, if possible, as great a tyrant as his patron the captain; the second lieutenant was a mild, amiable, and excellent seaman, but detested by the first lieutenant; and, before a month was out, I became a mark for both captain and first lieutenant because I attempted to shield the seamen from unjust punishment.

"Before we reached the West Indies, there were not thirty men aboard the ship but had either felt the cat, or received some sort of punishment. I confess, at this period of my life, I was not of a very patient temper under unjust reproof. We had aboard a young midshipman of the name of Radcliff; he was a sweet, pretty, amiable boy, fair and delicate as a girl, no more fit for the sea than one of his sisters, and he had seven, and two elder brothers. 'My poor boy,' said I to him one day, seeing him shed tears at some cruel words addressed to him by Parker, the first lieutenant, 'what tempted you to take to the sea for a profession?'

"The boy sighed. 'My father has a large family and very small means,' and he hesitated; but, knowing I was very partial to him, he added, 'and, too proud to put his boys to a trade, he had interest with a certain member, and

* The name of this ship and her captain are fictitious, though the principal incident is true.

I was made a midshipman, and my brother an ensign in a
foot regiment.'

" ' Pride is the bane of the human race,' thought I. ' Pride
makes our commander a tyrant.'

" One day it was blowing very fresh indeed, and a terribly
tumbling cross sea. Poor little Radcliff offended the first
lieutenant; he ordered him out to the end of the bowsprit
for four hours : the poor child looked at me with tears in his
eyes, and walked forward. I remonstrated with Mr. Parker,
for the ship plunged so violently into the head seas that I
feared for the boy's life — besides he was ill.

" ' Sir,' said my superior officer, ' you are perpetually interfering with me and my duty; you had better take care,'
and, turning on his heel, he went below.

" I watched the boy anxiously, and an old quartermaster
said to me, ' The poor boy will be washed off, sir; he has
been under water several times.'

" I went for'ard and called him in : he was half dead,
drenched to the skin — for it was piercing cold — and he
shook as if in an ague. We were then cruising off the coast
of North America.

" Captain Scot came on deck. After a moment he looked
over the ship.

" ' Where's that good-for-nothing young Radcliff ?' said
he, turning to me. ' Mr. Parker told me he had sent him
out on the bowsprit.'

" ' I called him in, sir,' I replied ; ' he was nearly washed
off, and he is almost inanimate with cold.'

" Amongst Captain Scot's accomplishments was swearing
— his oaths I shall not repeat. His face grew inflamed with
passion as he said — ' How dare you, sir, call in that young,
good-for-nothing rascal? Send up young Radcliff; he shall
have eight hours instead of four.'

" ' The surgeon says, sir,' I replied, keeping my temper, ' that he is in the ague.'

" ' He lies, then ! ' said the captain furiously. ' I'll have him up here if he dies. I'll give him an ague of another kind.'

" ' Then you will be answerable for his death, Captain Scot,' said I firmly ; ' for he had the ague when ordered out.'

" ' Hold your tongue, sir ! Consider yourself under arrest ; and, if I live to reach the station, I'll break you.'

" ' I shall thank you, Captain Scot, even if you do ; but I defy you ! I have merely stated the truth ; the boy is in a fever,' and, turning round, I quitted the deck.

" The poor boy was actually forced from his berth by orders of this tyrant, but he could not stand, and the surgeon positively asserted it would be his death if ordered out. Determined to wreak his vengeance upon some one, the captain ordered all hands to reef topsails ; the men ran up, and, as they lay out, the captain called out with a fierce oath — ' Lazy rascals ! I'll flog the last man off the mizen-topsail yard ! '

" The men knew quite well that he would do so ; two of them, in their eagerness to escape, being in a bad position, missed their hold, and fell on the quarterdeck — both were killed.

" The captain turned away, saying brutally, ' Throw the lubbers overboard.' *

" The men were horror-struck, and the officers rather staggered. Repeated floggings occurred after this ; in fact, the ship became a perfect Pandemonium.

---

* In Brenton's " Naval History," Vol. II., page 436, our young readers may peruse a similar catastrophe happening aboard the *Hermione ;* the crew afterwards mutinied.

" I remained three days under arrest, and then I resumed my duty ; but a storm was brewing aboard that doomed ship.

" One night I was roused from my slumbers by a tremendous cheering ; I jumped up, and young Radcliff, who was on deck, it being his watch, rushed in to me, saying, ' A mutiny has broken out, sir ; they have disarmed and secured the marines.' Seizing my pistols and sword I rushed to the captain's cabin, where I found him, the first and second lieutenant, the master, the captain of marines, and three or four petty officers — petty tyrants in their way.'

" ' Ah ! ' said Captain Scot, who was pale as death, ' you knew of this, sir ; go, bring the men back to their duty, or you shall be hanged for it ! '

" ' What do you accuse me of, Captain Scot ? ' said I indignantly ; there was no time for more words. We heard the shouts of the men as they came cheering, and shouting, and exclaiming, ' Death to the tyrant and his cronies ! '

" The captain trembled with rage and fear. The doors of the cabin were barricaded ; but the mutineers brought a twelve-pounder into a certain position, and, loading it to the muzzle, fired it through the bulkheads ; a horrible crash ensued — the timber was driven in every direction, and the iron shower stretched the captain, mortally wounded, on the floor of the cabin ; killed the first lieutenant outright, and two petty officers ; I was severely hurt by a splinter ; young Radcliff was the only one in the cabin untouched.

" In rushed a body of the mutineers ; and one, a tall, powerful fellow, who had often been flogged innocently — at least his offences would have passed unheeded by any other commander — rushed at the captain and struck him a tremendous blow over the head with a heavy brass-mounted pistol ; they then seized the wretched man, still alive, dragged him and the body of the first lieutenant by the legs out of the cabin, and, as I afterwards understood, pitched them overboard. I had just perception enough to see and understand what passed; four other officers were killed and thrown overboard.* The surgeon, second lieutenant, two midshipmen, and myself, were spared.

"I lay in my cot several days. I asked Mr. Maxwell, the surgeon, what was doing aboard. 'They are all dead drunk,' said he, 'from morning till night, except the marines; they have thrown all the arms overboard, flooded the powder magazine, and the ship is lying to under her double-reefed topsails.'

"Young Radcliff scarcely left the side of my cot; the frightful scenes upon deck, and the horrible orgies of the half-maddened crew, drove the boy's wits away.

"The frigate, at the time of this horrible mutiny (which, thank God! rarely occurs in the British navy, for there are few such officers as Captain Scot), was in the Gulf of Florida, about fifteen or twenty leagues from the group of islands called the Bahamas.

"These islands were discovered by Columbus, in fact they were the first land descried by that great navigator; but few of them are inhabited, some are mere barren rocks. After six days' hideous drunkenness, the mutineers came to the determination of running the frigate upon one of the Bahama group, the Island of Providence, a Spanish settlement.

"As soon as I was able I went on deck; some of the men were sober and reasonable enough — that is, they evinced no intention of injuring any one else aboard. I implored them not to destroy the frigate, but in this they were fully determined. 'Our lives are all forfeited,' said a topman, 'and

---

* In the case of the British frigate *Hermione*, the mutineers threw the captain, Spigot by name, out of the cabin windows, and barbarously murdered eight of the officers, mangling them horribly. — *Brenton.*

we are sworn to stand by one another. We are quite aware that all would not be hanged, but we shall all pull in the same boat for all that.'

"As the marines had no hand in the cruel treatment that they had received, they did them no injury. They killed those that made them what they were, and they did not repent the act.

"It was quite in vain I argued with them : they offered no violence, left us the cabins to ourselves, but freely indulged in the ship's stores. After this they squared away the yards, and, with a favorable wind, steered direct for the Bahamas. Not a vessel of war did we meet on the passage, and, on the 29th of December, the frigate took the ground with a terrible shock.

"Though it was blowing very fresh there was little or no sea on, as the breeze blew over a group of small islands.

"I was on the deck the next morning, with the second lieutenant and the rest of us, looking anxiously around. The island the frigate was on (now totally dismasted from the shock she received) was a perfectly barren one ; the frigate appeared firmly wedged. In the far distance we could just perceive the highest summits of the Island of Providence, then belonging to the Spaniards. It was somewhere on the Island of Providence that they intended running the frigate ; but most of the men got drunk, and the night, being exceedingly dark, puzzled them. I was on deck at the time, and did all I could to persuade them to let go their anchors, and leave the frigate, and not eternally disgrace themselves by a second crime. Some of the men then began to threaten, and finally, as I told you, they run her right on the rocks.

"Two brigs and a schooner were seen two leagues off the island, but they did not appear to notice us, or alter their course.

"I several times tried to encourage our party to recover the ship, but forty-seven against a hundred and seventeen armed and savage men, deterred them ; and yet I feel persuaded it could have been done during one of their drunken fits.

"During the day the mutineers got the boats out, and stored them with provisions and plunder, all the officers' clothes and money, and a considerable booty besides ; they tried to persuade some of the marines to join them, but the men remained firm.

"Several proposed to fire the frigate — we, upon this, determined to sell our lives dearly ; but some, less vindictive, said, 'Let her alone, the Spaniards will settle her!' So, crowding into their boats, they pushed off with a cheer, and, hoisting sail, steered direct for Providence.

"The men and officers now aboard the frigate amounted to forty-seven. She was half full of water, but plenty of provisions could be got at. Our men were perfectly obedient to control, and the second lieutenant, Mr. Marston, and myself, proposed clearing the deck, getting some of the guns to bear seaward, and hunt for some dry powder and shot, and endeavor to defend the ship from the Spaniards, who would surely come from Providence to plunder her ; to this they all agreed."

CHAPTER VI.

"Our first work was to clear away the wreck of spars and rigging, and this we did readily, and then the deck presented an orderly appearance.

"Fortunately, the mutineers had not completely succeeded in flooding the powder magazine, for we rescued several barrels of dry powder, and an abundance of all kind of shot, round and grape. We felt certain that some English vessels of war would soon make their appearance; for we knew it was in contemplation of the government to retake Providence. We got two twelve-pounders aft, and four of the starboard guns looked well seaward : there was remarkably fine weather, and no sea running; indeed, the frigate was run with such force against the rocks, that, chancing to run in between two ledges, she sat perfectly upright, with water all round her at all times of tide. The island was not more than three miles in circumference, and quite barren.

"The day after the departure of the mutineers two Spanish merchant craft hove to, off the island, and after looking at us for some time, one ventured to send a boat alongside, and asked us if we wished to be taken off the wreck? They seemed surprised at our refusing, but we strongly suspected they intended plunder; so we told them we intended to stay where we were, and were well prepared to resist. The boat returned aboard, and shortly after they made sail.

"The next day, about noon, a very handsome, long, raking schooner made her appearance; this we knew to be an armed craft — she was either a privateer or a pirate.

" She first hoisted English colors; we did the same on a flagstaff we erected. She then replaced it with a Spanish flag, and fired a shot from an eight-pounder, which hulled the frigate. Now this was evidently to try what we could do, and have a guess at our numbers; for we kept below, only a few on deck. She then edged a little nearer and gave us a couple more; having got her comfortably in a position we liked, we suddenly commenced returning the compliment with one long twelve-pounder; and, though we had no gunners aboard, we knocked her main boom and her gaff to splinters: this completely opened her eyes, for she squared away at once, and bore away for Providence.

" ' That fellow has had enough of it,' said Mr. Marston. ' I hope there is no vessel of war in Providence, and we shall do very well, and can beat off those small craft easily; the only thing startling is, those huge rocks before our bows prevent us defending ourselves from an enemy landing on the island on the other side.' We, however, after a little difficulty, got one of our guns to command the approach on that side.

" The next day we had a heavy thunder-storm, afterwards a very heavy gale, with a tremendous sea on the other side of the island; the frigate rocked heavily, but evidently settled herself, for she lay quiet during the night-tide, and the water increased inside.

" The two following days remained quiet; but the next showed us three schooners, and a lateen-rigged craft, coming from the direction of Providence. ' Ah!' said Lieutenant Marston, ' now, my lads, comes the tug of war; stand by for a tough struggle — we will defend the old ship as long as we can.' To this the men assented cheerfully: we had procured plenty of powder, some forty or fifty muskets, taken out of the water and cleaned, were ready, lots of cartridges made ; in fact, we all took a pride in defending the old *Kangaroo* from the enemy ; at the same time we looked anxiously to seaward, hoping to see some friends arrive to our assistance.

" With a fine leading breeze on came the two schooners and the lateen-rigged craft — we recognized one as our former antagonist, the other was a very large schooner indeed ; we were greatly afraid she might have a pivot-gun of long range ; if so, we should be riddled. The lateen-rigged craft was full of men, we could see by our glasses. I hoped none of the *Kangaroo's* former crew would lend their aid to the enemy, and, as we afterwards learned, they did not.

" As they came nearer, we made out those in the lateen craft, a vessel of one hundred and fifty tons, to be soldiers.

" ' You see,' said Lieutenant Marston, ' they intend taking us on the land side ; that lateen is edging away to land the soldiers on the other side of the island ; ' and this was the case. We loaded our single gun heavy on that side with grape and canister ; and those facing the schooners with two shots in each. We had eight active seamen who had often served the guns, though not regular gunners, and these we divided, putting four, and fifteen marines with their muskets, to defend that side. I fancied they did not know that the ship was surrounded with water, which would present an almost insurmountable obstacle to their boarding ; but we soon perceived that they had prepared for this ; for, as the lateen craft anchored on the other side, protected from our guns by a range of rock, we saw that they towed after their boats, which were full of soldiers, four light, broad, and, no doubt, flat-bottomed boats. The two schooners, to divert our attention, began peppering us with their eight and twelve pounders; but the old *Kangaroo* took as many of them into her old hull as they liked, whilst our shot told desperately in their spars and rigging. We so completely crippled one, that she hove off out of shot; the large one, however, being armed with eight twelve-pounders, boldly stood in and gave us a broadside, which ripped our bulwarks pretty considerably, and wounded three of our men slightly with splinters.

"We then gave him our four altogether, and were so fortunate as to knock his mainmast's head to splinters, and bring down all his top gear; for this schooner carried topsails on her main-topmast. This broadside sent him off to repair damages. In the mean time, full one hundred and twenty men were advancing over the rocks, carrying the four skiffs between them, and sheltering themselves as well as they could; at last we were able to get our gun to bear on them —they either expected or feared this, for they divided into four parties. We, however, let drive a shower of grape at the nearest; this astonished them, and two dropped, and several threw themselves flat amid the rocks, whilst the other three parties made a run for the high rocks, about sixty yards from us, and from whence they could command the decks of the frigate.

"However, we gave them such doses of grape and musketry that they fairly dropped the boats and made a rush for the high rocks — we afterwards learned, they lost nine men in getting to a place of safety; but it was now our turn to feel and to face the brunt of war. From between the rocks they commenced a desperate fire down upon the decks of the frigate, with their muskets, although we peppered the face of the rocks with our grape, so that a mole, if he showed his nose, would have been hit; but they kept down, and, poking their muskets between the crevices, they killed two of our men and wounded six at the same time; while the two schooners, having repaired damages, again approached and opened fire upon us.

"We could no longer keep the deck to work the guns against the schooners; and, to make matters worse, we saw several smaller craft coming up from Providence, no doubt to lend a hand in the contest.

"The Spaniards now kept up from the rocks such an incessant fire that we were, unless resolved to sacrifice life uselessly, forced to go below, upon which the enemy gave a loud shout of triumph; but the frigate was not gained yet, for, to get aboard, they must either swim or go back for their boats.

"The schooners still kept up their fire, and hulled the old ship repeatedly; but, finding we did not reply, they ceased, and waited, we supposed, for some signs of surrender — but we gave none. The firing from the rocks also ceased. We bound up our wounded, eleven in all, five unable to do any thing more. We could watch the proceedings of those on the rocks. Some twenty or thirty ventured out, and on them we opened fire from our muskets, thrust out through our ventilators in the ship's hold, they took to their heels immediately back to the rocks; and then we reposed ourselves, ate our dinner, and a glass of grog served round — for, thanks to haste and drunkenness, a good many things escaped the mutineers.

"During all this time the wind from the sea came in fresh, with a heavy surf on the sea side of the island; and presently, just an hour before sunset, a gun from the lateen craft no doubt announced to the soldiers that they must be quick and re-embark.

"Presently we saw them stealing off for the boats, dividing into parties. We had no desire to sacrifice life, now that the attack was abandoned. We watched them embarking, which they did with great difficulty, leaving their few flat-
5

bottomed skiffs behind them. There was a gale brewing; so, as soon as all were embarked, the three crafts made sail, and we soon lost sight of them in the distance.

"We congratulated each other after their departure, and determined to go ashore and destroy all but one of the boats, and see if they left their killed and wounded behind. The whole of the night it blew very heavy, and the frigate leaked so rapidly that the water became three feet deep in the cabin, and our guns were dismounted; and, altogether, we felt satisfied we could not make as good a resistance again, as she heeled over considerably to starboard, and the spray of the sea flew over her deck, and made us pass a very uncomfortable night.

"We could not swim ashore the next day owing to the surf; but the gale fell in the evening, and, the following day, we beheld four sail in the offing: these we watched anxiously, for they were large ships. We hoisted our colors on our flagstaff, and waited to make them out with our glasses. Before one, P.M., we clearly made them out to be two frigates, a corvette, and a brig, and under British colors.

"They were standing in right for the island, under easy sail, and, when within two miles of us, they all hove their topsails aback, and shortly after two boats pulled in towards us.

"We now congratulated ourselves upon our deliverance. On the boats coming alongside, we learned from the two officers in them, who came on board, that they were about to attack Providence. The officers listened to our account of the mutiny with great astonishment and disgust. The commander of the squadron was Commodore ———. An examination of the frigate was made by order of Captain J———, and it was then pronounced impossible to do any thing with her; her bottom was evidently too much injured, and also her whole frame, for she was an old ship. All the stores we could save were taken out, and some of the guns, and, finally, she was set on fire. We were taken aboard Captain J——'s frigate, and then we sailed for Providence.

" It will be sufficient to say, that the island and chief town, Nassau, surrendered after a sharp conflict; and then a strict search was made for the mutineers of the *Kangaroo*, but only seventeen were taken on the island, the rest had gone over in various vessels, and were landed on the Main.

" The seventeen mutineers were sent in chains to England some short time after, in the ——— frigate, in which Lieutenant Marston and myself, and the others belonging to the *Kangaroo*, also returned.

" A court-martial was held, and we were all examined touching the mutiny and loss of the *Kangaroo*. The mutineers were all condemned to be hung, but only four suffered; the rest were banished to our penal settlements. We officers were all, of course, acquitted respecting the mutiny and loss of the ill-fated frigate; but in the late Captain Scot's books, memorandums, &c., he had mentioned my name, censuring my conduct, and accusing me of tampering with the men, and disobeying the orders of the first lieutenant.

" For this I was most unjustly censured and reprimanded; in vain I brought forward the testimony of the second lieutenant, the surgeon, and others.

" I felt excessively disgusted, knowing I by no means deserved this public disapprobation of my conduct — as the solitary instance of my interference was in the case of the young midshipman. I therefore retired from the service.

" I now made some inquiry after my family. My brother was alive, married, and had two sons. Again I tried to be reconciled, but in vain. I then proceeded to Bristol, and was joyfully welcomed by my dear Mary and her kind-hearted parents. Mr. Grantley told me he quite approved of my retiring from the service — told me not to feel annoyed: I should have his daughter Mary if I had not a sixpence in the world; and, very shortly afterwards, we were married, and I was truly happy and blessed in the affection of a most amiable woman.

" My father-in-law soon after got me the command of a fine ship, he himself retiring from an active life. In her I made several very successful voyages, when again misfortunes pressed upon me. My father-in-law lost all his savings by the failure of two mercantile houses and a bank; this so affected the old man's heart that he died the following year, and dear Mrs. Grantley two years afterwards. At this time my dear Mary was the mother of two children. I then sailed for the West Indies, and, after a couple of years, I had hopes of providing for my little family, when the war broke out, and I was captured on the way home, but released by a privateer — a very fine and heavily armed ship — that put us ashore with all the crew upon one of the islands, from whence we made our way with heavy hearts to Old England.

" Alas, my trials were not over! In giving birth to her fourth child, I lost my beloved Mary; her loss nearly unmanned me. I gave myself up to a torpor of grief; but the endearments of my poor bereaved children recalled me to a sense of my duty. I then accepted the berth of lieutenant aboard this privateer; on the promise of being her commander the next cruise, and also that Captain Driver was only to exercise a limited control over me. You now, my dear young friends, have listened to the third epoch of my eventful and somewhat sad life, during which I have to thank Providence for some years of unalloyed happiness whilst my lamented Mary lived. Still, you will acknowledge that my life has been a checkered one."

" In truth, my dear sir," said Henry, " it has ; and I trust the happiness you will enjoy with your dear children for the future, will repay you for the sufferings you endured in the loss of their mother."

" I hope, Lieutenant Ross," said Alfred earnestly, " *if it* pleases God that we shall all get ashore out of this privateer, that you will permit me to keep up an intercourse with you and your family. I shall inherit much more wealth than I can well know what to do with, and "— Alfred colored to the temples ; he knew not how to continue, for he feared he might wound the feelings of their protector.

But Lieutenant Ross took his hand, saying, with a look and tone of gratified affection —

" Your heart, my dear boy, is at all events in the right place, and I thank you. If you reach your native soil, and it should be my lot to fall in any coming strife, tell my beloved children that their father's last thoughts were fixed on them, and their never-forgotten parent."

CHAPTER VII.

"A sail, ho!" was sung out from the fore-topmast cross-trees of the *Fury* privateer, one fine morning shortly after the events of the preceding chapter. The privateer was then off Rochelle; two frigates with British colors flying had passed within musket-shot the day before, and Lieutenant Ross had a fierce altercation with Captain Driver about signalling one of them, and putting the boys aboard. But Captain Driver got into a furious passion, swore no man should handle a signal except by his orders; and, finally, Henry stepped up and said that they were content to stay where they were till the schooner returned to England.

"Yes," returned the skipper, with a frightful torrent of oaths, "I'll take care you shall; but I trust your brains will be blown out before that."

"There is something more in this unnatural animosity of Captain Driver to you, Henry," said Lieutenant Ross, "than we know of — it is quite incomprehensible."

The sail soon turned out to be a large schooner standing in for the land, probably making for Rochelle. Preparations were made for cutting her off, but, when within shot, the schooner opened fire from a pivot-gun heavier than the *Fury's*, which knocked away her jib-boom. Captain Driver swore furiously, and a smart running fight took place; but the French privateer schooner sailed remarkably well till a shot from the *Fury* brought down her main gaff; at the same moment a round shot from her struck the *Fury's* boom, knocking it to smash, killing one man, and, to Henry and Alfred's horror and grief, felling Lieutenant Ross to the deck. They rushed to his side, but he was insensible, and was carried below instantly.

The *Fury* then wore round and gave up the chase, the captain and mate exchanging looks of horrid satisfaction. Anxious and trembling for the safety of the kind-hearted lieutenant, Henry and Alfred were proceeding to his cabin, when Captain Driver, who had just swallowed a large potation of pure brandy, came up, followed by Higgins.

"Where are you going?" fiercely exclaimed the skipper, putting his hand on Henry's shoulder; "and you, you cowardly lubber," growled the mate, pushing back Alfred — "you shall now go to the cook and clean his coppers, you are fit for nothing else."

Alfred staggered back with the push the mate gave him; whilst Henry, boiling with indignation, shook off the skipper's grasp, saying — "You will one day or other pay for this outrage upon us. My cousin is no coward; your valor comes from drink."

Furious with rage and drink, Captain Driver, with a terrible look, drew a pistol from his belt, and presented it against the unshrinking boy's head.

"No, no," said the mate, seizing his arm, "this will not do; the men are looking on — let him alone," and then he whispered some words in the skipper's ear.

"Young reptile!" said the skipper, gazing at Henry as if his look could crush him, "I've not done with you yet. You wonder, no doubt, why I hate you; and, before we part, you shall know why. Come here, Peters," he said to one of the men — "come up; stand at that cabin door, and, hark ye — if either of these boys attempt to pass you, shoot them!" he then walked forward.

"I do not think," said Alfred to Henry, pressing his hand affectionately, "that there ever were two such brutes as the master and mate of this vile craft."

"Yes," said Henry, "there was another—that Captain Scot of whom poor Ross told us; but, my dear cousin, summon all your courage and energy; for I now foresee, if poor Lieutenant Ross dies—and I fear he will—we shall be made to suffer cruel persecution."

Alfred's cheek was pale, but he said, firmly enough, "For your sake, dear Harry, I will bear it. If our kind friend dies, and it pleases God to restore us to our homes, I will seek his children: they shall never want for any thing whilst I have it; but God spare him to them. Oh! why did he come out in this frightful craft?"

"No doubt," said Henry, "for the purpose of accumulating a fund for the future support of his children."

"It appears incomprehensible," observed Alfred, "that, with the very best intentions, and with an honest upright mind, as Lieutenant Ross always appears to have had, his life should have been so checkered by misfortune; and now, alas! the three epochs of his life close, I fear, in death."

"Those whom God loves he chasteneth—but I trust he will not die; it would be better to be prisoners to the French than live under this inhuman skipper's orders."

"I fear, dear Henry," said Alfred, "that he will do you some mischief."

"Not he, the savage! You see he has a motive, as he says, for his brutality. Nevertheless, he will not dare to commit an act that would hang him."

That night poor Lieutenant Ross died; he never recovered his senses. He was buried, alas! with no other ceremony than the body sewn in a hammock, and sunk beneath the wave, where many a brave heart has rested, and where many more will find a grave. The two cousins were deeply moved as the body splashed into the sparkling waters, and sunk, drawn down by the round-shot sewn up in the hammock. No form of prayer was uttered, or thought of, by the reckless crew of wild spirits clustered round. But, from the hearts and lips of the two lonely lads, a fervent and heartfelt prayer ascended to the throne of grace.

From that moment the lives of the two boys were made as wretched as the brutality of the skipper and his new lieutenant, Higgins, could make them. Alfred would have sunk under the severities he now experienced, had not Henry, with untiring spirit and energy, supported him. The crew were now under no restraint; they indulged in drink as long as the stores of brandy taken from the *Heureux* lasted.

The two cousins were now forced to eat, drink, and sleep with the crew. Henry had to reef, steer, splice, and do the meanest work; he did it cheerfully to save Alfred, who was evidently sinking under his hardships—he could not go aloft, like Henry, and reef topsails, but, to save himself from the brutality of Higgins, he did all he could.

But the days of the *Fury* were drawing to a close. It was time—for a more brutalized community never existed than the crew of the privateer.

The *Fury* was cruising one morning in sight of the East Penmarks. These numerous little islands, or rather cluster of rocks, lie off the coast of Brittany, and protect the fine Bay of Quiberon from the heavy seas of the Atlantic.

A large merchant schooner, evidently deeply laden, was observed running alongshore. The *Fury* gave chase, and, coming within shot, opened fire with her bow-gun; but the schooner carried on every stitch of canvas packed upon her masts; and, suddenly bracing up sharp, she ran into a deep bay, which Captain Driver called St. Guidaft, but he was mistaken. It was blowing fresh from the eastward; but the water was smooth with that wind, the islands and projecting land breaking the send-in of the sea. The captain of the *Fury* did not know the coast near so well as poor Lieutenant Ross; so now, depending on his own knowledge and the charts, he committed a great error.

The French schooner ran on, and the *Fury* followed, firing continually; and the schooner returning fire from a brass carronade she had aft, which wounded two of the *Fury's* crew.

The captain and mate had been drinking all the morning. The former vowed he would have the schooner, if he was to die for it; but the chase suddenly rounded to close inshore, and let go her anchor, furling her sails at the same time.

"Hurrah, she is ours!" exclaimed the mate, or lieutenant as he called himself; but, as he said the words, a wreath of smoke curled out from the high land behind the schooner at anchor, and a thirty-two-pound shot knocked the maintopmast of the *Fury* over the side; another quickly followed, passing between the masts. In the confusion of thus getting exposed to a heavy battery, the helm was suddenly put down, and the schooner, going rapidly through the water, shot up in the wind, striking with considerable force upon a sandbank, and there sticking fast.

Bang went the thirty-two-pounder from the battery, knocking the fore-topsail yard to splinters.

It was now all up with the *Fury;* she was hard and fast, and the tide ebbing rapidly. A scene of intense confusion, and cursing and swearing, ensued, every one for himself. Luckily, the *Fury* heeled over, with her side exposed to the battery, which in a measure protected the men; the three boats were got out, for another shot hulled the schooner below the water-mark, settling her fate.

Pitching food and water, some muskets, and powder and shot into the boats, the privateer's men crowded into them. "Keep those lubbers out!" roared the skipper, furiously drunk; for the first thing they all did was to drink all they could; but neither Henry nor Alfred showed the least inclination to join them — they preferred captivity to living with such fiends. Just then, Higgins came up from the fore-hatch and jumped into the yawl — "Shove off, and leave these young beggars to the charity of the mounseers, a French prison will tame them."

The boats pushed off under oar and sail, with a cheer of defiance and a volley of oaths.

Scarcely had they left the side of the schooner before they became exposed to the battery, which, now satisfied of having the schooner, turned their two guns upon the boats. The two first shots dashed the water over the nearest boat's stern. Henry and Alfred watched them eagerly; they saw the skipper stand up in the boat he and Higgins were in, and shake his clinched fist in impotent and drunken rage.

The thunder of the gun pealed through the air. "Oh!" exclaimed Alfred, "the boat is struck!" and such was the case, the heavy ball sunk her, and the entire crew were struggling in the waves.

The other two boats did not even stop to pick up the two or three that floated after the accident; for not only were they crowded, but they feared the same fate for themselves.

"Oh, see! what heartless wretches!" said Alfred with a shudder.

"Ah," said Henry, "they have gone where many a brave and better went before them; it's terrible to think of dying thus. Fierce as that captain and his mate were, I could not wish for them such a fate as that."

"What will become of those in the other boats, Harry; they can never expect to reach England in that crowded state, and in such small boats?"

"There are numbers of cruisers outside," said Henry; "very likely they will be picked up by one or other of them — but what smoke is that coming out of the fore-hatch?"

As he spoke a burst of flame rushed up, and then dense volumes of smoke.

"Ah!" exclaimed Henry, "that wretch Higgins has fired the vessel before he left, and there is a lot of gunpowder in the hold." Alfred turned pale, and staggered against the main-mast.

"Do not be alarmed, Alfred," said Henry; "we are nearly dry, the bank shows between us and the shore, and I see lots of boats pulling out. Now, let us swing down by this back-stay," casting the rope loose as he spoke. The flames spread rapidly, catching the rigging and the sails, which remained set just as she ran aground.

The water was only three feet deep under the schooner, so the two boys waded through it till they reached the dry part of the bank, and then they paused to gaze round them.

The *Fury*, by this time, was wrapped in a sheet of flame. Several boats were pulling round the sandbank towards the schooner, but paused when they beheld the flames, fearing she would blow up. The two boys proceeded towards the boats, the men in them shouting to them to come on. Just then the *Fury* blew up with a loud explosion, for she had a large quantity of powder in barrels, taken from a French vessel some days before. Her fore and main mast were driven into the air, and her timbers and planks scattered in all directions; the two cousins narrowly escaped being crushed by a mass of flaming timber.

After a moment's pause, one of the boats pulled in to

where Henry and Alfred stood. Two Frenchmen, in the dress of sailors — they belonged to the schooner the *Fury* had chased — jumped ashore.

"How's this, you *jeunes gens*," said the men, "is it you that set fire to the ship?"

We have said that Henry spoke French fluently and well — so well, indeed, as to surprise Frenchmen themselves — his father using him as his interpreter with prisoners and others aboard his ship.

"I should think not," said Henry in reply; "you scarcely suppose we incurred voluntarily the chance of being blown up?"

"Eh! are you English?" said the man, staring at Henry.

"Oh, yes! there is no mistake in that: but we did not belong to that privateer."

"How's that? what brought you aboard?" inquired the men, several of the others crowding round the youths.

"Ill luck," said Henry; and then in a few words he explained their situation.

"Well, then," continued the man, "jump into the boat: we do not want to leave you to be drowned; but, nevertheless, you will be prisoners."

"That we expected," said Henry.

The other boats had pulled up to the shattered and still blazing hull of the *Fury*; but the one with our young adventurers pulled in for the shore under the battery.

As they landed on the beach, amidst a crowd of men, women, and children, collected from the village near, four artillerymen came forward, one of them saying — "Ah! that was a bad job, Captain Goulet, the blowing-up of our prize; but who have you got there with you?"

Whilst the captain of the French schooner was explaining, a tall, good-natured, and comely dame, with a very strange head-dress, pushed her way close up to the two boys, and, looking them in the face, said, " Eh! what handsome lads: it's a pity to take them to prison, Sergeant Beaulieu."

" Thank you, dame," said Henry smiling, " for your good wishes, at all events."

" *Ça!* how well he speaks the language," said the dame.

" But they look like real aristocrats, and they are English, and as pretty heads as theirs have been put under the guillotine," said one or two fierce-looking fishwomen; " you are half an aristocrat yourself, Dame Moulin."

The dame said something in the worst *patois* of Bretagne, and walked away, whilst the sergeant of artillery said to Henry, " Come, my lads, I must take you to the fort; our commandant will know what to do with you."

" Very well," said Henry; " we will follow you."

" Why, you speak French," said the sergeant, " like a native; does your comrade?"

" A little," said Henry; " is there a prison near here?"

" No, *mon garçon*," said the sergeant; " but I suppose you will be sent on to Vannes, where the prisons are. I am sorry," said the good-natured sergeant, " that two lads, so young as you are, should undergo imprisonment; but it's the fortune of war."

" True!" said Henry, with a sigh, and his thoughts, despite his natural high spirit, reverted to home and England. Alfred walked by his side, resigned, but sad; perhaps — if asked — preferring captivity to the horrid life he had just escaped from.

The path they followed led in a zigzag course up the side of the steep hill to the little fort, if fort it could be styled, which, Henry now perceived, was quite hid from vessels entering the bay.

" You did not expect this little battery was here?" said Sergeant Beaulieu: " you were caught in a trap — eh, *mon garçon?* "

" Yes, that is true ; but the schooner would have escaped," said Henry, if she had bore round instead of going in stays ; * there was plenty of water astern of us."

" Yes, that was a mistake, caused, I suppose," he added, laughing, " by our little thirty-two-pound shot. Ah ! we have two nice little pill-boxes here," pointing to the guns.

They now entered into the space behind the little battery of two guns ; there was a small low house, built almost into the rock, and into this house the two lads followed the sergeant, and then into a scantily furnished room, in which sat the commander of the fort — a little stout consequential personage — eating his dinner, a very meagre one, and washing it down with bad wine at four sous the bottle.

" Ah ! who have we here, Sergeant Beaulieu?" said Captain Polard, for so he styled himself, though only a sub-lieutenant.

" These two boys were left in the schooner we riddled so nicely, captain," said the sergeant ; " the fellows blew the vessel up, and left these two lads behind."

" Are you sure? — but stop ; do you speak French?" said the commander of the fort, leaning back in his chair, and looking at Henry inquisitively.

" Ah ! he speaks like a Frenchman, captain," put in the sergeant.

" *Bien !* Well," said the captain, " you're English, of course."

" Yes," said Henry ; " we are."

" Then you're prisoners of war, that's clear ; to-morrow I

---

* That is to say, if she turned round on her heel, instead of going round with her head to the wind.

shall send you to the commandant at Blavet; we can't keep you here — can scarcely keep ourselves. Besides, we are always expecting an attack from those wolves the Chouans — they are in great force within a few leagues of this. Now, sergeant, you must lock them up above-stairs till to-morrow; give them a share of your rations. I can do no more."

The sergeant bade the boys follow him, which they did up a flight of stairs. On reaching the top he unlocked a door.

"Come, *garçons*, here's your resting-place for to-night; it's not worse than you will have at Vannes or Blavet; it's our lock-up. There's a pallet to sleep on, and by and by I will bring you something to eat, and, if I can, a bottle of wine."

"Thank you, sergeant," said Henry, after a glance at the desolate room; "but who are those Chouans your commandant was talking about?"

"They are the royalists," said Sergeant Beaulieu. "They are fighting against our noble republic — they want to put the king on the throne again. and the rascals expect the English will send them ships and arms; but they will be made mince-meat of by and by." So saying, he closed the door, double-locked it, and drew two heavy bolts besides.

Alfred threw himself on the straw bed, and burst into tears. Henry took his hand, and, pressing it, strove to soothe him.

"I am worse than a girl, Harry," said the poor boy, looking into the handsome, serious face of his cousin. "I have no energy; I never shall be fit for any thing — you always told me so."

"But I told you wrong, Alfred; for I have seen you bold, and active, and energetic, when you rouse yourself. Never despair — with God's blessing we may get out of this yet."

"And what should we do, dear Harry, if we were out of this miserable den?"

" Why, get to those Chouan royalists, to be sure; the moment I heard that little corpulent captain say that the Chouans were near, my heart leaped with joy. If we could get to them we should be quite safe, and get to England."

" But how get out of this? These are stone walls," said Alfred, looking round him; " and the window full nine feet from the floor, and crossed with strong iron bars."

" Hush! the door unlocks," said Henry.

The door opened, and the sergeant entered the room.

" Here, *mes enfans*—here is the best we have, it's our fare;" and he placed a small loaf of brown bread, a piece of boiled salt meat, and a bottle of wine on the bench, for table there was none.

" Thank you, sergeant; but your fare for a brave soldier is not very luxurious — what had you before the revolution?"

" *Ça*, what's that you say — do you mean, what had we to eat before our glorious revolution?"

" Yes, I ask from curiosity."

The sergeant rubbed his head, and then said, " To be sure we had white bread, and wine ten sous a bottle; this wine is *vin de quatre sous.*"

" Then," said Henry, " as far as eating and drinking goes, you are not so well off; but, of course, you have better pay?"

" You are droll," said the sergeant, looking puzzled. " No, we do not get any pay at present, till things settle; but, you see, it was easy for the king to pay and feed his soldiers when he taxed the people hard for them."

" Oh!" said Henry, " who's to pay you now? I suppose there will be no taxes?"

" You had better eat your supper, *mon garçon*," said the sergeant, looking half-inclined to laugh; " to-morrow you may have a long walk."

"Then it is very far to Blavet?" said Henry.

"No, it's not far; but you see we must keep away from the seashore — the Chouans are lurking about there — so, *bon soir!*"

"That's just what I wanted to know," said Henry; "then we must keep by the seashore."

"How sanguine you talk, Harry!" said Alfred; "let us get out first."

"Well, to enable us to work we must eat; so eat some of this tough beef, Alfred, and drink this four-sous wine."

The two boys ate as youth will eat under all circumstances; and tough the meat was and sour the wine. Then Henry got on the bench and had a look at the window; the window looked on the little battery and the two old thirty-two pounders.

He was then attracted by the chimney; he looked up this, and then joyfully said, "This is lucky, Alfred; we can get out on the top of the house through this chimney: we are not very fat after our cruise."

"Why, Harry!" exclaimed his cousin, "you do not suppose we could ever get up a chimney!"

"So you thought about the masts of the schooner; and yet, you see, you surmounted that difficulty."

"Yes! but, even allowing we were on the top of the chimney, what could we do there?"

"Why, get on the roof; and, by tearing this coarse quilt and blanket into strips, we shall make a famous rope, and then get down."

Alfred sighed. "You were made for a life of adventure, Harry — the greater the difficulty, the greater your energy and spirit."

"Does not Livy say, Alfred, that there is no less grandeur in supporting great evils than in performing great deeds?"

"Genius is the gold in the mine," said Alfred, "and talent works and brings it out; but I have neither genius nor talent, and you have both."

"And both to be displayed," said Henry, with a cheerful laugh, "in getting up a chimney and down again. We must wait till dusk," continued Henry, "and then we will commence making a rope of this quilt; the height of the house is trifling — two stories, say twenty feet: then the garrets, if there are any — say thirty feet rope will take us to the bottom."

"Ah! how shall I get up that chimney?" said Alfred, after taking a look up it. "I have often wondered how the little unfortunate sweeps manage it."

"I will show you how, and help you; there is not room, certainly, for a full-grown man, but that's all the better for us. You must put your back to the wall, and work yourself up with your feet."

The remainder of the daylight wore away: the boys climbed to the window, they beheld the last rays of the setting sun lingering on the bright sea; beneath, the hull of the *Fury*, or the piece of it left, was still visible, but the tide had covered the bank; they could see several boats about the spot, doubtless picking up what they could from the wreck.

"I wonder," said Alfred, "if that horrid skipper and his mate perished when the shot struck the boat!"

"Not a doubt of it," said Henry; "probably crushed to death by the shot itself. They lost the vessel through their own negligence and drunkenness; they might have guessed — seeing the vessel we chased anchor so coolly, and take such a sweep to her anchorage — that she considered herself safe, and made the sweep to avoid shoal water."

It grew very rapidly dark, and the two poor solitary prisoners sat beside each other, talking of home, and of their dear parents, wondering if they would think them dead; and, oh! thinking what joy would fill their hearts if Providence blessed their efforts to escape, and that once more they should be folded in their embrace. Every remembrance of their happy home was talked over, every familiar spot spoken spoken of — nothing was forgotten — till at last Henry thought it time to set to work.

"They visit us no more to-night; let us make the rope, and then you, Alfred, take an hour or two's sleep, to enable you to bear the fatigue before you."

"What, and leave you watching, dear Harry? No, no! I really am beginning to be ashamed of my weakness, and want of firmness and energy. I do not feel any inclination to sleep. I would rather listen to one of your stories of sea life. Ah! by the by, do you remember my asking you — oh! how happy we were then — to tell me the story of your adventures aboard the *Boston*, and the pirate-ship you were in — the cause of your getting that splendid piece of plate and richly mounted pistols? I love to hear you speak of your adventures; it will soothe my mind and spirits."

"With great pleasure, dear Alfred. I always consider myself the cause of your present situation; and, depend on it, without you my foot shall never be set on the shores of England."

Alfred pressed his cousin's hand and sighed, Henry commencing his narration, which we give our young readers in the next chapter.

CHAPTER VIII.

"I was about fourteen years of age when I sailed in the *Boston* as midshipman. This twelve-pounder thirty-two-gun frigate, was but a poor cramped-up little ship, and I heard her officers say that she was a bad specimen of our thirty-two-gun frigates, to send out where we were sure to meet some dashing American ships. But we had a gallant captain, and a brave and skilful set of officers. On reaching our station off the American coast, Captain Courtenay, our commander, heard so much of a French frigate called the *Embuscade*, that he became extremely anxious to meet her. At length we heard she was at anchor in New York; we then commenced working up, for the wind was contrary for that harbor. The *Boston*, though she was a cramped ship, could go along pretty fast in a stiff breeze; so, in three days after receiving the information about the *Embuscade*, we came in sight of our destination.

"We stood pretty close in; and there, sure enough, she was. The *Embuscade* was considered a most successful cruiser, having, during the period she was out, already captured sixty-four British vessels, of one kind or another. In fact, she had become a perfect pest to our commerce; and, no doubt, it would be considered a first-rate exploit to capture her, or, at all events, put an end to her further cruising.

"Just before we came in sight of New York, Captain Courtenay proposed, in order to deceive the pilot-boats on

the coast, especially those out of New York, that those officers who could speak French should dress up in French uniforms.   As I could speak the language pretty well, I was
one of those so attired.   As we stood across the entrance to
the harbor, we passed very close to a pilot-boat; so we began conversing eagerly and loudly in French, the crew looking up at us, and remarking that we were a French ship.

"As we found out afterwards, Captain Bompart, who was
the commander of the *Embuscade*, caught sight of us, and
supposed we were his consort, the *Concorde*.   He at once
summoned his lieutenant, and desired him to take a boat's
crew and pull out to the supposed *Concorde*, and tell her commander that there was a pirate on the coast, committing
great depredations; that the said pirate had boarded and
sunk — killing all the crews — two French and three American vessels, and plundered them of their cargoes.   The *Concorde* was therefore to search for this pirate, and, if successful in catching her, to hang the whole crew without any ceremony whatever."

"Dear me," said Alfred, interrupting his companion,
"what atrocities those pirates commit!"

"You shall hear," returned Henry.   "I am happy, at all
events, to see that my narrative diverts your mind.   But, to
continue: the first lieutenant of the *Embuscade*, with his
boat's crew, pulled out, and soon came up with the very
pilot-boat that, half an hour before, passed us.   'Hallo,
pilot!' hailed the lieutenant, 'is that a French ship you
passed just now?'

"'Ay, ay, sir! I guess she be a mounseer, and no mistake.'

"'Give way, my lads; all right!' said the lieutenant of
the *Embuscade*.   'It's the *Concorde*,' and on flew the boat;
we were intently watching her.   In a few moments she was

alongside, but, to their infinite rage and disgust, they were all made prisoners. This was most provoking to Lieutenant Whitynow, for he was a Bostonian by birth.

" After the first little flurry of vexation had passed over, our commander said to the lieutenant that he was extremely anxious to meet the *Embuscade* at sea. ' Well,' returned Lieutenant Whitynow, 'I can assure you that Captain Bompart is equally anxious for the same meeting, and if you will permit me to write to my commander, by yonder pilot-boat still in sight, I have no doubt but that your wish will be complied with.'

. " This was done, and, besides, Captain Courtenay sent a verbal message to Captain Bompart, to the purport that we would wait three days for him.

" The pilot-master, it seems, was very exact in delivering both letter and message ; he also caused a written copy of the message to be posted in one of the public coffee-rooms of the city.

" In the mean time we bore away from the port, and stood out to sea — the sight of a French squadron, however, caused our captain to alter his course. Determined not to lose the chance of this encounter, we bore up, and ran within a few leagues of the Long-Island shore.

" You may imagine, my dear Alfred, how anxious we all were, and what a sharp look-out we kept. On the 31st, about three in the morning, we observed a ship coming down before the wind in the direction of north-east. We then immediately cleared for action. As the ship approached, nearing us by three miles, she commenced making signals by false fires."

" Pardon me," interrupted Alfred ; " what do you mean by false fires ? "

" They are lights hoisted at night as signals ; they m⸱

true or false signals, as the case requires, so as to mystify or distinguish a friend or enemy. But the ship was the expected one; for, shortly after, she ran up at her peak a blue flag with a white cross, and thus we at once recognized her as the long-wished for *Embuscade*. Our ship then set her mainsail, and so did the enemy; we thus manœuvred for a short time till, about five o'clock, the *Embuscade* bore up and ranged along the *Boston's* larboard and weather side. We now commenced peppering away with our larboard guns, and the enemy with their starboard, with her main topsail to the mast. A fierce fire was thus kept up for a short time; we were, at this period, about four leagues from the high land of Neversink, in the Jerseys.

" The fire of the *Embuscade* did us considerable mischief in our rigging and spars. Before six o'clock our cross-jack-yard was shot away, then our jib and fore topmast-staysail, with the stays themselves, and braces and bowlines, and thus the control of the ship was lost; about six o'clock our main topmast was struck by a shot, and fell with the yard on our larboard side; then followed our mizzen-topmast and mizzen-staysail; whilst, each moment, we expected our mizzen-mast to fall over the side.

" But our misfortunes were not confined to our rigging: our two lieutenants were both forced to go below, severely wounded; Lieutenant Edwards with a contusion on the head, that rendered him senseless at the time, but Lieutenant Ker had one eye entirely destroyed.

" For want of officers we were thrown into some confusion, so I ran down below and found Lieutenant Edwards recovering. I told him the state they were in on deck, and he at once, though suffering much, came up with me to look at the *Embuscade;* she appeared to have all her masts uninjured, but such was far from the fact, as we afterwards found out.

"We were now in a sad way. Our gallant captain, and Lieutenant Butler of the marines, were both killed by the same shot, standing on the forepart of the quarterdeck. In this crippled state — our principal officers disabled, our guns rendered useless by our main-topmast lying over them, ten men dead, and twenty-four wounded — Lieutenant Edwards ordered the ship to be put before the wind under all the sail available. The *Embuscade* made an attempt to follow, but was evidently too crippled; for, after a couple of miles, she hove up in the wind, and shortly after we lost sight of her. Thus ended our action with the *Embuscade;* we certainly failed in taking her, but we effectually prevented her taking any more prizes, for, after getting back to New York, she had to take out all her masts, and was not able to leave port till the month of October.

"In the mean time, we continued our course for the Delaware, to refit in that river; but, hearing that two French frigates were lying at anchor opposite Mud Fort, we hauled up for St John's. That evening there was a fog; we had a boat towing astern, having made use of her to stop some shot-holes; she was the only boat we had, the rest being knocked to pieces. We were going dead before the wind, near six knots, when one of our boys named Jack Porter fell off the fore-yard into the sea. This poor lad was a favorite of mine, and, knowing he could not swim, I kicked off my shoes and went overboard after him.

"Several of the men ran to haul up the boat, but, in the confusion, they let go the painter. This I did not know, however, for many a long day after. In the mean time, I came up with Jack Porter; he was a cool, courageous lad, and was making prodigious efforts to keep himself afloat.

"'Do not grasp me, Jack,' I called out; 'lay your hands on my shoulder; look, here is the boat.'

" ' Ay, ay, sir ! ' sputtered Jack, as he bobbed up and down, his mouth full of water, but he contrived to place his hands on my shoulder.

" The boat had drifted down to us, and, in a moment, I got within reach of her painter, which hung over her bow ; but the frigate was not to be seen, the fog was so dense. ' Lay hold of this rope, Jack,' said I, giving him the painter ; and he did so, whilst I began scrambling into the boat over the side, rather anxious for fear of the sharks.

" I had just got in, and was running forward to haul him in, for he was greatly exhausted, when a fearful shriek rang upon my ears, that filled me with the utmost horror ; for I knew at once Jack Porter was seized by a shark. I rushed to the bows — Oh ! what a sight ! the poor lad was floating in a pool of blood, the next instant he disappeared ; the sea was alive with hideous, monstrous sharks. I sunk back in the boat, with my face hid by my hands, shuddering. The sound of a gun from the frigate, and a heavy squall rushing across the boat, did not even rouse me, so horrified was I by the loss of poor Jack, and the frightful death he had met.

" When I recovered from my stupor, I found I was driving before a strong gale, and that another gun fired by the frigate was to windward of me. This was startling ; for she must thus have shot up in the wind and lay to, whilst I drove past them in the boat ; by the sound of the gun I must have got nearly a mile from them. There were four oars in the boat, but it blew too fresh, and the sea was too rough, for a single hand to do any thing. I listened, but no more guns were fired. ' So, then,' thought I, ' they think us drowned.'

" My situation drove even the fate of poor Jack Porter from my mind. It was warm enough, but there was no food in the boat, or a drop of water. I shipped one of the oars into the scull-hole, and kept her before the wind, thinking to myself they may see me if the fog clears; but the day ran on, and nothing did I see save the fins and then the heads of several sharks following me, and eyeing me with positively a ferocious expression of countenance, though you may think that was imagination.

"You may be sure, before night, though the gale lulled, still keeping thick, that I began to feel thirsty and hungry; but there was nothing for it but patience and resignation. Night came on, and, feeling tired and weary, I lay down, and let the boat drift before the breeze, and, soon after, fell into an uncomfortable sleep. It was daylight when I awoke, hungry and miserable; the fog was gone, the sky tolerably clear, but not a craft met my anxious gaze — I appeared alone on the wide ocean."

"I should have died from despair," said Alfred; "my poor Harry, what you must have suffered in mind and body!"

"Not so much as you think, Alfred; I was a strong, hearty boy, and not given to a despairing mood; I roused up and began thinking. I then remembered that the two carpenters who used the boat had eaten their food in it, and, perhaps, had left a bit in the lockers; so I went and groped, and found, stowed away in a piece of old canvas, four pieces of biscuit, a piece of boiled salt-junk, and a small jar of water. What luxuries they were to me! I eat and drank sparingly, and stowed away two half-biscuits, half a pint of water, but no beef, the piece was too small to divide.

"That night passed, and the following morning saw the end of my provisions: another day passed; but, before sundown, I beheld, to my great relief, a sail approaching. I put my jacket on an oar, and stuck it in the mast-hole, and then I watched — you may imagine how anxiously — the distant sail. It came rapidly on, and then I perceived it was a schooner, under all the canvas she could set. She was not steering towards me, and I trembled as I watched her; when, almost on the point of giving her up, I saw her square away.her yards, and bear towards me. I knelt down, and from my heart I returned thanks to a kind Providence. I did not fear facing death on the deck of a frigate, fighting for my country; but facing death by starvation is a trial few can stand with resignation. As the schooner bore down I got a clear view of her; she was a long, very long, low craft, with great raking masts, and immense mainsail; as she came near she brailed her foresail, and hove her topsails aback, so that I drifted up to her. As I came alongside I was rather startled, for a more ferocious set of men I never beheld than I saw looking over the side at me.

" ' Hilloa ! my hearty,' said a tall, powerful fellow in his shirt, with a broad belt round his waist, in which was a broad two-edged knife, and a brace of pistols, as with a boat-hook he hooked on the boat — this man was an Englishman — ' Here's a young middy,' said he, as he grasped me by the arm and lugged me on deck, swearing at the same time terribly.

" ' Hang him ! it's the best thing we can do,' said several voices; whilst a dozen others, mulattoes and Frenchmen, vociferated in French and broken English all kinds of threats, and for what it puzzled me to say.

" ' Is this the way,' said I to the fellow that pulled me aboard, ' you treat a lad of my age in distress ? '

" ' Stand back, there, you rascals ! ' said a shrill voice behind the men; and then a middle-sized man, thin, and about forty years of age, his face covered with beard, whiskers, and mustaches, pushed his way through the men, and stood right before me. ' From what ship do you come, youngster ? ' demanded this man, covered with weapons; he spoke in French, and I knew by his language that he was a Frenchman.

"'I belong to the *Boston*, English frigate,' I replied in French.

"'And where is she?' he demanded; 'and how do you come to be alone in this boat alongside?'

"I, of course, told him the truth. 'Do you know,' said he, 'where the *Embuscade* is — did you fall in with her?'

"'Yes,' I returned; 'we fought her four days ago, off New York. Where she is now I cannot say, for we left her so crippled that she must seek a port.'

"'Give a cheer, my beauties!' said the captain of the pirate, for such she was, and the very identical one Captain Bompart wished his consort, the *Concorde*, to go in chase of. At once a tremendous cheer rent the air from the throats of sixty or seventy as ferocious-looking fellows — a mixture of English, French, blacks, and mulattoes — as were ever packed together aboard one craft!

"'Now, my lad,' said the captain with a grin, 'you will have to fight under another flag: but you will have a jolly life of it; your hand will soon come in. You're a stout-built youngster, and, belonging to a king's ship, you may think yourself lucky you are not run up at once to the yard-arm — a method we have of showing our loyalty.'

"'Send me adrift,' said I; 'for I tell you plainly, I will never fight under the bloody flag of a pirate.'

"The Frenchman drew a pistol from his girdle and cocked it. I looked him firmly in the face, and thought my doom was sealed. 'A sail, ho!' shouted a man on the topgallant-cross-tree; all turned to look in the direction pointed out. 'A large brig, going free,' said the man aloft.

"'Cast off that boat,' said the captain, 'and square away the yards, and let drop the foresail;' he then turned to me, and, putting his pistol close to my heart, said — 'Hark ye, youngster, if you are not one of the first aboard yonder brig when we bring her to, and show that you can cut a man down as well as one of us, I'll not shoot you, for I see you don't wink — I'll hang you by the heels to the foreyard,' he then turned away."

"Ah, what a monster!" said Alfred; "and what a horrible situation to be in! What should I have done in such a position? He was a thousand times worse than the *Fury's* skipper."

"No one knows till he is tried, dear Alfred; circumstances make the man. The pirate captain then left me. I stood leaning against the bulwarks; I saw the boat of the *Boston* drifting to leeward; how I wished I was again in her! but that wish was useless; I was weak with hunger, and my lips parched. I turned to a huge black standing near me; he had on only a check shirt and a pair of duck trousers; he had an enormous head, covered with a thick crop of curly hair as thick as the wool on a sheep; he was sharpening a huge broad two-edged knife. I spoke to him in French, but he stopped me saying — 'Speak de English. Me no jabber French.'

"'Will you give me something to eat? I have neither eat nor drank for nearly thirty hours.'

"'You no eat tirty hour? dat no good. You no fight if you no eat — eh? Come dis way?'

"This man was the cook; he took me to his cooking-place, and, opening a locker, gave me two large slices of fat pork and two biscuits, and, showing me the water-butt, walked off.

"I sat down on a gun-carriage, and began eating sparingly of the food, but drank a glorious draught of water. I then looked round the schooner's deck — she was a beautifully modelled craft, but filthy dirty; her decks disgusting. She had a formidable pivot-gun, a long eighteen-pounder,

She had four six-pounders, and two large brass swivels on each quarter, and two for'ard. She appeared quite a new vessel, her spars lofty, and her sails all new. She was going through the water at a prodigious rate; the crew — and such a crew — swarthy, hirsute ruffians, clothed in all kinds of garbs, but covered with weapons — they were cramming the pivot-gun with grape and canister; and shouting and swearing in a manner awful to hear; they more resembled fiends than human beings. I then looked after the brig; she was going dead before the wind, with studding-sails alow and aloft, but she had not the slightest chance of escape — with only her ordinary sails, the pirate schooner was coming up with her hand over hand. I looked all round the horizon, hoping to see some man-of-war to save the doomed brig; but the sea sparkled and rippled, and the sun shone bright in the clear, blue vault above us — alas! it was to shine on a deed of cruel bloodshed.

"'Stand by, there!' roared the captain; 'hoist our jolly flag, and fire a gun, and let the rascals aboard that brig know who we are.'

"The foresail, which was of no service going before the wind, was brailed; up went the blood-red nag of the pirate, and the loud boom of his gun, no doubt, smote many a heart aboard that brig with a cruel pang. Still on she went, a large and handsome brig, till we were within half a mile of her.

"'Now, pitch a shot or two into her,' said the pirate captain, swearing frightfully. 'Does she imagine we are going to dance after her till sundown?'

"The schooner yawed, and her two six-pounders were fired; crash went one of the studding-sail booms, and the sail fluttered in the wind. A shout — a savage shout — gave the pirate crew, and again she yawed, and the other two guns were fired, bringing down the brig's main-topgallant mast.

" ' Now, my lads,' said the captain, ' stand ready to board ; but, just as we run up, give her the contents of our beauty.'

" My heart felt sick, for the doomed brig now shot up in the wind, and laid her fore-topsails aback. Within pistol-shot the pivot-gun was fired, sweeping the brig's deck, for she was low in the water, with its iron shower ; the next instant we were alongside, when the captain, thrusting a cutlass into my hand, and holding his cocked pistol to my head, said, ' Now, boy — up the side, or '—— As he spoke the words, and the crew of the pirate were preparing to rush aboard, two ports in the side of the brig opened, and a gush of fire and smoke burst forth, and then the contents of two eight-pounders, crammed to the muzzle with every species of missile, old iron, nails, pieces of lead, shot, were poured out with a horrible roar right amongst the pirate crew swarming up the sides.

" More than ten lay dead ; and, shrieking with fearful imprecations, the captain lay beside me, his shoulder torn off, and his face fearfully shattered ; for an instant he writhed frightfully on the deck, and then was still. Providentially, and almost miraculously, I was only hit slightly in two places — the shoulder and my left side ; but with so little pain, that at the moment I did not know I was hit.

" Oh ! the yell with which those wretches rushed up the side of the brig — it was horrible ! Then followed shouts, pistol-shots, and fearful screams ; amid the terrific din I thought I heard the wild shriek of a female voice. What could I do? nothing — and yet, with an impulse irresistible, I stooped and seized the dead captain's pistol and cutlass, and sprang into the brig's rigging ; as I did so, the loud boom of a heavy gun pealed over the deep. I paused, and gazed back in the direction of the sound, and beheld, coming down before the wind, a large ship under a perfect cloud of canvas.

" The noise of the gun alarmed the pirates ; they saw the ship, and knew her to be a vessel of war. With a torrent of imprecations they threw themselves over the side, whilst I, watching my opportunity, gained the brig's rigging, at first unperceived ; the lashings holding the schooner to the brig were cut, and, as she shot ahead, the huge English mate caught a glimpse of me as I hastened to get behind the head of the mainmast. With a savage oath he levelled his pistol at me, but the ball only cut the rigging my hand was on. I was turning to discharge the pistol I had in my waistband, when a whole volley of balls rattled and cut away the rigging on every side of me ; but I was again untouched. By this time, the thunder of another gun roused the pirates to action. The schooner shot clear of the brig, and every stitch of canvas was set to the fine breeze blowing, and away she went close-hauled, evidently her safe point of sailing when pursued by a superior ship. I then looked at the stranger, and beheld a large frigate ; she had been coming up all along, but, so intent were the pirates upon the brig, that she was quite unnoticed, especially as a thin mist lay over the waters towards the horizon.

" She was now taking in her studding-sails, and running in her booms, and, in less than three minutes, she was in pursuit of the pirate on the other tack. Thus they would pass tolerably close to each other, by the pirate's keeping his wind, but scarcely within shot ; this convinced me the wretches knew right well that they had no chance with a frigate going free."

7

CHAPTER IX.

"I was now, my dear Alfred, safe from the frightful wretches congregated aboard that terrible schooner, and I returned thanks to God for my singular escape. I then turned my gaze from my lofty perch down upon the scene below. What a sight presented itself! I closed my eyes for a moment, and then looked again. Young as I was I was accustomed to the sight of death, but not to see human beings so mercilessly mutilated. I will not shock you with the description. I counted on the deck below, thirteen dead bodies — and two females — four, however, were pirates; the deck was horrible to look at.

"She was a fine brig, nearly four hundred tons burden, but I saw only the two eight-pounders, both on the one side. She was evidently an English vessel, by the rigging and the cut of her sails. It was blowing fresh, but there was not much sea; it had not time to get up. The brig's fore-top-sails were aback, her main-topsail full, her main top-gallant mast and sail hanging in wreck over the rigging.

"As I moved to descend, I felt the wound in my left shoulder a little painful; I saw my jacket was torn, and, putting my hand under my clothes, I felt they were saturated with blood, but the wound itself, I found by feeling, was nothing of consequence, and made by a piece of ragged iron, no doubt. Descending the rigging, I stood upon the deck, and gazed at the dead; the sun was by this time dipping in the wave, and the strong breeze, as it rushed through the rigging, had an ominous sound in my ears, for I saw clearly it was about to blow hard.

"There was not a sign of life in one of the bodies; they were English sailors. 'Oh!' prayed I, 'God help their wives and children, for surely some of these poor fellows have such!'

"With even a greater feeling of horror, I stooped and turned over the body of one of the females. I felt sick, and turned away. She was a young woman, and handsomely dressed; the other was an elderly female about fifty, also very well attired. As I stood, pale and almost stupefied, I thought I heard a little cry from below; I started, and ran to the companion and listened — yes, I could not mistake it, I heard the cry of a child.

"I ran hastily down the stairs, and fell over the body of a man, which rolled with me to the bottom; I heeded it not, for I still heard the cry. I rushed into the cabin, and, by the light from the windows, I beheld a table upset, and under it the motionless form of a female, and next her the body of a man, her arm round his neck; and, lying against one of the sides of a sofa, or couch, an infant undressed, and not more than a year old: its little eyes were open, and, as they rested upon me, it set up a piteous cry. 'O God, help the little thing!' said I, as I lifted it up; 'what shall I do?" As I uttered the words, a low moaning sound came from beneath the table. I started, and instantly placed the baby in one of the berths and covered it up, and then began lifting the table; the female beneath was moving, her garments were covered with blood, but I saw no wound on her face and neck like those on the deck. The man, to judge by his attire, was the captain of the ship; he also was not dead, though he bled profusely from a cutlass wound over the temple, and, may be, other wounds besides. ' Perhaps,' thought I, ' the woman has only fainted.' I raised her in a sitting position, with her back to the lockers; the captain, as I supposed him, was groaning heavily and moving his limbs; presently the female opened her eyes, and some words escaped her lips.

" The child's cries instantly attracted her; with a shudder she made an effort, and, holding out her hands, cried, ' My child! my child! '

" 'The child is safe,' said I; ' are you wounded?'

" ' No — no! ' she murmured; ' give me my child! I only fainted; but oh! the wretches, they have killed my husband.' And then, with an effort, she raised herself up, and instantly, though the light was fading, saw her husband; for, with a cry, she threw herself on him, saying, ' He is not dead — help me to save him, whoever you are, and God will bless you! Go, get water.

" I ran upon deck and found the water-butt, and then hastened back to the cabin after taking a draught; for I was weak and ill myself. When I entered the cabin, the female was' on her knees, wiping the blood from the captain's face; he was recovering his senses rapidly; the child saw its mother from the berth, and was quiet.

" The captain's wife was a very handsome young woman, and totally unhurt; she took the water from me; the light was now very faint, for the sun was down; but she looked earnestly at me, saying, ' Who are you — are those fearful wretches, the pirates, aboard?'

" 'God forbid! ' I replied; ' they are gone, chased by a frigate,' — and then I helped her to raise the captain, a man about thirty-six years of age. He opened his eyes, and his lips moved, but he did not utter a word; his wife gave him a small quantity of water just to moisten his lips, and then said to me — 'Open that locker, you will find wine; and in that other, candles, and means for striking a light. God bless us! I suppose they have murdered all the crew, and my mother and sister, or they would be here.'

" ' We are the only persons aboard alive,' said I. She shuddered, but her husband rapidly revived. I gave him a small cup of wine, she took some also; indeed, I found a little of it revive me wonderfully. I lighted a candle, and then the cabin-lamp, that hung from the beam, and then went on deck to see if there was any chance of the frigate's return; but it was a long chase, the chase of that pirate, as I heard afterwards.

" There was not a sail to be seen; the sea was rising, and the horizon getting heavy and overcast. I looked up at the sails, and thought what should I do; if a gale sprung up, the masts would go by the board.

" I now determined to get rid of the dead bodies; it would be horrible to see them rolling about with the motion of the ship; but, first, I would hear what the captain might say, perhaps he would recover sufficiently to come on deck in the morning.

" When I returned to the cabin, I found the captain's wife with her child in her arms, and her husband stretched on one of the couches; he looked shockingly bad — pale and ghastly. He held out his hand to me, saying in a weak voice, ' I see you are belonging to the navy. You have saved our lives; but how came you here — are you alone, young gentleman?'

" ' Yes,' said I ' I am;' and I briefly told him how I came aboard.

" ' You are a brave boy,' said he, faintly. ' I am not mortally wounded, I think; it nearly killed me to get up here, for I have pistol-balls through my right side, and, besides this gash over my temple, I have several knife-stabs, but they are flesh-wounds. My wife tells me all are dead aboard,' and, closing his eyes, he groaned heavily.

"His young wife cried bitterly, knelt by his side, kissing his clammy brow with fond affection, whilst I took the little babe, then fast asleep, and put it in a berth. A little more wine revived the captain, and yet I feared to see him take it, for fear of heating his blood and doing him harm, but he merely kept moistening his lips.

"'How is the ship?' said he anxiously; 'for it is blowing hard I perceive.'

"'As you left her,' I replied; 'her fore-topsails aback; she is lying to: if it does not come to a gale, she will do.'

"'Yes, young gentleman; she will do, as you say; but, if it blows into a gale, her masts will go.'

"'I hope it will keep quiet till morning,' I returned; 'it's easy then to cut away the wreck of the main-topgallant mast, and brail up the fore-topgallant sail. I can even lower the main-sail.'

"'Ah!' said the skipper, 'if you could do that, it's possible she might hold on till some craft comes in sight.'

"'Had I not better get the bodies overboard,' I remarked?

"'No, no, no!' sobbed the young wife of the captain. 'Oh! let me see my poor mother and sister once more.'

"'No, indeed, you had better not,' said I; 'I will throw a sail over them, if you choose; perhaps we may reach land in a day or two.'

"'No,' said the captain with a deep sigh; 'that is impossible. Many sleep where they will sleep; but it's a horrid task for you, my dear young gentleman.'

"'Better than see them washing about the decks if it comes on to blow; besides '——— I saw the captain's wife shudder, so I said no more, but I recollected the body lying at the bottom of the stairs; I could not move that. As I felt it was necessary to look for some food, I asked the captain where some could be procured.

" ' True, true,' said he; he then told me where the provisions were kept. ' You will find plenty; we are only four days out, and yesterday we had a round of beef cooked, and some roast fowls. Just take a look on deck,' he continued; ' the frigate may be standing back, which she surely will, after they destroy those horrible pirates.'

" I went up on deck, casting a look as I went upon the poor body — one of the crew — lying at the foot of the stairs, thinking how on earth I should be able to remove it. The moon was now and then seen, struggling to cast its rays through dense broken masses of stormy clouds, that, by their motion through the sky, showed that there was a storm brewing. There was no sail in sight, but, just as I was turning round, I heard a voice from for'ard say —' This way, my hearty, and lend us a hand to get on our pins; blow the lubbers, they nearly stove in my upper works.'

" Astounded at these words, I ran for'ard, and beheld by the light of the moon, striking full at that moment on the fore-part of the ship, a man's head and shoulders above the fore-hatch: it was a ghastly sight at first, for his face was covered with clotted blood. I ran to him, however, and then he looked at me, passing his hands across his eyes.

" ' My poor fellow, how glad I am to see one more of you alive ! '

" ' Ay, ay — I'm alive, thank God ! but, dear me, I think my skull is broke by that black nigger's hatchet. But who are you? be my messmates all murdered by those bloodthirsty pirates?'

" ' Every soul but the captain, his wife, and little baby.'

" 'The Lord save us !' said the sailor solemnly; ' but

lend us your hand, my lad, whoever you are. I think if 1 had a souse of my head in a bucket of water, and a stiff glass of grog, I'd be all right, and able to do something.'

"With some difficulty I got him out of the fore-hatch ; at first he staggered from weakness, occasioned by the quantity of blood he had lost ; there was a frightful blow from the sharp edge of a hatchet on the side of the head ; it was wonderful to think how he survived it — the blow had tumbled him, luckily, down the hatchway, and there he lay insensible in a pool of blood. I got him a bucket of water, and it seemed to revive him wonderfully. He was a tall, fine, strongly-built man, and not more than thirty.

"'I'm second mate of this unfortunate ship,' said he, sitting down to recover himself, 'and I had as fine a set of young fellows, comrades, as you need see, and there they lie ;' and, bending his head down on his hands, he remained several moments without stirring, but then looking up —'My lad, is my captain much hurt?' said he.

"'Yes — very much ; but if you will keep quiet, I will go and bring you a mug of wine, and tell the captain you're alive. What's your name?'

"'John Morgan,' said he ; 'but give us a grip of your arm, I'll go see my captain ; we must try and save the ship. It blows hard, and, if it comes harder, why she'll carry away her masts. My poor fellows ! Oh, the villains ! if I could only have given them a second dose of the two eight-pounders ; but we were short-handed, having lost four hands from Yellow Jack.'

"I went down just to tell the captain, who seemed to be reviving greatly, that one of his men, John Morgan, was alive, though badly hurt.

"'Thank God for that !' said husband and wife ; 'he is an honest, fine seaman. Will you, if he is able to come, bring him down here?'

"' Ah! but for you, sir,' said the captain's wife, ' we should all have perished.'

" Not to weary you, dear Alfred, by minute details, I shall merely say that the night passed over without a very strong wind; and, the next morning, John Morgan was so much better, having got a plaster from the medicine-chest, that, with his assistance, we got the bodies of the pirates overboard through one of the port-holes. John, poor fellow! would sew each of his comrades up in their hammocks, which he did after a labor of several hours, and then we committed them to the deep, with several eight-pound-shot sewed up with them — the poor females the same way; but the captain's wife came up, knelt by them, and prayed — oh! with such sobbing and tears, that poor John had to go away; he was as soft-hearted a creature as ever lived.

" This sad duty performed, John — who would work, it was no use trying to stop him — began clearing the decks, and lighting a fire in the caboose. I never saw a man of such indefatigable energy as that fine fellow. He could not yet go aloft; but I went, and, with a good knife, I cut away the ropes that held the wreck of the main-topgallant-mast, and then, by using tackles, he braced round the yards; and, as the wind was due west, we let the brig go before it, lashing the wheel.

" John Morgan knew where every thing was. Not a sail was in sight, which surprised me, for I fully expected to see the strange frigate come back.

" John and I prepared some coffee, &c., for Mrs. Stanley's breakfast; and, besides that, some soaked biscuit and prepared milk for the little baby. John was every thing, he thought nothing of himself; the ship and his captain seemed to be ever in his thoughts. We got the body of the first mate up with a tackle from the bottom of the stairs — and he, poor fellow! found his last resting-place beneath the wave.

"I then learned from John, as he took the wheel (for the brig yawed terribly with the wheel lashed, as it was blowing very fresh, with a good tumble of a sea), that the brig was called the Eliza of London, and belonged part to the captain, and part to owners in London. She was returning home with a valuable cargo when chased by the pirates. Knowing that, if the pirates got aboard, they should be all murdered, they determined, as John said, to give them a dose; so they crammed the two eight-pounders to the very muzzle with every thing they could muster destructive, in the shape of iron and lead, and then fought to the last gasp.

" We had a fine fair breeze. We managed to get down the driver, and stop it, so that we went along nicely under our two topsails only. Mrs. Stanley was in deep affliction; the loss of her mother and sister — coming home, as they were, after many years' residence in a foreign land, and to perish so miserably — cut her to the heart; her husband's situation also frightened her, for, though he seemed to mend, he still suffered exceedingly from the wound in his side, though his wife dressed it as well as she could from the contents of the medicine-chest.

" As night came on, John and I agreed to lower the maintopsail on the cap. 'She will then steer steadily,' said he, ' with the wheel lashed; for neither of us are fit to stay up all night. We shall be able to work it up again with the windlass — if we can't, its no matter; we must fall in with some craft, or some homeward-bound ship will overtake us, and spare us a couple of hands.'

" In this manner we ran before a steady, strong breeze for seven days, without any thing particular occurring. The captain's wound in the head healed well, so did the knife-stabs, and he was able the fifth day to come on deck ; but the wound in the side would not let him use the slightest exertion.

" The eighth day the wind fell, and, before night, we had a strong south-east gale and heavy rain ; nevertheless, by prodigious exertion, John and I, before it came on, got in two reefs in our topsails, and lowered our fore-topgallant mast, the captain, steering by tackles, &c., we managed to heave round the yards, and get them tolerably well up. This was a very heavy gale, and lasted three days ; but we got her to lie to, and, though the sea was tremendously heavy, she bore it wonderfully well, for she was a fine sea-boat. We had the boats washed overboard, and part of the starboard bulwarks knocked away.

" Whilst lying to, the last day of the gale, we observed, for the first time, a sail to windward — and, very shortly after, made her out to be a man-of-war, steering right for us. She was under double-reefed topsails and housed top-gallant masts. In an hour's time she was close up with us, and showed English colors ; we did the same. She then hove to, about a quarter of a mile from us, and, as wind and sea went down that night, she sent a boat aboard us the next morning. The frigate was the ——, Captain Percival, the identical frigate that chased the pirate.

" The second lieutenant of the frigate it was that boarded us ; he was surprised when he saw me, and heard that I belonged to the *Boston*. I stated how I came in the situation I was ; he seemed interested, but said I had, as well as the captain and his wife, and John Morgan, a very fortunate escape ; that the pirate schooner was one of the fastest crafts on a wind he ever fell in with — they chased her for three days, and would not have caught her but for a shift of wind, and some very severe and heavy squalls.

" The pirates refused to surrender, killing two of the

frigate's crew with a shot from their long pivot-gun, and cutting their rigging and sails ; and, finally, they were forced to sink her with a broadside. The frigate spared us six hands, and the lieutenant offered to take me aboard their ship, but I felt a wish to see the brig safe to port, so I remained ; and, five days after, we made the Scilly Islands, and ran, twenty-four hours afterwards, into Falmouth.

" Captain Stanley staid in Falmouth some time to recover his health ; placing himself under the skilful hands of Surgeon Vigors, he recovered his health and strength. In the mean time I reached home, to the great joy of my beloved mother and father, who were then at home. Two months afterwards, I received from London a very handsome letter from the owners of the *Eliza*, and, enclosed in a box, the beautiful piece of plate you so often remarked, and the history of which I so often promised you, and somehow was prevented from telling you till now.

" Mrs. Stanley sent me a very costly watch, and a very pretty letter expressive of her deep and lasting gratitude. Captain Stanley, also, sent me a very beautiful case of pistols and a valuable chronometer. The *Boston* arrived safely in England some time after. I did not join her again, but I met one of her officers in London. He said my loss was greatly deplored ; that, immediately after the loss of the boat, they hove the ship to, but, in the wretchedly crippled state of her masts, when the wind freshened they were forced to bear up, and the fog completely put it out of their power to find us ; they fired several guns, and, for several hours, thought to come across the boat, but in vain ; they then concluded we had perished, or else we should have reached them with the boat."

CHAPTER X.

"Well, my dear Harry," said Alfred, as his cousin finished his narrative, "I cannot imagine how you endured all the perils you have gone through."

"Custom, Alfred, and being brought up to witness scenes of strife and peril; but now, do not let us forget that we are prisoners to the worthy Captain Polard, and that we intend giving him the slip."

The two boys then commenced cutting up the quilt and the sacking, and fastening the strips together. They tested the power of their rope when finished, and Henry became satisfied that it was sufficiently strong.

Climbing up to the window, Henry Barlow perceived that it was a very dark night, and blowing very fresh against the front of the fort. There was not a sound of human voice to be heard within or without, so Henry judged that the inmates had all retired to rest.

"Now, Alfred, I will go up first," said Henry, "and then I will lower down the rope to you; if you fasten it round your waist, I shall be able to haul you up."

"You think of every thing, dear Harry, and have a head full of expedients; I am absolutely a useless piece of lumber."

"Very far from that, indeed," said Henry; "you are rapidly improving, and now you see the benefit of exerting the faculties God has bestowed upon us."

Henry Barlow, having completed his preparation, commenced pushing himself up the little chimney, which, after a little squeezing, he managed to do. He was a broad-shouldered lad, strong and hearty; but this was his first experience in chimney climbing. We can safely assure our youthful readers, that ascending a chimney is by no means an easy exploit. Neither is it a pleasant or profitable one to the knees and elbows, which are more required in this act than any other members of the body.

His first enemy was a cloud of dust, and cobwebs, and loose mortar; luckily there was no soot. So, after some vigorous efforts and some bruises, he reached the summit, bathed in perspiration. "It's lucky," thought Henry, "that I have the cord to assist Alfred; he would never get up." Lowering down the rope, he waited till Alfred had made fast, and then, sitting astride on the chimney, which was not more than four feet from the roof, he commenced hauling his cousin up; this was not done without exceeding labor and difficulty, for poor Alfred made but a miserable attempt at the climbing. At length they both sat upon the summit of the chimney, with their legs into it, to recover themselves after their exertions. "I should never have got up without your tugging at me, Henry," whispered Alfred.

"You did famously," returned his cousin; "how lucky it is so dark! Now, be very careful how you come on the tiles, they are slippery; I see there's a parapet at the back, so, if we can fasten our rope, we are all right."

They soon got from the chimney, and then slid down quietly to the parapet without any noise; groping along, Henry found an iron spike driven between the stone copings; to this he fastened the cord, on which there were several knots.

"Now, I shall go first," whispered Henry, "and be ready

to assist you ; be careful, and do not let the cord slip through your hands, but cling with feet and knees."

Henry began the descent, rubbing against the rough walls as he went ; but, active and accustomed to going down ropes, it was easy enough to him ; he found the rope was long enough, and, looking up, there was not one window to the back. He anxiously watched Alfred. He, however, managed remarkably well, and reached the ground safely, losing a little skin from his hands, but of no consequence.

They now perceived that they were in a very circumscribed little back-yard, with a door leading into the house ; the hill rose like a wall at the back ; in fact, the rock and clay had been blasted away to make the little yard. There was a large water cask, and several tubs, and a low wall, and over this they got without making any noise, and, after a short time, came upon the path they had ascended some hours before, under the escort of Sergeant Beaulieu.

The wind blew very strong, and the sky was obscured by dark masses of clouds. They continued descending till they suddenly found themselves on a good broad road, leading to the right and left.

"To get to Quiberon," said Henry, " we must go to the left ; but, as soon as daylight appears, we must get off the road and hide ourselves somewhere during the day. I have the rest of the bread and tough beef, and I suppose we shall find water in plenty."

"It's so dark," said Alfred, " there's no making out what kind of country we are traversing." They walked on briskly for two hours, when, to their surprise, they perceived that day was breaking.

"Dear me," said Henry, " we delayed two hours too long! I wish we had started off sooner."

As the light increased, they perceived that they were

traversing a bad road, through a very deserted and barren tract of country, within view of the coast, which they judged was a league from them; on their left was a wide moor.

"There's somebody—it's a woman and child," said Alfred, "crossing the moor, and coming towards us, with something on their heads."

Henry looked, and said, "Yes, a woman and a young girl—they will cross close by us; and yonder is the spire of a church—it will not do to go near a village yet. Let us keep off this road, and make for the shore."

"Let me speak to the woman; for it won't do us any harm to ask her a question or two."

In a few minutes the woman and the young girl were close to them, and all stopped. Henry, to his surprise, beheld the tall woman who spoke so kindly to him the day before on the beach, and who was called by the other woman Dame Moulin.

The woman recollected them at once. "Ah, *Ca! mon joli garçon*, how is this? have you escaped from the fort? I am so glad."

"Yes, dame, we have; we want to get to Quiberon, to join the royalists."

"So do we, *mon joli garçon;* but if you keep on this road they will catch you. You are English, and I love the English and hate the Blues;* so come with us, and I will put you where you will be safe during the day; and, when night comes, we will go on to Quiberon."

"How good you are!" said Henry, joyfully; and then he cast a look at the little girl. He started with surprise, for he beheld two large and singularly beautiful dark eyes

---

* The revolutionary soldiers were so called from their blue dress; the royalists wore white.

fixed upon him with great interest; the girl was about thirteen, and extremely lovely. She was dressed in the coarse garments of a Bretagne peasant girl, and her small neat feet were thrust into a pair of wooden sabots. Seeing Henry looking so earnestly at her, she cast down her eyes.

"Come let us move on," said Dame Moulin; "it will not do to be loitering here: you will have the 'Blues' after you presently. I can't think how you got away from the fort."

"By climbing up a chimney, dame, then cutting up a quilt into a rope."

"You are a brave *garçon;* but move on, quick, right before you, for yonder trees."

"Then let me carry your basket, little girl," said Henry, wonderfully attracted by her sweet countenance. .

"Oh!" said the little girl, with a pleased smile, and such a pretty genteel manner, "my basket has only fern leaves and a few eggs, and is as light as possible."

Henry was surprised; there was not a particle of the rude Bretagne accent or expression in the young girl's words. "There is some mystery here," thought Henry.

"What a very pretty child!' said Alfred in English to Harry.

"She is positively beautiful, and I am sure she is no peasant girl," remarked his cousin.

"Do you know," said the little damsel, with her cheeks the color of a rose, "that I can speak and understand English? therefore you must mind what you say," and she looked up into the face of the surprised Henry with such an innocent, sweet expression that was quite captivating.

"Come, come, you young things: you must stop chattering, and walk faster," said the stout dame, walking at the rate of four miles an hour, "or we may get caught yet: heads are very cheap in France now, and it would be a pity such handsome heads as yours should feel the axe."

"How can you talk so, Dame Moulin?" said the little girl, trying to keep up with her; though she gave her hand willingly to Henry to help her on.

They soon reached the summit of the cliff. Over the beach there was a magnificent view: the promontory of Quiberon was distinctly visible, and in the distance, the numerous islands off that part of the French coast.

"Now, *mon garçon*," said Dame Moulin, "take care of the little girl down these cliffs; the path is not an easy one."

Henry promised to take the greatest care of her; Dame Moulin led the way down an extremely difficult, tortuous path, with the sea roaring on the beach some three hundred feet below them. Henry had to lift his little companion over many a critical spot, which puzzled even Alfred. She was so pleased with his kindness and care of her, that they became quite familiar, and like as if they had known each other for a long time: it is so with youth; the young heart unchecked, not controlled by the dull restraints and cold formalities of after years, beats with a pure love and confidence for its own kindred age.

"What name shall I call you by, my dear little girl?" said Henry, as they nearly reached the beach: he still spoke in French.

"Oh, call me Rosina!" said the damsel in perfectly pure English; "and you — what shall I call you and your brother?"

"Call me Henry, and my cousin — he is not my brother, though I love him as one — call him Alfred; but how well you speak English!"

"So do you French; but perhaps Dame Moulin — though

that is not her real name, only she is called Moulin, which you know is the French for mill, because she owns a very large mill: but I was going to say perhaps the dame will tell you all about me — oh! here we are," and Henry lifting her over a huge split in a rock, jumped down on the fine pebbly beach. "Ah, ça, here we are," said the dame; "a rough road, very few ever try it. Now follow me into the caves of St. Gueltas."

She walked on some few hundred yards, and then paused before what appeared a cleft in an immense rock. Stooping, the dame pushed her way in, and all the young folks followed. The passage was very narrow at first, but gradually widening, and passing under a very low arch, they at once found themselves in an immense lofty cavern, well lighted by two or three very large fissures near the summit.

"Well, here you are, *mes enfans*, in the famous caves of St. Gueltas, which they say beat those of Oderque. People say there is a passage here that runs five miles under the cliffs, but I can't say it's truth, for I never went far into them; and mind, none of you must go rambling about here, for fear of losing yourselves. So now sit down, for I want to speak a word or two to you all before I go."

"Oh! then you intend to leave us here," said Henry, "and little Rosina, too?"

"Ah, ça! How soon you found out her name," said Dame Moulin, smiling good-humoredly. "Tell me," turning to Henry, "all about how you got away from the fort, and what you wish to do, and who you are."

This Henry did, and then said he wished to join the royalists, and then get to England.

"Well, well, poor things!" said Dame Moulin, "how that horrid wretch of a captain hated you! The fish will make a meal of him and his comrade, anyhow, so that's satisfactory."

. Henry smiled at the good dame's way of settling the skipper, but she continued —

" As to getting to Quiberon, I hope we shall get there to-night, or to-morrow morning. Well, now, wouldn't it be curious," she looked with a placid smile at little Rosina as she sat close to Henry, listening eagerly to every word of his narrative — " now, wouldn't it be curious if you two pretty creatures were to love one another by and by?"

" Oh! I am sure," said little Rosina, with all the innocence and beauty of a child's nature, " that Henry and I, and indeed Alfred — though he does not understand what we say — we'll all love one another like brothers and sisters."

" Yes, my dear little girl!" said Henry, in his affectionate tone and manner, and stooping he kissed the fair forehead of the girl; " yes, I promise you I will be a brother to you, and take care of you as long as we remain together."

" Oh, you will not part so soon as you think!" said the dame. " This little girl's mother is an Englishwoman; she married a French marquis, who is a determined royalist, and he, luckily, escaped to England through Germany, from Paris. But madame was at their château Delancy with this little girl, her daughter, and a friend sent her warning to escape to England with her child; but, before she could do any thing but just pack up her jewels, &c., the horrid Blues came into this part of the country. I was the foster-sister of Monsieur le Marquis, and I lived in a fine mill, which, with twenty acres of land, he gave me and my son, for my poor husband died some years ago. So I found out that the Blues were going to plunder château Delancy, and send madame and her child to Paris; so I got them both to my mill, and clothed them like our farm-servants. Yesterday I went to St. Guidaft to get information of their movements, and the blowing-up of your schooner attracted me to

the beach, where I saw you. From the information I picked
up, I found it was necessary to move madame and the
child here for a day or so, and then get to Quiberon, where
the royalists are in force, and where an English fleet is expected, and where madame's father-in-law, the brave old
Marquis Delancy, now is, and one of the royalist commanders. So I brought Rosina this morning, and madame I shall
bring to-night, and then we will move on to Quiberon."

" Well, indeed, you have a noble, kind heart, dame!"
said Henry; and then he briefly explained to Alfred the parts
of the narrative he did not understand.

" Now," said the dame, getting up, " I will show you that
I have not brought you here to starve;" so saying, she began unpacking her huge basket that she had carried on her
head, Rosina eagerly helping her, and in which the two boys
joined; both were quite happy, and actually delighted with
their adventure, and freedom from the horrid association they
had endured aboard the *Fury* privateer.

The basket contained four fine fowls roasted, a nice tongue,
plenty of bread, and two bottles of wine, with knives and
forks.

" Ah! *ça mes enfans!* there's good wholesome food; you
see I did not know but that madame and mademoiselle might
have to pass two or three days here — and, over there, is
some wood to light a fire if the night air is cold in the cave;
and, to-night, I will bring two blankets to keep madame and
Rosina warm, if they have to pass the whole night here.
Now, I dare say you are all hungry, *mes enfans*, so sit down
and eat, for now I can go back and bring madame myself, as
I shall not have to leave Rosina alone — if I had not met
you, I would have staid with her, and my girl Joan would
have brought madame when dark, but now it will be better
arranged."

Dame Moulin looked quite happy when she saw the three young people so pleased and so familiar. Rosina placing a white napkin on a rock, Henry and Alfred laying a fowl, and the tongue, and the knives and forks, and laughing with all their hearts; thinking only of the moment, and driving away with smiles all thoughts of the perils that were before them.

Kissing all three with the affection of a mother, the good dame brushed away the tears from her eyes; for she thought —though they did not —and she knew that there was yet danger in their path, but she would not for worlds check their spirits. So, bidding them farewell till dark, and telling them on no account to leave the cave, or go out on the beach, and that there were candles and materials for striking a light in Rosina's basket, and plenty of eggs, she departed.

CHAPTER XI.

" Thanks to you and good Dame Moulin," said Henry to
Rosina, helping her to some fowl and tongue ; " this is a vast
improvement on our supper last night in Captain Polard's
fine fort."

" Indeed," said Alfred, " we ought to be greatly obliged
to the said commander's nice thirty-two-pounders ; for without their agency we should not now be enjoying our breakfast with mademoiselle."

" Oh, how terrified I should have been ! " said Rosina,
" had I been near when your ship was blown up into the air ;
but how shockingly distressed both your papas must be, not
knowing what occurred to you ! How you must long to see
them, as I do to see my dear papa ! "

" Was your papa, Rosina, with the poor king of France
during those terrible times ? "

" Oh, yes ! he had a command in the poor king's guard,
and they were nearly all killed at the Tuileries ; but, thank
God ! papa escaped, and afterwards got to England. Oh,
how rejoiced mamma will be to get to England ! "

" May I ask you what was your mamma's name, Rosina,
before she married the Marquis Delancy ? "

" Mamma's name, was Trelawny," said Rosina.

" Trelawny," repeated Henry, " then, very likely, she is a
Cornish lady by birth, and perhaps one of the Trelawnys of

Polgreden Manor, a place very close to our mansion, near Penzance."

"I cannot say I ever heard those names," said Rosina. "But mamma will tell you all about Cornwall, for she often speaks to me of that part of England; but latterly we got so terrified about papa, till we heard he was safe in England, that our lives were wretched — and then the fear of the horrid Blues, who committed such frightful deeds, killing whole villages of poor people because they loved poor King Louis and our beautiful queen — ah! what a life hers must be, and the young dauphine."

"But surely the royalists will conquer in the end," said Henry: "they dare not in reality touch the king."

"Oh! I hope not," said Rosina; "but, when we get to Quiberon, we shall be quite safe, for grandpapa is there — oh! such a grand, good old man, is grandpapa — he is seventy years old, and-yet he is fighting for the king; and then there is the handsome Count de Sombreul, who was such a friend of papa's, though much younger — and the Count de Herville — all at Quiberon."

"But how is it, that these gentlemen, having soldiers with them," said Henry, "did not take your mamma from the château, instead of leaving her there exposed to such danger?"

"Because," said Rosina, "that cruel and terrible General Moine's army is between the château and Quiberon; and the Royalists, I heard Dame Moulin say, were not strong enough to fight the Blues, so they kept within the walls of Quiberon."

Conversing in this manner the day passed; they certainly, to some extent, disobeyed the good dame's injunctions, for they examined several caves, some of great length, but too dark to explore.

As the sun declined, and the sea-breeze found its way into
the cave, Henry and Alfred lighted a good wood-fire, and, as
it grew darker, a couple of candles.   Rosina began to get a
little uneasy ; but, scarcely an hour had elapsed after the
night set in, when they heard the sound of footsteps in the
outer cave, and, the next instant, Rosina sprung forward and
threw herself into the arms of a lady who accompanied Dame
Moulin into the cave.

By the strong glare of the wood-fire the two cousins had a
clear view of Rosina's mother ; though vested in the costume
of a Bretagne peasant, and wearing the strange head-dress
so disfiguring to the face, they could see that she was a remarkably handsome woman, in age about two or three and
thirty ; and the expression of her features was extremely
pleasing.   After embracing and kissing her daughter, she advanced towards the two youths, and, holding out her hand,
said in English, "I have to return you many thanks, young
gentlemen, for your care and attention to my little girl ; and
I am sure, as a countrywoman of yours, I need not say how
rejoiced I am at your escape from the hands of Captain Polard, who would assuredly have sent you to the prison of
Nantes."

Henry replied that he and his cousin were deeply indebted
to the kindness of Dame Moulin ; for without her most oppor-
tune assistance, they would, no doubt, have been recap-
tured.

" She is a kind, generous creature," said Madame Delancy ;
" but we have no time to lose, for we have determined to
push on to-night as far as we can towards Quiberon, for the
republican soldiers of General Moine are rapidly spreading
over the whole of this part of the country."

Dame Moulin was, during this time, putting a pair of
walking-shoes on little Rosina ; she said they had to walk at

least three leagues before they could say they were safe. The party were soon ready, the fire extinguished, and then, by the aid of a candle, they passed out into the open air, little Rosina holding Henry by the hand.

The tide was at full, and rolled in with a loud splash upon the pebbles to their feet; it was not a very dark night, but there was no moon. "We must go along the beach a short distance," said the dame, "till we come to an easier path up the cliffs, and where they are not so high."

Having reached the desired spot, they all ascended to the summit of the cliffs without much trouble or difficulty. They then, under the guidance of Dame Moulin, proceeded across a waste and barren piece of land, and at length came upon a very indifferent horse road; indeed, like all the roads in Brittany at that period, scarcely deserving of the name. Along this they proceeded, keeping a strict silence, for nearly a league.

Of all the provinces in France, without exception, Brittany is the one which retains even to the present day, and most vividly, the ancient impress of its national character; the ardent and wild superstitions of the past still exist in almost their original force; together with the singular festivals, and even the costumes, of the middle ages. The feudal system, though extinct in principle, yet lives in many of its local customs.

Our travellers were crossing a most extensive heath; they had just come up to some druidical remains surmounted by a huge stone cross. As they were passing this monument of the past, Dame Moulin paused, and, crossing herself, repeated some strange formula preserved by local usages. As she did so, a figure suddenly started out from behind the mass of stones, and, facing the somewhat startled travellers, tossed its arms wildly in the air, and then cried out in a strange plaintive voice, in the *patois* of the province, a whole torrent of words.

Madame Delancy and the young people drew back; but Dame Moulin, after crossing herself, addressed the figure in the same dialect, and in a soothing tone.

The figure was certainly sufficiently uncouth to startle Rosina, who clung to Henry in great alarm. It was that of an exceedingly tall, emaciated girl, with her person scarcely covered by a few rags, that fluttered about her in the strong night wind. Her hair, which was long and abundant, was hanging in matted strings all over her person; whilst her long skeleton arms, bare to the shoulder, were waved over her head in the wildest gestures.

"Who is this unfortunate creature?" said Madame Delancy to Dame Moulin; "I think, now I see her features, I have some slight recollection of her — can it be possible she is Madeleine d'Ailby le Grange?"

"Yes, madame, it is her, but she is off again;" for the poor maniac no sooner heard her name pronounced, than with a sharp cry she fled across the heath.

"What did she say, dame?" demanded Madame Delancy as they continued their journey.

"The Madonna preserve us!" said the dame; "though she is crazy she knows what is going on better than any one, and sees things other people can't see — but so the Lord wills it. But we must turn back, we can't go the way I intended."

"Why, what has happened, dame — what did the poor crazy creature say, that causes you to turn aside here?"

"She says, madame," said Dame Moulin shuddering, that she saw this night the *karrequel-an-ancow*,* and the

---

* The chariot of death.

saints keep us from such a sight, for he or she that sees it never lives long after the terrible sight. She says, she saw in the chariot the three great leaders of the Royalists."

"Poor unfortunate!" said Madame Delancy; "her disturbed imagination creates visions."

"And yet, madame, she named the three chiefs," said the dame, shaking her head.

"But what is there in this to make you turn off in this direction?" said Rosina's mother.

"Because, madame, Madeleine says she saw twenty mounted troopers of the Blues, half a mile from here, in the little Wood of Grouan, the very place we were going through, and that the men were dismounted, and their horses were picketted, as if they were on the watch. We will now keep down nearer the coast; it is a little longer, but safer as things turn out."

As they walked on, little Rosina said to Henry, "Did you ever hear of this terrible chariot of death that the people of this country believe so firmly in?"

"No, indeed, Rosina! I know I have read something about Bretagne, and that they are a very strange people."

"Pray, Dame Moulin," said Madame Delancy, "who did Madeleine see in the *karrequel-an-ancow?*"

Dame Moulin hesitated, but at length said, "She saw the Bishop of Dol, the Count de Sombreul, and"—she paused.

"Well, dame!"

The dame sighed, and then in a low voice said, "The old Marquis Delancy."

"Ah! my dear grandfather!" said Rosina, in a tone of grief, "and the brave, handsome Count Sombreul."

"But, my dear Rosina," said Henry, "you do not give credit to such a foolish superstition—the poor girl is a maniac."

"But I am a native of Bretagne, Henry," said the little girl.

But Madame Delancy observed, "Dear me, dame, do not give way to such fancies; this poor girl is in the habit of following the soldiers of the Royalist army, and she has picked up these names, and they float about in her confused brain!"

"What is the tradition of this 'chariot of death'?" said Alfred to his cousin, after listening and catching as much of the observation as he could.

Madame Delancy heard the question, and immediately said — "Dame Moulin shall tell you Master Alfred, and also who this poor girl is; it will beguile the way; for I assure you, three years ago — indeed, two — she was a very smart, pretty girl, and married well." Then, addressing Dame Moulin, she requested her to tell the two cousins how Madeleine became crazy.

"Ah, ça, poor thing! she may well curse the Blues," said Dame Moulin; "but poor Madeleine's story is soon told. But first to tell you about the *karrequel-an-ancow* — there are some things never pass away, and this tradition is one. The karrequel is a chariot drawn by a half-starved cow (Henry smiled, but kept his thoughts to himself); on the cow sits an old wrinkled sorceress, with a scythe and a lantern in her hands, and a terrible spur on the heel, with which she goads the cow into fearful speed, throwing up showers of mud and stones. Sometimes the chariot contains the ghosts of the departed, sometimes the likeness of those who are to die a violent death soon. After the chariot come fiends yelling and screaming fearfully. May the blessed saints save me from such a sight! Madeleine has seen it, and her doom is fixed."

"Strange," thought Henry to himself, "that any mind,

save a diseased one, could entertain so absurd a belief;" and yet, had Henry conversed much with the peasantry of England, Ireland, Wales, or Scotland, he would have heard just as improbable legends steadily believed in. "As to poor Madeleine," continued Dame Moulin, "she is the daughter of a farmer well to do, and, on her bridal night, the farm was surrounded by a body of General Moine's troopers, for they were all known to be stanch royalists. They broke into the house, and, in the scuffle and brutality that ensued, the Blues massacred the girl's family, and burnt down the farm, leaving the poor girl herself insensible, and carried off her husband, and forced him to be a soldier; but by Madeleine's help he escaped — but, alas! overtaken by General Moine's troopers, they seized him in Grouan Wood, and hung him to one of the trees, tying his wretched wife to the same tree. They left her; she, when released by some peasants, was a maniac: ever since she has wandered wild about the country, her fits at times returning; they say she spies all the movements of the Blues, and betrays them to the Royalists: if the Blues catch her they will shoot her."

"What monsters!" exclaimed all the young people. "Before I leave this land," said Henry, indignantly, "I hope to to fight a battle by the side of the royal troops."

Madame Delancy looked into the fine youthful features of the high-spirited lad, saying, "Alas! my dear boy, you are young to mingle in fierce strife: this is a vile war, an unnatural one, as all civil strifes are — father against son, and son against father."

"Surely, Henry," said Rosina in her low, pretty voice; "surely, you will not think of mingling in this terrible fighting. Had you not better try to get to England as soon as possible? your papa and mamma must be fretting themselves to death."

"Yes, my dear Rosina, so I will; but in the mean time, let me see one fight by the side of true and loyal men — seeing fights is nothing new to me, young as I am."

Rosina shook her little head; but they walked on rapidly, and in another hour reached the front of a large farmhouse and out-offices.

"This farm belongs," said Dame Moulin, "to a good man, and here you will be safe till we learn where the forces of the Count de Herville are."

The people of the farm were soon roused, for it was near their time of rising, and Dame Moulin, explaining to the good people how Madame Delancy and her companions were situated, they immediately showed them every hospitality they could; at the same time, they gave them cheering intelligence that the way was clear: that General Moine's army had retired further from the coast, so that they might, after a couple of hours' rest, easily proceed to Quiberon.

After a few hours' rest and refreshment, and thanking gratefully the honest, kind-hearted people, who seemed so willing to do them all the kindness in their power, they prepared for departure. The farmer harnessed a horse to one of his waggons, with a bed on it, to take them to Quiberon; and here they parted with good Dame Moulin, who shed many tears at bidding farewell to her mistress; "but," she said, "the day would yet come when peace and tranquillity would be restored to unhappy France, and Madame Delancy return to the old château, and make her people happy."

Little Rosina shed many tears as she bade the kind dame farewell, and said, "Why not come with us, dame, out of this terrible country?"

"Because, dear child," said the dame, "it is my country still, and I love it! It is not the country's fault, but of its wicked rulers and the wicked blues — God blessed the land, but man brings a curse upon his gifts! Farewell, young gentlemen," said the good dame, embracing them, "when you get home to your own dear land, do not forget Bretagne. If there are bad men trying to destroy its simple happiness, recollect that there are true and honest hearts in it still. May the blessed saints protect you!" and drawing Henry aside, she said in a low serious tone, "I know you do not believe in the *karrequel-an-ancow*; but remember this, it's the prophecy of Margaret of the Mill. In Rosina Delancy you behold your future wife — love her, cherish and protect her. She will be a treasure your heart will guard as eagerly as a miser does his gold. Now, farewell again," the dame kissed his brow, wrung his hand, and departed.

CHAPTER XII.

QUIBERON was at this time the great rendezvous of the Royalist forces, and many of the nobility and gentry of the province, faithful to the Royal cause, took refuge there from the cruel persecutions and outrages of the Blues.

The town of Quiberon was seated at the extremity of a peninsula; it was an ugly old French town, with walls and gates, and houses with strange gables and chimneys, and a quaint, antique-attired people; but they were a simple, loyal race, and the town commanded a noble view over a splendid bay, with a peep of Bellisle in the distance to the north.

The town was guarded by a strong fort called Penthière; this fort had just been taken by the Count de Herville, and great rejoicings were taking place in consequence.

The wagon containing the Countess Delancy, her daughter, and Henry and Alfred, reached Quiberon in safety. Henry, with his high spirit and untiring energy, cheered them on the way; whilst Alfred, relieved from fear of falling into the hands of the revolutionary soldiers, gave way to the inertness of his disposition, and thought of nothing else but the near prospect of getting home to his former life of ease and quietness.

On reaching Quiberon, the countess was joyfully received by her father-in-law, the gallant old Marquis Delancy. He became at once interested with the two boys introduced to him by the countess, and insisted upon their taking up their abode with his daughter-in-law, in a good and comfortable house which was immediately got ready for them, and a servant to attend upon them. The marquis took, in a few days, a prodigious liking to Henry; his eager, ardent spirit was completely roused by the martial and stirring scenes he witnessed from the windows of their house, which looked out upon the great square where the Royalist troops assembled. An English fleet was expected at Quiberon to bring help to the Royalists; and those families that eagerly wished to fly from France were anxiously watching its arrival in the bay.

Alfred passed his days quietly reading and chatting to little Rosina; but the enthusiastic little girl was more bent upon following the movements of Henry, for whom she evinced a singular attachment. Henry soon became acquainted with many of the Royalist leaders, especially with the Count de Herville and the handsome and gay Count de Sombreul. His perfect knowledge of French, his lively manner, and ardent desire to acquire some knowledge of military affairs, pleased the leaders of the Royalists. The Marquis Delancy insisted on supplying them with a complete outfit in garments, theirs being worn out and thread bare. When dressed in his new garments, which were made after a military fashion, little Rosina looked at Henry with a very serious air,—

"Surely, Henry," said his pretty examiner, "you are not now going to turn soldier! Mamma is only waiting for an opportunity to get to England and join papa, and you and Alfred are coming with us?"

"But, my dear little girl," said Henry, "you would not wish me to remain idle; we cannot get away yet, for there are no ships, and two French men-of-war are watching the mouth of the bay. Don't you see, I am quite as tall and as stout as many of the brave young men training every day in the square, and the Count de Sombreul has promised to take me out to have a brush with your old persecutors, the Blues."

"What!" said Alfred, laying down his book, "you are not in earnest, Henry, surely — what have you to say to Royalists and Blues? I wish we were aboard an English ship."

"My dear Alfred," said Henry, "you forget that England is sending over soldiers to help these brave Frenchmen against the cruel wretches that have killed the best and noblest in the land — then, think how kind they are to us; we ought to show our gratitude."

"But," said Rosina, with tears in her eyes, "you might be wounded — ah, dear me! you might be killed!"

"If I am wounded, Rosina," said Henry, "you will nurse me; and, if I am killed, I shall die in a good and righteous cause. Did I not brave death often with those horrid privateer's men: I was not afraid then — why should I now? Besides, Rosina, you ought to rejoice at my being permitted to fight for your father's countrymen. Remember poor Madeleine, how cruelly she was treated by the Blues!"

"But you are so young, Henry; you see Alfred is content to remain with us quietly, and take care of us: if you were a man it would be different."

"But Alfred, dear Rosina, was reared differently from me; he is equally brave, but I have been accustomed from my very early years to face danger, and, with God's blessing, I have hitherto escaped."

"Indeed, Cousin Henry," said Alfred with a blush, "I confess I am not naturally brave; left to my own choice I would never go in the way of danger — aboard that horrid privateer, the *Fury*, I had no help for it."

"Then, my dear Alfred, the courage you displayed was the more worthy of praise; yours was moral courage—mind against the weakness of the body. I do not wish to see you join me, because it is not your natural inclination. You love peace and tranquillity; you can enjoy both, and do good besides; all I wish to see is, that you refrain from that listless inertness of disposition you feel inclined to submit to."

"No fear of that, my dear Harry," returned Alfred with a smile; "whilst under your care, I have had a very good apprenticeship."

"Ah!" said Rosina, "Alfred is right, Henry. What a blessed thing peace and quietness is! Look out of this window: look how lovely the bay looks, with the sun shining so bright on its waters, and they so blue and calm; what do you call those two lovely little islands?"

"Hoedic and Houat," said Henry; "and that long range of black objects, away to the right, are called the Cardinal Rocks. You see, they seem to shut out the waves and the gales from this fine bay."

"I sincerely wish," said Alfred, "that we had an opportunity of letting our dear parents know that we are safe; they must be in terrible anxiety."

"If we had the means of sending a letter," said Henry, "we could go ourselves; but, depend on it, we shall soon have plenty of English vessels here, and then the Count de Herville will drive away the Blues, under General Hoch; his army is posted on the Heights of St. Barbe. Ha! there is the sound of drums and trumpets," continued Henry, starting away from the back windows of the house they lived in, and which commanded a fine view of the bay—"let us go to the front and see the troops."

That night, the 16th of July, it was determined by the

Count de Herville to make an attack upon the right flank of General Hoch's army. The English fleet was expected back in the bay, and his little army was re-enforced by two hundred British marines. The Counts de Sombreul and de Herville came in the evening to see the Countess Delancy before their departure. The old Marquis Delancy was sitting with his daughter-in-law, and the three young people, Henry, Alfred, and Rosina. Henry had overcome all the opposition of the countess to his going with the troops — the Counts de Herville and de Sombreul promised to take every care of him ; but, in truth, the high-spirited boy of seventeen was, from early experience and development, already a young man. Alfred, of the same age, looked a mere boy — but such has often been the case ; some of our greatest military heroes, in all countries, have fought their first field ere sixteen years had passed over their heads.

"The *Robust* and the *Thunderer*," said the Count de Herville to the marquis, "have just anchored below Cramee ; we shall have five British launches with twenty-four-pound carronades to cover our retreat, if retreat be necessary."

" I rejoice at that," said the old marquis, then in his seventieth year ; " for, if we are driven back, we shall be able to get the countess and these young folks aboard a British ship. I know you are anxious, my dear child, to quit this land of strife."

" Yes, dear sir," said the countess with a sigh ; " it is not only a land of strife, but of famine — the accounts from Paris of the sufferings of the people, from want of bread, is fearful."

" Yes," returned the Count de Sombreul bitterly ; " the regicides are howling for bread and the constitution of '93. There has been a terrible day of reckoning for some of the monsters — Billaud, Collot, Barère, and Vadier, are, we hear, condemned to be transported to the pestilential colony of Cayenne. In fact, my dear madame," said the Count de Herville, " every thing is turning out hopefully for the restoration of the monarchy; there is scarcely a single province of France that has escaped the horrors of civil war — the pursuits of industry are paralyzed, the chief seats of commerce and manufacture purposely destroyed. In fact, but for the superiority of England on the seas, our foreign commerce would have expired altogether. Then, look at the horrors waiting in the interior of France, and in our great cities — alas ! liberty has been a great chimera ! "

The little party now broke up. The marquis embraced his daughter-in-law with much emotion — did a feeling pervade his aged heart that they parted for the last time on earth ? The countess wept bitterly, and could scarcely utter a word; little Rosina clung round her grandfather's neck, sobbing bitterly; but the brave old Royalist stood erect — " Courage, *mes enfans !* " and, lifting his right hand to heaven, he said in a touching voice — " The Lord fights for us, why need we despair ? and, if we die, it's in a glorious cause ! "

They departed ; and Rosina, with her arms round Henry's neck, the tears rolling down her cheeks, said, " But you, Henry — you, so young — you need not thus sacrifice yourself. You are entirely English ; you ought to stay and protect mamma and poor Rosina."

" I shall best protect you, dear child," said the young soldier, " by helping to drive away from this place those who oppress you." Kissing the sorrowing little girl, and shaking Alfred's hand, he rushed after the Count de Sombreul.

It was an extremely dark night for the season of the year, as the royal troops, under the Counts de Herville, de

Sombreul, and the Marquis Delancy, marched forth to attack the Heights of St. Barbe, intending to take General Hoch by surprise. But in this the Royalist leaders were deceived, for treachery was already in their ranks. General Hoch was quite aware of their intended attack. Henry, with a sash round his waist containing a brace of pistols, and a cutlass in his hand, walked by the side of de Sombreul with a steady step and a cheerful, hopeful heart.

"You are young," said the count, "for a night attack, my dear boy, though you have stood fire before now, and seen balls fly about like hail; yet in an attack of this kind, in the darkness of night, it's trying — I was younger than you, though," added the count, "when I first drew my maiden sword."

"Oh, never fear for me, count!" said Henry. "I will follow you close; this is not worse than boarding an enemy's ship amid a storm of grape and canister."

He had scarcely spoken the words than, from both sides of the road, a stream of bright light flashed across their eyes, and then followed the rattle of musketry, and a storm of balls clattered in amongst the advanced troops, and many a brave heart was laid low. "You are betrayed, count," said Henry, as for an instant the troop were brought to a halt, and then a tremendous fire was poured in upon the ambushed enemy.

In vain was courage, gallantry, and skill displayed by the Royalists; they were surrounded. In the terrible confusion that ensued, Henry, whose gallantry and coolness amazed the men, got separated from de Sombreul, and fell in with a party of men headed by the Count de Herville; at that moment a ball struck the count and he fell. Henry rushed to his side, and called loudly to the retreating soldiers that their commander was down.

"Fly, my dear boy," said the count, "while you have yet time."

"No, no," said Henry, raising the count's head. "I trust in God you are not seriously hurt."

"Not severely, my brave boy; here are some of my men." A party in full retreat now came up, and, lifting the count, they bore him rapidly along. Henry was following, when a spent ball struck him on the leg and he fell; he was not much hurt, and, after a moment, he rose again on his feet, but the men that bore the count were out of sight. Before he could stir, a party of the Blues rushed by him, one aiming a blow with his sabre at him, but Henry shot the man down; the next instant a blow from the butt of a musket stretched him senseless on the sod.

The Count de Herville, as the men bore him along, kept anxiously inquiring if Henry was following. The men, too anxious to escape, said, "Yes." On approaching the shore, the English launches at once opened fire upon the pursuing enemy, and this saved the remnant of the royal army. The rage of the Count de Herville was great when he found out that Henry was left behind, and doubtless a prisoner in the hands of the Blues. The Countess Delancy was shocked—as to Rosina, she was inconsolable, and wept bitterly. For a moment Alfred appeared stupefied; then, stealing forth from the house, he disappeared.

CHAPTER XIII.

Henry Barlow, in the mean time, lay stretched upon the field of battle : he quickly, however, recovered his sensibility ; for, though the blow stunned him, he had only received half its force, the Blue having slipped in aiming his blow at the youth. It was still night ; he could hear the shouts and shots from the pursuing enemy, and the loud boom of the British carronades. He tried to rise, but his leg was now swelled from the blow of the spent-ball ; the effort to rise made him dizzy, and he sunk back fainting upon the ground. He was in the midst of the dead and dying ; for, in the pauses of the strong blast that swept over the field of strife, he could hear deep groans — and, alas! fierce oaths and imprecations — from the wounded, at their comrades for deserting them.

As the pain and dizziness in his head subsided, he made another attempt to rise, so as to get out of the way of the retreating enemy ; but, hearing voices and shouts, he again lay down, and, in the dim light, he saw bodies of men cross the field, stooping, and either lifting some wounded comrade, or rifling the dead ; these passed on, and so did others. He lay perfectly still, and again all became silent, save the breath of the gale as it swept over the dying and the dead.

He thought of home, of his dear father, and of merry, happy England ; and the tears, despite his courage and high spirit, rolled down his cheeks. He did not weep for pain, nor from fear — the latter was a sensation unknown to him; but his heart was softened by recollection of those dear to him, and whom he might never see again.

Of the dead he felt no sensation of dread; for he, unconsciously, was leaning on the dead body of the very soldier he had shot. As the gray of the early morn crept over the earth and sky, Henry beheld a figure wandering with unsteady steps amid the dead, stooping every moment as the dawn increased; he started up on his elbow, and gazed at the slight figure advancing towards him.

"Ah, happiness! it is my dear Cousin Alfred," exclaimed Henry, shouting with all his might, and, making an effort, he stood up.

With a cry of joy, Alfred rushed towards his cousin, his face pale as death, and, throwing himself into his arms, he wept passionately with joy.

"My brave, kind-hearted Alfred," said Henry; "and you have been wandering here amidst the dead, looking for me!"

"Yes," replied the boy with a shudder, "and, thank God, I have found you, dear, dear Harry! I knew not how I loved you till I thought I had lost you; but you are hurt — you are wounded — the blood is running down your face!"

"It is nothing — it's a scratch on the head. My leg is bruised by a spent-ball, but with your help I can hobble on right well; don't talk any more of want of courage, dear Alfred: is not this a noble proof of both courage and love?"

"Ah!" exclaimed Alfred, "how often have you shielded me from danger, exposing your own body! how often done double duty to give me a night's rest! But come from amongst the dead — oh! how horrible and ghastly they look! you have been lying on a dead body!"

"Never mind, poor fellow! I could not hurt him now,"

said Henry; " he tried to kill me, and I was forced in my own defence to kill him — it's the fortune of war."

" *Arrête*, you young dogs!" shouted a voice behind them, " or I'll give you the contents of my carbine."

Both youths turned round with a start, and beheld, coming towards them, a tall, strapping soldier of the Blues, with a cocked carbine in his hand. " Pick up that musket, Alfred, and give it me; perhaps it's loaded."

" Let us run — let us run!" said Alfred anxiously. " Alas! I forget, you can't run."

" Ah!" roared the republican soldier, " rascals! do you think to escape me?" and, lifting his carbine, he was about to fire before Henry could lift his musket and cock it, when a figure lying flat upon the ground suddenly sprung up behind the Blue, and, throwing its arms round his neck, dragged him back. The man, with a savage oath, raised his carbine to strike the strange figure dead, but Henry raised the musket and fired; the man was not badly wounded, but he staggered forward and fell with an oath.

" Alfred," said Henry, limping up to the wounded soldier, " this is the mad girl Madeleine."

" Ha, ha, ha!" wildly shrieked the unfortunate girl, spurning with her foot the wounded Blue — " Come," said she, waving her naked arms, " follow me — quick, quick!"

This Henry and Alfred did, as well as the latter could with his swelled ankle, and then, scrambling through one of the low, thick hedges, Henry, in considerable pain, leaned back against the hedge, and then looked earnestly into the wasted features of the wretched maniac.

" Cannot we get back to the fort, Madeleine," said Henry, " by a longer road, and thus avoid meeting the Blues?"

" No, no!" exclaimed the girl, " Blues between us and the

fort now — see," and, pointing to a distance, they beheld the ruins of an old château — "safe there."

But Henry and Alfred were intensely anxious to get back to Quiberon ; his leg, he fancied, was getting much better ; but Alfred, who had climbed up a steep bank, said, " Here is a woman coming this way, and I do verily believe it is the same dame we met when we first landed — yes ! I am sure it is."

Madeleine was sitting with her head leaning on her hands, singing a strange melancholy ditty, and rocking herself to and fro.   She now started up, though she did not understand the words, and, climbing up, looked where Alfred pointed.

" Dame Moulin — Dame Moulin !" said Madeleine to Henry ; " and, see — Blues ! "

Henry contrived to get up, and saw Dame Moulin quite close to them ; and, looking back, he saw a body of cavalry, in the uniform of the Blues, scouring across the plain, and long files of infantry descending from the Heights of St. Barbe.

Dame Moulin at once recognized the party, up to whom she advanced in great haste.

" Are you here, my children ? " said the dame, with a look of profound amazement, " and Madeleine — how is this ? "

Before Henry could explain, Madeleine wildly cried out, " The Blues — the Blues ! let us fly ! "   All looked round, and, sure enough, they beheld a body of horse wheel round and gallop towards them.

" Woe to us all ! " said Dame Moulin, wringing her hands ; " last night I lost my only son — he lies dead yonder — he was a Blue, poor boy ! he will be buried where he fell.   Well, the Lord blessed all the earth ; one spot is as good as another. I kissed his cold face, and have seen the last of him; come along, *mes enfans*, we must move from here," but Madeleine seemed in a stupor, she kept muttering strange words, in a *patois* unintelligible to Henry, till he took her by the arm to get her to come on.

"My hour is come — my hour is come!" said the girl wildly. "I saw my husband in the *karraquel-an-ancow*, and he beckoned me to come — woe, woe to the land!"

As they hurried her along, the troop of cavalry gained the side of the low hedge. "Run, run, in the name of Madonna!" said Dame Moulin; "let us get the other side of yonder hedge, and the cavalry cannot cross."

"Alas! dame, I can scarcely walk, let alone run," said Henry; "but do you all go on, for it is better for only one to be taken than all."

"I will stay with you, Harry, if I die," said Alfred.

"*Arrêtez vous!*" shouted the horse-soldiers from the other side of the hedge; "stop, aristocrats, or you are dead;" but the little party pressed on across the field, Henry resting on Alfred and the good dame

"Ah, cursed rebels!" snouted the dragoons; and, raising their carbines, they fired a volley.

Madeleine alone was hit; she fell postrate on her face. Henry stooped; he raised the girl's head, and looked into the poor, wasted, emaciated features. She was released from her troubles — she was dead!

Dame Moulin, wringing her hands, exclaimed in a voice of terror, "Lost, lost — all lost!" and ran on by herself for the hedge, saying, "Alas! God alone can save them — I cannot."

Four of the troopers had leaped their horses over the fence, and now, with loud shouts of derision, galloped up alongside the two youths.

"Ha, you young rascals, we have caught you! You are young at your work, but quite fledged enough for mother guillotine. As the carbineer spoke, he threw himself from his horse and approached the youths, who stood patiently awaiting their fate. "So," said the man, "you two and that imp," spurning the body of poor Madeleine with his foot, " thought to murder Sergeant Le Croix, to plunder him, you young butchers!"

"What do you mean?" exclaimed Henry, indignantly.

"Eh? then you speak French like a native, my young cock, and you crow loud, too! Hold out your wrists: you will be taught before long not to plunder the dead."

"It's false!" said Henry, with a flushed cheek, putting his hand on the remaining pistol in his sash.

"Ha! young villain, would you fire upon us? Come here, comrades! Take them over the hedge, tie ropes to their wrists, and drag them after us to the camp." This was literally done, Henry suffering exquisite pain from his leg.

"You have no right," said Henry, "to treat even an enemy in so brutal and cowardly a manner: I am wounded in the leg, and cannot keep up with you."

"We'll drag you after us. You had no pity for Sergeant Le Croix when you shot him down because he wanted to hinder you from rifling the dead — he heard you speaking English, you young whelps!"

"Take the boy up, Jaques — take him up!" said one of the troop more humane than the rest; " do you not see he cannot walk, and the perspiration pours from his head and face?" The trooper who thus spoke rode up, and, offering his hand, said, "Come, lad; give me your hand, and get up behind me."

With a brutal and coarse jest the man who held the rope attached to Henry's wrist let it go, saying, "Kill your horse, if you like, comrade ; I'll take care mine shall not carry any of the brood of aristocrats."

The two boys were, however, mounted behind the troopers, and then they moved on at a smart trot for the camp of General Hoch. The troopers rode back towards the late field of strife ; there were parties burying the dead, and conveying off the wounded. Henry, as he rode close to poor Alfred, who looked the picture of despair, tried to raise his spirits by words of encouragement and hope — " When we get to to an officer," said Henry, " we shall be treated differently."

" Hold thy tongue, spawn of an aristocrat ! " said the fierce trooper who had behaved so cruelly to Henry ; and, putting a cocked pistol to his head, he added, " None of thy heretical prayers, or I'll blow thy brains out."

Henry had too much good sense to bandy words with such a ruffian, therefore he remained silent ; passing across the plain, they began their ascent to the camp. On reaching the outposts, before which were several wagons loaded with wretched prisoners — some actually dying of their wounds — the troop halted. Henry and Alfred were put down and fastened together with a cord by the wrists.

" Who have you there ? " said an officer with a most repulsive and savage countenance, stopping and eyeing the two youths with a most sinister scowl.

" Two spawns of heretical aristocrats," said the trooper. " Sergeant Le Croix says he saw them rifling the dead after the night attack. They doubtless came out of Quiberon : they are English. The sergeant saw them pilfering, and, when he called out to them, this young fellow fired a musket at him and wounded him. Here is the sergeant coming ; he can scarcely walk, he is wounded in the thigh."

" All this is false, captain ! " said Henry resolutely. " We are English, but we came out — that is, I did — last night, and fought by the side of the Counts de Sombreul and de Herville. This young lad did not fight at all, but came out to look for me, his cousin; we only defended ourselves."

The Blue gave a scornful laugh — "What do you say, Sergeant Le Croix?"

"That young viper and his comrade, with that mad girl, Madeleine, who has so often betrayed our soldiers to the Royalists, did their best to murder me."

"Wretch!" said Henry, with indignation, "dare you tell, before God, so great a lie?"

"Bah!" said the French officer contemptuously; "why did you not shoot them at once, Jaques Mercecourt, instead of bringing them to pester me? There, Sergeant Dubois, take a half a dozen men, march them to the foot of yonder rock, and shoot them like young rooks — such are General Moine's orders: any one, no matter friend or enemy, stripping the dead, to be instantly shot."

"You dare not commit such a crime!" said Henry indignantly. A burst of laughter broke from the lips of those savage revolutionists. "At least," said Henry earnestly, "let my comrade here have justice and mercy. It was I shot at Sergeant Le Croix in my own defence."

"The rebel owns to the deed at last," said the officer; "take them away, our time is precious."

"Come, march! I have no music for you," said the brutal Sergeant Dubois, "but you may whistle if it relieves you."

Alfred burst into tears, and, with his unbound hand, he pressed Henry's neck, bowing his head on his shoulder, sobbing — "O, Henry, Henry, this is too hard! O my poor father!"

"Heaven knows I would die twice over for you," said Henry bitterly; "but God still beholds us."

" Halt ! " said a loud authoritative voice to the men, as they were about to push on the lads with the butts of their muskets. An officer in the uniform of a colonel of chasseurs stepped forward, saying, " You are too hasty, Captain Gerard ; this must not be : I have listened to what that noble boy said, and I believe him. Come here, Sergeant Le Croix " — the man hobbled up, looking startled ; " what did you see those two young lads strip off the dead ? "

The man looked confused, but he said, " I saw them stooping and pushing over a dead soldier of our regiment, and that stout lad picked up a musket and shot me in the thigh."

" And that is your reason for saying, rascal, that they were stripping the dead ? Begone, sir ! and feel grateful I do not strip you of your sergeant's stripe. Who are you, young gentlemen ? " said the colonel, mildly addressing Henry.

Henry, in remarkably few words, told their real story. The colonel was interested. " You see, Captain Gerard, you might have committed a great crime."

" Nevertheless, colonel," said Captain Gerard doggedly, " they are prisoners of war, and I must obey General Moine's orders, and send them on in these wagons to Nantes." ·

" To that decision I can offer no check," said the colonel, " but treat the lads kindly. Farewell, my poor boys," said the colonel ; " I shall not forget your courage. You may yet see your country and your homes."

The near approach of death could not bring tears from the noble-hearted Henry ; but, as he pressed the kind colonel's hand in his, it was bathed in tears.

10

CHAPTER XIV.

The Countess Delancy, when she learned next day the disastrous events of the night's encounter, and that the Royalists were not only defeated but many slain, her brave old father-in-law taken prisoner, and the Count de Herville wounded, was distracted; her own sorrows for a time rendered her oblivious of the disappearance of the two youths.

Rosina wept without ceasing. She wept for her grandfather, and for her young companions, but especially for her favorite Henry.

The Count de Sombreul did all he could to soothe the countess; but he was sorely hurt, and cut to the heart at the state of affairs, for the cause of the Royalists in Quiberon was desperate. Desertions were constantly taking place, and treachery at work in every quarter. The ships of war were in the bay, ready to embark the principal Royalists and emigrants, but the weather was dreadful.

On the night of the 22d of July — a night long remembered by those who suffered during its terrible hours — the storm howled over the bay, the waves rolled on the shore with a noise like thunder, the darkness was intense, and a pitiless rain added to its horrors.

A party of emigrant soldiers who were on guard deserted, and shortly after returned with a large body of republican troops. A scene of confusion and horror ensued. Whilst the faithful were staining the ground with their blood, the cowardly laid down their arms, and joined the assailants in the terrible cry of " Vive la Republique! " and, in the end, even helped to massacre their officers. About one thousand of the royalist troops, led by Pusage, fled to the seashore, leaving the brave de Sombreul fighting to the last; one thousand of the fugitives fled with the troops, to get aboard the shipping, to escape captivity or death.

The countess, roused from her couch by the horrible tumult, and by an officer and some men sent by the Count de Sombreul to conduct her and her daughter to the seashore, and to see to their safe embarking, hurriedly dressed herself and child, and, amid the darkness and storm, they were guided to the beach to await daylight.

" Oh! what a scene of horror! " exclaimed the countess, clasping her child close to her side. Some flaming houses threw a fearful glare over the streets, peals of musketry rattled on all sides, the shouts of a furious enemy were heard above all. Screams of terrified women, flying with children in their arms, altogether presented a sight appalling and bewildering.

A vast crowd pressed upon their rear; the countess could scarcely keep her feet, though the officer and his men did all they could to save them.

As the dawn appeared, the wretched fugitives gave a shout of joy. The British frigates, who feared to approach the shore during the storm and darkness, were standing in under double-reefed topsails; and soon numerous boats and launches covered the waters, and were run in on the beach to embark the tired, worn-out, and dripping fugitives.

Then came a fearful rush to the boats, for the Blues were assembling and firing on the wretched people.

During all the hours of the night, little Rosina clung to her mother; she was nearly dead with fatigue, when a terrible rush of the crowd threw her down; the next instant she was separated from her mother. With a wild shriek, mother and child were torn asunder — bruised and faint, Rosina lay prostrate; as the crowd passed on, she was left alone; but when she tried to rise, terror deprived her of strength, and she fainted.

How long she remained in that state the poor child knew not; for the terrors of the night, the separation from her mother, the soaking wet she endured, brought on a fever.

When she opened her eyes, so as to be conscious of objects around her, she perceived she was lying on a very humble bed, in a small low room, and, sitting at the foot of the bed, was a female knitting. Rosina sobbed out, "O mother, mother! where are you? Your poor Rosina will die."

The woman started up, dropping her knitting, and, running to the bed, Rosina beheld Dame Moulin. "Ah, the blessed Mary be praised!" said the dame, bending over the bed and kissing the child's cheeks, "you are coming to."

"But where is my mother — my beloved mother?" sobbed the little girl; "and where am I, Dame Moulin?"

"Be patient, my poor child, and I will tell you every thing. Now, drink this," and she handed her little patient a mug filled with some refreshing drink.

"Only say is my dear mother safe, dame," said Rosina, "and I will bless you, and do any thing you ask me."

"Yes, little one," said the kind-hearted dame; "she must be safe, for she was put into a boat, and carried aboard one of the great English ships of war.

"Alas! alas!" exclaimed Rosina, "why was not I also put aboard?"

"My child, you were found insensible on the shore by a good town's-woman of Quiberon, who knew you; the boats were all full and pulling off for the ships, and the Blues were firing at those left on the beach; so she took you up, and, with her daughter, carried you here: you are in one of the little cabins outside Quiberon."

"And how came you to know I was here, dear dame? Ah, my poor mother! what she must suffer."

"The good woman of this cottage," said Dame Moulin, "is my poor son's mother-in-law; her daughter is his widow. I came to Quiberon, anxious to inquire how your dear mother got away that dreadful night, and naturally I came here, and here I found you, poor child! in a high fever; and heard that your two brave little comrades are both prisoners to the Blues."

Rosina threw her arms round the dame's neck, and wept herself to sleep. Youth, extreme youth, recovers more rapidly from shocks that rend the heart than mature age; hope almost always lives in the young heart, uncrushed by repeated sorrows and trials. Rosina in a few days was able to leave her bed; she was very thin, looked sad and thoughtful, but still she was gradually gaining strength.

"And now, dear dame, what is to be done — how am I to be got aboard the ship where mamma is?"

"Alas! my child," said Dame Moulin sorrowfully, "the ships have sailed away. The Blues have complete possession of Quiberon and all the places on the coast; the Royalists have all fled."

Rosina clasped her hands in despair; her large and beautifully expressive eyes filling with tears. "And am I never," said the child bitterly, to "leave this wretched, blood-stained land — never to see those so dear to me? Oh! better, better I had died on the beach that terrible night."

"Ah! my child," said Dame Moulin, crossing herself devoutly, "do not be unjust to the mercy of God; your life has been spared, and so, I firmly believe, has your dear mother's. Pray to the saints, trust in their intercession, my poor bereaved little one, and you may yet be happy in your dear mother's arms."

"Ah, Dame Moulin!" said Rosina with a sigh, "misfortune has made me wicked; I do trust in God, and though we pray differently, dear dame, the *bon Dieu* will still listen to us both."

The poor child's sorrow and despair for the first few days were in truth overpowering: in the midst of her own grief she still thought of Henry and Alfred, and begged the dame to try and find out what became of them. After a time she discovered, and told Rosina, that they were both carried prisoners to Nantes. Rosina wept; her little heart was full.

When able to leave the cottage, Dame Moulin dressed her in peasant's attire, and, taking leave of the good folks of the cottage, the dame and her little charge set out for her own home and her mill, and there they arrived safely; and in this quiet retreat we must leave them, to return to our unfortunate prisoners.

Henry and Alfred were placed in a wagon with nearly thirty other prisoners — many severely wounded; so severely, that it appeared scarcely possible that they would survive the journey.

The two youths were handcuffed, and fastened together by a short chain. The wagon was an uncovered, long-bodied cart; the wretched prisoners had neither a mattress or even straw to lie upon; and, as it began to rain heavily after dusk, and they were to travel all night, their sufferings may be imagined.

Poor Alfred was greatly dejected in mind, neither had he the bodily strength to endure the same hardships as Henry.

Some of the prisoners bore their fate with patience and wonderful resignation ; others, with tears and moans ; and a few with imprecations against their merciless conquerors. A troop of horse surrounded the four wagons ; and, if an unfortunate prisoner murmured loudly against the cruel way they were treated, he received a blow from the flat of a sabre, or a poke with the butt of a musket.

Henry tried to shelter Alfred from the rain by sitting at the windward side, for it blew hard, and, by the most hopeful expressions, to cheer the dreary hours of the night.

" Alas ! Harry, we are doomed ; depend on it : we were only saved from instant death to suffer a prolonged one."

" No, dear cousin, I do not think so ; that colonel who saved us was a noble-looking soldier : I have great faith in his words. I do not deny that these Blues — as dear little Rosina called these hard-hearted wretches — are a bloodthirsty, merciless set, and that they commit horrid atrocities ; still, as prisoners of war, we shall have a chance of being released in time — or, perhaps, contrive to escape."

" I am dead to hope," said Alfred ; " the horrid jolting of this frightful cart into ruts deep enough to founder a horse, kills me. I only wonder how our vehicle holds together."

The weary night drew to a close, and, as the morning broke, they halted for a few hours in a miserable village, the inhabitants of which were roused from their slumbers, and forced to find food for the entire escort of prisoners. A mug of sour wine, and a small amount of oaten bread, was the allowance for each prisoner.

A poor fellow died during the halt ; his body was handed out and thrown on the ground, and the country people ordered to bury him — then, after two hours' halt, they again proceeded.

Alfred was now fairly worn out, and Henry getting him to lay his head upon his lap, he sunk into an uneasy slumber.

"That *pauvre garçon* will not trouble our guard long," said a wounded soldier, lying near Henry. "You are English, and too young to be soldiers; how came you into this trouble? But you have a good friend in the colonel that saved you from that brute, Captain Gerard."

"What is the colonel's name?" demanded Henry; "he appeared a kind, good man."

"Ah, and so he is! his name is Moreau, a brave, gallant soldier: we were both born in Morlaix, and we both listed as private soldiers in the same regiment on the same day, and see how different our fates are."

"Then how comes it," said Henry, glad to beguile the time, and if possible divert his thoughts from their sad situation, "that he is now a revolutionary colonel, and you a wounded royalist soldier?"

"Such is life, my lad," said the Royalist with a sigh. "Colonel Moreau's father was an avocat; he didn't choose his son to be a soldier, so he procured his discharge. I had run away from home, too; but my father was a poor baker, so I remained in my regiment till the revolution. The revolution brought young Moreau out. I would not fight against my king, so I deserted and came back into Brittany. I afterwards joined the Chouans, and so on, till I entered the regiment of Royalists commanded by the Count de Herville, and fell the night of our unsuccessful attack upon the Heights of St. Barbe: they will find out who I am when we get to Nantes, and then *ce finis* (it's finished), they will shoot me!"

"I trust not — but what do you think they will do with us?" said Henry.

“ Hard to say, my lad,” returned the soldier. “ You speak French so well, you might pass for a native of one of the southern provinces. You are too young to be very particular; therefore propose to join the revolutionary army, and that will save your lives.”

“ What !” exclaimed Henry, “ join an army of regicides ! No, no ! I do not fear death ; but I wish to save this dear cousin of mine.”

“ You are a brave lad, at all events,” said the man ; “ but still that butcher, General Moine, will have little pity : once within the walls of the strong prison of Nantes, there will be no escape.”

“ Nothing is impossible with the Almighty !” said Henry cheerfully ; “ we are born in hope, and it lives with us as long as the breath of life remains.”

The soldier sighed, saying, “ You are a young philosopher ; but, as you say, why, we hope to the last, and I trust sincerely you will escape the doom that assuredly awaits many of us here — but, behold, there is Nantes !”

The wagons were descending a hill, and, turning an abrupt angle, they beheld the great suburbs and town of Nantes before them, with the mighty Loire winding, like a huge serpent, through a very fine country ; the immense bridge of boats, three miles in length, spanning its broad surface, looking like a dark thread stretched across it. Alfred looked up with a shudder ; he was pale and ill, and exhausted. “ I’m a miserable traveller, Harry,” he added with a faint smile ; “ I feel as if I had an ague.”

“ I trust not,” said Henry anxiously, gently taking hold of the feverish hand of his cousin. “ Alas ! alas !” thought he, “ this cruise of the yacht, to which we looked forward with so much pleasure, see to what it has led — and my fault, too,” he added bitterly.

"Why do you look so sad and stern, Henry?" said Alfred, reading his cousin's expressive features. "You are thinking of me, not yourself, I know."

Harry pressed the boy's hand, and brushed away the tear from his own eyes.

Nantes was reached, and, as they entered the long suburb, crowds collected round the wagons; some uttered expressions of pity, but numbers of fierce sanguinary republicans joined as they entered the town, and mocking remarks and shouts of derision were uttered against the Royalists and soldiers. "Food for the guillotine!" screamed a pack of horrid-looking women, mocking those who seemed to suffer most.

"Shout, ye curs!" said the Royalist soldiers beside Henry. "A month ago, you shouted 'Vive le Roi' when Charette entered the town with his victorious Royalists — curse ye!"

The wagons filed in through the prison-gates into an immense court surrounded by lofty walls. The prisoners were then delivered over to the prison authorities by the officer of the escort, and then began the dismal unloading.

Henry watched the proceedings, and he distinctly saw the officer of the escort point with his sword to him and Alfred; and the official, a jailer no doubt, took a steady look at them, and then said, with a very sinister smile — "*Bien* (very well)!"

"That fellow means no good," thought Henry. Two jailers then came up, and the same man, pointing to the youths, said, "Take them to No. 2 corridor, cell 12 — you understand — by themselves!"

The men nodded, and then desired the youths to follow, one walking before, the other behind.

Passing across the central court, a space capable of containing five hundred men, they entered a smaller yard, and then by a side-door into the great building. After passing through ranges of dismal passages and corridors, they mounted an immense flight of steps, and, finally, the jailer unlocked one of a range of cells.

" There, *mes garçons*, you see your chamber ; " and, un-locking the manacles that kept the two lads together, they entered a very small chamber, with a window heavily barred, and some two feet square ; there was a bench and a straw pallet, or rather a frame like a long box, containing straw and a coarse coverlet like a horse-cloth.

" You are young, *mes enfans*, for captivity," said the jailer ; " but thanks to General Moine, who commands here in Nantes, our prisoners do not long languish in our prisons, we have always a change of guests," and, with a very significant grin, he closed, locked, and bolted the door.

The two cousins stood for a moment gazing upon the limits of the cell and the furniture — if, indeed, you could call the bench and bed-box by that name — with a troubled look. Alfred, overcome by illness and despair, threw him-self in a passion of tears upon the straw, and buried his face in his hands, sobbing in uncontrollable agony.

Henry Barlow knelt by the side of the pallet ; every argu-ment that affection and devotion could use, he tried to soothe his cousin, but the poor boy was really ill, and be-fore morning was quite feverish and delirious.

Henry, naturally of an iron constitution for one so young, bore all his suffering till now without flinching ; but Alfred's situation overcame him, and, with tears, he implored his hard-hearted jailer to afford him the aid of a doctor, or even medicine, but in vain.

" Bah ! " said the brute, " boys never die of illness : he'll get well before he's wanted ; " and, with a malicious grin, he left him to his bitter reflections. Again, the next day, he renewed his solicitations.

“ Miserable wretch !” said Henry, exasperated, “ the day will come when you will implore aid and be refused — then, remember this.”

“ Ha, viper ! do you bite ?” said the jailer ; “ take care, the axe of the guillotine is not far off.”

Youth and the mercy of Providence, however, restored Alfred to his loving and devoted cousin. When quite sensible of all Henry’s care and affection, he threw his arms round his neck, and, sobbing with emotion, said — “ Dear, dear Henry ! what do I not owe to your devotion and love? You have now beheld the last of my weakness, my want of courage, but, above all, a firm reliance in the mercy of Providence. I thought I was dying, but God spared me, and your love and care — sharing your own food to nourish me. Ah ! I have learned a lesson of life that will last me to my grave. Henceforth I will deserve your friendship ; and, if it is the will of God, that these wretches do condemn us to die, I will die like a Briton,” he added with a smile. “ No, dear Harry ! you shall not be ashamed of poor Alfred.”

“ I’m proud of you, my cousin,” said Henry, much moved, and embracing him. “ But I trust with confidence in the justice and mercy of God : we shall not perish here, depend on it, and by the hands of regicides.”

Some days after this conversation, as Alfred gradually regained strength, the door of their prison opened, and the jailer entered, followed by a tall, handsome youth, in an English naval uniform. “ There,” said the jailer, “ is a companion for you.” Henry and Alfred gazed upon the stranger, and he upon them ; and then, with an exclamation, they all started forward, grasping each other’s hands, which they warmly shook, “ Magnus O’More,” exclaimed Harry, “ can this be possible ? ”

“ I am so amazed and confounded,” said Magnus O’More,

their old comrade at the school near Exeter, "that I am like one in a dream."

"There, jabber away at your jargon," said the jailer, who beheld the joy and surprise of the three lads with some degree of vexation that he had been the means of gratifying them, though in truth he could not have helped it. An assistant turnkey then threw down a sack of straw and a quilt, and the three friends were left to themselves.

"We cannot rejoice," said Henry, "at your captivity, Magnus; but, since this misfortune has occurred to you, we rejoice at having your company in our solitary cell."

"Ah!" said the young midshipman — a remarkably noble, handsome lad, of seventeen or eighteen — "if you knew the relief I feel at being with you, after days spent in a wretched cell, with nearly two hundred condemned wretches, dragged out daily to execution and others thrust in their place — such a den of horrors may I never see again! But what on earth brought you here, Alfred?" continued Magnus O'More — "Henry, being in the navy, I can fancy becoming a prisoner, but you."

"Ah!" said Alfred, "it's a strange story, and one, a month ago, I would have thought a dream; and indeed, if I awoke to-morrow morning and found myself in my own bed, I should positively persuade myself I had dreamt."

After some further conversation, the three friends agreed to tell each other their adventures. Henry began his and Alfred's, to which Magnus O'More listened with great attention and interest. On finishing, Magnus said, "You have certainly gone through some severe trials, and met with cruel usage. To you, Henry, knowing your disposition, these trials only give firmness and endurance; but to Alfred, totally unaccustomed to meet or face adversity and danger, the trial must have been severe indeed, and proves, after all, that that courage gained by mastering the mind is the one most worthy of admiration."

"You are kind to say so," said Alfred with a pleased smile; "for in truth, when I left the shores of Cornwall, I possessed as little courage as any other youth of my age — but now let us hear your adventures."

A shade passed over the intelligent features of the midshipman, and for a moment he remained silent. But then looking up, he said — "You may remember, Harry, when we were at school near Exeter, you frequently spoke to me about my country and my home — had I brothers or sisters — and why I resided with Captain Broomsley? I always avoided giving any direct reply to these natural questions, because my kind protector considered it better I should say nothing of myself or my previous history, and I strictly obeyed his wishes, though I often wished to make you a confidant of my strange history: there is no barrier now, and I will do so, it will serve to pass the hours of our tedious confinement."

As Magnus O'More's narrative occupied a considerable time, and was frequently interrupted, and as the first person is not always agreeable to youthful readers, we will in our next chapters relate the young midshipman's story in our own words, hoping it will be equally acceptable to our readers in that form and style.

CHAPTER XV.

On the borders of Lough Corrib, one of Ireland's most picturesque lakes, stood, in the year 1786, the mansion of Mr. Roderick Magnus O'More. This gentleman was of very ancient descent, possessed a fine property, and was next heir to the title and domains of Courtown, then in the possession of his cousin, Lord ——, a somewhat eccentric nobleman, near sixty, and unmarried. At this period Mr. O'More was a widower, with an only son about nine years of age. A great deal of mystery involved the early life of Mr. O'More. At the age of one-and-twenty he inherited the family estates; his only brother, Mr. Gorman O'More, having a sum of ten thousand pounds left him by will, retired into another county, married a Miss Hamilton, a Roman Catholic like himself, and from that period had but little intercourse with his brother, who was a Protestant, his mother being one, though his father was of the Catholic persuasion.

Mr. O'More, after inheriting the family estates, put an agent of excellent character over his property and went abroad; little was known of his wanderings, save that he travelled over Europe, visited Africa, and finally, at the expiration of six years, returned to his mansion of Ashgrove, with a young and exquisitely beautiful bride.

All that was known of Mrs. O'More was, that she was a Spanish lady; spoke little, if indeed any English, when she first arrived; but her sweet and amiable disposition soon won the love of her people, and the admiration of the surrounding gentry. Six months after her arrival at Ashgrove, she gave birth to a fine boy, named, after his sire, Roderick Magnus. Great rejoicings took place in consequence, and the tenants received many favors. Some months after this event, to the great surprise of the neighboring gentry, two events took place that occupied public attention in their vicinity a great deal.

Mrs. O'More renounced the Catholic faith and became a Protestant, and, immediately after, the rector of the parish performed the marriage-ceremony between Mr. and Mrs. O'More. This created intense surprise; but the Rev. Mr. Creagh, the rector, was heard to say that Mr. and Mrs. O'More were previously married in Spain by both a Protestant and Catholic minister.

Still a mystery existed, and many said it was a pity, for the sake of young Magnus, that the ceremony was not performed before his birth, for fear any difficulty should exist respecting his succession; but time wore on, Mr. O'More at times looking troubled, and receiving many letters from abroad, when a terrible blow was inflicted upon the happiness of Mr. O'More. Young Magnus had reached his second year, when a malignant typhus-fever, raging through the country, carried off Mrs. O'More. The despair of Mr. O'More was terrible to behold; then, for the first time for several years, his brother, Mr. Gorman O'More, visited him; but his cold calculating disposition was ill suited to soothe the high-hearted and generous O'More, who was accounted one of the handsomest men in Ireland.

For eighteen months Mr. O'More remained plunged in a stupor of grief and seclusion; but the exhortations of Mr. Creagh, the rector, at length roused him from his apathy. He turned to his beautiful boy, the image of his mother, for consolation; and, thanking God he was spared to him, he resolved from that period to be resigned to the will of Providence, and do his duty.

When five years old, a most accomplished and amiable woman was selected to superintend Magnus's early education; and, two years after, his brother recommended for a tutor his wife's brother, a Mr. Hamilton. He was accordingly installed as tutor to Magnus, and took up his residence in Ashgrove. Mr. O'More then left home, and was absent a whole year, and returned much more depressed than before his departure; he loved his boy with an intense affection, and the child, a noble boy, adored his parent.

At this period Earl Temple, afterwards Marquis of Buckingham, was viceroy of Ireland. The new governor of Ireland was of severe but just administration. It was a period of great speculation in the castle of Dublin; and embezzlement of military stores, which were ingeniously carried out of one door and brought in at the other as newly-purchased articles. Clerks, receiving one hundred a year. managed to live in splendid style.

Earl Temple's return terrified these worthies. Some fled the kingdom, and some actually committed suicide. At this time *Peep of Day Boys*, and another society, calling themselves *Defenders*. made their appearance, and committed great outrages.

The viceroy at once summoned to Dublin the most influential of the Irish gentry. Mr. O'More was personally known to the viceroy; in fact, they had been very intimate in former years, having met abroad. He therefore prepared for a journey to Dublin.

Young Magnus was, as a child, extremely precocious and sensible; he frequently spent an hour in the red drawing-room, gazing up into the lovely face of his lamented mother

11

till the tears came into his eyes; he also would talk to Mrs. Hudson of his mother; and, as even the best of servants will gossip, the housekeeper of Ashgrove, in speaking to a gossip of hers, little Magnus being present at the time, frequently said, shaking her head, "It's very strange master should marry the mistress after Master Magnus was born!"

"Uncommon strange!" returned her companion; " it's a great pity she sould her soul to please the master and became a Protestant; faith though they may have been married abroad, yet it would have been better the master had married the mistress here afore Master Magnus was born; some mischief will come of it, surely."

Magnus, though he could not understand these gossiping conversations, nevertheless retained them in his memory, where, like motes in a sunbeam, they floated about without any distinct form.

On the day of his father's departure for Dublin, Magnus was in the red drawing-room by himself, gazing into his mother's face. So absorbed was the child that he did not hear his father's step on the soft Turkey carpet.

A heavy sigh from Mr. O'More caused the boy to start and turn round, and then to take his father's hand.

" You are fond, Magnus," said Mr. O'More, sitting down and drawing his beloved son to him—"you are fond of coming here and looking at your poor mother. Ah!" he added, struggling with his emotion, " my heart has never enjoyed an hour's peace since it pleased God to take her."

Magnus wiped his eyes, and in his little, touching, sweet voice said, " I come here, papa, every day. I think mamma looks at me; I often think she does. Her beautiful black eyes seem to speak to me—tell me, papa, why she is dressed in that strange, grand dress, so beautiful but so different from all the ladies I see?"

"It was her first bridal dress, my child; it is the costume of her country where we were married."

"But, papa," said the child thoughtfully, the motes floating in his little brain, "I heard Mrs. Turner say you were married here, in the church of D——, and that it would have been better if you had married mamma before I was born "—the motes had assumed a distinct shape.

Mr. O'More started, and looked for an instant very stern, his fine features clouded; but with a sigh, he said, as if to himself, "Yes, the old gossip is right; but who can anticipate?"

Magnus watched his father's countenance, and he saw the change. "You are not angry, dear, dear father?" and he threw his arms round his neck and kissed him fondly.

"Angry, my own boy! Oh, no! worlds would not make me angry with Fernanda's child. You are too young to understand the reason of my second marriage with your mamma, and yet you are a very sensible child, and I see retain things you hear in your little mind. Rest satisfied you are my own beloved and lawful child; if it please God, the difficulty I at present labor under will soon disappear. I am going now to Dublin, but shall not be long." Alas! who can ever say such words and be sure that they will be fulfilled. "Whilst I am away, Magnus, do not go into the boats, keep from the lake, attend to Mrs. Stanmore and Mr. Hamilton, and be a good boy — as indeed you always are."

"But I may ride my favorite pony, papa, may I not?"

"Oh, certainly! but always take Phelim with you, and do not go out of the park, for there are naughty people prowling about the country."

"Then there is danger in your going to Dublin, dear papa?" said the boy anxiously.

"Oh, not much, my child! I shall be well armed, and so

will my two attendants; but come, there is the chariot at the door."

Holding his son by the hand, Mr. O'More descended; and after passing a few moments in his library, talking to Mr. Hamilton, he came out on the hall steps.

A travelling chariot and four fine bays, with postilions, stood at the door; and two attendants with pistol-holsters on their saddles, were holding their horses ready to mount. Mr. O'More again embraced his son, looked earnestly into his sweet face, kissed him again passionately, and stepped into his carriage. The postilions received a sign, and the four bays started off down the long smooth avenue at a smart trot; the attendants mounted and followed, whilst Magnus stood with the tears rolling down his cheeks, and his little heart beating strangely, though he could not tell why.

"Come, my dear child," said Mrs. Stanmore tenderly, taking him by the hand and leading him into the house, "you have often seen your papa leave home and not seemed so grieved as you do now, and yet his absence will only be for a week or two at most."

"I am older now," said the boy seriously, "and I know better what it is to part from one we love: I have only one parent now, and papa is gone away armed, and there is danger."

"There is no danger to him," said his governess, looking surprised at the child's words; "your father is too much loved: no one will hurt him.'

"He would not carry pistols if he thought that," said little Magnus. "Oh! if I was big enough, he should never go from home without me."

"Well, my love, you will grow by and by, if God spares you," said Mrs. Stanmore kindly. "Now go and pass your

two hours with Mr. Hamilton ; and, as this is a very fine
day for the month of October, Phelim shall have your pet
pony ready, and you can ride round the park and have a
canter across the lawn."

Magnus proceeded to the study with a very serious expression of countenance, and Mrs. Stanmore, herself somewhat thoughtful, retired to her own room and took up some
needlework.

Magnus O'More's governess was the daughter of a highly
respectable and much lamented clergyman in the town of
Mallow ; she was reared and educated in England for a
governess, for they were seven in family, and a curate's
salary in Ireland at that period was not nearly so much as
a good workman earns at the present day. Having received
a very careful education, she prepared to commence the
arduous and generally ill-paid career of governess.

She struggled on, really talented, amiable, and handsome.
She pleased everywhere — it was her fortune to find an
amiable employer ; but Cupid interfering, and being desir-
ous of imparting his stock of information, introduced the
lieutenant of a marching regiment to the pretty governess,
and thus she became Mrs. Stanmore. After several years'
trial, although they had no children, they found the pay of
a lieutenant in a regiment of foot was hardly sufficient for
their support. Lieutenant Stanmore, therefore, exchanged
into a regiment going abroad, in hope of promotion, but
would not permit his wife to accompany him to Jamaica, as
it was unhealthy at that time. Poor fellow ! he became a
captain, but was soon laid beside many another — a victim
of yellow-fever.

Mrs. Stanmore mourned the loss of an affectionate husband sincerely and deeply ; and, after a time, resumed her
previous occupation. Having accompanied a lady and her

two daughters to Dublin, she remained several years in that city, paying an occasional visit to her father; at his death she was the only one remaining out of the seven children, and a good friend introducing her to the notice of Mr. O'More, she became the governess of his little boy, with a very handsome salary. Mrs. Stanmore at this period was just forty.

Magnus, thoughtful and serious, proceeded to the study, where Mr. Hamilton waited for him. This gentleman was not more than one or two and thirty; he was certainly, neither in manner or appearance, an agreeable-looking person : he was tall and thin, wore spectacles, had a very keen cold gray eye, and a very sallow complexion. In his manner he was obsequious, never maintained an opinion of his own, but gave up every argument at once with an air of humble resignation; though, had a keen observer looked at him fixedly at the time, he might have caught a very rapid glance of supreme contempt flashing from his deep sunk eyes. That he relished the luxuries of life was very evident, though he tried to conceal this predilection. Magnus disliked him exceedingly; he had a way of looking over his spectacles at him that made him feel uncomfortable.

Entering the study, Magnus commenced the lessons for the day. Mr. Hamilton was undoubtedly a good scholar and a good teacher, and was highly recommended by Mr. Gorman O'More, being his wife's brother.

" Pray, Mr. Hamilton," said Magnus, as he finished his lessons, " what are *Peep of Day Boys?* "

" *Peep of Day Boys!* " repeated the tutor, looking over his spectacles, and then saying, — " It would be difficult, Magnus, to make you understand what they are. However, they are bad Protestants (Mr. Hamilton was a Roman Catholic); the law does not permit Catholics to possess arms, therefore the Protestants unlawfully hunt the houses of Catholics for, or under pretence of, seeking for weapons. These visits are made very early in the morning; and for this reason they are called *Peep of Day Boys*."

Magnus thought a few moments, and then said, " As papa is a Protestant, and there are plenty of arms in the house, there is no fear of *Peep of Day Boys* coming here; and yet guns and pistols are loaded every night on the great hall table, and men watch all night — what is that for?"

" Oh! for fear the house should be attacked by *Defenders;* but you are too young to understand these things: you may now go and take a ride on your pony."

Magnus put aside his book, and left the study without a word more, but the motes were afloat in his brain again, for he was a thinking child.

CHAPTER XVI.

As soon as Magnus left the library, Mr. Hamilton thoughtfully drew a writing-desk towards him ; and, after cogitating a few moments, took up his pen and commenced writing a letter. Having the gift of invisibility we look over his shoulder, and give our young readers the contents of the letter, as it will show Mr. Hamilton in his true character —

"My dear Gorman, — Your brother has this day left for Dublin, having received a private letter from the viceroy ; but he has other objects in view — he intends making a will while in Dublin. I am now perfectly satisfied, from careful observation, and other means I need not mention, that he has no possible chance of legitimizing his son Magnus. I feel confident that he *was* married in Spain ; but whether a legal marriage or not I cannot determine, or whether it is that he has failed in procuring proofs. He appears greatly excited and deeply concerned ; and, strange to say for a man of his strong and powerful mind, gives way to a feeling or a presentiment that his life will be short and his death very sudden.

"He has no power, as you are aware, of willing away the Ashgrove estates ; but he has the two properties he purchased in Clare two years ago, and which yield a rental of £2,000 a year — and all his personal property besides, and this is considerable. I have not been able, notwithstanding all my efforts, to discover the name or the rank of the late Mrs. O'More; and yet I am satisfied Mrs. Stanmore, the child's governess, knows it. She is a very handsome and . fascinating woman. I thought she was playing her cards to become mistress of Ashgrove, but I wronged her; and besides it would be a losing game, for your brother is devoted to the memory of his lost wife. He is a noble-hearted man, there is no denying; still that is no reason why you should romantically believe in your brother's marriage without proofs of it, or acknowledge an heir who may really after all be illegitimate. Your brother is still what may be termed a young man — forty, perhaps; but with an iron frame and constitution — and yet I do not think he will live long. I cannot say that he has affected me with his own belief, though it is my opinion that he will die early. The times are working in our favor. The Marquis of Buckingham is getting vastly unpopular; the spirit of the oppressed is again becoming roused, and the *Defenders* are working their way; slowly but surely our time is coming. Should any thing happen, and Mr. O'More's prognostic of his own fate turn out correct, this boy Magnus should be got rid of at once; he is shrewd and precocious beyond his years. If possible, the very memory of his origin should be obliterated from his mind; he has a fierce spirit within him now, child as he is, and he thinks and asks questions rather startling. I shall probably see you in a short time. Give my love to Mary. She may be mistress of Ashgrove yet, and the title of Courtown your son's. The present holder of the title will never marry; his habits of life are confirmed though he is but fifty-two. — Yours sincerely,

"GEORGE HAMILTON."

Magnus O'More on leaving the study proceeded to the

hall, and, taking up his cap and whip, he prepared for a ride on his favorite pony, attended by a young lad for whom he had a great partiality.

Phelim M'Farlane was coming up to the hall door as Magnus came out. "Ah! what a very fine day it is, Phelim," said the young boy, rousing his somewhat depressed spirits.

"Yes, sir," said the lad, "it's mighty fine, intirely," and he helped his young master up on the pony's back.

"My papa has gone to Dublin, Phelim, and his absence has made me very low-spirited."

"Sure it's only for a short time, Master Magnus," said the lad. "I heard my father say it's all about putting down those uneasy *Peep of Day Boys*, and those other queer fellows calling themselves *Defenders*, bad cess to them! Can't they keep easy in their beds, without prowling about at night like uneasy cats — but which way will you, *darlint?*"

"Along the path by the lake, Phelim, and then round the park."

Phelim M'Farlane, then about fourteen, was as good-looking and well-made a lad as could be met with in any county of Ireland, and wonderfully attached to his little master. Phelim's mother, a fine healthy young woman, and the wife of a small farmer on the estate, nursed young Magnus, weaning her little boy for that purpose. Phelim thus, as is the custom in Ireland, considered himself as particularly bound to the family; and indeed Mr. O'More took care that his family should be gainers by the transaction. Phelim's father was an industrious, sober man, and Mr. O'More made him a kind of under-steward over the Ashgrove property, and had his son Phelim to the house as Magnus's attendant only, and Mr. Hamilton gave him an hour's instruction each day, so that Phelim could write and read well, and was very proud of his accomplishments.

Phelim rode a sturdy pony by the side of young Magnus, who was now able to manage his spirited little animal right well. The two lads proceeded down the avenue, and, without going outside the lodge-gate, took a broad path leading along the borders of the lake.

The scenery of this beautiful sheet of water — stretching away to the north, where it nearly meets Lough Musk — was delightful to the eye, though late in the month of October. The sun shone brightly on its waters, which came rippling pleasantly to the eye and ear upon the pebbly shore, and the light fishing-boats in the distance, with their white sails, on which the sun shone brightly, looked like great birds sporting on the waters. Protected by a little quay was the cutter yacht, lying at anchor ; and a well-built boat-house contained a couple of boats, and a very handsome barge for pleasure excursions or rowing parties.

Magnus's spirits roused as he rode along, and then had a canter through the fine park, full of deer, till he was tired, and returned to the house. Several days passed in this manner, and letters were received from Mr. O'More stating that he was quite well, and sending a hundred kind and loving messages to his son. The country about Ashgrove remained tolerably quiet, with the exception of a few visits from the *Peep of Day Boys* to the Catholic gentry ; but there were no outrages, as in Clare and Munster.

Mrs. Stanmore took advantage of a fine day, and set out in a car for Galway, distant thirteen miles, to make some purchases : this was the beginning of the third week after Mr. O'More's departure ; and for the last eight days no intelligence had been received from him.

Some three hours after the departure of the governess, a post-chaise and four drove up the avenue, and pulled up at the hall-door of the mansion. Magnus was taking his lesson in the study, and Mr. Hamilton — who had received letters the previous day, and was giving very little attention to his pupil's instruction, no sooner heard the noise of the wheels than he started to his feet, throwing down his spectacles, and was hastening from the room, when Magnus jumped up, saying, whilst his eyes sparkled with joy, "Papa, perhaps!"

"No, boy!" returned Mr. Hamilton, sharply, "stay where you are; this is not your papa;" and immediately he left the room, locking the door.

Magnus's little cheek flushed with anger, both at the harsh manner of Mr. Hamilton, and at his being locked in; he got up from his chair and went to the window; he saw the post-chaise, it was a common one with four smoking post-horses.

"Why am I locked in, in my father's house?" thought Magnus. "I detest that man!"

An hour passed, and at length Mr. Hamilton returned; he looked pale and excited; he carried a mantle in his hand, and Magnus's cloak and cap.

"Why was I locked in?" said Magnus, looking at his tutor with surprise; his countenance was so changed for want of the peculiar spectacles he wore.

Mr. Hamilton picked up his glasses and put them on, and, giving Magnus the cloak and cap, said — "Put them on and come with me: your father is ill in Galway."

Magnus clasped his hands and burst into tears, but, putting on his cap and cloak, he said — "Come, let us be quick!" and the poor little fellow shook as if in an ague.

Mr. Hamilton took him by the hand and went out of the room; but, turning to the left, he passed out through a private door, and, gaining the front, opened the door of the chaise and let Magnus in. Several domestics, looking startled and even pale, were coming out of the front door when Mr. Hamilton jumped into the chaise, closed the door, and signed to the postilions to drive on. Away went the posters at a canter, the lodge-gate was passed, and Magnus was thus torn away from the mansion of his fathers.

"Is my papa very ill?" said Magnus. "Why did he not come on to his own home?"

"Your papa is dead!" said this man without heart or feeling, and in a tone sharp and cutting.

A wild cry escaped the wretched boy's lips. "Dead! dead!" he repeated. "Oh! you cannot be speaking truth!" and the child sobbed till he was almost convulsed.

"Yes," returned Mr. Hamilton, "you have lost your father, but you will be taken care of. You have no longer a right to stay at Ashgrove. Your mother was a low woman, and not the wife of your father."

Cruelly beat to the earth as the child was, and his little heart bursting with grief, these words smote upon his brain with a strange feeling for one but little more than nine years old. "My mother a low woman, and not my father's wife! You tell a falsehood, Mr. Hamilton, and you are a bad, bad man, to tell so great a lie!"

"Tut, foolish boy! what do you know of your mother? Your mother was Jane Muggins, and you are going back to your grandmother.

Magnus stared bewildered at his tutor; he could scarcely breathe. The shock he had received, and the frightful words he heard, that seemed like a hot iron to burn his brain, rendered him sick and dizzy; he grew quite hysterical. Mr. Hamilton gazed at him without one particle of feeling in the expression of his countenance; seeing the child almost insensible, he pulled a bottle from his pocket and poured some of the contents down the child's throat. After a time his sobbings ceased, and, finally, he lay back in the chaise in a kind of stupor.

CHAPTER XVII

LATE on the evening of the same day that beheld the heir of Ashgrove thus rudely torn from his home, Mrs. Stanmore, returning from Galway in the car, was stopped at the lodge-gate by the keeper's wife running out, and wringing her hands, exclaiming in a tone of deep, unaffected grief — " Och hone! Mrs. Stanmore, dear — the master's dead — the Lord have mercy on his soul! Ah, wirra stru! where will his like be seen agin? "

Mrs. Stanmore grew sick and pale as death, unable to utter a word; while the domestic driving dropped the reins, crying out in all the vehemence of Irish grief, " Och, murder — murder! the master dead — and he in the pride of his manhood! "

" O, Mrs. Murphy — where did you hear this news? Go on, Dennis — go on! " exclaimed Mrs. Stanmore in an agony. " Let me see my boy, my poor boy! " and the tears ran down her cheeks in streams.

The man drove on. Mrs. Murphy, the gate-keeper, had not seen the child in the chaise; so Mrs. Stanmore drove up to the house, and jumping down, hurried up the steps to the door. A domestic, looking stupefied and bewildered, let the governess in. " Where is Master Magnus? " she exclaimed in an agitated voice.

" Oh, ma'am! sure he is gone; Mr. Hamilton has taken

·him away four hours ago in the chaise — have you heard of the master's death, ma'am?"

"Why, what is all this, William?" exclaimed Mrs. Stanmore bewildered, and entering a small chamber off the hall.

" Oh, ma'am!" said the footman, " we are all struck dumb like ; the master's — the Lord receive his soul in glory," and the man piously crossed himself — " the master's brother, Mr. Gorman O'More, arrived here this afternoon, and said his brother was dead six days ago, was killed coming out of the castle-gate in Dublin ; his horse took fright and threw him, and killed him on the spot."

Mrs. Stanmore clasped her hands and bent her head upon them, weeping bitterly. " Send Mrs. Flood to me, William, I am stupefied ; but how dare any one take away the child?"

William looked-confused, and, stooping, in a low voice he said to the governess — " Mr. Gorman O'More's own man says, Master Magnus has no right to be here — that he's a —"

" It's a falsehood! a vile, inhuman lie!" exclaimed Mrs. Stanmore, starting from her seat, her fine features flushed, before so pale. " Has Mr. Gorman O'More the hardihood to dare to say this to my face?"

" Yes, madam," said a strong unpleasant voice without the door, " he has!" and the speaker entered the chamber. The footman started back, looked frightened. " Leave the room, sir," said Mr. Gorman O'More, for he it was, and then he closed the door. Mrs. Stanmore did not shrink an inch. She stood her ground firmly, gazing into the cold and apparently passionless features of Mr. Gorman O'More with a feeling of curiosity and disgust. It was the first time she ever beheld him.

He was a tall man, though not so tall as his late brother ;

he was handsome, certainly, but it was disagreeably so —
for the fine and well-formed features were rendered unpleas-
ing by the peculiarity of their expression. There was an icy
coldness in his look, and the upper lip, excessively short,
expressed so much haughty contempt that the beholder felt
an unpleasant feeling creep over him as he met the steady
glance of his very penetrating eyes ; he was younger by three
years than his brother — his age, probably, about thirty-
six.

"I presume, madam," said Mr. Gorman O'More, "that
you are Mrs. Stanmore, the person selected by my late
brother to take care of a child of his?"

"My name is Stanmore," returned the governess. "My
occupation here was to educate and take care of Master
Roderick Magnus O'More, the only child and heir of my
lamented benefactor."

"No doubt, madam," returned Mr. O'More quite calmly,
"for such a purpose you engaged with my late brother.
But I heard you just now make use of a most unwarrant-
able assertion, which reflects on my word. I now tell you,
madam, that my late brother left no legitimate child ; unfortunately no doubt for this child, falsely reared as his heir,
he died before signing a will drawn up by a solicitor in
Dublin."

"And do you tell me, Mr. Gorman O'More," said Mrs.
Stanmore solemnly, and gazing steadily into Mr. O'More's
eyes, though her heart beat painfully, "that you believe in
your heart the monstrous assertion you have just now made?
O man!" she added passionately, "without pity or heart
for the orphan child you would rob of his inheritance — do
you dare to tell me, knowing the contrary, that your brother's son is not the lawful heir of this property you would
seize ; and, not content with even that, you would blast

your noble brother's name, and throw a slur upon his innocent child and its mother?"

So passionate and vehement was Mrs. Stanmore in her
declamation and manner, that Mr. O'More made no attempt
to stop her; he turned very pale, and his lip trembled with
suppressed passion; he was startled also, for he could not
tell what Mrs. Stanmore might know. But, mastering his
emotion, for he was a man of deep penetration and of exceeding cunning, he said, "I am sorry, madam, that your
passion has induced you to forget yourself. I can excuse it,
however; I am robbing no heir of his just rights, being
quite ready to surrender this and all the property of my late
brother into the hands of whoever the law may appoint as
guardian to the heir, if there is one, provided any legal
proof of my brother's marriage, previous to the birth of his
child, can be brought forward. I am not quite so romantic,
however, madam, as to yield my birthright to imaginary
claims, and deprive my children of their inheritance. My
brother married the Spanish girl he brought to Ireland with
him after the birth of this child. This is a forcible proof
that if there ever was a marriage of any kind previously, it
was not a binding one in law; thus, then, you expect me to
yield the property of my fathers to a child born of a foreign
adventuress."

"That assertion is false!" said Mrs. Stanmore, bitterly.
"Mrs. O'More was a Spanish grandee's daughter."

A smile of scorn passed over Mr. O'More's features as
he abruptly said, "Of course! all foreign adventurers,
male or female, are counts, dukes, duchesses, and count-
esses; but, pardon me, this war of words is quite useless.
To-morrow, madam, I shall be happy to settle whatever
claims you may have against my late brother for the care
of his child."

12

"Ah!" said Mrs. Stanmore, vehemently, "you think there is not a God hearing and seeing you, and who knows every thought of your heart — you may triumph now, but, though the ways of the Lord are inscrutable, your fall will be greater than your triumph."   .

With a look of rage Mr. O'More threw open the door, and left the room. Mrs. Stanmore sunk back into a chair, and covered her face with her hands.

The following day, at noon, she left Ashgrove after a vain attempt to see Mr. O'More; he refused either to see her or to let her know where the poor child was sent to — merely sending her a message, desiring to know what sum was due to her from her salary.

Mrs. Stanmore indignantly declared that nothing was due from the late Mr. O'More, and she required nothing from him. Packing up her effects she sent to the next village for a car, and, taking an affectionate leave of the upper domestics, who were all much attached to the governess, she left the house, stopped for near an hour at the tidy and prosperous-looking little farm of Phelim's father, in earnest conversation with himself, and then proceeded to Galway.

The sudden death of Mr. O'More created exceeding surprise and deep regret over the neighborhood, but the succession of his brother to the estates created less wonder; for, long before Mr. O'More's death, it was singularly diffused over the neighborhood that his son Magnus was illegitimate. Mr. O'More's marriage after his birth first gave rise to many surmises, and, after Mrs. O'More's death, strange reports about herself and child began to be circulated all over the country in a singular manner.

Many of the surrounding gentry felt exceeding pity concerning the fate of the poor boy; but as, three weeks after Mr. O'More's death, all the servants were discharged, without one solitary exception, and replaced by others, nothing could be learned respecting him. Phelim's father was removed from his stewardship, and would have had notice to quit his farm, but it was secured to him in a lease impossible to break.

Six months after his coming into possession, Mr. O'More's family arrived and took up their residence in Ashgrove, which was refurnished in splendid style; new carriages were purchased, and the establishment put upon a very handsome footing. There was nothing to say against Mr. Gorman O'More; he was therefore at once visited by the Blakes, Bells, and other first-rate county families, and even Lord Courtown became a visitor. A domestic chaplain, in the shape of a comfortable, sleek-looking priest, was added to the establishment of Ashgrove; he was an exceedingly good kind of man, loved ease and quiet, was not at all particular about fast-days; his penances were very light and easily borne; so that, like all the rest of the world, the people on the estate began to think that, after all, as their lamented landlord was gone, and they hoped to heaven — notwithstanding Father Malachi Macnamara shook his head, and said he was afraid not — that his successor was a good man, and one of the ould faith, and so it was God's will. Some indeed there were who could not forget; and some also remembered the beautiful boy and his lovely mother, and shook their heads, muttering, " It was a queer world — people were soon forgot" — and " Who knows what would come yet?" and " Where was the poor child?"

Before twelve months were over " a change came o'er the spirit of their dream;" some leases required renewing; and the run-out farms were put up to let. An attorney, from Cork, came and settled in the village, which before only boasted of a grocer and apothecary conjoined, and one or two other small shops, with a couple of ale-houses, or rather whiskey stores, for ale is not much drank in Ireland.

Mr. George M'Grab was employed by Mr. O'More in all transactions with the tenants, and it was soon discovered that Mr. M'Grab was quite up to his name. The rents of all the renewable farms were nearly doubled; no new lease was granted unless under very hard terms indeed; and the small farms were let so high that poverty stared the possessor in the face in a very short time. An engineer and surveyor re-measured the farms — acres were cut off here and there, to the dismay of the holder of the land — in fact, before the third year of Mr. O'More's possession of the property, the happiness and prosperity of the tenant farmers declined, and the cotters of Ashgrove Estate bitterly bewailed their change of landlord.

The same effect was working on the estate in Clare. Thus, at the expiration of the fourth year, no landlord in the whole of Galway and Clare was more detested and feared than Mr. O'More. His family did not increase; but his wife indulged in great extravagance, assisted by her brother, Mr. Hamilton, who lived six months of the year at Ashgrove, the other six in Dublin, where his dissipation and extravagance rendered him notorious.

He no longer wore spectacles — his manner and appearance became so changed, that no one could well recognize him; he kept the best hunters, and also one or two bloods for the race-course, visited most of the resident gentry, and was paying very serious attention to a Miss Blake, a spinster of good fortune.

The family of Mr. O'More consisted of one daughter and two sons — the eldest son was about fourteen when his father obtained possession of Ashgrove, the daughter seven, the youngest boy about five. Young Gorman O'More, at seventeen years of age, was one of the most finished puppies the county of Galway could produce; he had just entered Trinity College, which at this period excelled in producing wild spirits.

This was a period of wild excitement, and a species of *furor* respecting liberty; the business of parliament was carried on amid tumult and acts of rioting, and outrages scarcely to be credited at the present day. The very members of parliament were attacked openly in the streets; the House itself was violated by mobs forcing into the gallery. The populace seized upon obnoxious persons, and tarred and feathered them — a savage practice borrowed from America. The soldiers called in to quell the riots were houghed — a fearfully savage act; but this was done by the brutal butchers of the metropolis — a set of miscreants, as Lord Carhampton * said, requiring no other qualification for their infamous acts than a strong arm, a sharp knife, and a hard heart.

The boys of Trinity, though they never joined in these infamous acts, yet nevertheless were partakers in the wild scenes enacting in the metropolis, their young bloods inflamed with the spirit of liberty; and young Gorman O'More came hot from college and the metropolis, to astonish the natives of Galway by his eloquence, and his violent imaginary ideas of liberty.

Norah O'More, the daughter, was but a child; but she was one of the loveliest children that ever sprang from the stock of the O'More's: young as she was, her disposition was loving and kind. Every one loved Norah — the cottagers blessed her sweet face with its dark clustering ringlets, over a forehead of snow; and her large liquid dark eyes beamed with such sweetness, and her smile, as she thanked the cot-

---

* Lord Carhampton, formerly General Luttrell.

tager who ran to open the gates to let her pony pass, was so fascinating and endearing, that many a peasant would exclaim, as he gazed in wonder at her beauty — " Shure, if the father is bad, the daughter is an angel ! "

CHAPTER XVIII.

We left little Magnus sunk in a stupor, both from grief and the sedative mixture given him by his tutor — Mr. Hamilton.

How long he remained in that state, or whether he awoke in a high fever or not, of course he could not say. But when he began to recover, and was able to look about him, and to understand things, he gazed around him with a bewildered and stupefied look ; he rubbed his eyes and looked again, and gradually the power of recollection, and of understanding what he saw, came to him. He perceived he was lying on a plain unpainted wooden bedstead, with coarse but clean clothes over him ; he looked at his little hand, as he put it out to push back the thick coarse woollen quilt from him, with surprise ; it was white and wasted — even he perceived it was so. He then looked round the chamber, which was very small, with one window of four panes of glass ; the walls were whitewashed, an old, very old set of drawers, blackened by time and smoke, filled one corner, two chairs and a deal table completed the furniture of the room. There was a fireplace and a large turf fire. Sitting on a three-legged stool, stirring something in a saucepan with a wooden spoon, sat an old and wrinkled-faced looking woman ; she had her nose up the chimney, smoking a pipe not two inches long, and making strange faces as she puffed away some very bad tobacco.

Magnus gazed at this apparition of an old crone, for such he thought at first she must be, and that all he saw was in a dream. But the old woman turned suddenly round, and her eyes met those of Magnus.

"Och, my conscience!" she exclaimed, "it's myself is proud to see you coming to, Jack. Faix, I've had a hard time o' watching you day and night, but you'll come to now, darlint!"

Magnus was confounded; his large eyes opened to their widest extent as the old dame got up, poured the mixture into a mug, stirred it, and then swallowed a spoonful herself. "Now, avick! take this," said she, holding the mixture to Magnus; "it will warm your poor stomach."

Magnus pushed the warm mixture away with disgust, saying, "I won't drink such stuff — who are you — and where am I?"

"Stuff!" repeated the old woman, making grimaces — "Stuff — boderation! call my beautiful gruel, stuff! Ochone, my poor boy! you mustn't starve yourself."

"Who are you?" angrily repeated Magnus, sitting up, and immediately falling back from weakness, while his lips were parched with thirst.

"Who am I, avick? Musha, Jack, I'm your own ould grandmother, the Lord be good to us !"

Magnus closed his eyes with a shudder, and began to think — "Oh! my papa — now I recollect — my own papa is dead!" and he sobbed and cried, the old woman administering comfort after her own fashion, in a string of half English, half Irish expressions. But Magnus was inconsolable; he again demanded where he was — where was Mr. Hamilton — and why was he in such a hole of a place, and under the care of such an old woman?

"Save us! it's hard when one's own disowns us," muttered the old dame in a voice of reproach. "Sure, darlint, I told you I was your own grandmother; your mother was Jane Muggins—rest her sowl in glory!—and you're my poor grandchild, Jack Muggins!"

"It's false, woman!" exclaimed the child fiercely; "I am Magnus O'More!"

"Hush, hush, acushla! true for ye. Your father was a Mr. O'More, but your poor mother, who was taken away from me, and dressed in fine clothes like a great foreign lady entirely, and lived in great style till she died, poor thing! she was my own daughter, Jane; and the unnatural people as got your father's lands turned you adrift, avick, becase you were a natural child like, and no right to any thing but scorn, acushla — and so your poor ould grandmother took you, and you ill of the fever, and nursed you; and, if you have patience, my darlint, you'll get well and strong, plase God!"

Magnus listened with a look of scorn, and contempt and disgust on his fine but wasted features; he put his hand up to his head, and closed his eyes. The motes were dancing in the sunbeam; his little brain was dizzy and confused with thought; he would not open his eyes — he lay still and thought.

"Jack Muggins!" he repeated to himself; "my beautiful and stately mother, that my own papa told me was his own beloved wife, and I his lawful child, and this horrid old witch to dare to say my mother was her child!" and then the tears ran down his cheeks in streams. But nature demands support — in childhood or manhood, in old age or in second childhood it is all the same — the body must be nourished; even the deepest grief will give way to the wants of the human frame.

Magnus before night was forced to eat something; he

closed his eyes and refused to talk or listen to the old woman, but he took milk and bread in the mornings and evenings, and as he grew stronger, which he ardently longed to do, she gave him broth. He brought himself to eat any thing she gave him, but never for one moment was she able to shake his belief as to who he was; he scorned to make even a reply: the old woman would glare at him strangely at times, sometimes almost savagely. She did not sleep in the room with him, but locked him in at night.

In a week he was able to leave his bed. She gave him a pair of thick pea-cloth trousers, check shirt, and jacket to put on. Magnus gazed at them, but made no remark, and put them on; he found he was getting strong and well, but his heart was cruelly wrung — yet, with a spirit beyond his years, he seemed to defy the misery inflicted on him; in vain the old woman called him Jack, and talked of his mother — he looked upon her with scorn, but made no reply: his thoughts were far away from his lonely prison, for not a soul entered his room save the old crone — he sometimes heard voices in the next chamber, but they spoke in Irish; and from his window he could see nothing but a dreary heath, though at times he heard a dull roar that he could not account for.

Thus passed a fortnight and more, and the child longed to breathe the fresh air; he was well, but pale from confinement.

"Will you let me go out in the open air, woman?" he always called her *woman*, though she did all she could to make him call her grandmother, but in vain.

"Yes, avick!" said the old dame; " you shall go out and play on the sands, and see the great sea, if you will call me grandmother, and be a good boy, and promise to come back when you get tired."

" I will promise to come back," said the boy ; " and when
I promise," he added proudly, " I will do so — but I will
never tell a lie, so do not think I will ever call you grandmother."

The old woman eyed the child savagely ; her bleared eyes
seemed to dart into him, but he never flinched or showed the
slightest fear — in truth, that sensation seemed unknown to
him. She muttered some strong expression in Irish, which,
if translated, would mean, " Faith, and may be I'm wrong —
but it will not be easy to break him in. Well," she added,
" you may go ; but take care how you go down the cliff by the
path from the garden."

She opened the door, and then Magnus saw that there
were several rooms in the cabin, but all on the ground-floor.
He passed out into the open air, and then stood gazing before
him, drawing his breath with a powerful impulse acting upon
him to fly and leave the frightful old woman and her eternal
pipe far behind him ; but recollecting that he had said, " I will
return," the boy's proud spirit conquered, and he walked
slowly on, and, turning the angle of the cottage, a sight met his
gaze that rooted him to the spot : he beheld the sea, the wide
unbounded sea, for the first time, and he stood gazing at it
with a breathless wonder : he had read of it, seen pictures
of it, but all fell short, so short of the reality that he stood
spell-bound. He then walked to the end of the garden, if it
could be so called, being only a long strip of potato ground,
and found that he was standing on the summit of a cliff —
not very high, but formed entirely of huge masses of rock —
the sandy beach was beneath, upon which the tide gently
rippled. It was a small bight or cove, with noble lofty rocks
bounding it on all sides, and the heads, east and west, jutting
far into the sea, shutting out all view beyond them. He
looked back, the cottage was the only habitation his eye could

rest on, all before it was a wide and seemingly intermina-
ble down or heath, without a shrub or a tree to break its
dreary surface.

There was a path, almost like steps, down the cliff, and
down this he went and got on the sands, and then sat down
on a rock, and gazed out as if in a dream on the sparkling
waters of the Atlantic. There were ships in the far distance,
and their white sails shone in the sunlight : it was a bright
day in the first week of November, such a day as sometimes
comes to wile us into the belief that winter is yet distant.

The motes were in the sunbeam ; and the child's thoughts
floated about in his brain so wildly and confusedly that not
one fixed idea became permanent. He remained in this
apathetic state nearly an hour, and then he rose to his feet,
ascended the cliff, and re-entered the cottage.

" Well, acushla ! " said the old woman, " do you feel better
after your nice walk on the sea-sands ? "

" Yes," said the boy ; " I like the sands — you will let me
go there again ? "

" Yes, Jack, avourneen."

Magnus's cheek flushed, and his dark eyes flashed, but he
said not a word.

The next day and the next passed, and then the storm-
king rode over the face of the deep, and the huge swell of
the Atlantic rolled in on the beach ; the dark clouds hung over
the ocean, and its white waves rose up, and their snowy
crests toppled over in foam, and the boy gazed on them in
wonder. " How different a storm on the narrow waters of
Lough Corrib ! " thought the boy, and he felt a wish stir
within his young breast to glide over those storm-tossed
waters to other lands, to grow to manhood far away from
the home of his childhood, and then to come back and face
those who had so cruelly and wrongfully driven him from his
inheritance.

" Where is Phelim, my faithful Phelim?" thought Magnus; " surely he has not forgotten me. Do they think I will forget my home, or forget my father and the beautiful face of my mother?   My dear father taught me to pray every night to God, and I do pray, and I pray that I may never forget that my name is Magnus — Magnus O'More!" and his cheeks flushed, and his pretty features became so fixed and stern, it seemed scarcely natural to see that look in a child of ten; but Magnus O'More was a noble boy, and thought and looked beyond his years.

One evening Mrs. Muggins was puffing away at her pipe, with knees up to her chin, and her nose poked up the chimney to let the smoke — which Magnus said was detestable — go up the aperture; for somehow the old woman began to feel an awe of the child, and did as he wished her. Magnus was sitting on the side of the bed, his eyes bent upon the clay floor, his thoughts ever on his father and mother, when he heard a strange rumbling sound as if beneath him: the old woman no sooner heard the sound than she started up, knocked the ashes out of her pipe, exclaiming: " Ah! the saints in glory — they are come!" and jumping up she left the room, locking the door after her. There was a candle, a remarkably thin one, in an old tin case on the table, which threw but a faint glow over the small chamber. It was a wild night without, though the gale blew off the shore, but it drove the shower at times hard against the small panes of glass in the window; Magnus raised his eyes, for he thought he heard a tap, unlike the rain, against the pane of glass, and, as he looked steadily at it, he saw a face — a human face — pressed against the pane, as if peering into the room.

Magnus could not say whether it was a man's or a woman's face, but he was satisfied it was a face: he got up, and was moving towards the window, when the rough, deep, guttural sounds of a man's voice in the passage caused him to pause; the next moment the chamber door opened, and the old woman entered, followed by a huge, bulky, broad-chested man, his immense whiskers covering half his face. He wore a great rough pilot coat and trousers, and on his head that nondescript kind of a covering called by sailors " sou'-westers," but quite as good in nor'-westers or easters either; he had a thick woollen wrapper round his neck, and the long nap of his pilot coat was glistening with moisture. Magnus gazed with astonishment upon this sea-monster, who appeared as if just then to have emerged from the deep. Having cast aside his sou'-wester, woollen wrapper, and given himself a shake, he unbuttoned his over-coat, and showed a strong untanned belt round his waist, in which was stuck a pair of pistols.

" Now, Jack," said the old woman, " here is your uncle, Bill Muggins, come to see you; he is your poor mother's brother."

Magnus drew back as this sea-monster held out his huge paw, saying in the voice of a bear, " Give us your fin, Jack; I'm blowed if I ain't glad to see you, though the priest did not tackle your mother to your father."

" My mother your sister ! " said Magnus; " you will never make me believe that ! " and he drew back to the bed.

" Ho, ho ! it's squally weather with you, my bantam," said the smuggler; " it's squally weather and a head sea: never mind, my lad, though you're too proud to own your mother's kindred, I'll make a man of you yet. Wait till I get you aboard the *Nancy*. He's a fine boy, mother," continued the man, turning to the old woman, " so make yourself easy, I'll take care of him; he's as like his mother as two double blocks."

"So he is, acushla, though, faix, at times he puzzles me; but he has the bad blood of his father in him, or he wouldn't turn from his ould grandmother, who nursed him when sick and like to die, and left at my door to die like a dog, *becase* his father died, and the new master wouldn't look at him."

"Magnus listened bewildered; his child's mind could not comprehend exactly whether the old woman was playing a part, or whether she really and truly believed he was her grandchild.

"Never mind, old girl," said the smuggler; "it never blows the same gale throughout the year. I'll make a man of him, or my name's not Bill Muggins!"

Magnus cast a glance at the window, but the face was not there.

The smuggler then took some parcels out of his capacious pockets, saying, "There's some prime tea and baccy, old girl, as never paid the king duty, and there's a bottle of prime brandy as will warm the cockles of your heart."

"Faix, acushla, I'm glad of the baccy and the tea — the boy will have a drop of good stuff for his breakfast."

So now, mother, I'm off; take care of Jack till I'm ready for sea, and I'll make a man of him;" and, taking Magnus by the hand, though he strove to avoid him, he shook it quite hard enough to dislocate it. "Cheer up, my hearty!" he exclaimed; "don't look so down in the mouth; it doesn't always blow hard; a thribble-reefed topsail gale at night, is often a topgallant breeze in the morning."

Magnus made no reply; he was thinking of the face he had seen against the pane of glass, and wondering if he should see it again, and whose face it was.

The smuggler and his mother then left the room, and presently Magnus heard the same sound as before in the other room, and beneath him ; shortly after, the old woman returned and Magnus went to bed, and then she blew out the candle and retired, locking the door.

Magnus could not sleep ; he lay on his back with his eyes fixed upon the window, from which, however, no light came, for it was a very dark night ; but a faint gleam was sent over the room from the embers of the turf fire ; the gusts of wind were still violent, but it did not rain. As he lay thus, half an hour after the old woman had retired, he heard a pane of glass break, and the pieces fall on the floor. He lay quite still, for he felt no fear, but very curious ; immediately after the breaking of the glass, a voice cried out, "Hush, avick — Hush ! It's I — it's Phelim ! "

Oh ! how the boy's heart leaped to his throat as he heard those words ; his pulse beat wildly as, with a bound, he sprung from the bed and rushed to the window, and thrust his little hand out, sobbing, " Phelim — Phelim ! is it you at last ? "

Phelim could have cried like a child ; he covered the little hand with kisses, and put it back as tenderly as he would an infant's ; saying in a low, affectionate voice, " Hush — darling ! or the ould woman will hear you. Oh ! the Lord is good to us — I've found you at last."

" Ah, Phelim ! I can't see you," said the boy. " Oh ! how I long to see a face I love ; and is it true, Phelim dear, quite true, that my own papa is dead ? "

" Ochone ! avick, it is too true ; but the Lord will protect you yet, now I have found you, and sure good Mrs. Stanmore is waiting till I — Hush ! I hear a noise ! Be to-morrow on the sea-beach, if fine ; I will be there every day — Hush ! jump into bed, darling."

Magnus sprung into bed and covered himself up as the door opened, and the old woman — by no means improved by being half-dressed — entered the room with a piece of candle between her fingers, and gazed round, saying, " Didn't I hear a voice — did you speak, acushla?"

" Yes, said Magnus, " a pane of glass has fallen into the room, and I got out of bed to see what it was."

" Bad cess to the wind, then, to break my glass, there's no fear of his paying for another ;" and, picking up a pair of old stockings, she thrust them into the hole, saying, " that would keep the wind out, anyhow ; so go to sleep, avick ; it's a bad night intirely, but it's a safe wind, and won't hurt the *Nancy* ;" and, finding the flame of the candle unpleasantly near her fingers, she blew it out, and then, shutting and locking the door, retired grumbling at the loss of her pane of glass.

18

MAGNUS slept little that night, watching the daylight through the little window; a glimpse of sunlight made his heart beat with joy, for it promised perhaps a fair day. The strong north-westerly wind had cleared the sky.

That morning the old woman gave him some tea for breakfast, and told him his uncle would take him to sea in the *Nancy*, and then he would become a fine hardy boy, and be a man soon, and go to France and Spain. Magnus made no reply: he was thinking of Phelim; and, as soon as his breakfast was over, he said he would like, as the sun was shining, to go down on the sands and gather shells.

"Well, avick, do so; but don't go out on the rocks for fear of the tide."

"Oh, no!" said Magnus, in a more cheerful tone than usual, and his bright speaking eyes sparkling. The old woman looked at him and then said, "Be sure to come back — mind your promise — you said you would never tell a lie."

"I will come back," said the boy, with a slight blush on his cheek, and then he passed out. Though the sun shone at intervals, it was a wild and stormy-looking day: the little bay was sheltered, but he could see, beyond the headlands, the white waves rolling along under a stiff gale at northwest, and the distant barks scudding under very low canvas.

Magnus descended the path and was soon on the level sands, and then he gazed around him anxiously. Presently he perceived a cap waved to him from one of the many caves in the lofty rocks that lined the bay. "Ah! there is Phelim;" and Magnus walked rapidly up to the mouth of the cave, and the next moment he was in the arms of his young follower. Phelim's expressions of joy were truly characteristic of his country.

Magnus wept with joy — he considered himself as good as freed from his persecutors, once under Phelim's protection.

"Ah! my poor Master Magnus, how the villains have treated you; but, the Lord be praised, we will now be able to get you away from them — and they have cut all your hair off, bad cess to them! and you look thin, avick!"

"Oh, no matter for that, Phelim! I fear nothing now; they wanted to make me believe my name was Jack Muggins, and that my noble, beautiful mother was a daughter of that horrid old woman up at the cottage, who calls herself Muggins; and her son, a frightful, huge sea-bear, called me his nephew, and said I should go to sea — horrid monster!"

"Ho, ho, ho! so I'm a horrid monster," exclaimed a voice as thick and as guttural as the growl of a half-strangled bear. The boys started, and in walked Bill Muggins himself, for the lads had gone farther into the cave to avoid observation.

"Double blocks and grapnell irons! who the dickens are you?" said Muggins, seizing Phelim by the collar.

Poor Phelim was like a shrimp in the claw of a lobster, but he answered stoutly, "Let me go; you're a smuggler, I know; but, take care, you will pay for kidnapping my young master!"

"Stop your jaw, you whelp!" said Muggins, giving Phelim a shake, "or I'll put an ounce of lead in your mouth, you sneaker."

Magnus snatched one of the pistols out of the smuggler's

belt, and in a delirium of passion cocked it; and, before the smuggler could interfere, he fired full at his foe, crying out — "You sha'n't touch or hurt Phelim, you monster!" Bill Muggins only escaped by rolling himself and Phelim over on the pebbles of the cave, whilst the ball knocked splinters of rock off the opposite side. No sooner did the shot echo through the cavern than two men vested as sailors rushed into the place, and for an instant stood stupefied; seeing Bill Muggins scrambling upon the gravel, still griping Phelim by the collar, whilst little Magnus stood pale, but with an air of perfect defiance on his expressive features.

"There's a young firebrand! tacks and sheets! By the powers the young spawn wanted to murder his uncle!" said the smuggler, giving himself a shake.

"Are you hurt, skipper?" said one of the men advancing, and taking the pistol from the hand of Magnus.

"Hurt, no; but if I hadn't ducked like a diver this precious nephew of mine would have stopped my log, I'm blowed if he wouldn't: but I bear no malice; give us your fin, Jack — blow me if I don't like to see pluck, though it ain't pleasant having an ounce of lead in one's trunk."

"You're no uncle of mine!" said Magnus stoutly, "and I will not be forced to stay with you."

"Oh, you won't!" said the smuggler; "very good! But who's this lubber here, that has thrust his oar into a rullock not meant for him?"

"It's nothing to you who I am," said Phelim. "I've found you out, anyhow; so take care what you do to this young boy, who is the son of a real gentleman; and, faix, no more a nephew of your's than I am."

"Then, for that speech of yours," said the smuggler, "if you don't cross the salt water my name is not Bill

Muggins, whatever yours is; lay hold of the lad," continued Bill, "and bring them along; faith, it looks as if they came purposely into the trap."

One of the men laid hold of Phelim, whilst Muggins tucked poor Magnus under his arm, and on they went farther into the cave, and then, stooping very low, turned into another branch of the cavern. Presently they were in total darkness, when one of the men opened a dark lantern, and then they proceeded through several intricate low caves, and then, of a sudden, the shade was turned over the light and they were again in darkness; but in a few moments they paused, Magnus heard a key turn in a lock. and the next instant Muggins put him down, saying, " You have brought this upon yourself, Jack, and this lubber also; but don't take on, I'll make a man of you yet." A door was then slammed to, the key turned, and the prisoners were left in total darkness.

"Avick, acushla!" said Phelim, "this is too bad entirely; I've made things worse for you — bad cess to the whole boiling of them!"

" I do not mind it, Phelim," said Magnus, groping about till he got Phelim's hand; " now let us sit down here ; here is a great box — they will not leave us long here, I daresay, and my dear papa always told me that God never deserts those that trust in him."

" True for you, dear — glory be to his name! so our priest says; but faith, avick, you have a great spirit; I wish you had shot that big man."

" Well. I am glad I did not, Phelim. I was in a passion, and that was wrong. I thought he was going to hurt you, but I would not like to have killed that man, for somehow he seems to think I am his nephew."

" Oh, bother, Master Magnus, that's impossible!"

"I know I am not so," said Magnus; "but tell me, Phelim, how you found me — who's at Ashgrove — and where's dear Mrs. Stanmore? I am so longing to know. Oh! my poor dear papa — I shall never see him again."

"Ochone! no, avick; but, please God, you will see those who will love and cherish you, and take care of you till you grow a man, and get your own lands again."

"Now, tell me how you found me, Phelim; I'm longing to know that."

"Well, dear, you remember the day the 'chaise' and four drove up to the hall door? Well, avick, in the chaise was your uncle, Mr. Gorman O'More. I was at the door when he came into the house, and I heard him say to his own man who was with him, 'Send for Mr. Hamilton; but Mr. Hamilton came out of the study, and then, my dear, we all heard the terrible news. The Lord save us! We were all dumbfoundered; but when I overheard that you were to be taken away by Mr. Hamilton in the chaise, I made out of a back-door, and never stopped running till I reached my father's. Unfortunately, father was so bad with the rheumatiz that he could do nothing himself; but says he, 'Phelim, they wants to put our young master out of the way; you must follow the chaise, Phelim; it will pass the farm-door, hide behind the hedge and jump up behind it, and keep after it some way or another; here's money, and I'll see Mrs. Stanmore when she comes back from Galway. Run, boy; bedad you will be too late, it's coming along the road! I seized my cap and bolted out, my mother calling out to me never to give up till I saw where they put you. I hid behind a hedge, and, as soon as the chaise passed I got up behind; and, when we came out on the turnpike road to Galway, it turned off and went away in another direction, and after six or eight miles it changed horses, but I managed to hide till they came on again.   It was then dusk, and faix I managed it well, for we drove ten or twelve miles farther, and came into a village with an inn in it, but I got off before it stopped, and I asked a man, ' What do you call the town ? '

" ' Arrah,' says he, ' what would you have it? it's Screeb, my boy.'

" ' Screeb,' says I to myself, ' I never heard of the place,' but I saw the chaise go into the yard ; and so, after a time, I goes into the place and sees the chaise put under a shed, and a boy and man taking the horses into the stables ; so I knew they was going to stop for the night anyhow, so I went to a little ale-house and got some food and a bed, and tould them to call me afore daylight.   But, bad scran to them ! it was broad daylight when I awoke, and then I dressed and ran to the inn, but the chaise was gone ; I thought I'd drop. I sees a boy sweeping the yard, so says I, ' May be, lad, you would tell me which way the chaise went ? '

" ' Arrah, what chaise ? '

" ' Why, the chaise that came in with the gentleman and the young lad.'

" ' Oh, I see ; the one as brought in the sick lad from Galway.'

" ' Sick lad,' says I, ' and from Galway ! ' frightened in- tirely ; ' sure,' says I, ' the boy was well and hearty, and the chaise did not come from Galway.'

" ' Bedad that's droll,' says the boy ; ' may be you'll tell me I'm blind, agra ! '

" ' Sure there might be another chaise,' says I.

" ' No, there wasn't,' says he ; ' and sure the chaise went back to Galway with the gentleman, and the sick boy went away two hours ago, wrapped in blankets, to Ballytanget, in a cart with straw in it.'

" 'Ballytanget,' says I, rubbing my head ; ' arrah where's that ?'

" 'Faix,' said the boy with a grin, ' you ax as many questions as the priest does at Easter ; sure Ballytanget is away by the sea-coast ; when you get out of the town turn to the left, and follow that road, and anybody will tell you where's Ballytanget.'

" Not to weary you, acushla, with my wanderings for six long days — sometimes sleeping under a hedge or a haystack — faix, I came to this part of the world, out on the heath, and I see'd a boy watching sheep, and away on the edge of the cliff was the cottage you were in, though I didn't know it then ; so I sat down by the boy. I had tracked you to within six miles of this place — 'What's the next village to this, gossoon ?' said I.

" ' Be sure there's no village nearer than Ballytanget, and that's seven or eight miles off.'

" ' How's that ?' says I ; ' it's a wild country intirely ; and who lives in yon cottage ?'

" ' Oh, you had better not go there ; the ould woman is a regular ould screed : I see'd them take a young lad there in a cart, wrapped in blankets, more than a week ago.'

" Musha, how glad I was to hear this ; so, after getting all kinds of information from the boy, who very knowingly told me to take care of myself, for the smugglers came to those parts at night, and if they caught any one prying about, they would half kill him.

" So now, avick, you see that's the way I found you at last, and faix we have gotten into worse quarters ; that great baste of a smuggler has a grip like a bear, bad cess to him ; and here we are in the dark, in this hole of a place, and never a morsel to eat or drink."

" Never mind, Phelim," said the stout-hearted boy ; " now

we are together we shall be able to get away from them, they can't keep us always locked up."

"No, faix, that's true for ye, my darling; but what kind of a place is this? may be we could get out of it."

"No, no," said Magnus, "they have locked us into the cave where they keep all their smuggled goods. I read a story not long ago about smugglers; they will come for us presently."

Still several hours passed away, till the prisoners judged it was night; and then they heard the key turn in the lock, and, the door opening, Bill Muggins, with his lantern open, and two men following him, entered the cave.

"Well, Jack, how are you, my hearty? you see what this lubber has brought upon you," holding his lantern so that the light fell upon Phelim. "Come, you're a sizable lad, and may be of use; now come along with us, and take care of Jack."

Magnus looked round him, and beheld a lofty and spacious cavern, stowed almost as full as it could hold with boxes and kegs; barrels piled one on the other; coils of rope, new and old; kedge-anchors; cables, sails, oars and spars — in fact, something of all things appertaining to the sea, and a smuggler's life. They passed out of the cave through a most ingeniously contrived door, covering a very limited slit in the rock, into which two great iron bars were inserted, upon which the door swung.

"You will be a broth of a boy yet," said Bill Muggins to little Magnus, seeing him follow so fearlessly; "you will take to your uncle by and by, like a young calf a week old; give us your flipper," and, as the light went out, he took him by the hand, and led him out through the entrances of the cavern till they gained the outside of the caves. The two men followed, carrying a kedge-anchor and two heavy coils of new rope.

It was a very dark night, the wind blowing very fresh indeed off the cliffs. The tide was up nearly to the cave's mouth — indeed, at high springs, it flowed many yards within them : a four-oared boat lay close to the shore, with two men in it. The smuggler lifted Magnus in his arms, and, having boots half-way up his thighs, he waded into the water, and deposited Magnus on the stern-sheets. Phelim was lifted in, the coils of rope deposited on the bottom, and then the boat was shoved off. Magnus and Phelim, knowing how useless either complaint or remonstrance would be, sat close to one another and remained silent ; but the young child's eyes were full of tears, as the boat, impelled by four oars, flew from the shore ; probably, he thought, " When shall I again set foot upon the shores of my father's land ? "

As they receded from the shore the puffs of wind came strong and frequent over the boat, driving her along, the oars scarcely touching the water.

" It blows hard, skipper," said one of the men ; who was pulling the stroke oar.

" Ay, ay," returned Bill ; " a double-reefed mainsail breeze ; but give way, there's the *Nancy*."

CHAPTER XX.

MAGNUS O'MORE, as the boat pulled out from the land, caught sight of a vessel with one mast lying at anchor, her sails down; in a few minutes they were alongside. She was a smart-looking craft of some fifty or sixty tons.

"Now Jack, my man," said the skipper, lifting Magnus up, "here's the *Lively Nancy*, as light a craft as ever swam or topped a sea. There, get your sea-legs;" so saying, the skipper deposited the boy upon the deck, Phelim and the boat's crew followed, and then the men commenced reefing the sail and hoisting it.

Magnus and Phelim stood, regarding the preparations for making sail in a very thoughtful mood; Phelim, however, doing and saying all he could to comfort the young boy.

"Oh!" said Magnus, rousing himself, "I am not at all afraid of the sea, Phelim; I have always wished to sail on the great sea, and aboard a large ship, and this one is much bigger than our pleasure-boat on the lake; but there are ships with three masts, a great deal bigger."

"But if we get sick, Master Magnus, what shall we do?"

"Dear me," said the hardy boy, "sea-sickness will not last long. I do not think I shall be sick."

"I shall," said Phelim; "I can't bear a boat rolling, and this one here makes me feel very queer even now."

"Now, my lads, go down below," said the skipper, coming aft to take the tiller; "it's not very warm off this coast in a nor'-wester; there's a light in the cabin; and do you," touching Phelim, "keep your weather-eye open. What's your name?"

"My name's Phelim M'Farlane; and faix, as to having my weather eye open, I'm not likely to keep either of them shut as long as we're under your orders, and faith you'll pay for this kidnapping yet."

The skipper burst into a hearty laugh, saying, "Go down, my lad, and keep your mouth shut for fear the salt water should get in; that's my advice, unless you want to have your jaw closed with a stopper on it. Now, Jack, go below," he added, in a softer voice; "that's a good boy, and stow yourself away in one of the berths." Magnus made no reply, but descended the stairs followed by Phelim, and entered the cabin of the smuggling cutter. It was a small place for the size of the craft, but convenience was sacrificed for stowage. A dirty lamp, emitting a small amount of light, let them perceive that the cabin contained four rough-boarded berths; there were a variety of articles scattered about, coils of small rope, pea-coats and sou'-westers thrown on the small table screwed to the floor, and a keg of some kind of compound lashed down on one of the lockers.

"I am tired and cold," said Magnus, "and will get into this curious box and cover myself up."

"Do, my poor child," said Phelim, helping him in, and then covering him over with blankets; fatigue and past excitement, and the motion of the cutter, then gliding through the water rapidly, soothed Magnus, and in a few moments he dropped off into a fast slumber. Phelim, who by no means admired the increased motion of the cutter, looked very wistfully about him, wished the sea would keep quiet, and not be disturbing his head, which began to swim; for, after passing the headland, she began to pitch into a tumble of a sea with considerable violence.

Magnus, notwithstanding the violence of the motion and the noise of the gale, did not awake till morning. Phelim, though exceedingly sick, being afraid that Magnus would be thrown out of his berth, remained below watching him. Our young hero looked around him at first, confused by the novelty of his situation, and trying to collect his thoughts. "Why, Phelim, how we are tossing about; what's the matter? It's blowing a storm."

"Musha, aren't you sea-sick, avick?" said Phelim, groaning at every lurch the little cutter gave. "I'm most dead—troth, it's the worst sickness ever I had!"

"No," said Magnus, "I am not sick; but I am very hungry—are not you?"

"Oh! don't talk of *ating*, Master Magnus; it turns me inside out. Oh, blessed saints! if we was once on dry land."

"I will get up and see the great waves, Phelim, and see if they are as big as they are represented in my great picture of a storm."

"Well, faix, you have great courage, intirely, but you couldn't keep your legs on the deck. To me it's like if I had sorra a leg to stand on at all, and then—oh! there she goes down—it's like as if my heart was in my throat."

Magnus nevertheless got out of the berth, and, just as he was steadying himself by holding on to the table, Bill Muggins descended the stairs and entered the cabin, his thick pea-jacket dripping wet, and only his nose and eyes to be seen outside the thick wrapper tied round his neck.

"So, Jack, here you are, alive and hearty, trying your sea-legs, eh? and looking as if you could eat a piece of fat

bacon and take a stiff glass of grog ; and this here lubber ”
—giving Phelim, who was making wry faces when he
heard of the fat bacon, a slap on the shoulder — “ looks as
pale as a dead codfish, and his eyes as if bunged up. Stir
yourself, boy, and open that locker near you, and pull out
the bread and beef and the jars that’s there ; we can’t light
a fire this morning, the sea is every now and then making a
breach over us.” So saying, he unrolled his wrapper,
wiped the spray from his bushy whiskers, and threw aside
his sou’-wester.

Phelim, more dead than alive, pulled out a huge piece of
boiled beef and a loaf, and laid them on the table ; from
thence the roll of the sea deposited them on the floor.
“ Why, clumsy, do you think the beef and the bread have a
marlinspike driven through them to keep them on the table?
hand them up, you land-lubber, and not stand staring at me
as if I was a sea-horse ! ”

“ Sure,” said Phelim, picking up the loaf and the beef,
and handing them to the skipper, “ every thing in this here
craft seems to be rolling about as if they had life in them ;
bad cess to the sea — it’s the worst place I ever was in ! ”

“ I’ll lick seamanship into you, Mister Phelim, as you
call yourself, before a week’s out. I’ll make you find your
legs,” said the skipper, cutting off with his knife a slice of
beef and bread, which he handed to Magnus, who took it
very quietly and began eating it, for he was very hungry,
and not at all sick.

“ Do eat some, Phelim,” said the boy ; “ you must eat.”

“ Oh, faix, I can’t eat, Master Magnus ! ”

“ Avast there ! ” said Bill Muggins with a savage look at
Phelim ; “ if I hear any of your outlandish names given to
my nephew Jack, I’ll thump your ugly head into putty, and
stop a leak with it.”

"Then, faix, you may do that as soon as you like," said Phelim stoutly. "The Lord save us! call my master's son Jack! no, I'll never do it!"

"You won't," growled Bill Muggins, stretching out his huge hand to get a grip of Phelim, who got so completely sick that he bolted up the stairs as nimbly as a regular sailor.

"If you beat or hurt Phelim," said Magnus resolutely, "I'll jump into the sea."

"Well, if you ain't a precious pair! Come, come, Jack, take it easy, I'm not so bad as you think me; I won't touch the boy, I only want to make a man of him, not a useless lubber skulking about and shooting cats." *

"Shooting cats!" exclaimed Magnus; "Phelim would not hurt a cat, or any other animal."

The skipper happened to have a very large piece of beef in his mouth, which, in the excitement of laughing, he bolted; it stuck in his throat, and his face grew so frightfully red with the laughing and choking, that Magnus fairly thought it was all over with him; but, opening a locker, the skipper pulled out a jar, and, putting it to his capacious mouth, swallowed nearly half a pint of strong whiskey, and then breathed a sigh of great relief. "Well, youngster, if you hadn't nearly choked me. Here, take a pull at this," and he poured out what appeared to Magnus clear water; but the smell satisfied him it was whiskey.

"No, I will have a drink of water," said the lad; "I cannot swallow that."

"Ah, you will take to it yet like new milk," said the skipper; "but you shall have a mug of water." Opening a

---

* A common term amongst seamen when they see any one exceedingly sea-sick.

locker he took out another jar, and, filling the mug with water, gave it to Magnus.

Wishing to see the great waves, he was ascending the stairs when the skipper, resuming his sou'-wester, took Magnus in his arms and carried him up on deck, and placing him down, said, "Now, Jack, my lad, what do you think of the great waves?"

Magnus was so utterly amazed that he stood holding on by Bill Muggins's hand, gazing at the storm-tossed ocean without uttering a word. The little cutter was lying too under a thribble-reefed trysail and close-reefed foresail. No land was visible, for the weather was far from clear, though the gale was a nor'-wester. To Magnus the mighty waves were a wonderful sight, and yet they did not frighten him. The monstrous wave came rolling on like a mountain, with its summit breaking into foam — it was like a hill of ice, covered with a crest of snow, over which the little *Nancy* rose like a sea-bird on its own element.

"Ain't she a beauty, my boy?" said the skipper with a feeling of pride, as the wild gust whirled past, driving the spray like a snow-drift over her deck. "Sit down there, boy," and putting Magnus against the weather bulwark, alongside the miserable Phelim — who would rather have stood on the wildest hill in his native country, exposed bareheaded to the fiercest tempest that ever blew, than spend a summer's day aboard the *Lively Nancy* — and yet Phelim in the end became as good and thorough a seaman as any in Great Britain.

With a rope passed round his little waist, Magnus sat looking at the huge waves as they came rolling towards the little vessel, threatening to overwhelm her, but she gallantly rode aloft, and passed gently into the deep trough of the succeeding wave.

Magnus observed the four men upon deck taking it as coolly as if it was a summer's breeze. Presently one of the men called out, " A sail in the south-west!" in a few min utes, two more made their appearance, and the skipper shortly after said they were men-of-war under their fore course.

It was a time of peace with France, so their appearance created neither much surprise nor curiosity. They very soon came full into view, and in the foremost vessel, Magnus, for the first time, beheld a seventy-four gun-ship. He was astounded; though her topgallant-masts were struck, and her topsails furled, to him her masts appeared to tower to the sky; and her gigantic hull, as it rose and fell on the billows, looked a fabric so immense as to defy the utmost force of the raging seas.

" Well, if these ain't French men-of-war!" said Bill Muggins to one of the men standing by the tiller, which was fastened down, "and the gale and sea is increasing. See! they are rounding to, and setting their close-reefed topsails."

In a short time the great seventy-four had brought herself to the wind, and lay to about a couple of miles to leeward of the cutter, the others doing the same at some distance from each other. Before four o'clock in the day the gale had increased to a hurricane; to attempt to scud back to the land would have insured the destruction of the cutter, whose only chance of safety lay in lying to. The gale had shifted two or three points, and about half-past four o'clock, a tremendous sea struck the *Nancy*, her tiller broke loose, and the rudder-head split in pieces; as the cutter broached to, another sea struck her, and her weather-shrouds giving way, the mast went over the side.

Phelim, terrified out of his sickness by the danger, dragged Magnus down the companion-stairs, followed by a rush of

14

water that threw them both on the cabin-floor, which became half filled with water. "Oh, murder — murder! what shall we do?" exclaimed Phelim, lifting Magnus up; "my poor boy, you are kilt entirely!"

"Come up — come up — if you wish to save your lives!" shouted the skipper from above.

Magnus and Phelim crawled up the stairs and gained the deck; the cutter was careering before the storm like a startled steed. Several of the men had got a spar over the traffrail, and were striving with might and main to turn the cutter from her fatal course. Magnus and Phelim looked before them — they were on the very summit of a giant wave — beneath them, as it seemed, was a great black mass, with its monstrous masts — it was the seventy-four gun-ship! Magnus beheld a crowd upon her decks, he heard the roar of the breaking sea as it bore them on — on — in its snow-white crest. Suddenly he was grasped in the strong arms of the skipper; he heard a wild shout and a fearful cry as the doomed craft shot down the roaring breaker — he felt as if Muggins leaped into the sea — a world of waters rushed over him — the next moment a blow on the head left him senseless and ignorant of what followed.

CHAPTER XXI.

WHEN Magnus opened his eyes and came to his recollection, he found himself lying in a cot with his head bound up, but the extraordinary place he was lying in amazed him. He was in the sick ward of a line-of-battle ship.

"Ah! you come to de life, *mon garçon*," said a tall thin man, bending over him. "Now you take dat," and he held a glass with some mixture in it to Magnus, who took it at once.

"Where is Phelim?" said our young hero, feeling roused from the cordial he had taken.

"Feel him — Feel him! what dat for — ne bones broken, *mon garçon*, only de thump on de head. How you feel now?"

"A great deal better, sir," said Magnus, wondering how he got where he was; "but Phelim — is he saved?"

"Ah! Feel him again — who is dat Feel him? one of de *garçons*, saved, eh?"

"Yes," said Magnus joyfully, "Phelim is the young lad that was in the smuggling cutter with me."

"*Ah, bon! de contrabandists*, you too young to be what you call smugger."

"I am no smuggler," said Magnus anxiously, "nor Phelim; we were carried away by the people in the cutter against our wills. My name is Roderick Magnus O'More."

"Ah! what a name dat," said the surgeon; "but you

keep quiet and go *dormir* — that is, sleep — and I bring you one countryman who can talk de English, because he is an Irishman. *Soyez*, tranquil — sleep, *mon enfant*." So saying, the good-natured surgeon left him to sleep, which he did, the mixture he had taken making him feel drowsy.

Magnus slept well, and when he awoke felt not much the worse excepting the consciousness of having had a smart blow on the head. A man brought him some good broth, but shook his head, saying to Magnus's questions, "No Anglais." But shortly after the surgeon came, and with him a naval officer, a very handsome man, not more than two-and-twenty.

"Here, *mon enfant*," said the surgeon, "is a countryman; he understands you."

"Well, my lad," said the lieutenant, looking surprised at the uncommonly handsome and preposessing features of Magnus, "tell me all you told the good doctor; I am, no doubt, a countryman of yours. What is your name, and how came you in that unfortunate smuggling cutter?"

"Oh! I am so glad to hear you speak," said Magnus sitting up; "but do, sir, tell me if there is a young lad saved named Phelim M'Farlane?"

"Eh, *garçon* — dare is dat Feel him again," said the surgeon.

"Yes," returned Lieutenant O'Brien; "there was a lad, three or four years older than you, saved, if that is the one you mean, and the skipper and one other man — the rest foundered with the cutter, which was knocked to atoms against our sides; but what is your name? The skipper, whose leg and ribs are broken, says you are his nephew, and he is very anxious about you, for he certainly saved your life by jumping with you into the rigging."

"I am grateful to him for my life," said Magnus, in the

sweet quiet tones of his little voice; "but I am not his nephew — indeed, indeed, I am not: Phelim will tell you the same. My name is Roderick Magnus O'More."

"What a name, dat!" muttered the surgeon.

"Not half as long as your own, *mon ami*," said Lieutenant O'Brien, laughing; and then, sitting down on the side of the cot, he listened with exceeding attention to the artless and truthful tale of poor Magnus. "My poor boy," said the lieutenant, "I believe every word you have told me. I will have you removed to my berth, and will take every care of you till I get you back to your friends; though, upon my conscience, I think you have more enemies than friends."

"Oh!" said Magnus, "if I could get to my governess, Mrs. Stanmore, she would take care of me. I am quite able to get up and walk, the blow I had on the head is nothing ; I long to see Phelim."

"Dat Feel him is *un grand garçon*," said the surgeon; "what is he?"

"The faithful follower of this young gentleman," said the lieutenant; "I suppose he may get up? I'll swear to his being Irish — not a hair he cares for a thump on the head! I always told you, André, that we Irishmen have thicker skulls than you Frenchmen."

"*Ah, oui*, and *leetle* brains!" said the surgeon, laughing.

"But the leetle is very good, *mon ami;* you may have as much brains as a bullock, but, like that interesting animal when cut up for the table, very little wit in them. Now, Magnus, jump up," he added, "and come out of this berth; I'll get the ship's tailor to make you a new suit of garments now this strong and lasting gale is going down."

Magnus, rejoicing in his little heart at getting rid of the name of Jack Muggins, was soon up and dressed; he then felt a little sore, as if he had been knocked about, and a little giddy. The huge ship he was in rolled exceedingly, and her bulkheads and cannons, as the ship rose and fell, made a tremendous creaking noise.

The number of men Magnus met on his way through the ship, and the immense guns, amazed and bewildered him; such a monstrous fabric was to him wonderful. On gaining the deck his wonder increased; it was still blowing a gale, but its tremendous violence had ceased.

Magnus gazed up at the enormous masts, the great sails —though close-reefed, for the seventy-four was now making head-way through the still heavy seas —the roar of the wind, as it swept over the ship and whistled through the rigging, all was matter of wonder and almost awe to the young boy.

Several officers were walking on the quarter-deck; and Lieutenant O'Brien, still holding Magnus by the hand, walked up to a fine-looking officer, past middle age, but still vigorous and active, and, touching his hat, spoke to him in French. This officer was Captain François Doré, commander of the *Temeraire*. He looked at Magnus attentively, then, with a smile, patted him on the head, saying something in French, which ended in " beau garçon ; " and then Lieutenant O'Brien took him with him to his own quarters.

A couple of days made Magnus quite at home in the great seventy-four gun-ship. He was likely to become a favorite with all the officers ; for, though he did not understand them, he was so intelligent and quick, that he almost comprehended what they said by their looks. Lieutenant O'Brien had questioned Phelim, who was getting better, having been desperately bruised, and would have perished had not one of the crew hooked him with a boat-hook, and, others assisting, he was hauled aboard half dead with the shock.

Magnus would sit for an hour at a time by his bedside, so rejoiced was he to see that he had escaped. Though Lieutenant O'Brien strictly questioned Bill Muggins, he stoutly stuck to his assertion, with divers oaths, that Magnus was his nephew, and the child of his sister Jane, though he did not deny but that Mr. O'More was his father. Lieutenant O'Brien thought there was some strange jumble in the affair, or that the smuggler was bribed to play the part of uncle to the boy; for Phelim's account was so very clear about Magnus's mother being a Spanish lady that came from abroad with Mr. O'More, and the child being born soon after, satisfied him that it was out of the question his being the child of Jane Muggins.

"Well, my dear boy," said the lieutenant, one evening as they sat together in their cabin, "we are returning to Brest; our cruise is now finished; we shall be in port after to-morrow. I really am puzzled what to do with you. To send you to England — for we are at peace now — with only Phelim to protect you, and your home in the possession of those who evidently wished to get rid of you, would be cruel. Are you a Catholic or a Protestant?"

"Papa went to church," said Magnus, "and so did I and Mrs. Stanmore; Catholics go to mass. Are not you a Protestant?"

"No, by the powers! I'm what they call in Ireland a Papist, and my father's great-grandfather before him."

"But why are you an officer in a French ship?"

"Because, my dear Magnus, the English would not let us worship God after our own fashion, and they persecuted us and our priests; and when my great-grandfather fought for his rightful king, and he was driven away from his kingdom to die in France, a great many of his Irish subjects followed him — our estates and entire property were confiscated, and lost to us. So, though we are Irish at heart still, and love the dear old country, we have taken service in the country that protected us. My father died a colonel in the French service; and I, when very young, entered the navy, and am now a lieutenant. Now, if you will stay with me, I will share my pay with you, and get you, in a year or two, to be a midshipman."

"You are very kind, Mr. O'Brien," said Magnus, pressing the lieutenant's hand affectionately, "but I would not like to fight against England."

"Faith, you are right, my little friend. You have not the same feelings as I have, neither have your forefathers suffered like mine; however, when we get to Brest, we must see what can be done for you."

Magnus dearly loved to ramble about on the quarter-deck of the *Temeraire*, looking up at the pyramid of canvas she carried, and to watch the other five ships following in her wake.

The *Temeraire*, and five frigates, were out on a cruise, exercising their crews, when a succession of heavy gales separated the ships, and drove the *Temeraire* and three others nearer to the coast of Ireland than they intended; the *Temeraire* was now returning to Brest, having picked up the missing ships in the Bay of Biscay.

The following day the *Temeraire* approached the roadstead of Brest, the strongest and most magnificent harbor in France. Magnus was on deck, placed on a gun-carriage, so that he might look about him as the ships made for the Goulet, the narrow passage between the Promontory of Finisterre on the north, and the Peninsula of Quiberon on the south. In the middle of this narrow passage rise the

Mengan Rocks, which renders the navigation even more difficult to line-of-battle ships. An enemy attempting the passage would have to pass close under the guns of tremendous batteries, which line the passage on either side.

After running through the Goulet, the *Temeraire* and the frigates came to an anchor in the roadstead, one of the finest in the world, and where all the fleets of France might anchor in safety.

Magnus was too young to feel sufficient curiosity concerning this remarkable and magnificent harbor, so full of objects memorable in history. To the south of the Goulet, where the *Temeraire* anchored, is the Bay of Camoret, one of whose formidable batteries is called Mort Anglais — because 900 men, under General Tollemache, when landed in 1694 under this fort, were all cut to pieces.

The next day Lieutenant O'Brien went ashore, whilst Magnus remained under the care of Phelim, who was now able to walk about the ship, but at a sad loss to make himself understood. Bill Muggins was taken ashore to the hospital. After two or three days, Lieutenant O'Brien had leave to stay a week on shore, so he took Magnus and Phelim with him. There never was a kinder-hearted man than Lieutenant O'Brien ; he became singularly interested in Magnus, though at the same time he felt greatly puzzled what to do with him. But, fortunately for him and for Magnus, he encountered one day an English officer, who, during the late war, was greatly indebted to him, having rendered him every assistance in money and otherwise, during a long imprisonment. This officer, who was now in possession of a handsome income through the death of an elder brother, had been travelling with his only son, a young lad of Magnus's age, through Brittany, and was stopping for a few days in Brest, on his return to England.

Lieutenant O'Brien mentioned Magnus's history to Captain Broomsley, and so interested that gentleman — who was of the most generous, noble disposition — that he at once proposed to take the young boy with him to England: — " I will employ my solicitor," said Captain Broomsley, " to make inquiries in Ireland, and, if I can find no friends willing to protect the child, I will put him to school with my own son, and, afterwards, put him a midshipman aboard a man-of-war; if he lives to be a man, he may yet fight his own battles.   I have but one child, and am independent; I can, therefore, afford to offer this protection to your little *protégé*, so let me see him to-morrow."

" My dear Magnus," said Lieutenant O'Brien, when he returned home that evening, " I have found a kind protector for you, who will take you to England, and, if he cannot find your friends, he will take care of you and make you a midshipman aboard one of your own king's ships.   You know you often say you would like to be a sailor."

Magnus's eyes filled with tears; he was about to leave one he was beginning to love dearly; he jumped up, and, throwing his arms round the lieutenant's neck, kissed him — " I shall never forget you! I never forget any thing I love, and I love you next to my dear, dear papa; you have been so kind and good to me.   Oh ! I wish you commanded an English ship, I would stay and fight by your side."

Lieutenant O'Brien was moved; he kissed his favorite affectionately, saying — " Who knows, Magnus, we may meet again when you become a man. I shall not forget you, depend on it; but you will go with Captain Broomsley, his son is a fine little fellow, a year older than you, but neither so tall or so stout : by the powers, you'll make a fine man, Magnus; you're as tall and strong as a boy of thirteen !"

" If I live to be a man," said Magnus, his bright eyes

kindling, "I will see my own land again, and those who so cruelly turned me out of my home may be sorry for it yet — but will your kind friend take poor Phelim?"

"Oh! I have a place for him; there is a schooner here bound for Cork. I will get him a passage and give him money to travel home to his father; he may do you service yet — his parents must be anxious about him." Magnus sighed; he had too much good sense to ask his new protector to burden himself with poor Phelim.

The next day Magnus, neatly dressed in a new suit of clothes, purchased for him on landing by his generous protector, proceeded to the hotel with Lieutenant O'Brien, where Captain Broomsley lodged. The captain was at once struck with the aristocratic beauty of Magnus's features and his graceful little figure. There was a strong mark of his Spanish origin in his dark clear complexion and brilliant dark eyes. It was impossible not to be interested in him, especially after conversing with him; and Captain Broomsley felt highly pleased as he saw the two boys become great friends during the evening.

"I shall have to thank you, indeed, O'Brien," said the captain, "for putting this interesting boy under my care, and I feel sure Mrs. Broomsley will be equally so."

The idea of parting from Magnus was more than Phelim could endure; the generous-hearted Irish lad was willing to forego home and country, to work, do any thing, suffer any privation, sooner than leave his young master.

"I like that lad," said Captain Broomsley, looking into the open, honest, and comely face of Phelim; "I don't see why he should not come with us; he can attend on the two lads — they will want some one — and when we get to England he can visit his parents, and return and ship aboard the same ship as his young master." Phelim threw himself at the feet of Captain Broomsley, and kissed his hand with all the passionate earnestness of his countrymen.

Magnus wept a good deal in parting with his generous friend, Lieutenant O'Brien; who himself was evidently much moved, and, as the carriage drove off containing Captain Broomsley and his *protégé*, Phelim mounted on the dicky in front; he felt a sense of loneliness steal over him, quite unusual to his general gay and thoughtless character.

CHAPTER XXII.

AFTER a pleasant journey through Normandy, Captain
Broomsley and his party reached Calais and embarked for
Dover. During the journey — stopping here and there to
enjoy the scenery, &c. — the two lads became greatly
attached to each other; and Captain Broomsley also found
Phelim M‘Farlàne a clever, intelligent lad, who soon made
himself exceedingly useful. A post-chaise carried the party
into Devonshire, where Captain Broomsley resided in a very
handsome mansion, called "Broomsley Lodge."

Mrs. Broomsley received her husband and son with the
warmest affection; and, though surprised, welcomed her
husband's *protégé* with great kindness. She was a most
amiable, handsome woman, cheerful and agreeable in her
manners. In this happy and kind family Magnus O'More
passed the first six months after his arrival in England.
Mrs. Broomsley soon learned to love and admire the young
lad so strangely committed to their care, and Magnus returned her kindness with the deepest gratitude and love.
Phelim was sent home, but Captain Broomsley promised to
put him aboard the same ship as Magnus O'More, when the
time came for him to become a midshipman.

Captain Broomsley's son and Magnus were then placed in
a very superior school, near Exeter. In this establishment
Magnus found Henry Barlow and Alfred Hammond; between Henry and Magnus a great friendship took place —

remarkably similar in tastes, habits, and spirit, the two boys soon learned to love each other. Magnus, as Captain Broomsley advised him, refrained from confiding his family history to any of his companions. Henry Barlow was destined for the sea, so was Magnus, and they both wished that they might commence their novitiate as midshipmen in the same ship. Alfred Hammond, as related in our first chapter, became heir to immense wealth, and quitted school; but Magnus and Henry remained four years together.

Captain Broomsley had employed his solicitor to make inquiries in the county of Galway concerning Magnus's relations, having made him first fully acquainted with all the particulars related to him by his *protégé ;* he also instructed him to make inquiries of Phelim M'Farlane's father; but, above all, to seek out Mrs. Stanmore if possible.

Mr. Lucas, Captain Broomsley's solicitor, on his return from Ireland visited his employer. As they sat over their wine after dinner, Captain Broomsley said, " Well, Lucas, how did you get on?"

" Why, I was greatly surprised with Galway; do you know it put me greatly in mind of Malaga and Cadiz? In Galway you have quite a Catholic population, priests and monks, nunneries, churches, and convents, and such a look of antiquity about the place — great arched doorways — really, without a great stretch of imagination, you might fancy yourself in Spain; even the people wear a costume different from all the other towns I visited. I had hired a car and a guide to visit the shores of Lough Corrib; I hired a guide purposely, for one picks up strange and useful hints from these kind of people. Galway appears to belong exclusively to the families of Blakes, Burkes, Butkins, and Birdeens — these families have all their traditions in the mouths of the peasantry. I found that the O'More is not a

Galway family originally, though a family of great antiquity. As we approached the village of D——, we got sight of Ashgrove, a splendid mansion, standing on a slight eminence above Lough Corrib, well wooded at the back, with a noble park and extensive pasture-grounds along the borders of that beautiful lake. 'Who lives in that mansion?' I questioned of my guide, a very respectable man, and quite a scholar in his way.

" 'That's Ashgrove,' said my guide; 'the seat of the O'Mores.'

" 'That's not a Galway name,' said I.

" 'No, your honor; the great O'Mores came out of Ulster. But in the times of Elizabeth the O'Mores and the O'Neils rose in arms, but the English overpowered them, and the family became scattered and their estates were confiscated.'

" 'Who lives now at Ashgrove?' I questioned, finding my companion very much inclined to give me a history of all the O'Mores that ever existed.

" 'Faix, your honor, the owner of Ashgrove and the Clare Estates now is a Mr. Gorman O'More; but it's whispered through the country that he has no more right to it than you or I, your honor.'

" 'He's a very lucky man, then,' said I; 'perhaps you can put me up to the way of getting such a handsome residence and estates to boot.'

" 'Oh, faix, your worship, maybe after all it's all blarney!' But, not to weary you, my dear sir," continued the solicitor, "from this man I heard very nearly the same particulars I received from you. The fact is, Mr. Gorman O'More has made himself so thoroughly detested by various acts of oppression, that he would never hold his ground in the county were he not protected by the priesthood, although he is a Roman Catholic — and a most bigoted, narrow-minded one too, giving large sums to convents and monks, &c. The consequence of his tyranny is, that the story of his brother's death, although strictly true, and the assertion of his child's illegitimacy, are alike discredited. The former is firmly believed to have been accomplished by unfair means, while the latter is held to be a mere pretence for driving from his home the son of his brother; and many boldly declare that the unfortunate child is the real and lawful heir of the O'More Estates.

"I visited Phelim's father, a respectable intelligent man; his wife is ready to declare, on oath, that she several times heard the late Mr. O'More say that his lady was a Spanish grandee's daughter, and that they were married somewhere in Spain, by a Protestant clergyman and a priest; but, you see, this is all hearsay; we have not one single tangible proof to work upon. M'Farlane gave me Mrs. Stanmore's address in Dublin, and assured me she would furnish me with names and particulars that would materially assist me; but when I reached Dublin, and sought out Mrs. Stanmore, to my intense vexation I found she had gone out to India with the care of two young ladies, to join their father, who was governor of some British settlement. Thus, though I am perfectly persuaded of your *protégé's* rights to the O'More's Estates, I see no possibility of dispossessing the present holder of them, or of proving Magnus's legitimacy."

Captain Broomsley agreed with his solicitor — "At all events I will give the poor boy a profession; he is a remarkably high-spirited, clever lad, and, if spared, will rise in the service; perhaps, in the course of time, Mrs. Stanmore may return to England, and give us some clew which we can follow up to the fountain-head."

"Well, I do not see that you can do better," said Mr.

Lucas; " by the by, I find that the present possessor of the O'More Estates is likely to succeed to the great Courtown property, and the title of Lord Courtown. The present Lord Courtown is a man of strange habits, near sixty I believe, and in delicate health."

" Upon my word it's a very hard case," said Captain Broomsley, " but we must leave the issue to Providence."

At the age of thirteen, Captain Broomsley obtained for Magnus a midshipman's berth aboard a thirty-two-gun frigate, of which vessel, Captain J——, a great friend of his, and a most experienced and gallant officer, was commander.

Magnus was fitted out in every way as liberally as if he was Captain Broomsley's son. Aboard the same ship Phelim M'Farlane, then a stout, able youth of eighteen, and more attached than ever to his young master, shipped as second-class seaman — having purposely passed three years in a merchant-vessel, in order to become a thorough seaman before entering aboard a man-of-war; and Captain Broomsley spoke of Phelim in high terms to his friend Captain J——, so that after a short time he would have the prospect of becoming a seaman of the first class.

It was not without feelings of deep regret and earnest gratitude that Magnus parted from his kind protectors, and his young companions, Charles Broomsley and Henry Barlow, who came to spend a week with Magnus and Charles at Broomsley Lodge. Henry, on his return home, was also to be entered aboard a man-of-war, and the two friends ardently hoped that they might meet aboard the same ship. He would speak to his father on his return to Cornwall. Henry bid adieu to all, and soon after Magnus joined his ship at Portsmouth; he had a letter from Henry Barlow, stating he was to sail aboard the *Madagascar* — thus, their

15

first wish was frustrated. The *D*—— frigate, aboard which was Magnus and Phelim, sailed for the West Indies.

We pass over the first four years of a midshipman's life; it was a time of peace, so — except in becoming a good seaman, and distinguishing himself by diligent and active service — he had no other opportunity of showing his spirit or enterprise. In 1792, the *D*—— frigate returned to England; in 1793, the war broke out with revolutionary France, when Magnus, after a short but very happy visit to his benefactors, who received him with unaffected pleasure, rejoicing to see their *protégé* grown almost to manhood, so tall and strong was he for his age — while his friend Charles Broomsley was pursuing his studies at Cambridge — prepared again for sea.

Magnus was now to sail with Captain James Cotes, in the thirty-two-gun frigate *Thames* — his old comrade and most attached follower, Phelim, being still with him, having shipped as able seaman aboard the *Thames*.

The *Thames* sailed to join the British fleet off Brest. During the years that had passed, Magnus O'More never for one moment allowed the recollections of the past to fade from his memory. Every incident of his early life was treasured in his mind — his loved home, his lamented father, and the features of his beautiful mother, were ever before him; while the many hours of leisure he enjoyed in his first years of a midshipman's life, were devoted to the acquirement of French and Spanish; he studied with a perseverance and an ardor that soon conquered the difficulties in both these languages.

Remaining for some months amongst the Spanish settlements, he had opportunities of speaking the language; and, being remarkably quick, he surprised his brother officers by his talent and power in picking up the accent and idiom of the natives. Thus, when he returned to England after an absence of four years, he was able to converse fluently in Spanish and French, and was improving himself in Italian; the two previous languages being a great help to the latter.

Phelim, as he increased in years, became a thorough seaman, and the *beau-ideal* of a smart blue jacket; he was a general favorite, full of life and spirits, and was always ready and willing for any species of service for which he was required.

The coast of the Spanish main was infested with pirates, and many a one was destroyed by the boats of the *D——* frigate. Magnus's spirit and love of enterprise was often shown in these boat actions, and in one he most particularly distinguished himself.

It was the month of October; the *Thames* had taken several prizes, and sent them with prize-crews to England; thus she became very short of hands. The second lieutenant, George Robinson, was extremely partial to Magnus, who greatly esteemed him, his manner and conduct being so kind and considerate.

One morning, as the *Thames* was standing away to the southward, the wind west south-west, the weather rather hazy, Magnus made out a craft right ahead of them.

"What is she like, Magnus?" said Lieutenant Robinson, taking the glass from our hero's hand, and directing it towards the stranger.

"I think she's a frigate, sir, with a blue flag at the fore, going away large."

"You are right," said the lieutenant, "and she sees us. She is now hauling her wind."

All became roused aboard the *Thames*. Captain Cotes came upon deck, and, after a look at the stranger, declared her to be a French frigate. The *Thames* now cleared for action.

"I say, Mag," said a young midshipman of Magnus's own age, of the name of Dale, "how do you feel? This will be our first trial of nerves — and, Jemima, she's a whopper! She's as large again as we are."

"The more glory in beating her, James," said Magnus, his cheek flushing with excitement.

The two ships now passed each other on opposite tacks, and as the stranger went by, she fired her broadside, and then wore round on the opposite tack. This was the first real broadside between frigate and frigate our hero had ever seen or heard. Young Dale, the midshipman, was standing beside him, when a splinter struck him down, bleeding from a sharp wound it inflicted on the side of his head; Magnus anxiously raised him up, and some of the men wished to carry him below.

"No, no, Magnus!" exclaimed the gallant boy, "just wipe the blood off my face, and let me sit on a gun-carriage for a few minutes, and I shall be as well as ever; I'm not going to be done out of my first battle by a splinter."

The *Thames* now blazed away in right earnest, though it was easy to perceive that she had a most formidable antagonist to contend with. She looked five or six hundred tons larger, and her crew were no doubt nearly double in number, but this only excited the crew of the *Thames* to greater exertion.

Phelim, when he could, kept his eye upon his young master; for such he persisted in calling him in his own mind. He saw him as busy as possible, and as cool and collected during a terrible raking fire as the oldest officer aboard.

At this moment the French frigate, crossing the stern of the *Thames*, fired into her two raking broadsides. But the British ship poured an admirably directed fire from several of her main deck guns. This seemed to stagger the Frenchman, for she at once threw all her sails aback, and then hauled off to the southward. Phelim M'Farlane tossed his hat in the air, and at once the whole crew gave three hearty cheers.

The French frigate had evidently received considerable damage, and, for the time, was quite satisfied; but the *Thames*, in this somewhat unequal contest, had suffered severely. She had ten seamen and a marine killed; Magnus found Lieutenant Robinson, and his comrade James Dale, the midshipman, both wounded; also several of the seamen. Captain Cotes immediately began to see to the damage the *Thames* had received; for she appeared to be quite in a disabled state. Her three lower masts were shot through in several places; she had not a stay standing, and, excepting a few shrouds, all the main rigging was gone. A double-headed shot had carried away her main topsail-yard; even the hull had its share of damage; all the gangways were gone, whilst the main deck in front of the mainmast was torn up from the waterway to the hatchways. Every man aboard had his work to do; meanwhile, the ship was put before the wind, the only way she could be made to steer.

" Faix, we have had a peppering, and no mistake, Master Magnus," said Phelim, as the young midshipman was overlooking a party knotting and splicing the riggings; " but I think we gave mounseer as much as he wanted for one day's dinner."

" Any how, 'twould *spile* his digestion, Phelim, as the doctor says," said a topman with a grin.

" Yes, I think he had a pretty good dose," said Magnus; " but look sharp, he's perhaps only taking a snooze, and will blaze away again in a few hours."

" Lord love ye, not he!" said an old quarter-master; " our guns were pointed lower than his'n, and I'll swear he'll have enough to do to keep Davy Jones out of his bread-lockers; I see'd several men over her sides stopping the shot-holes, and we could hear her pumps going with a vengeance."

When he had time, Magnus ran below to see how his friends Lieutenant Robinson and Midshipman Dale got on, and was delighted to hear the surgeon say there was no danger whatever to be apprehended.

"Where's the French frigate now, Mag, old boy?" said Dale.

"She's out of sight somewhere or other," said Magnus; "they can't see her from the tops."

"She's gone down, then," returned the mid; "how could she get out of sight by this time?"

"Well, our commander himself is puzzled about that; at all events, she's not to be seen; however, we're just like a man whose crutches are knocked from under him; we haven't a leg to stand on. We are going before the wind like a Dutch dogger, and quite as fast."

"If any thing came up with us now," said young Dale, "it would be U—P, eh?"

"I hope not," said Magnus, hurrying on deck, hearing an unusual bustle. On gaining the deck, he perceived that the breeze had freshened from the south-west quarter; but the worst of it was, four sail had made their appearance, and were coming up fast under English colors; the crew of the *Thames* looked with great suspense on these new-comers, whilst Captain Cotes seemed extremely uneasy. The *Thames* could carry no after-sail, having all her runners carried forward and crossed, to serve as stays and shrouds, therefore she could not haul upon a wind.

The leading frigate of the four now hauled down her English colors, and hoisted the tri-color, and, ranging up under the *Thames's* stern, gave her a broadside. The crew, still eager, and thirsting for a blow at their saucy enemy, were turning to return the broadside, even in their miserably crippled state ; but Captain Cotes, seeing that resistance was utterly hopeless, and would cause a sacrifice of life to no purpose, hailed, saying she was in a disabled state from a previous action, and then hauled down her colors.

" Well, I'm bothered," exclaimed a topman, dashing his hat on the deck, and dancing on it in his rage, " if them 'ere lubbers should have had us without giving them a taste of our pill-boxes ! Here's a go ! brown-bread and water, and as many hoppers in them as would tow a three-decker in a calm, if you could tackle them on in a row."

CHAPTER XXIII.

The hauling-down of the British ensign, and surrendering to the French frigate, caused a profound sensation of disappointment and vexation amongst the crew of the *Thames*, to no one more so than Magnus O'More; his day-dreams of glory were all dispersed by this untoward event. After so gallantly defeating and beating off a powerful antagonist, to have to surrender to an enemy who had no hand in disabling them was galling in the extreme.

The French frigate was called the *Carmagnole*, and commanded by Jaques Theodore Allemand. She had for consorts the *Resolue* and *Semilante*, both frigates. The *Carmagnole* at once hailed, and ordered Captain Cotes to send his boat aboard. The reply was, the *Thames* had no boat fit to stand. The French commodore then ordered his two boats to be hoisted out, and, being manned, they pulled alongside and took possession. It was then decided to take the *Thames* in tow, and proceed for Brest; Captain Cotes and most of his officers and men were removed aboard the other ships, the rest were left unconfined aboard the *Thames*. Magnus was one of those left, because he spoke the language; those of the crew who were left were forced to knot and splice part of the rigging; they were stripped of all their clothes, not even left a spare shirt; the officers of the French ship seemed to have no control over their men.

The night that followed the action was intensely dark,

with a thick mist. Magnus was walking the deck in a most disconsolate mood; the thought of a French prison, to be endured perhaps for years, struck a chill to his young heart. He was leaning over the bulwarks, when a low voice beside him said — "Go aft, Master Magnus, without speaking to any of the mounseers; they are half of them drunk, and their officers are taking it *aisy* in the cabin." It was the voice of Phelim M'Farlane, and, as soon as he said the words, he glided noiselessly away.

It was so intensely dark that, except for a few battle lanterns here and there, not a mast could be distinguished at a few yards' distance.

Several of the French crew were lying, half drunk and asleep, under the bulwarks, and some in the boats. The *Thames* was going dead before the wind, in tow of the *Carmagnole;* it was a very light breeze, the ship not going through the water more than four knots an hour. Magnus could see the lights of the French frigate, but not the vessel herself, owing to the thick haze.

Over the quarter-deck was strewed a vast quantity of the rigging, and spars and lumber of the *Thames*, which the prize-crew had piled up and not cleared away, so that the space before the wheel was clear, though the rest of the ship was in a sad state, the crew not having had time to do any thing before the *Carmagnole* came up.

Magnus O'More passed along the deck, keeping amongst the lumber, and gained the stern without being noticed; stowed away amongst the mass of rigging were three men, Phelim was one.

" There are two boats towing astern, Master Magnus," said Phelim in a low voice, "and we have stowed away a bag of biscuit and this small keg of water — any chance is better than a French prison. There is a man in one of the boats now, close under the stern; here is the rope, slide down it, sir, and we will follow."

Magnus understood the plan at once, so without more words he passed out of one of the stern-ports, and, sliding down the rope, was in the boat the next minute. So well did they manage it, that all four got into the boat without creating the slightest alarm aboard the frigate. "Now, cut away the painter, boys," said Phelim, "and let us drop quietly astern."

"Cut away the other boat also," said Magnus, "and then they will not have one fit to pursue us, if we are missed; and the delay before the alarm spreads to the other ship will give us a start in this thick fog."

"Ay, ay, sir," said one of the men; "it's not a bad notion;" and so both boats were cut adrift. It was not till they had been left astern a few hundred yards, that they became aware how dense the fog was. As they lay tranquil, having still a glimpse of the frigate's lights, showing like small stars at a distance in the fog, they heard sounds of alarm come upon the night air; they then took four oars, and pulled steadily away in a slanting direction; presently the loud boom of a gun was heard, and then a rocket, scarcely visible, but heard distinctly, shot up into the air; then followed blue-lights, and another gun, but, owing to the dense fog, the lights scarcely showed fifty yards from the ship.

" We are quite safe, my lads," said Magnus; "but give way, let us get as far as we can; is there a sail in the boat?"

" There's a mast and a lug, sir," said Phelim.

" Then step the mast and hoist the lug, we will run out to the nor'-west; this wind is about south and west, and we may fall in with some of our cruisers in the daylight."

"That is just what we expected, sir, when we planned this here escape," said one of the men. "Confound those French lubbers! they plundered us like robbers. I've seen the inside of a French prison during the late war, and I'm bothered if you'd ever fall in love with your companions in them."

The mast was now stepped and the lug set, and the light pinnace flew through the almost calm water; but there was a heavy roll from the northward that betokened a shift of wind.

"If this fog holds on till daylight, we shall be clear of our enemies," said Magnus; "but if we have any weather, this is a poor boat; what kind of one was the other?"

"A heavy launch, sir," said Phelim, "and we didn't like to take her."

"They are sure to cruise about looking for us," said the old man-of-war's man who seemed so well acquainted with the inside of a French prison; "our only chance is the fog."

"Faith, then, there's fog enough, and thick enough to cut a slice of it," said Phelim; "shall I take a spell at the tiller, sir? two of us sleep and two keep watch?"

"You can do so, my lads, as you like," said the midshipman; "I am not inclined for sleep, though sleep is a very necessary thing; but one or two nights' loss of it is not of much moment."

"No, your honor," said an Irish sailor, one of the four, "if they were not to be followed by three or four more of 'em. I've gone four days and nights without a wink when chasing pirates on the coast of Africa; but faith we weren't worth our broth when we came to the scratch! Sleep's a great thing, intirely." So Paddy and another of the men stretched themselves along the bottom of the boat with a quid of tobacco in their jaws, and appeared as contented as if in their hammocks. Magnus sat steering and talking to Phelim, and watching all round for fear any of the frigates might stretch after them in the direction they were going. He would be able to detect their lights, he thought, time enough to avoid them. Two or three hours before daylight the wind suddenly shifted, first into the south-east, and then rapidly into east and north-east, and began blowing in squalls which roused the sleepers.

" This boat will not carry sail on a wind long," said Magnus, as the men lowered and close-reefed it; " it's dawn, and it's inclined to blow." And so it did, the fog lifting a little with the advancing of daylight. The wind and sea kept increasing, and the boat took in water rather abundantly.

Magnus had given the helm to the old man-of-war's-man, who was named Martin; he was a fine, hardy seaman, about seven or eight and forty; the rest were young men.

" We must keep her before the wind, sir," said Dick Martin; " she's a poor boat — where will this wind drive us, sir?"

" In upon the coast of France," said Magnus, " but where, precisely, I cannot say; I should think somewhere near the mouth of the Loire."

In another hour they were forced to drive right before the gale, with only a wing of the lug to steady them. The fog was rapidly lifting, and, in less than half an hour, not a streak remained, but they had a clear uninterrupted view of the ocean seaward, and of the coast of France, which they were rapidly approaching. The gale blew steadily from the north, with a clear sky; they were about twenty miles from the coast; not a ship was to be seen in the offing, but a long promontory to the eastward bounded the view in that direction, which subsequently turned out to be Belle Isle, as the boat going rapidly through the water opened out the land.

Magnus now knew that they were running for the mouth of the Loire River, with Belle Isle to their left, and the Isle Nourmontier to the right. If they lowered their sail the boat would fill, for the sea and wind increased every moment till it blew a perfect gale.

Having eaten a biscuit or two, and taken a draught of water, all hands were employed baling the boat, for the sea made frequent breaches over her—indeed they expected her each moment to be swamped.

Towards two o'clock in the day they were so close in with the land that they could clearly distinguish the mouth of the Loire and the forts in the southern head; but the fog was coming on again thicker than ever, and the wind, being more to the north-west, increasing in violence.

"She will go to bits the moment she touches," said Dick Martin, "and I see'd a lot of small islands before this confounded fog came on; it's not a French prison we have to steer clear of now, but Davy Jones's locker."

"If the wind does not blow any more to the westward," said Magnus, "we shall run right up the river; it's over three miles wide at the mouth."

"But there's sure to be a terrible sea, your honor," said the Irish sailor; "I have heard it spoken of."

"Yes," returned the midshipman; "with an ill tide and this gale we should be swamped; we are running in with the flood—though those rascals aboard the *Carmagnole* took my watch and money, we can judge the time of day."

"Faith, sir, they would take our skins if they could get 'em off aisy," said Phelim.

The pinnace was now running through a tremendous breaking sea, which compelled them to keep baling with might and main, and forced them to carry more sail to lift them over the seas.

"I am sure we are close in with the land," said Dick Martin; "I think I hear the roar of the surf on the banks."

"Sink or swim, we cannot alter our course a yard," said Magnus; "I hear the surf on all sides, which makes me think we have entered the mouth of the river; there is a town called St. Nazaire on the left bank, and Fort Meudon on the right; but this dense fog, so unusual with nor'-westers, will not let us see a yard."

As Magnus spoke, a heavy sea lifted the boat, and dashed it amongst the breakers; but, carrying sail till it blew out in ribbons, the light boat was driven high up on a fine sandy beach without overturning, and all leaping out, they ran her, with the help of a heavy sea which drenched them to the skin, high up, and out of reach of the waves.

"Well! it's a French prison, and no mistake!" said Martin, giving himself a shake; "for as soon as the fog clears the beggars will be upon us."

"Faix, this is unfortunate, Mr. Magnus," said Phelim anxiously. "May be, after all, I had better have staid with you aboard the old *Thames*."

"The attempt was a bold one, Phelim; its failure does not lie at our door; we cannot control the will of Providence — here we are, and we must make the best of it."

It was now the last week of the month of October, and the wind felt exceedingly cold as it drove the soaked garments of the party next their skins.

"I should like to know where we are," said Martin; "I think a horn of stiff grog would not choke us."

"Well, it will not do," said Magnus, "for us to stand on this wild beach, which may be after all only a sandbank — let us move on; we can retrace our footsteps, at all events, by the marks in this soft sand. Let us keep our blood in circulation by moving."

The disconsolate party moved on from the water, and as they proceeded the bank rose considerably. The course of the Loire, from Nantes to the sea, runs through and between immense sandbanks on each side; as Mr. A. Young, in speaking of this river, says — "It exhibits a stream of sand, and rolls shingles through the valley instead of water." "Quel torrent revolutionare que cette Loire!" said the democrat, Barrère, and well might he say it, for the monsters of the revolution made it run blood.

The party soon found that they were on the main land at all events, for the shore gradually lost its sands, and, rising rapidly, they came upon what looked to be a marsh or waste land. If they proceeded farther they would evidently be unable to retrace their steps, so a halt took place, and a consultation ensued; Magnus very clearly proved to them that, even supposing the gale fell during the night, they could not possibly put to sea again without provisions. To this they all agreed with very rueful countenances — but what was to be done? Magnus spoke French well, but then he had no money or valuables of any kind.

"Be the powers of Moll Kelly, your honors!" said Denis Fagan, the Irish sailor, "sure we are in an inemy's country, and have as much right to take a house as a ship! Bedad! let us attack the first habitation we come up with, and victual our ship and then put to sea."

This proposal met with the approval of all except Magnus, who differed with Denis — he had no objection to procure food at the first house they came to by quiet and peaceable means, but deprecated force or ill-usage of the inmates. Accordingly it was agreed to keep along the banks of the river till they came to a house; for food, Magnus acknowledged, was absolutely necessary, and must be had — quietly and by persuasion, if possible; but still, as Denis

Fagan said, "Bedad! they mustn't starve themselves in an inemy's country."

It still blew with extraordinary violence, but evidently shifting into the south-west; for the rain now began to fall, though, driven along by the violence of the wind, it soon ceased. The marshy track they were pursuing was at times traversed by dykes full of water, all leading into the river. After nearly a mile of this salt marsh being traversed, without seeing a human being, or habitation, or animal of any sort, they heard the report of a gun to their right; this was a heavy gun, as if discharged from a fort or vessel, and immediately after, passing over a strong palisade, they came out upon a broad track leading to the right and left.

"If we go much farther in this way, my men," observed Magnus, "we shall lose our track." Before they had time to deliberate, they heard the sound of many steps, and whilst wondering whose they could be, a body of revolutionary soldiers, dressed in blue uniforms, emerged from the fog. .

The first impulse of the party, excepting Magnus and Phelim, was to leap over the paling and scud; the moment they did so, bang went half a dozen muskets after the fugitives, and half a dozen of the Blues in pursuit; whilst an officer and the rest of the men at once summoned Magnus and Phelim to surrender.

"You are the persons, no doubt, who made the land half an hour ago in an open boat. You are English, I see," said the officer commanding the detachment.

"Yes," said Magnus, surprised how this could be known, "we are English, and we landed, or rather were driven by the violence of the wind ashore."

"Ah!" said the young officer, "you speak French well; you belong to some ship, doubtless."

"Yes, we belong to the *Thames*, thirty-two-gun frigate. She surrendered to the *Carmagnole*, having fought the forty-gun frigate, *Urania*, previously."

"Then how came you and your comrades here?"

"Well, that's easily answered," said Magnus, seeing the men returning after their chase of the fugitives, which proved unsuccessful. "We tried to escape in a boat, and the storm blew us ashore; how did you know where to find us?"

"Ah, *ça!* easily enough: you were seen from the watch-tower of St. Luz, before the fog came on, making for the mouth of the river; and, knowing you must make land somewhere here, our commandant sent us by this road, and half a dozen men and a sergeant are gone by the lower road — so your comrades will be caught in a trap."

"It was a very unnecessary and cowardly act," said Magnus, "to fire upon three or four unarmed men, though they are your enemies."

"If they had stood their ground," said the officer with a sneer, "they would, like yourself and comrade, be treated as prisoners of war — when men run, it's our duty to bring them down any way we can. So now, fall in, you are prisoners of war; I will conduct you to St. Nazaire, which is close by, though, I dare say, you did not know it."

"Well, bother the mounseers!" said Phelim, as he walked by the side of Magnus O'More; "we have just hopped from the frying-pan into the fire; they are sure to catch Martin and the rest."

"It's very unlucky, Phelim, but it's past remedy. We must now wait till we are exchanged," and Magnus sighed; his spirits a good deal depressed at the prospect of imprisonment.

In half an hour they entered the dirty, miserable suburbs

16

of St. Nazaire, which was at the period of our story a wretched place, and very little better now, only that a steamer plies, when high tides permit, between it and Nantes. The people came out to gaze at them as the Blues passed by with their prisoners, looking with surprise and pity at them; for the people of this district, and the opposite side of the Loire, were all Royalists, and only put down by the most revolting cruelties.

After passing through several streets they stopped before the gates of the town prison — a gloomy, miserable-looking building. Here the prisoners were handed over to several jailers, who conducted them into a chamber where sat an official before a desk. This man looked up, and eyed the two prisoners keenly. "Who brought these prisoners here?" demanded the governor.

"Captain Marmande: they are English sailors."

"*Sacre bleu!* I can see that," said the governor. "Can either of you speak French?" said the surly official.

"Yes," said Magnus.

"What's your name, and rank aboard ship?"

"Magnus O'More, and I rank as a midshipman."

"And your comrade — common seaman?"

"Yes," returned Magnus, who was both tired and hungry.

Having written some lines in a book, he turned to the jailer, simply saying, "Nine and ten;" they were then led away, and, despite the remonstrances of Magnus and the violent rage of Phelim, who overturned two of the jailers in his passion, they were thrust into separate cells and locked up.

CHAPTER XXIV.

Tɴᴇ period of Magnus O'More's incarceration was one of profound horror and dismay throughout the district on which he and his party were thrown. The great battle that had decided the fate of the gallant Vendéans had just been fought, in which the Vendéans were defeated, and their generals were mortally wounded ; the fugitives fled to the banks of the Loire, to escape the frightful massacre inflicted upon them by the army of Turreau — called, most justly, the " infernal columns." It was a party of these troops that intercepted Magnus and his boat's crew.

After three days' confinement Magnus was sent on, under an escort, to Nantes. On arriving in that ill-fated city, he was thrown into a prison, with one hundred of doomed wretches, as an English spy, the commandant of Nazaire wishing to propitiate the bloodthirsty Carrier, who ruled at Nantes, and who was just commencing his fearful career of blood, and dying the waters of the Loire as far up as Saumur with the blood of his victims. Fortunately for Magnus, two or three days previous to the wholesale butchery that consigned twelve thousand innocent victims to a cruel death, a commissioner arrived from Paris to examine the prisons and prisoners confined in them.

The chamber in which Magnus was confined was about thirty feet square, and in this were thrust nearly two hundred persons of all ages and sexes — the next day most of these were to be guillotined or shot.

Magnus O'More bore his hard fate with manly fortitude; he could not conceive how he — an Englishman — a prisoner of war — should thus be thrust amongst those unfortunates, ruthlessly condemned by the atrocious demons composing Carrier's band, whose duty it was to find victims for this monster.

On the morning that was to decide their fate, the commissioner, as a matter of form, went through the prison, merely examining each book containing the names (many of them false ones) of the unfortunates within. This man, not a jot more humane than any other of the terrible leaders in those times, but a shade less bloodthirsty than Carrier, was accompanied by an officer in the navy, a young man and a commander, who had just come to Nantes from Brest, bearing an order to the commissioner for the release of Lieutenant Jaques-Marie Leveque, an officer in the republican service, who was supposed to be in the prisons of Nantes, having left his ship, hearing that his father, mother, and sister were under sentence of death, for which Carrier had at once added him to the list of condemned. The officer accompanying the commissioner was a bosom friend of Leveque's, who was known to be a most gallant officer, and had procured with immense difficulty an order for his and his family's release.

The commissioner and this officer having gone through several cells and chambers, at length stopped before the one in which Magnus O'More was confined. The jailer shewed his book previous to an examination of the poor wretches.

"These are all condemned, citoyen commissioner," said the jailer, " *sent teris Girondists*, to be guillotined and shot at one o'clock." The young officer shuddered, and uttered some expressions betokening his disgust, the commissioner, shrugged his shoulders, merely saying, "*Que voulez-vous, mon ami!*"

Taking the book, both ran their eyes over the names, designations, trade, &c., of the condemned — when the officer started, and in a voice of intense agitation said, "Stay! what name is this?" laying his hand on a curiously spelt name, intended for Roderick Magnus O'More, and after it — " English spy — dangerous."

" This is not the person you seek, captain," said the commissioner — " this is a vile English spy ! "

" Bah ! " exclaimed the officer, " this is false ! this is a lad — a boy — not more than seventeen ; he is, or rather was, an officer aboard the *Thames* frigate, taken by the *Carmagnole*, and brought into Brest eight or nine days ago. This will not do — to murder this young lad, a subject of Great Britain, and a prisoner of war ! "

" How is this, jailer?" demanded the commissioner, not much interested as far as humanity was concerned, but willing to find something to do to show his authority. " Go, bring out that lad, if you know him."

" Eh, monsieur, I know him well enough ; he has the spirit of a tiger; he struck Jean Marlot, the man who first had the care of him, a blow with his chained hand that nearly brained him ; that's what chiefly got him in here."

The officer ground his teeth with rage, muttering to himself, " Would that he had brained him, and all the monsters that are making my heart sick in this doomed land.   Your friend, Lieutenant Leveque, is not here, I perceive," said the commissioner, " neither are any of his family, for this is the last of the batch : he must have escaped with them out of this district."

" I trust so," returned the officer; " but, thank God! I came here to save this noble boy's life " — as he spoke, the jailer returned, followed by Magnus. The moment the midshipman raised his eyes, and they rested on the officer's face, he uttered a cry of intense joy, and, springing forward, threw himself into the arms of the officer, saying, " Ah, God be praised ! I do not fear to die — but, oh ! how happy I am to see you, O'Brien ; I never thought to see the face of a friend again."

" My poor boy ! and have they reduced you to this, the murderous villains ? " said O'Brien with much emotion, for he it was, having been recently made a commander, and was proceeding to Rochelle to take the command of a fine corvette, but, anxious to release his friend and brother officer, he stopped on his way at Nantes.

Before another word could be spoken, Carrier, the monster whose name will ever be held in execration, entered the corridor, followed by the governor of the prison and several of his satellites.

" Well, Citizen Vergeneau," said Carrier, in his rough brutal manner, " what's the matter? You are keeping *mes enfans* from their good mother the guillotine."

Captain O'Brien turned round with a look of abhorrence, and gazed into the bloodthirsty, ignoble countenance of John Baptiste Carrier, who was at this period about forty-two. Nature had legibly written on this man's features his character and feelings ; there was a brutal coldness in the look of his pale gray eyes, and a hanging of the under lip, showing his large ill-shaped. teeth, that almost created a shudder in the beholder.

The entreaties of the most beautiful women had no effect on this demon, and the cries and tears of childhood only drove him to greater fury.

In answer to his question the commissioner said, " Why, citizen, here is a lad from the condemned cell — an English youth — that Captain O'Brien says is an officer of an English ship, taken the other day by the *Carmagnole,* and brought into Brest."

" That's a lie !" said Carrier brutally.

" How dare you say those words to my face ?" said O'Brien, his eyes flashing and his cheek flushed, as he faced Carrier and laid his hand on his sword.

" Nay, Captain O'Brien," said the commissioner, " keep your temper ; Citizen Carrier means that you must be misinformed."

" This is a spy of Pitt's," said Carrier, pale with rage ; " he was caught near Nazaire, and was sent on to me as a dangerous spy, as he speaks the language like a native, and on account of his youth is well calculated to deceive."

" What an absurdity ! " said Captain O'Brien.

" Yes, a cruel falsehood ! " said Magnus indignantly. " The commander of the fort of Nazaire knew I was driven ashore in a boat, with five sailors belonging to the *Thames.*"

" *Par bleu !*" laughed Carrier scornfully, " I'm not going to delay, *mes enfans ;* the guillotine is thirsty ; so, to end this matter, as there may be a mistake, jailer, take this English aristocrat, and lock him up with those other young cut-throats that were sent here."

Captain O'Brien knew well he had no power to dispute Carrier's orders ; having stated that Magnus was a British officer and a prisoner of war, and having vouched for the truth of his assertion and written his statement in a book, was all he could do ; but he said to Carrier, " I shall get an order for the removal of this youth to Brest, where his captain and brother officers are confined."

" Do as you like about that, captain," said Carrier with a sneer ; " let me to my business — take him away, jailer ! "

O'Brien could have felled the brutal Carrier to his feet,

but he thought he would not only imperil his own life, but destroy his *protégé*; therefore, taking Magnus aside whilst Carrier spoke with the commissioner, he pressed his hand warmly and affectionately — " Cheer up, my poor friend," said he, " as the villains have half-starved you, put that in your pocket," thrusting his purse into Magnus's hand; " you don't know how you may want it. Carrier dare not hurt a hair of your head now I have declared who you are; I will go back to Brest this very day, and get an order for your being sent there; you will then have a chance of being exchanged."

" Come, come, lad, I can't stay here all day," said the jailer; " come with me, you're lucky." Embracing the kind-hearted O'Brien with the tears in his eyes, brought forth by recollections of the past, and which no fear of death could cause to flow, Magnus turned away, but first implored Captain O'Brien to inquire what became of the five men — Phelim M'Farlane amongst them — who came ashore with him in the boat near St. Nazaire.

" Make your mind easy, I will do so — so God bless you, my boy! and send us better times and fewer monsters to devastate this unhappy land."

Magnus cast a last look at his gallant, kind-hearted friend, returned thanks to Providence for his unlooked-for escape from a cruel death, and followed his jailer.

" My lad," said this man, " you have had a narrow escape of your life; you must keep your fingers quiet; and mind, Jacques Marlot is not to be played with;" so saying, he threw open the prison-door, and, as related, Magnus, to his intense joy, found in his fellow-prisoners his old school-fellows, Henry Barlow and Alfred Hammond.

Such was the substance of Magnus O'More's narrative — not related at one time, but at various periods. His young friends listened with interest and surprise, and many were the comments and remarks made upon the cruel treatment he had received from his unnatural uncle ; and sincerely did his friends hope that the day would come when he might be able to prove his right not only to the name but to the estates of the O'More. Day after day passed over ; and the three friends wondered at no change taking place in their destiny. Magnus, though it would grieve him to the heart to quit Henry and Alfred, was surprised that he heard no more from Captain O'Brien, for he secretly hoped he might be able to return himself, and then he would be sure to be interested by the history of Henry and Alfred.

One morning, however, their jailer, Marlot, who did not often visit them, entered their cell with a malignant smile on his surly countenance. " Now, aristocrats," said he, mentioning Henry and Alfred's names, '' it's your turn now. You will grow too fat. So, come, you will see the sun to-day — your new friend is not so fortunate," he added with a grin.

" What do you mean?" said Magnus O'More, grasping the hands of Henry and Alfred ; " why separate us? whatever is the doom of the one, let us all share it."

'' Oh, that's it — is it?" said the jailer, with a savage look at Magnus ; " pity I must baulk your heroic inclination. So, you are tired of your head. Ah ! if it was my will, you should all three meet the axe of the guillotine ! "

'' Oh, that I had my hand upon your throat, reptile ! " said Magnus fiercely, and none of your myrmidons present, " you should not require the executioner's axe to stop your foul breath."

Jacques Marlot stamped with rage. " Nay, dear friend," said Henry, embracing him, " keep quiet, a day of reckoning will come."

"Shove the aristocrats out," shouted Marlot; two or three jailers pushed the two boys out, and the last words they heard were, "God bless you!" from the lips of O'More.

Henry looked at Alfred, but the poor boy's eyes were bright — his cheek, it is true, was pale from recent confinement, and, no doubt, many and bitter thoughts : for who can die so young, and know besides that his doom is an unjust and cruel one, without a feeling of intense bitterness? But the seeds Henry had sown in his heart had taken root, and, with a firm step and even a cheerful manner, he said to Henry, "Come, beloved cousin! do not fear for me, let them do their worst ; I shall die, blessing my dear parents, and thanking God for having, through you, gained sufficient firmness to meet the fate his will designs to be ; " and, holding out his hand for the manacles, the brutal and heartless wretch put them on laughing, and saying at the same time — "Oh, ho ! my lad, you seem to take it quite easy. Do you really think you are going to a party of pleasure? Ah, ça ! to be sure you are ; you will have a jolly volley of musketry to announce you."

"Brute ! without one particle of humanity about you," said Henry, his eyes flashing with indignation ; " take that, it's my last remembrance ! " and lifting his hand, before the jailer had time manacle it, he smote him in the face with such power as to strike him down, his face covered with blood. The men started back, surprised at such audacity and such power in one so young. Alfred rushed before Henry, for the furious jailer sprung to his feet, and, foaming with rage, lifted his ponderous bunch of keys, and, raising his arm, prepared to brain his victim with a blow ; but just then an officer hastily entered the corridor.

"Hallo ! Jaques Marlot, what is all this about — what is

delaying you — have you been fighting amongst yourselves, that I see you covered with blood? Are these the two youths sent here by Captain Paul Gerard?"

" Yes," returned the jailer, wiping his face, and trembling with rage; " a pair of vipers they are; lucky their time is short — that young reptile has dared to strike me! "

" A stout boy and a strong blow; but come along, my lads, you have struck your last blow at all events?"

" You do not know that," said Henry, whose generally calm temper and forbearance was forgotten, as he heard the cruel, unfeeling words addressed to them; " for I may live when you will cease to be! "

The lieutenant stood for an instant gazing at the excited features of the youth; in truth, he was a noble boy — his high fine forehead, and dark clustering hair; his head, without covering of any sort; his fine intelligent features; and, above all, the steady, lightning glance of his dark eyes, awed the officer: he turned pale, for he was superstitious. " Young firebrand! " said he, slowly recovering himself, " it is time to quench your fierce spirit : bring them along, and be quick, jailer," and, turning round, he hastened away.

" Now, move on, aristocrats! " said the jailer, glaring at Henry; " my turn comes now! "

" Hold me by the hand, Harry," said Alfred in a low voice. " Mind, to the very last — press my hand, dear, dear cousin; our spirits will go together before the throne of grace."

" Hope, Alfred, to the last," said Henry firmly : " I have a presentiment that our time is not yet come; these wretches may, through the mercy of God, be even now balked of their purpose! "

CHAPTER XXV

On entering the immense court-yard, enclosed by lofty walls, the two cousins gazed around them with an eager, and even curious eye. They perceived that the prison court was lined with troops under arms. In the middle were congregated a group of prisoners, most of them in the royalist uniform, white — a few in plain garments. Mounted on a powerful gray charger was General Moine; several other officers were mounted and stationed behind him in a row. Henry guessed at once that he beheld the famous revolutionary general, a man who has left a name sufficiently notorious to posterity for his savage persecution of the Royalists.

As the two youths were led into the circle, the soldiers opened a passage, and the officer who commanded them was Captain Paul Gerard; he looked into Henry's face with a scoffing smile, as much as to say, " You have not escaped me, after all ! "

" Ah ! " said Alfred, who also recognized him. " Ah ! there is that cruel officer who first ordered us to be shot at St. Barbe — well," he added, with a slight sigh, " there was little use, after all, in sparing us. Colonel Moreau has forgotten us."

" No, no ! " said Henry, " the fault lies not with him; he was a noble gentleman ! " .

As the two youths advanced into the circle some of the prisoners turned round, and then Henry perceived, with feel-

ings of deep regret, the old Marquis Delaney and the gallant
and handsome Count de Sombreul.   They were pinioned, as
were all the captives, amounting to fifty in number.

"Oh! can this be possible," said both the marquis and
the count; "you here, my brave boys! How is this? surely
there is some great mistake; they cannot condemn you."

"Alas, my lord!" exclaimed Henry, looking sadly into
the venerable features of the marquis, "what signifies our
lives compared to yours?"

"But this is a monstrous and iniquitous proceeding!"
said the Count de Sombreul out loud, and in a fierce,
excited tone; "this is a wanton sacrifice of life — it's contrary to the usages of war! These boys are English,"
continued the count, advancing almost to the horse of General Moine; and, addressing that general in a loud voice,
clear as a trumpet, every word heard by the assembled
troops — "You have condemned us after agreeing to an
honorable capitulation,* but does your boasted republic war
with boys?"

General Moine spurred his horse fiercely in advance, and,
raising his arm, a file of soldiers drove the count back with
fixed bayonets, whilst a scornful laugh of derision burst from
this remorseless general's lips.   He was then about to give
the word for the troops to form and the procession of victims
to proceed, when the quick tramp of a horse in a gallop was
heard; the next minute an officer, mounted on a horse covered with foam, dashed into the court-yard, and reined up
alongside of the surprised General Moine, handing him at the
same time a folded paper.

"Ah, Alfred — beloved cousin!" said Henry in a low
voice, "we are saved! that officer is Colonel Moreau."
Alfred now trembled all over, and tears, despite his efforts,

---

* Fact.

ran down his cheeks. The poor boy again thought of his home and his beloved parents.

Henry watched keenly General Moine's countenance; he could see that a dark frown sat on his features, and that he pressed his lips together firmly. At length he said, loud enough for the prisoners to hear, " Take care, Colonel Moreau, lest your false humanity does not yet cost you your head."

" Ah, general ! " said the colonel, " heads are trifles in these times ; we keep them as long as we can ; at all events, my head is my own ; " and, throwing himself from his horse, his eagle eye espied the two youths, and he advanced towards them, their young hearts beating with intense emotion. " Come here," said the colonel, calling a jailer; " undo the bonds from these boys — these lads are English, and are entitled to the courtesy of warfare. Deeply I regret, gentlemen," said the brave Moreau, lifting his plumed hat and bowing with respect to the old Marquis Delancy and the Count de Sombreul — " deeply I regret your fate."

" Thank God, these boys are saved ! " said the handsomest man in all France, the noble de Sombreul ; " we thank you, colonel, for you are a soldier and a gentleman ; we will carry to our graves the recollection that we have, at all events, left one gallant spirit in the ranks of the regicides. The drums beat, comrades ! " said de Sombreul in his trumpet voice, " Let our last words be — Vive le Roi ! "

That cry, once so loved, rang through the air with an electric sound ; in vain, by the incensed general's orders, the drums beat and the trumpets sounded, " Vive le Roi ! " rose full and clear above all. Henry, with a feeling of uncontrollable emotion, threw himself on the breast of de Sombreul, weeping passionately.

" I cannot press you to my heart, brave boy, for the villains have pinioned a soldier who knows how to die without bonds," said de Sombreul; "but I can bless thee!" and, bending down, he kissed the forehead of the boy; the old marquis did the same, and then, with the mien and port of men walking to ascend a throne, these noble hearts marched to their doom. A few minutes afterwards successive charges of musketry were heard — those noble spirits had ceased to exist, and France added to her list of crimes as foul a murder as ever a nation committed.

"Come with me, young gentlemen," said Colonel Moreau in a sad voice, for he was much affected and amazed by the fate of de Sombreul. "I cannot restore you to liberty, I deeply regret to say; but I have secured you good treatment, and you will be sent on to Paris to-morrow — I would not leave you here."

"Ah, colonel!" said Henry, speaking for Alfred, who could not express himself well in French, "can we ever repay you for your noble and generous conduct to us? If ever we return to our own land, the name of Moreau will ever be venerated, and loved, and remembered with the deepest gratitude."

"By my faith, my brave boy," said the colonel, "such a disgrace to the nation should not have taken place as long as I had the power to prevent it. I cannot think why Captain Gerard felt such malignant satisfaction in getting you both included in the list of the condemned — it was most unjust to treat you as rebels. You fought against France as the enemy of your country. There was no plea could be urged to justify your condemnation. I sent a courier to Paris stating facts; and only received the order for your release and conveyance to Paris this morning, and I had to ride nearly ten leagues in little more than two hours."

Henry and Alfred pressed the colonel's hand, deeply grateful for the interest he took in their fate.

"I regret," continued the colonel, as he proceeded to another wing of the prison, "that I have been able to do so little. I would have saved that noble-hearted de Sombreul; but, alas! in the fearful excitement of feeling against royalty, it was impossible."

They now entered the prison by another gate; and the colonel summoning the head of that part of the establishment, he delivered over the two boys to his care, showing him the orders for their release, and for the future care of them. "They are to go on to Paris under an escort," said the colonel, "the day after to-morrow. So treat them well — you are answerable for their health and safety." The sub-governor bowed. Colonel Moreau then took a most kind leave of the two youths, telling them to be of good heart, he had secured them a protection in Paris, and he would shortly see them there himself; and, holding out his purse, he made Henry take it, saying, "You will find the contents useful." Before Henry could say a word about their friend Magnus O'More, an orderly called the colonel away, so, pressing their hands, he hurried off.

".What a generous, noble being!" said Alfred. "What a pity we could not get him to let Magnus come with us!"

"At all events," said Henry, "I will ask this sub-governor to put us back with him," and he did ask him.

"Can't do so now," said the governor, shaking his head; "he goes away to-morrow, perhaps, with other English prisoners, to Blavet. You shall have a good room now, and good food. Come along!" The boys were grievously vexed; they could only think of Magnus's loneliness. They were then shown into a good room. "Now," said the governor, "if you wish for wine, you can have it; that is, if you can pay for it," — and he eyed Henry with a greedy look.

"Well," said Henry, who thought good food and a little wine would restore Alfred's strength — "we are willing to pay for good food and wine."

"Eh! but have you means of paying?" said the worthy sub-governor. Henry took from his purse a gold-piece of twenty francs, and handed it to the man, who quietly pocketed it, saying, "You shall have a bottle of good wine, and a good dinner."

The chamber they now occupied was small, but clean, with a tolerable bed, table, and a couple of chairs; with a window — barred, certainly, but looking out over the walls, and over the Loire, just below the bridge of boats.

"We are likely," said Henry, "to see more of the world than we bargained for when we left Penzance for the Scilly Islands, my dear Alfred!"

"In truth, yes!" said Alfred, "and, were it not for the grief our dear parents must experience at our uncertain destiny, and the melancholy fate of those brave men to-day, and the loss of poor Magnus, I should scarcely regret it. I think, if it pleases God to spare us, and to restore us to our homes, I shall grow up a very different man. I should assuredly have been an indolent, weak, and good-for-nothing individual, but for your good example, in proving to me that energy, perseverance, and faith in the justice and goodness of God, are the real foundations on which to rest our future felicity."

"You underrate yourself, dear Alfred; those good qualities were natural to you, they only required to be brought out by circumstances."

In about an hour the jailer entered the chamber with a tureen of soup, some other viands, and a bottle of really good wine; so that the young adventurers sat down to the first good meal for several weeks, and, with gratitude in their hearts, drank Colonel Moreau's health. The next morning

17

they had a good breakfast, when the jailer informed them that their twenty-franc-piece was exhausted. Henry gave the man another, thinking, however, that provisions were either very dear in Nantes, or the sub-governor's fees were high. He looked into his purse, and found ten remaining. "Well," said he to Alfred, "if we are to go to-morrow, it matters not; but if we had to stay much longer, our worthy caterer would soon exhaust our purse." ·

The next morning the sub-governor entered the chamber. "Well, *mes enfans!* you look better, eh. My mode of feeding does you good. I regret we part!"

"No doubt," thought Henry; "we are become profitable. When do we go, monsieur?"

"In an hour. You will go in a covered wagon with two guards. Colonel Moreau was forced to leave for Paris in haste yesterday; there was a disturbance. I am sorry — but I cannot help it — General Moine orders you to be handcuffed, as you will be under the charge of only two men in a covered wagon."

"What!" interrupted Henry; "are not two armed men sufficient to take care of two unarmed boys, without handcuffing them?"

"*Mon cher!* you are as strong and as vigorous as any man. You broke Jaques Marlot's nose the other day with a blow — besides, if you should happen to run away — young lads run fast; and the guard might be obliged to use their pistols, which would be unpleasant."

"If Colonel Moreau was here," said Henry, "we should not be subjected to this useless indignity; but, *n'importe!* do as you are ordered. It's all for the best."

The under jailer now brought in separate handcuffs, and the two youths were fastened in them, like felons. Henry and Alfred bore this cruel infliction with burning cheeks.

The former said within himself, "If ever I am free, and the war still continues — if I go as a volunteer — I will serve against these vile revolutionists, and strike a blow for the noble fellows they have so wantonly butchered!"

Henry and Alfred were then conducted into a back court, where stood a light covered cart with springs. Two men, besides the driver, were standing, talking together; as they turned round, Henry at once recognized in one of the men the coarse, brutal features of his guardian jailer, the man he had struck in the face. He had a black belt round his waist, in which were a brace of pistols, and a seaman's cutlass strapped to his side.

"So this fellow is to be one of our guard," said Henry to Alfred; "this does not look well — I strongly suspect our good friend the colonel knows nothing of this."

"We must be on our guard, Harry," said Alfred; "I am sure they mean us mischief."

The cart was divided, so that a small space remained at the back for the prisoners, whilst the two guards sat in the front with the driver: there were two stout horses to draw it.

"So I have got the care of you again, *mon garçon*," said the jailer with a grin; "forget and forgive is not my motto, I can tell you."

Henry made no answer, but got into the vehicle; there was no window, but a round air-hole in the back, crossed with iron wire. It was a machine evidently built for the carriage of prisoners; for it was crossed and reversed with flat bars of iron. There was a slide in the front boards that divided the prisoners from their guards; they got in at the back, the door being locked after they were in — in fact, it was an extremely secure little vehicle, especially with handcuffed captives. It was not possible to see any thing of the country they travelled through; for the wire grating over the place to admit air was so very close that scarcely even light entered.

"This is a dismal mode of travelling, Henry," said Alfred, as the vehicle, having left the streets, proceeded at a tolerably smart pace over an execrably paved road.

At this period the whole interior of France was in the most fearfully disorganized state — the laws set at defiance, religion disregarded, man preying upon man, trusting to brute force to establish right, roads were scarcely passable, and infested to the very gates of Paris by the most ferocious troops of brigands; in the cities and towns "The Company of Jesus" and of "The Sun," committed the most frightful massacres, in retaliation upon the revolutionists, calling themselves Royalists, whilst, in fact, they were the worst description of robbers and assassins. To travel from one end of France to the other was a miracle, if performed; but none attempted this feat unless protected by military escorts. There was not much danger, however, from brigands to be apprehended by our two unfortunate prisoners; but they feared there was some other design on foot than taking them to Paris.

The two cousins passed the day conversing on many subjects, chiefly of home; they both felt exceedingly curious and anxious concerning the fate of the Countess Delancy and little Rosina. Henry felt a strange interest in the young girl's safety. She was so innocent and *naive*, so young and so very lovely, and in manner and words so affectionate and graceful, that it was impossible not to feel a deep interest in her fate, especially knowing in what a troubled state he had left them. Henry had picked up from his jailer some little information concerning the fate of the Royalists at Quiberon, after the surrender of the Count de

Sombreul and the other Royalist leaders. All those families who could effect an escape aboard the English ships did; others fled into La Vendée; many were slain, many imprisoned, and the Blues had entire possession of the coast, not a single Royalist now remaining in those parts.

A vague idea entered Henry's head at times of an escape; he knew that if they reached Paris they might remain years in captivity, at all events till the war ended. But how were they to escape from two armed men while their hands were bound in iron fetters?

They stopped for the second night at a small cabaret; and, when the door of the vehicle was unlocked, all they could see was a dirty court-yard, and a very small house, at the door of which stood an old woman and a girl holding a light. The two prisoners followed their guards into the kitchen of the cabaret; and then the surly guardian asked the woman of the house to show them the best room she had.

The two youths found the handcuffs extremely tiresome, as it confined their hands nearly in one position. The old woman, who looked as sulky and as disinclined to be obliging as their guards, led the way up a flight of stairs into a moderate sized room with a bed in it. Jaques Marlot looked at the door, and then at the window, which he opened and looked out.

"Well, you can sleep here," said the man, "and you shall have something to eat? Have you any money?" he added, looking Henry full in the face, with an expression as much as to say, "I know you have."

"I have," said Henry quietly; "but I do not suppose prisoners pay for their daily food, and I am also satisfied that this is not the way we were ordered to be taken to Paris."

"And who told you you were going to Paris, my young cock, that crows so loud and hits so hard? don't think I forget your blow. Suppose, now, you are going to Brest, to be put aboard a convict-ship for a voyage to Cayenne — it's quite fashionable now — what would you think?"

Though Henry started at the mention of this horrible and pestilential settlement, he boldly replied — "I should think you a cruel, remorseless villain — which I always thought you; but it is more than your head is worth to dare to disobey the orders respecting us. Take care — you are watched, though you do not think it!"

The man started, and, with a savage scowl, said — "You think me a fool, but I'll convince you to the contrary;" and, grasping the youth by the collar, he commenced searching his pockets, whilst his comrade stood by, laughing with malicious satisfaction.

Henry remained quite passive, but, as he roughly turned him round, the small key of their handcuffs dropped from the man's waistcoat on Henry's foot without his perceiving it, and Henry contrived to put his foot on it. Pulling out the purse, with a laugh, he counted its contents, saying — "This will enable us, my lad, to drink both your healths, and a safe passage to Cayenne;" so, pocketing the money, they left the room, locking the door after them.

"Now, Alfred," said Henry, as he stooped and picked up the key, "this gives us a chance of escape."

"What do you mean?" said Alfred; "what key is that?"

"The villains are taking us as convicts to Brest, to be sent to Cayenne; this is the key of our fetters — hold your hands:" the key was like one of our latch-keys, simply a triangular hole in a steel key. In a moment both boys were free from their fetters: they listened a moment — they could hear the hoarse laughter and oaths of the men below, and felt satisfied they were drinking. "We must be quick, Alfred," said Henry; "remember the chimney — this time we must get out of the window; it's no use trusting these ruffians, they would never attempt to rob us if they were taking us to Paris. The night is intensely dark — so tie this quilt and sheets together, and let us get out of the window."

Alfred obeyed without a word; tying the sheet to a chair placed across the window, Henry slid down into a garden, as well as he could judge, and Alfred followed without any noise — it was the back of the house, they saw no light in any window — it was extremely dark, cloudy, and sprinkling with rain. Holding. each other by the hand, they turned along a rather extensive garden, and coming to a hedge they scrambled through it. "Now," said Henry, "we shall easily be tracked as far as this by our footmarks; this is evidently a pasture-field; let us keep away in this direction, and get as far as we can during the night, they will find it somewhat difficult to guess which way we have taken. At any rate we shall have only two pursuers, and I think, if we had stout sticks, we could manage them on a pinch."

"I won't flinch from any danger or difficulty, Harry," said Alfred cheerfully; "so, push along, and God direct us!"

CHAPTER XXVI

Young, active, and energetic, the two cousins, inspired by hope, and horrified by the thought of being sent as convicts to Cayenne, hurried on over every obstacle — hedge, ditch, and swamp — with untiring spirit. Presently they heard a loud shout behind them, but they could distinguish nothing.

" Surely they cannot be on our track already," said Alfred — " and yet, what is that shout for? " Leaping over a hedge, they found themselves close to a large barn, and, before they could recover from their surprise or turn round, were tightly held in the grasp of four men, armed with muskets, who started up from the heather like magic.

" Hollo ! who ever are you," exclaimed one of the men, " running like hares across the country at this time of night ? "

Astounded at this fresh misfortune, Henry hardly knew what to say, for he could not imagine who the men were. Whilst hesitating how to answer, a loud hoarse voice, at some distance, shouted — " This way, Jaques — this way ; the cursed young puppies have gone across this field ! "

" Ho, ho ! " said the men, " you are runaways, are you. Who are those pursuing you ? "

Making up his mind at once, Henry boldly said, " We are English ; we were prisoners, and escaped from two of the jailers of the Nantes prison."

"Ha!" said Henry's holder, swearing a savage oath, "is this it — then you are Royalists, eh?"

"Yes, yes!" said Henry, eagerly.

"*C'est bien!*" said the man. "Lie down, comrades; and you, boy, stand up on yonder bank, and shout out as if for your comrade. We must catch those ruffians; we owe them a debt."

Henry jumped over the ditch, while Alfred and the four men threw themselves on the ground, where they were hid by the long fern.

As Henry gained the top of the bank, and was about to call out, he caught sight of two dark objects running across the field below him.

"Curse them, there they are!" cried the voice of Jaques Marlot, and the next moment the report of a pistol, and a ball whistling past his head, satisfied Henry he was seen.

"Jump down, boy — jump down!" said the men; "you can stand fire, I see; we shall have them directly." As he spoke, several men came running out from the barn, calling out — "Who fired?"

"Hush! go back," cried the men in the fern. "All's right; hide yourselves!" The men went back into the barn. Two minutes afterwards Jaques Marlot and his comrade appeared on the summit of the bank.

"Which way now, think ye," said Jaques to his comrade, "have the young ruffians taken, for this is a wide heath?"

"They are perhaps hiding in yonder building — jump down," returned the other.

This they did, and the next moment they were in the grasp of the strangers, who sprung up, and, after a fierce struggle, mastered them. One of the strangers applied a whistle to his lips, and out rushed nearly twenty men, some armed, and two or three carrying lighted lanterns.

"Ha, ha! Jaques Marlot, *mon ami!* So you are caught at last," said one of the strangers, holding a lantern close up to the frightened villain's disturbed features.

"Vile wretch!" uttered another with a fearful oath, "he had my wife and three children butchered, and myself branded, and for no crime. Hang him, the reptile — hang him! Give him no time, he never spared others."

Alfred shuddered, whilst the trembling and doomed jailer on his knees implored mercy.

"Dog!" shouted another of the band, striking him a blow with the butt of a carbine, "did you show mercy to me when you branded me on the shoulder, and then pressed the hot iron upon my breast for sport, to see the flesh, as you said, hiss and curl? Hang the dog! Who's the other villain?"

"A cur of the same kind," said one of the band, whom Henry began to think were escaped galley slaves.

"Bring a rope from the barn, Pierre," said the leader, and search the ruffian's pockets."

The cries and curses of the doomed jailer were now horrible to hear.

"For mercy's sake," said Henry, horrified at the thought of this wretch being thus suddenly hurried into eternity — "for mercy's sake, do not take his life — bad as he is let him live and repent!"

"Hold your tongue, boy — that reptile repent! No; he would burn, or torture, or hang us all to-morrow, if he was let lose and could catch us."

A rope was brought, and, despite the prisoner's struggles and fearful imprecations, the rope was put round his neck; and, dragging him over the ground to a tree on the bank, one of the men climbed up and passed the end of the rope over a branch. Henry and Alfred turned away, hiding their faces in their hands, to shut out the horrid sight. There

was a howl of fierce rage — of frantic despair — and then the
doomed victim was swinging in the night breeze from the
branch of the elm.

" God forgive and pardon the miserable wretch ! " said
both Alfred and Henry, shocked at this tragical ending of
their brutal jailer, who was a much more guilty wretch than
they thought.

" Now, bring those boys and that other ruffian into the
building," said the leader of the band ; " we must put our
mark on him."

Henry and Alfred followed the men into the building, who
left, however, a guard outside as before ; Henry also understood that there were other sentinels posted farther off, on
the main road. On entering the building, the cousins perceived a good wood-fire burning in a large grate, and over it
a huge boiler, suspended from a stout beam across the chimney. There were a number of old rusty carbines piled
against the wall, a few pikes, and several muskets. As the
men entered the building — which appeared to be the interior
of a large farm-house, the division walls of which had been
demolished evidently by fire, and the rubbish cleared away
— Henry regarded them earnestly. They were a fierce and
desperate set of men to look at, variously attired, and all
with their beards, whiskers, and mustaches of immense
growth, hiding every portion of the face except the eyes. It
was impossible to say what their previous mode of life might
have been from their attire ; but they each wore a belt,
some of untanned sheep-skin, others of good buff-leather, and
all had a double-edged knife stuck in their belt. The only
uniform piece of clothing about them was their head-dress,
which consisted of a red woollen cap. The wood-fire threw
a strong glare over the building, but the men opening several
lanterns, the light was increased.

Dragging in the wretched comrade of the miserable Jaques Marlot, the leader of the band, a short, but remarkably broad-shouldered individual, with a grizzly-grayish beard and mustaches, called out, "Now, bring here those boys; let us hear what they have to say for themselves, and put the iron in the fire till we mark our comrade here. We like to have some token by which we can recognize our friends."

The man supplicated for mercy in a piteous tone. "Put a pike down his throat!" roared the leader. "Stop his talk; he ought to think it a mercy he's not swinging alongside his rascally cut-throat of a companion! Now, my lad," said the leader, "you who speak French so well" — turning to Henry — "let us hear what you have to say for yourself and comrade."

The strange, fierce-looking band gathered round; whilst their leader, seating himself on an empty cask, with a piece a plank on the top, fixed his fierce dark eyes upon Henry, who very calmly stated their having been taken prisoners after the attack of the Royalists upon General Hoch's army on the Heights of St. Barbe — their imprisonment at Nantes — and, finally, that they were ordered to be taken to Paris: that their guards stopped for the night at a cabaret, near where they then were — that Jaques Marlot robbed them of the gold given them by Colonel Moreau, and also told them he was taking them as convicts to Brest, to be transported to Cayenne, which so startled them that they made an attempt to escape, but came upon their sentinels unexpectedly.

"Now, you villain!" said the leader of the band, turning to the jailer — "were you going to take these youths to Brest? If you tell a lie, I'll hang you!"

"I'll tell the truth," said the jailer; "it was none of my doing, it was all Jaques Marlot's plans; he swore he would be revenged on that youth for striking him in the face when he had the care of him. The orders were to take them to Paris, but Jaques Marlot bribed me to aid him, and take them to Brest; he would get a bounty for bringing convicts for the Cayenne settlement."

"Precious pair of rascals! Is the iron hot, Pierre?"

"Yes, captain," returned the man named Pierre; "it's superb!"

"Strip off the rascal's garments from his back!" said the leader; "he has assisted to brand many a honest man—his turn is come." In vain the terrified wretch implored mercy, gazing with horror at the heated brand; even Henry ventured to intercede for him, but he was told roughly to stand back and hold his tongue, and look at an act of justice.

An iron rod with two letters, over two inches long, was now drawn from the fire in a white-heat. The jailer roared with terror, which only caused infinite laughter and amusement to the band. In this state the instrument was applied forcibly to the bare back of the jailer, held down by four stout hands. The wretch screamed in agony. The mark seared into his quivering flesh was a cross, and underneath "C. J." They then threw the man his coat, and forcing him to put it on, though he rolled on the ground in agony, they drove him out of the building with the butts of their muskets, and permitted him to go where he pleased.

"Now, my lads," said the leader to the disgusted cousins, "you have seen justice administered by the royalist *Company of Jesus*, * — for to that great band we belong. Many of us here were in the prisons of Nantes when Charette entered that town, and the prisons were thrown open. That villain, Jaques Marlot, escaped our vengeance at that time by flight; the ruffian used to torture us for his own amusement, after

---

* This company, so stated, existed in the south of France.

he had extorted all the money he could get from us or from our families; many of us he branded. We were then guilty of no crime but loyalty; we vowed vengeance against every revolutionist; all of us here — having lost our wives and children, massacred without mercy by the Blues — swore a terrible revenge; we enrolled ourselves in the Company of Jesus, and woe to the Blue that falls into our hands. We are now marching to join our brethren at Lyons; you two had better remain here till morning — you are three leagues from the coast. You speak French like a native. There are no troops nearer than Nantes on the west, and St. Sernin on the east, so you may be able to get off to sea in some fishing-smack. There is your purse and its contents — you will want it. The Blues call us assassins; but we are not robbers, at all events. We shall go to supper directly; after that take a sleep on the straw yonder, and then *en route!*"

Henry and Alfred retired to the farther end of the building, and sat down on a heap of straw, whilst the singular band with whom they were thus strangely associated, dragged several planks out from a recess, and, placing them across some empty barrels, in a few minutes placed upon this rude table various eatables, and some skins of wine. It was a wild and somewhat savage-looking banquet — the blazing logs throwing a crimson glare upon the strangely attired group, their great beards and mustaches, and high red caps, and bare throats and necks, giving them altogether a most banditti-like appearance.

"The idea of calling themselves Royalists is preposterous," said Alfred to Henry, " to say nothing of the profanation of the sacred name by which they distinguish themselves; they are more like a band of robbers. I trust we shall get clear of them to-morrow."

Just as the band were preparing to begin their supper,

the loud report of a musket startled all within the building; then followed another report, and in rushed the four sentinels left without. "Up and away!" shouted the men; "the dragoons of St. Sernin are coming down the road at full gallop; we heard the signal from our outposts."

The scene of confusion that ensued is indescribable; the boards placed over the barrels for tables, with their contents, food and drinkables, were overturned in an instant. Muskets, carbines, and pikes, were grasped with desperate eagerness and with terrible imprecations; all were rushing to the door, when a loud shout was heard without, and then followed a volley of carbines, which rattled and shattered the sides of the doorway into splinters, killed three or four of the band, and wounding several. With a wild cheer, the rest rushed through the great doorway, firing their muskets and pistols at their assailants, and shouting their various cries with a fury horrible to look at. Then followed the trampling of horses; shouts of "Kill, kill — spare none!" the firing of carbines following in quick succession, as if pursued and pursuers were retreating to a distance.

"We must be off, Alfred," said Henry — both youths having stood hitherto irresolute — "it will not do for us to stay here till the dragoons return; they are pursuing and massacring those wretches without mercy. See, there are several dead lying on the floor!" As they hastened towards the door they paused, for they beheld a figure enter the building. It was their late guard, the companion of the defunct Jaques Marlot! his face and neck were covered with blood, his coat hanging in stripes from his back, as if torn in a recent scuffle, whilst his wild and savage look was fixed upon the two boys with a horrid feeling of satisfaction. In one hand he grasped the long, sharp knife of the Royalist assassins, in the other one of their cutlasses. With a hideous laugh he flourished his cutlass, and then, with a frightful imprecation, rushed towards the boys, exclaiming — "Thus I revenge Jaques Marlot's death and my own branding, vile spawns of an aristocrat! You sha'n't escape me, at all events."

Springing on one side, Henry snatched up a broken rafter lying on the floor, and telling Alfred to pick him up a cutlass from the side of one of the dead men by the door, he stood his ground unflinchingly. With a laugh of derision the jailer rushed headlong upon Henry; but bold, active, and powerful for his age, he sprung aside and dealt the man a severe blow on the back of the head that caused the wretch to stagger forward, nearly falling on his knees; the next instant Alfred put a cutlass into Henry's hand, saying — "We had better fly now we have the door."

"No, no!" said Henry, "this wretch would pursue us, and set the dragoons after us — leave him to me; the cutlass is an old favorite, I fear no one with it: I am more than a match for such a wretch as this!"

The man, having recovered himself, came on with the rage and fury of a fiend; but Henry parried his unskilful blows with ease, and, as he rushed headlong upon him, throwing down the cutlass and grasping the knife only, he struck him over the temple with all his force — a stream of blood followed, and the man fell prostrate on his face.

Henry, notwithstanding his resolution, shuddered. "Now, dear Alfred, let us be off; that villain will not pursue us in a hurry — pick up that loaf of bread, I will carry this piece of beef," and taking up a skin of wine, unspilt, he took a small quantity of it, so did Alfred, and then both hastened from the place. On emerging into the open air, they perceived that the drizzly rain had ceased, the clouds were breaking, and the gray dawn struggling through the murky sky.

"Quick, quick, Alfred!" said Henry, after a hasty glance around; "keep the building between us and that troop of horse I see coming across the heath — the St. Sernin dragoons, no doubt, are returning here after the pursuit." Running across the space that divided them from a hedge, they threw themselves over it, and, to their surprise, found themselves on a broad paved road.

"This is the road by which, no doubt," said Henry, "the dragoons came so suddenly upon the Royalist band, and very likely the jailer they drove from the building met them and directed them to the attack. We must get off the road, and keep high hedges between us and them should they persue us." This our two young heroes did for about three miles, and then they paused on the brink of a wild and picturesque glen, covered on the sides by a quantity of brushwood and tall firs, and running down one of the sides was a clear, sparkling stream.

"Suppose, dear Alfred," said Henry, looking at his companion's pale face — for the poor boy, from recent illness, was not so strong as before — "suppose we hide ourselves in this glen — though I am sure we are not pursued — and take two or three hours' repose; you must also be hungry."

"It's a capital looking spot, Harry, and I do think a few hours' repose would be beneficial. I am weak as yet — and then we can talk over our plans. We have to thank God, also, for our safety under all the strange trials we have had to pass through."

"We ought, and indeed I know," returned Henry, "that we are grateful for the mercy shown us; let us get down under the shelter of yonder thick furze; the day is now fine, and the sun warm and pleasant, and there is a nice stream to drink from."

The two youths pushed their way through the furze till

they gained a completely sheltered spot, close by the stream of water; and, pulling a considerable quantity of dry withered fern, they made a heap and sat down, and, taking out the loaf of bread and piece of salt beef, they managed to divide it, and make a hearty breakfast.

"It was the month of July," said Harry to his companion, as they reposed themselves after their meal — "it was in the month of July we sailed from Penzance for the Scilly Islands, it is now October. What a strange succession of events have occurred from that period!"

"True, dear Harry, most strange: but now what course do you propose to take that we may get out of this country? It's getting late in the year, and the nights are long."

"I have been thinking," returned Henry, "that if we can make our way to the coast, near the village of St. Quentin, where old Dame Moulin resides, I am satisfied that good-hearted woman would procure us a fishing-smack to take us off to some English cruiser. There are sure to be vessels of war off the coast, till the winter gales drive them away. We have nearly ten pounds in French gold; that would bribe any of the fishermen or pilots, I know."

"Yours is a good idea," said Alfred, "if we could only find out where we are, and how far we are from St. Quentin or La Roche Bernard."

"In any of the farm-houses we can obtain that information," said Henry; "in their hearts all the peasantry are loyalists. Our only difficulty will be to avoid towns: besides, I think, according to the direction that we have come since we left Nantes, we are on the right road. Those villains were taking us to Brest, therefore St. Quentin must lie nearly in our road; I think I should know it, and the way to it, if I could get sight of the ruins of that remarkable old château Dame Moulin pointed out to us."

"Yes, I remember it well; and also that wide heath where we first encountered that unfortunate girl Madeleine."

Thus, chatting and talking over their plans and projects for escaping out of France, the two youths fell fast asleep. They must have slept three or four hours, when they were suddenly roused by the barking of a dog. Starting up, they beheld a small poodle dog snuffing and barking at their feet, and close by an elderly man, habited in black, with a staff in his hand, gazing earnestly at them. The stranger was probably sixty, with a fine benevolent countenance, and there was something about his person and look that banished fear, and. at the same time, induced the cousins to think he must be a priest of some religious community.

"Perhaps," said the stranger, in a mild, pleasing voice, "my little dog has disturbed your slumbers; he would not leave this spot, so I descended to see what was the cause of his anxiety."

Henry — the speaker on all occasions — stood up, saying — "We have slept long enough, monsieur; I see the sun is declining."

"Pardon me, my children," said the stranger earnestly, "but by your looks, manner, and dress, I do not think you claim France — unfortunate, misguided France — as your country. Do not be afraid of me, for I have been, and am, one of the persecuted. I was once a priest. Alas! neither God or priest are acknowledged in this once fair land!"

"We are not French, monsieur," said Henry; "your sacred calling emboldens me to speak the truth to you — we are English prisoners!"

"Ah! then, you are the two lads the dragoons of St. Sernin are looking after — don't be alarmed," continued the *ci-devant* priest, seeing Alfred turn pale and start — "you are quite safe with me; I guessed as much when I saw you."

"You are very kind, mousieur," said Henry; "we are the lads you speak of."

The old priest sat down beside the stream, saying—"Sit you down by me, *mes enfans*. I must hear your story, and help you as far as may be in my power; but you must stay here till dark, and I will send my little attendant for you and shelter you in my humble cottage, which is close by here, till I find means of doing you a service."

"How kind you are, monsieur!" said Henry, taking the old man's hand and pressing it.

"Not kinder than our blessed but disregarded religion teaches us to be one to the other. We are all brethren, no matter our nation, our creed, or our political opinions. Let me hear your story; for the officer of the St. Seruin dragoons, whom I encountered a mile from here, asked me if I had met or seen two youths—he said you were both escaped convicts, and had joined a band of Royalist assassins and murdered your two guards."

"Monsieur," said Henry indignantly, "what a vile falsehood! that miserable wretch, our jailer, no doubt gave this false information in revenge."

"Having now seen you, my children," said the priest, "and knowing you to be English, I feel quite satisfied of the impossibility of your having committed any such acts. Our government can certainly imprison English subjects in arms against the republic, but to make them convicts is against the laws. Now, let me hear all your story."

Henry made the worthy ex-priest acquainted with their mishaps from the very beginning.

"Poor boys!" said the old man tenderly, "you have been sorely tried; but God loves those who submit with resignation and patience to his decrees. All this, therefore, is for the best, though our weak understandings cannot comprehend the ways of the Deity. I say, also, with respect to the fearful horrors that devastate this land, that the Almighty has some great design in it, though his temples are polluted, his very name a mockery, and his ministers trampled on and driven from their once happy firesides and their faithful flocks."

The old man then rose up, and, taking the hands of both the youths, he pressed them warmly — " I regret to have to leave you here," said he ; " but you had better remain in this secure place till dark, for fear some one might see you pass from hence to my cottage. When it becomes dark, my little attendant and the dog — who will show her the way — will come for you ; so patience, my children, till then."

" I hope, monsieur," said Henry, retaining the ex-priest's hand, " that, in your kindness and hospitality to us, you will not bring suspicion and danger on yourself."

" Fear not for me," said the priest ; " God has shielded me through many and severe trials. But there is very little risk in giving you shelter ; the people of these parts would serve me with their lives. The only military in this part of the country are the dragoons of St. Sernin, and I know by what their officer said, that he does not much trouble about the escape of two lads ; he is waiting for orders to pursue and exterminate the Royalist assassins, as they are styled ; or, as they impiously style themselves, *The Company of Jesus.* So farewell, and keep quiet ! " So saying, the priest and his sagacious dog ascended the hill, and left the cousins to themselves.

CHAPTER XXVII.

The mill of Dame Scolet, or, as she was more usually called, Margaret of the Mill, or Dame Moulin — was situated within half a mile of the little village of St. Quentin, and this village was not more than a league from the ex priest's cottage.

Father St. Amand, as he was formerly styled before the revolution broke out, was the parish priest of St. Quentin and St. Sernin. No man was more loved than St. Amand; possessed of independent means, he was enabled to be not only the spiritual director of his flock, but their benefactor likewise.

Before the revolution, the Count and Countess Delancy resided in their château De Loyrency, a splendid residence within a league of St. Quentin. Monsieur de St. Amand was the spiritual director of the count's family; and though the countess was an Englishwoman by birth, and professing a different creed, yet the priest of St. Quentin was her most valued friend and adviser. When the revolution broke out, and the king's life became endangered, the Count Delancy hastened to Paris, and St. Amand accompanied him: both suffered persecution, but the count escaped to England. St. Amand, after imprisonment and incredible escapes, fled from the horrors enacting in Paris, and returned to his once loved home. He found the château De Loyrency plundered and half-consumed, his flock scattered and massacred, the countess and her daughter fled, the exercise of religious rights prohibited, the priesthood a byname, the churches desecrated and dismantled, and the very existence of God doubted and even denied!

" Woe to the land," said the horror-struck priest, " where such abominations exist! Out of evil cometh good: but, alas! out of such horrors what can come but desolation?"

Taking possession of a little cottage within three miles of St. Quentin, the heart-broken pastor furnished it from the little property still left him; and, taking a young peasant girl of fourteen or fifteen years of age to attend to his few wants, he sat down to await patiently, either the total annihilation of his beloved country, or its regeneration and return to God and righteousness.

On returning to his cottage after leaving our young adventurers, and wondering in his own mind and thoughts at the strange coincidence of his thus stumbling on the two boys, who had also so strangely become mixed up in the fate of those formerly so dear to him — though he made no remark to the cousins at the time, he found, on entering his little parlor, that Dame Moulin was there awaiting his return.

" Ah, Dame Margaret, is this you? it's a long time since we met. Alas! how memory travels back in one second to things and people, all gone — passed away! And you, I have heard, have had your troubles also, dame."

" Your blessing, holy father," said the dame, kneeling down, " as in the good old times — the blessed saints be merciful to us! will they ever come back again?"

" With God's blessing, dame — in the proper time, they will; our country is sore tried, and wicked, wilful men triumph. But I have a strange tale to tell you — however, first let me hear what has brought you here now, for you have not long returned to your mill."

"I am come to tell you a secret, Monsieur St. Amand," said the dame, "and to beg of you to visit the mill. I have a dear child ill, very ill, with a fever—more of the mind than the body, I think. I dare not get a surgeon from St. Sernin, for the dear child raves and speaks of names and of persons dangerous to be heard spoken of: but, the Madonna be praised! I have found you at home, for they told me you were gone to Vannes."

"So I was, dame," said Monsieur St. Amand; "but fortunately, as you will hear, I returned yesterday. But who is this child that is ill and talks so strangely: no relation of yours, dame?"

"Oh, no, monsieur!" but she will be dear to you when I tell you her name—it's little Rosina Delancy!"

"Eh! dame, can this be possible?" exclaimed the ex-priest in the greatest astonishment. "I was told, not an hour ago, that the countess and her daughter were left at Quiberon, and surely had embarked in one of the English ships, with the hundreds of other emigrants that fled at that period from the revolutionary army."

"Yes, Monsieur St. Amand," said the dame sorrowfully, " the countess escaped, I trust, but the unfortunate child was separated from the mother, and, by a miracle, escaped being trampled to death. There were two brave and noble boys with them at this time—English lads they were ; but one of them called Henry, and who spoke French like ourselves—Ah, Madonna! he was a noble youth, with a heart as tender and yet as bold as a lion—he went out to fight with the brave de Sombreul, and was left wounded on the field ; the other, a somewhat delicate boy, with a woman's heart, went out to look for him, and both—I witnessed it myself—were made prisoners, and I heard were carried to Nantes, and they say were — the Lord be merciful to them ! — both shot, along with the noble Count de Sombreul and the poor old Marquis Delancy. Alas, alas! father — what times — what monsters!" and the old dame wiped the tears from her eyes.

"Well, dame," said Monsieur St. Amand, greatly astonished, and no little mystified, "though I do not rightly understand you, yet I will relieve your mind on one subject; those two English boys you speak of were not shot — thank God! — at Nantes, for they are alive and well, and not a quarter of a league from here."

"Ah, Madonna be praised! Monsieur St. Amand, you give me great heart; but can it be possible that they are the two young convicts the St. Sernin dragoons say murdered their guards who were taking them to Brest?"

"Then you heard that story also, dame?" said Monsieur St. Amand.

"Yes, monsieur, as I came through the hamlet of Douay, which you know is about a quarter of a league from the farm of Troyin-ouse, which was burned down and its inmates all massacred in cold blood. Ah! you remember poor Madeleine's wedding-day. Alas! one thing or another, Monsieur St. Amand, reminds us of the past. But I was saying I passed through the hamlet, and I found a great crowd of the peasants round the little cabaret, and one or two of the dragoons with their horses tied to the hooks; these men were talking to the country-people, and telling them to disperse over the country, and try and hunt out two convicts — quite young lads — that had escaped from their guards who were taking them to Brest, and that these lads had got in amongst the brigands, who were carousing in the ruined building of Troyin-ouse, and, the two guards pursuing the boys, fell into the hands of the brigands, and the boys excited them to hang the one and brand the other — the one branded they beat with the butts of their muskets, and then turned him loose. It seems, as he ran along the road which is close to this ruined building, he met a troop of the St. Sernin dragoons going to Vannes, and he led them back to the building, and they surprised the brigands, and killed seven of them in the pursuit; and then, the guard going back into the building to look for the two boys, they both fell upon him with cutlass and knives, and hacked him till he was nearly dead, and then fled. The dragoons, coming back to Troyin-ouse, found the guard lying bleeding on the floor, so they brought him on to the hamlet of Douay, and left him in the cabaret. The dragoons, after telling the people they would get a handsome reward if they brought the two boys to St. Sernin, mounted their horses and rode off."

"I am sorry to hear this, dame," said Monsieur St. Amand seriously; "for the peasantry, believing this story, will hunt everywhere for the two poor boys."

"I am frightened now myself, monsieur; for we cannot explain the real truth to all who were present, and I heard many say they would scour the country for them — where are they, monsieur?"

"In a little glen or hollow about the third of a league from here. My little dog found them. They will be safe enough here for this night," continued the priest, "but it will be a great risk to keep them longer."

"I tell you what is best, monsieur," said the dame, after a moment's thought, "I will take them this very night to the caves of St. Gueltas; they were there before. No human being will dream of looking for them there: it is only a league and a half from here, and I can supply them with every thing myself till little Rosina is well, and then it's quite possible to hire a fishing-boat to take them out to some

As they had some hedges and ditches and some very rough ground to go over, before they found the narrow horse-track that led across the heath in the direction for the seashore, they did not attempt to converse; but after nearly an hour's search, for the night was not a very clear one, they came to the little wood; after that the dame soon came upon the right track.

"We may now talk a little bit, my children," said Dame Margaret; "for I long to hear all that has happened to you." Henry gratified the good woman's curiosity, and gave her a true account of all that occurred.

"Ah! that villain of a guard," said the dame, "that lies wounded up at the cabaret of Douay, what a pack of lies he has told! The villain wanted to murder you — pity the brigands did not hang him with that other wretch you call Jaques Marlot!"

"Well, he certainly deserved such a fate," said Henry, "and I am sure if ever that good Colonel Moreau catches him, he will surely hang him; but, dame, tell me about the countess and little Rosina, were they got away from Quiberon."

"*Eh, mon garçon,* that is a sad story!" said Margaret of the Mill with a sigh: "but, with the blessing of God, all will be right yet." She then informed the boys that the countess only had, as she supposed, escaped, and that poor little Rosina was with her, and ill.

Henry and Alfred — for the latter picked up enough, with a word or two from his companion, to understand all that was said — were both astounded and greatly grieved. "What must the poor mother suffer," said Henry, "separated thus from her only and beloved child! and the poor, dear, sensitive-hearted Rosina, what grief must be hers!"

"Yes, *pauvre enfant!* she is grieved, and very poorly;

but if good Monsieur St. Amand sees her, and gives her some medicine, and tells her you are here, she will recover rapidly, and then we will try and get a fishing-boat to take you out to one of the men-of-war off the coast; they will take you to England, and your parents will protect Rosina till her dear mother or father is informed where she is."

"Ah! how happy that would make us," exclaimed the two cousins joyfully, " to be able to take the dear girl to her mother; what joy would be in their hearts, to be thus re-united after so terrible a separation! "

It took the dame and her two companions nearly three hours to reach the summit of the cliffs, from whence they had descended with Rosina to the caves nearly three months back. It was a fine dry night, though cloudy and windy; but when Henry caught the sound of the surf rolling on the shingly beach, the tears came to his eyes, for the sound of the ocean-wave was one he loved well to hear: it bore many recollections in its sound — it spoke forcibly of his island home, of those he loved, and the perils of his early life. For the first time the spirit of the boy was subdued, and he wept audibly.

" Dear, dear Henry, what moves you thus?" said Alfred, affectionately pressing his cousin's hand; " here is your own element again. Does not its sound, as it rolls in on the pebbles, remind you of your own sea-beach?"

" It is that very remembrance, dear Alfred, that softens my heart, and makes me weep like a child. You know I am not one given to desponding, and that, in the hour of trouble and strife, my heart is high, and my spirit not easy to be conquered; but somehow, as the wave rolls in and dashes itself on the beach, and rolls back with that angry grating sound, I think of the wide space that yet intervenes between us and those we love.   Anxious thoughts and fears press upon my mind, but I will shake them off, dear Alfred ; there is energy and courage wanting yet to enable us to quit this land of strife, and cruel persecution of the good and brave."

CHAPTER XXVIII

" Now, my good dame," said Henry, as all paused on the summit of the high cliff, " it is quite needless for you to undergo the unnecessary fatigue of descending and ascending this steep path. I never forget a place I once visit; we shall stay quiet in the cave till you come again, for there is enough food in this basket for two days, and I dare say you did not remove the things we left in the cave, and there was wood, and candles, and things to strike a light in the place."

" Ah ! as to light, my children, you will find materials in that basket ; I thought of that, for though I have never been back to the cave since, because of many troubles, still damp would prevént you striking a light with the materials left. But, suppose you should not be able to find the entrance to the caves."

" Do not fear that, dame ; I took too good note of the peculiarity of the entrance to forget it."

" Well, as I am anxious to return to Mademoiselle Rosina, who will get frightened, I will go : here is the basket. Do not go outside the caves, and by dusk to-morrow I will be with you. Perhaps Father St. Amand may have hit upon some more comfortable place of concealment than those caves ; take the dog with you, for whilst you sleep he will watch, and he seems to take a fancy to you as it is."

Kissing both boys with the affection of a mother, they

parted. Henry and Alfred, with the little poodle at their heels — who seemed to follow them by instinct — began descending the cliff.

" I hope you will find the cave, Harry," said Alfred ; " I have not the slightest recollection of the entrance."

" Oh ! I remember it well," said Henry ; " take care how you come down this slippery path, there has been a great deal of rain since we were here. I am so glad I saved good Dame Moulin this terrible descent and ascent after all the fatigue she has had."

At length they reached the bottom, and, continuing along the beach — Henry regarding, as well as the light admitted, every rock they passed — came at length to the very entrance, though they passed several very similar, which deceived Alfred a dozen times.

" I should never have found it, Henry," remarked Alfred ; " what a memory you have ! "

" It's not exactly memory, my dear Alfred ; but, accustomed from my previous life to note and remark things connected with one's safety, I took particular notice of this certainly blind entrance by taking a mark above it for a guide. Thus, that rock above the cave, with its pinnacle like a spire, struck me, and I said to myself — ' I may never want to come here again, still I will remember the spot.' Now, let us in and strike a light. Ah ! Mignon," he added, as the poodle kept snuffing at the entrance, " do you smell any thing ? "

Entering the cave, and stooping under the arch, the boys paused ; and Henry, taking from the basket the tinder-box and a candle, struck a light, and then they entered the inner cave. There were no visible signs of anybody having been there since their visit, for the embers of the fire, and the very remnants of their last meal, lay as they had left

19

it; the poodle running here and there, and examining every hole and corner with the greatest anxiety and curiosity.

"Well, here we are once more," said Henry, seating himself on a huge piece of detached rock; "its but a short time, and yet we have gone through some unpleasant and not easily forgotten scenes."

"If ever we get home, Henry, we shall look back upon the events of the last few months as a dream."

"And yet," said Henry thoughtfully and seriously, "they may affect our whole life; but let us eat a bit, we have had plenty of exercise to create an appetite."

The basket was unpacked, and the boys had good reason to remember the kind Monsieur St. Amand, who had so well supplied them; but amongst the eatables Henry pulled out a parcel, carefully wrapped up. On opening it, to his extreme surprise and joy, he perceived it was the French version of the Protestant Bible, printed at Nismes in the year 1681. "How thoughtful and how kind of the good priest!" said Henry. "Ah! for months we have not read a line from this holy book; I will read you a chapter or two before we sleep," continued Henry, turning over the leaves. "Ah! this is singular; this book is a curious relic. See! there is the name of John Cavalier, the famous leader of the French Protestants in the frightful war carried on against them by the French King, Louis XIV."

"Dear me! I remember," said Alfred, "your giving me the history of the Camisards, and my reading of the great exploits of John Cavalier; who, born a peasant, yet defeated the great Marshal Villars in battle, with only rude peasants as soldiers. Could this have been his book? what a relic of the past!"

"No doubt this was his book; here is a bullet-mark in the cover! we will look over it after we eat. I would not lose this for any consideration; John Cavalier always struck me as a wonderful hero." Henry then cut up a fine fowl and a tempting loaf of bread; and, there being a cup in the basket, they took after their meal a small quantity of wine, giving the poodle — who sat on his hind-legs with the gravity of a judge — his share of the repast. Then Henry selected the fiftieth chapter of Genesis, beginning with, " And Joseph fell upon his father's face, and wept upon him, and kissed him."

Both boys were well and religiously brought up, and Henry read with a clear, steady voice, translating the chapter, which was in rather obsolete French, fluently and well.

It was a strange, wild picture — those two youths, with their fine, handsome, intelligent features, so calm and serious, the light of the lamp falling on their figures; for whilst the lofty cavern was involved in deep gloom, the huge shadows of its projecting rocks looked like giant figures in the dim light of a single lamp.

Having finished his reading, which gave great pleasure to both reader and listener, they prepared to take a few hours' rest, first lighting a fire, for the air was cold in the caverns. They found the wood Dame Moulin had collected on their first visit, and the blankets, which they aired at the fire, and then wrapping themselves in them, with the poodle at their feet, blessed with youth and innocence, they were soon asleep.

The day was considerably advanced when the two cousins awoke, the fire was out, and they felt chilly. It was soon relighted, and, having made their breakfast, Henry took a peep out from one of the great fissures in the rock, to which he climbed. He could see out over the wide bay, and the islands on which the bright sun shone; there were several fishing craft far out, but no large vessel met his sight. The day passed slowly away, the young lads amusing themselves with the tricks and gambols of the poodle, and teaching him some new ones — and then in talking of home and their hopes of reaching it.

It was scarcely dark when a low growl from Mignon warned them some one was entering the cave; in a moment the dog sprang upon his feet, and rushed out — it was Dame Moulin.

" Well, my poor children, I see you have made out one night in this dismal place," laying down a huge basket and a bundle beside.

" What a load you have carried, dame! how kind and thoughtful — but how is dear Rosina?" said Henry.

" *Eh, mon fils!* wonderfully better. Monsieur St. Amand was with her for two hours. It's only fretting the dear child is; for, when she heard of your being here, she was wild to come to see you, we could scarcely keep her quiet. The good priest gave her some little medicine, and promised her she should come and spend the day here after to-morrow. In the mean time we are to go cautiously to work, and get a pilot-boat from St. Quentin, who will engage to put you aboard one of the English vessels of war off the Island of Nourmontier, which is, they say, still in possession of the Royalists. But you must keep extraordinary close, for that villain of a guard you wounded in the head is not much hurt after all; for I heard this morning that he is up and actually out, and with several bad characters in this neighborhood, rank Revolutionists, prowling about the country looking for you both. But they will never think of coming down to this sea-beach, and there are few now left in the country who know the entrance into these caves; all the old stock is nearly exterminated in these villages round about."

"I wish," said Henry, "I had a brace of pistols. I would never let that wretch of a jailer take us, at all events!"

"The saints bless us! You are young," said the dame, crossing herself, "to have such a spirit. But, please God! the villain will give up his search after a day or so." Dame Moulin then unpacked her basket, and shortly after departed, after reiterating her instructions to keep close, and promising to bring Rosina to see them the next morning, and leave her till dusk. Dame Moulin was as good as her word: the next morning she entered the cave with little Rosina, again dressed like a little peasant-girl. With a joyful cry, she sprang forward, and, throwing her arms round each of the cousin's necks wept with joy.

She was thin and pale, but the joy she felt gave a brilliancy to her large and beautiful eyes, and a momentary color to her cheek. Henry felt rejoiced as he kissed the cheek of their former companion in peril, and soothed the young girl's sorrows; for seeing them brought back more forcibly the memory of her mother.

"I am going along the beach," said Dame Moulin, "to the fishing hamlet of Ouday: it's two leagues from here. I know a pilot there that was a prisoner in England three years; he was well treated there, and likes the English, and is beside a true Royalist. Monsieur St. Amand says we may trust him; so now you will have four hours and more to chat and talk over your adventures with Rosina."

"Oh! we shall do famously, dear dame," said Rosina, in high spirits; for her little heart was beating with the pleasure of seeing her old favorites, and in anticipation of going to England and rejoining her mother.

After the departure of Margaret of the Mill, the three young people sat side by side, Rosina with the poodle Mignon in her lap; whilst Henry gave the young girl a full account of their adventures. Rosina listened, with tears in her eyes, to the recital; for the death of her dear old grandfather, and the handsome, gallant Count de Sombreul, was recalled to her recollection most vividly.

"Ah! what you have suffered," said Rosina; "what cruelty those wretches in the prison showed towards you! and I suffered too. Oh! I shall never forget when the crowd on that dreadful night burst upon us, and tore me from my beloved mother's grasp. I fainted, or was rendered insensible, from fear and excessive fatigue. But, dear friends, though there are bad men in this land, there are bright and good ones also."

"Hark!" suddenly exclaimed Alfred, as Mignon jumped out of Rosina's lap and gave a low growl. "It's the sound and splash of oars!"

"Hold the dog," said Henry, "and keep him from barking; I will climb up to our look-out, for I hear oars certainly."

As Henry climbed up to the wide fissure above, Rosina caught up the poodle, whilst Alfred ran to the mouth of the cave and listened. Presently the sound of a man's voice was heard, evidently within a few yards of the mouth of the cave.

Henry, in the mean time, having reached the fissure in the rock, looked down upon the beach; at once he perceived eight men close to the cave, and a boat lying off held by an anchor, and a long rope ashore to regain possession of her.

The wind blew fresh off the shore, so that the water was perfectly still. As he looked at the men, he perceived that they were armed with various weapons; rusty muskets and pikes; four were sailors, armed with pistol and cutlass; but, as they moved on, to his dismay he recognized the Nantes jailer, the comrade of Jaques Marlot, his head bound round with a bandage, and surmounted with a red cap. Henry scarcely breathed as they passed beneath him; he heard one of the men say, " But who knows where the entrance is to these famous caves! We ought to have brought some one who has been in them; I have heard they reach to St. Gueltas."

" All stuff and nonsense!" said the jailer. " We'll ferret the young reptiles out; look well for any cave, and we will search all."

The caves, I know," said a sailor confidently, " are five . hundred yards below this, round that projecting mount; so come on."

Luckily the entrance to the cave where the fugitives were was extremely difficult to find walking towards the west; in returning was very easily made out; but the men, believing the assertion of the sailor, walked on, not looking back.

Henry got down as fast as he could; his first idea was to seize the boat, whilst the men walked on, and put out to sea; but this idea, he saw, would be frustrated, for about a mile or less from the beach were two fishing-boats at anchor, and the alarm would spread instantly.

" Oh dear! what shall we do?" said Rosina to Henry, shaking with fear, for she had heard the voices of the men.

" I am puzzled," said Henry, deep in thought; " they will find us as they return, but " — at that moment, to their intense surprise, Dame Moulin glided into the cave.

" Come!" said she, " not a moment is to be lost! I was hiding near here and saw the villains land; I have heard bad news, and returned as fast as I could. That wretch of a jailer has tracked you; but come, I have a better place of refuge for you all, and a protector for Rosina, one of her own sex. The villains are round the point and cannot see us — So, *allons!*"

In a moment all were ready, Rosina carrying Mignon and clinging to the arm of Henry. As they passed out from the cave, not a soul was in sight; so, keeping along the cliffs to the right, they hurried rapidly along till they turned a projecting rock.

"Now we cannot be seen," said the dame, "we may take it more leisurely. Rosina put down the dog. Now," said Dame Moulin, "we must get up the cliffs, and walk two leagues, but through a very wild country, on the borders of the salt marshes of Guerande. We shall not meet a human being most likely, except perhaps the poor cotter gathering salt. Those wretches with the jailer are bloodthirsty Republicans; they will, when they see the things in the cave, fancy you are hiding in its inner caverns, and perhaps spend hours in searching its intricacies."

"But how, my dear dame, did you return so soon and so fortunately?" said Henry.

"*Ah ça!* It was fortunate I met our good priest's little attendant coming to seek me; says she — 'My master says that the jailer of Nantes has found out that those they seek are in the caves. You must get them away, and take them to the old Château d'Ouden, on the banks of the Villaine; they will be quite safe there, for no living soul will go near it — there are spirits there!'"

"Ah!" said Rosina, looking up into Henry's face with a smile, "we shall not trouble about spirits and ghosts; God does not permit spirits to be wandering about old châteaux!"

Dame Moulin crossed herself as she cast a look at the little girl. "Well," said she, "it's well not to fear such things, and indeed I do not think spirits are permitted to hurt the innocent; however, you will not be alone in the old château, it's half in ruins and burnt down, but one wing is perfect; and the good priest says there is a lady hiding there, the sister of the Count d'Ouden, who is with the Vendéans in Nourmontier; and the people in those parts love the memory of the good Count d'Ouden, and she is safe there, and so will you be, young creatures; so now, no more talking, but move on just as fast as Rosina can comfortably do."

CHAPTER XXIX.

We must now return to Magnus O'More, who, after the departure of Henry Barlow and Alfred Hammond, remained in his solitary cell, a prey to regrets and disappointment; he could not imagine why he was not sent on as a prisoner of war to Brest, like his late companions. It was quite useless interrogating his sulky jailers; they gave him no satisfactory answer.

One morning, as he was pacing the narrow limits of his cell, he was roused from his thoughts by the loud reports of cannon; then repeated volleys of musketry, accompanied by tremendous shouts, cries, and vociferations, evidently in the court-yards, and even in the interior of the prison.

" What on earth is or can be the matter?" thought Magnus — " a popular tumult? in truth, I hope they will set all prisoners free!" As he listened, the firing of the cannons ceased, but volleys of musketry still pealed through the air; and the shouts and cries of the contending parties came nearer. Amidst the trampling of many feet, the locks and bolts gave way, and the door was burst open, while the gallery without was filled with a wild and excited mob, all armed with any available weapon they had the good fortune to seize.

" Liberty! liberty!" shouted these people; " come forth, *Grace à Dieu!* No more prisoners in Nantes now!"

Magnus O'More did not require any pressing on this point;

he joined the mob, who hurried on shouting and yelling, and smashing every thing that was to be smashed, and uttering fearful threats of vengeance upon Carrier and all his myrmidons. Magnus was soon in the streets, but what to do next puzzled him; he had money in the purse given to him by Lieutenant O'Brien, but how was he to proceed? On reaching a great square, he found it filled with thousands of the excited populace of Nantes, making a furious resistance to the Republican troops, just then returned, re-enforced by the regiments styled the "Infernal Columns."

Victory now changed sides, and the people fled in all directions. Carried along by a crowd of fugitives, Magnus reached one of the gates, when, to his utter amazement, he beheld Phelim, his old associate and humble friend, with a cutlass in his hand, in the midst of an armed group, pressing their way through the gate, eager to escape. Magnus, delighted to see his faithful follower, with difficulty made his way up to him, and laid his hand on his shoulder. Phelim turned, gave a shout of joy, and, grasping Magnus's hand, expressed his delight in such boisterous terms that he even attracted the attention of the armed band he was with. A tall, powerful, and handsome man, with dark whiskers, beard, and mustache, turned round, and, looking at Magnus, said earnestly — "If you are English, come with us; you will be massacred if you remain in the town. Carrier has returned at the head of two thousand men!"

"Yes!" said Magnus, "I am English, and will follow you." The party then, to the number of three hundred, made their way out, and gained the open country, but still continued marching at a quick pace. Up to this moment, Magnus could get no opportunity to speak to Phelim.

"How on earth," said he to him, "did you get with this party, and where have you been since we separated?"

"Faith, your honor," said Phelim, "you left me, you may remember, shut up in the old prison at the place they call St. Nazaire; dickens a much of a saintly odor there was about it, at all events! But after I knocked down the two jailers that separated me from your honor, they pushed and kicked at me, till they got me into a hole of a place as dark as pitch, and there they locked me in. I suppose I was there living on bad bread and dirty water ten days, when my door was burst open, and the tall gentleman you see, the head of this band — and a mighty nice man he is altogether; a count something, I believe — stood at the door, with several others. 'Who are you, my fine fellow?' says he — at least I suppose he said so — for faix, to tell the truth, the dickens a word I understood! but says I, 'I'm an Irishman, and a sailor!' 'Oh!' said the tall man, in a kind of English, 'you are an Englishman.' 'Not exactly, your honor,' says I; 'but we fight for the king, God bless him! all the same.' 'Well, come along; you're not a Republican, at all events.' 'No, faix!' says I; 'but if I ever catches a grip of a Republican — faith, I'll make him remember me!'

"Well, your honor, this gentleman was the leader of a party of Pandeans "—

"No!" interrupted Magnus, "Vendéans, you mean."

"Be sure, that's it; Vendéans, sure enough. They drove the Republicans out of St. Nazaire, and were going to make an attempt upon Nantes. We hunted the place, your honor, for you, and any of my messmates; but the jailers said you were sent a prisoner to Nantes, and that there were no more prisoners there; so the boat's crew must have wandered back to the boat and put to sea. I staid with the band of Vendéans till it was joined by another great band, and then we got into Nantes, and the people all rose up and took arms, and the Republicans fled. In the confusion, dickens a one of me knew where I was! I lost my companions, and kept asking every one where the prison was; for the count promised, if you were in the prison of Nantes, he would set you free. By great good-luck I stumbled on my companions — you see they are dressed quite different from the others, who wear blue — and then, by the powers! your honor, you joined us; and I hope, now we have got together, we shall get out of this country. I've had enough of it."

" Well, I think so too, Phelim."

" But where did you come from, Master Magnus? "

" Out of the prison, Phelim."

" It was lucky, at all events, Master Magnus, that they broke into the prisons."

As the band of Royalists continued on their way, their leader let the men proceed, and then walked on by the side of Magnus.

" Do you speak French?" said he, regarding Magnus with some surprise — " for my English is very indifferent."

" Yes!" returned the midshipman; " permit me to thank you for my deliverance from prison."

"Ah!" returned the Vendéan leader, " we were very unfortunate; there was a very large revolutionary force marching upon Nantes at the time we drove that wretch Carrier out. He returned with them, and unexpectedly attacked us when we thought victory ours. You are in the English navy, to judge by your dress?"

" Yes!" returned Magnus; "I fear your cause looks desperate."

" It does, indeed," said the Frenchman with a sigh, " unless your ministers fulfil their promise, and send us troops and arms. La Rochejaquelein is still alive — and

Chârette holds Nourmontier! I formerly held large estates a few leagues from here, and lived in the Château d'Ouden, on the banks of the Villaine, below La Roche Bernard. But the ferocious soldiers of Moine sacked the château in my absence, and reduced it partly to ruins; fortunately, my wife and children had escaped to England some months previously. I was then with Leseure; he has since perished, fighting for his king. Alas! it is nearly a hopeless cause!"

" Where, may I ask," said Magnus, " do you propose proceeding with so small a force? "

" To the forest and salt marshes of Zerbigue," said the Count d'Ouden,.for such was his title. " I do not know," he continued, after a moment's thought, " how to be of assistance to you and your countryman. May I ask how you came to be in the prison of Nantes?—for, with great difficulty, I understood a few sentences of your countryman's history."

Magnus told the count how he had been captured at St. Nazaire, and then sent on Nantes.

" At all events," said the count, " keep with us for a few days; perhaps we may recross the Loire. If you had run your boat ashore on the Island of Nourmontier, you would have easily procured a vessel to take you across the channel, for the island is held by the Royalists."

" But the fog was so great," said Magnus, " we knew not where we were running."

" Well! we must bear our lot with resignation," said the count; "if my followers were across the Loire, and dispersed to their homes, I should like to seek my wife and family in England, and wait for other and better times."

That night the whole party halted under the shelter of one of those thick and almost impassable woods that cover immense tracts of country in Brittany; fires were lighted, and sundry provisions the band carried were shared and eaten in a mournful silence. The royal cause was rapidly sinking. Overwhelming numbers on the other side, regular trained soldiers against undisciplined peasants, once clear of their impenetrable Bocages in La Vendée, soon stormed and destroyed the immense band that, but a few months before, crossed the Loire in hopeless flight. The band of the Count d'Ouden was the last remnant of the 80,000 exiles from La Vendée.

The following morning they resumed their journey, selecting a tract of country thinly inhabited and of dreary aspect; wide heaths and plains covered with broom, with here and there a solitary farm. From these farms they procured an abundance of provisions, simple, but sufficient for their wants.

Halting, some two hours after mid-day, within a mile or two of the great salt marsh that lies between Pont Château and Gueraude, to their right lay a tract of low forest-trees and thick brushwood; scarcely had they halted, and began to rest their weary limbs, when the notes of a bugle to the right of the wood caused each man to start to his feet, and grasp his musket; the next moment they beheld a formidable body of horse turn the wood in full gallop.

"The bloody dragoons of La Roche Bernard!" shouted the men. A panic seized all, and, throwing down their muskets, they fled to a man, dispersing in all directions for the salt marsh, where they knew the troopers dare not follow. In vain the Count d'Ouden stamped and implored them to make a stand. Four of the men seized the count and dragged him off towards the marsh, despite his struggles.

"Lie down — lie down behind this rock!" shouted Magnus to Phelim, whose first impulse was to seize a musket.

Magnus dragged him down behind a pile of natural crags that rose in singular forms and in clusters in different parts of the heath. They heard the hollow tramp of the horse, the shouts of the dragoons, and the incessant dropping shots fired after the fugitives. As the sounds receded, Magnus O'More raised his head and peeped cautiously over the rock ; the dragoons were in full pursuit, but the nature of the ground favored the fugitives, and the salt marsh, so treacherous to a horse, was within their reach. Still several fell from the carbine-shots of the dragoons.

"We cannot loiter here, Phelim," said Magnus ; "pick up some bread and meat, and let us make for that wood before the dragoons turn."

"Well," said Phelim, stuffing as much bread and half-roasted mutton into his pockets as he could, "if those mounseers had only made a stand behind these rocks, we'd have emptied half the saddles of those dragoons." The two youths then made for the wood, which they reached without attracting the notice of the dragoons.

"What shall we do now, sir?" said Phelim, as they paused to take breath ; "faix! it's a queer way we're in ; if we were on salt water, we could easily find out where we were — but here we are nowhere!"

"Nevertheless, we ought to be very thankful that we have our lives and our liberty."

"The blessed saints be praised, sir, that's true for us! I am not ungrateful ; but I wonder if we shall ever see ould Ireland and the fine lake again? Ah! Master Magnus, you will have your own one of these days, plase God!"

"I hope so, Phelim, for the sake of justice to my dear parents : I do not covet the estates. However, let us not talk of home ; let us trust to Providence and our own exertions to get out of this land — that's our present object. I wish we were with those two fine lads that were with me in the prison of Nantes, though that would be risking a long imprisonment."

"Who were they, sir?" questioned Phelim. Magnus O'More, to relieve his thoughts, related his meeting with Henry Barlow and Alfred Hammond.

"Faix, your honor! if they were with us we might reach the coast, and seize a fishing-boat, and make across channel."

"We may be able to do that ourselves," said Magnus; "we are not far from the banks of the Villaine River, and if we could find that Château d'Ouden the count spoke of, we might hide ourselves there for a few days; the peasants in those parts will always assist Royalists, and give them provisions."

Pursuing their way, before sunset they gained a view of the broad waters of the Villaine, and as the moon rose they reached its borders. It appeared a broad and rapid stream; for the tide was rolling down, the country on both sides dreary and flat.

"We will keep down towards the sea," said Magnus; "the count said the Château d'Ouden was close on the borders, and surrounded on three sides by a thick wood; and yonder appears the wood, extending very nearly to the river's edge, and there is a bend in the stream. I remember, by the chart, that La Roche Bernard must be away up the stream to the right, for the river is not near so broad there." They walked on — both strong, powerful youths; in fact, Phelim was now a man, and much improved since he had served aboard a man-of-war. Turning the bend of the river, and skirting the wood, they suddenly beheld the ruins of Château d'Ouden, for so Magnus set it down.

There was something striking and solemn in the look of the old ruined château as they approached its front, with the

20

bright moonlight resting upon its dilapidated walls. One part, the left wing, appeared still perfect; the rest was unroofed and blackened, apparently by fire.

"The people of Brittany," said Magnus to Phelim, "have a great dread of being in the night near ruins, especially where people have been slain. The Count d'Ouden said the ferocious soldiers of Moine murdered every soul within the walls — men, women, and children; but luckily — or rather providentially — his wife and daughters had fled to England some time before."

"The Lord save us, sir!" said Phelim, gazing at the blackened mass before them; and through which the night-wind whistled and moaned with a mournful wail. "I'm not fond myself of ould ruined houses and the like; they are dismal places!"

"You are not afraid of seeing spirits, Phelim?"

"No, faix, your honor!" said Phelim, with a quiet laugh: "a drop of whiskey wouldn't frighten me anyhow!"

Magnus smiled, and then mounting the broken steps, entered through the shattered doorway into a large and noble hall — at least it was such in the Count d'Ouden's time, and before the ruthless spoliation of the revolutionary soldiers of France left many such, over the land, as mementoes of the dreary past. The floor of the hall was strewed with the blackened ruins of the roof, the moon was high in the heavens, and a stream of bright silvery light streamed across the hall.

"The Lord save us, Master Magnus! what's that?" said Phelim, and he caught the young man's arms, his teeth actually chattering with fright; for, though bold as a lion, before a foe, he was a child in the lonely hours of the night, in such a place as within the walls of Château d'Ouden.

As Phelim spoke, Magnus caught a glimpse of a figure in white, on which the moonbeams played strikingly at that moment. Casting off Phelim's arm, Magnus leaped over the obstacles in his way, notwithstanding Phelim implored him not to chase a spirit — there was ill luck in it — but Magnus was gone. Phelim turned round and fairly rushed out of the hall into the open air, and then called upon half a dozen saints to protect his young master and himself from evil spirits.

Magnus O'More, who had not the slightest belief in spiritual appearances, bounded over the ruins, determined to see who it was that visited the blackened ruins of d'Ouden Château in the still hour of the night. The figure fled; but Magnus was too active to be distanced, and in two minutes he arrested the progress of the figure, which turned out to be a young woman carrying a large basket, which she dropped, uttering a faint cry. The rays of the moon fell full upon the spot where Magnus and the female stood; she was attired as a peasant, was about thirty years of age, and extremely pleasing in her countenance; though at first rather startled, as she gazed into Magnus's handsome features she regained her breath, saying — "*Qui voulez-vous, monsieur ?*"

"Pardon me," said Magnus, "if I have frightened you."

"What is the matter, Janette? Who has stopped you? I will be with you in a moment," said a youthful but manly voice from a window above, in that part of the château not in ruins.

Magnus O'More, when he heard the voice, started, and exclaimed, "Can it be possible?"

"Well, monsieur," said the young woman, taking up her basket, "who are you, and what do you want in this place at this hour of the night?"

"Only shelter, my good girl," said Magnus; "I am an Englishman!"

Just at that moment some one appeared in the doorway; and, as the rays of the moon fell upon the features, Magnus O'More recognized the countenance of his old school-fellow, and exclaimed, "Oh, Henry! is it possible we thus meet again?"

Henry Barlow, for he it was, darted forward, exclaiming, "Magnus O'More, how extraordinary!" and then the two lads shook hands with a delightful feeling of relief and joy at again meeting.

The young woman, perceiving this friendly feeling between the two youths, quite recovered her good humor; for, lifting her basket, she said, "Well, then, young gentlemen, since you seem to know one another so well, I will go on and tell madame and mademoiselle that they will have company to supper.

"Do so, Janette; and tell Alfred to come down to us."

"Yes, monsieur," returned the young woman, and then she disappeared amidst the chambers in the undilapidated part of the château.

"Well, Magnus," said Henry Barlow, "this is a most extraordinary meeting! Are you alone?"

"Oh!" interrupted Magnus, "that puts me in mind that I am not alone! I have with me my old boyish attendant, Phelim M'Farlane, whom you may remember I spoke of in such affectionate terms for his attachment to me when a young boy, or rather child."

"Where is he, then?" said Henry; "I am rejoiced you have found him again; fidelity is a rare quality! We must not neglect him."

"When I ran after that young woman who has just left us, Phelim, I suspect, bolted; for, like all seamen — and Irish ones especially — he has a profound belief in spirits."

"We will go and look for him; but stay, here is Alfred.'

"Magnus! how rejoiced I am to see you," said Alfred Hammond, springing to the side of the midshipman, and warmly and delightedly pressing his hand.

"Well! this is a most unexpected and delightful meeting," said Magnus O'More; "it repays me tenfold for the tedious and solitary hours I spent after your departure."

"What is it, your honor? In the name of the saints, Master Magnus, are you after talking to a spirit, or to real flesh and blood?" said Phelim's voice from the open portal.

"Oh!" said Magnus, "so you are there, Master Phelim! you are a very pretty specimen of an Irishman, to run from a petticoat!"

"The saints be praised! it was a woman then, after all," said Phelim, venturing within the hall; but, seeing three figures standing together, he paused quite surprised.

Henry Barlow immediately said, "I rejoice to say, Phelim, that we are not spirits; though I have never seen you, I have heard a great deal about you."

"God bless your honor!" said Phelim, greatly gratified —"I am much obliged to you; I suppose you are the young gentleman my master was so sorry to be separated from?"

"The very same," said Alfred, who, getting a clear view of the sailor's open, cheerful countenance, appeared pleased to take notice of him.

"Well, now let us," said Henry Barlow, "get to our residence; I will introduce you, Magnus, to the little Rosina you heard me speak so much about. She is here, and also a French lady, the sister of the Count d'Ouden."

"The Count d'Ouden!" said Magnus in great surprise; "why, it was to the count I owed my liberty from the prisons of Nantes; he is not very far from here, in the salt marshes of Gueraude — with some two hundred or more followers."

"How very singular!" said both Henry and Alfred; "but Madame Dupré — she is a widow — and will be rejoiced to hear of her brother's being in existence, and so near her."

The party now entered one of the lower rooms, and then a staircase, on the top of which stood Janette with a light. They ascended the stairs, and followed the young woman along a corridor, tolerably perfect, but stripped of every available article, into a large saloon; this also was bare of furniture, but there was a rudely constructed bench made from the fragments of plank and wood lying about, and the same kind of a table, on which was a lamp, and in the grate a good roaring wood-fire.

"Now, you stay here, Phelim," said Henry Barlow. "Janette will keep you company for a while. I think I heard you say you were not afraid of a petticoat; though I am afraid you will not understand one another very well."

"Oh, faix! we'll make shift, sir," said Phelim with a smile; "I was several days with the mounseers, and picked up a word here and there."

Henry Barlow then, to the great surprise of Magnus, approached the panelled wall, and, touching a secret spring, a square panel fell back; he then put his hand inside and pushed back two bolts, when a space opened, wide enough to admit any person through.

"You are surprised, Magnus," said Alfred; for Henry went on to apprise Madame Dupré and Rosina that they had another guest to supper, and who that guest was; for Janette had not gone further than the room they were in, having merely lighted her lamp to show them the way. "You are surprised; but there are few old châteaus in France, they tell me, without secret passages and secret chambers."

" So I have heard," said Magnus ; " I was surprised that this one should have escaped discovery during the pillage of the place."

" Unless they pulled down the wall," said Alfred, " it would be sure to escape observation."

Janette now told Alfred, who was making great progress in his French, that she would return to her brother's farm, as it was getting very late. She then pointed out the basket of provisions, and stated that, the next day, she would contrive to bring over some things for the new-comers to sleep on.

" Thank you, my good girl," said Magnus ; " but do not run any unnecessary risk for us. We are accustomed, at sea, to sleep on a soft plank, and will do very well."

Janette smiled, she looked pleased into the handsome features of the midshipman, saying, " I run no risk, monsieur, for my brother's farm is the nearest habitation to this place, and there are no soldiers or republicans nearer than La Rôche Bernard, near four leagues from this."

Henry Barlow now returned for Magnus ; so he and Alfred, lifting the basket, proceeded through the aperture, leaving Phelim a light and his share of the provisions, together with a bottle of wine. " With these, Phelim," said Alfred, " you will be able to pass the time till we return — for we all sleep here."

" Thank your honor ! " said Phelim ; " faith, with the help of this supply, I will be able to face the spirits, if there are any in this ould building."

Passing through the panel, the three friends entered a long narrow passage, evidently made between the walls of the château, which appeared immensely massive ; at the end of the passage, a door opposed their further progress. Henry opened the door, and admitted them into a long narrow room, without any fireplace or window, but ventilated by holes near the ceiling; this room led into another, where Rosina and Madame Dupré slept. The first room was tolerably furnished with tables, chairs, &c. Madame Dupré and Rosina came out from the inner room, and Henry introduced Magnus to them both. Madame Dupré was a very pleasing, agreeable looking person, and not more than thirty or two and thirty. She welcomed Magnus with great kindness of manner, and said she fancied she already knew him, having heard so much of him from Henry and Alfred. Magnus returned a suitable reply, and then the young cousins began spreading out the contents of the basket for supper.

Magnus O'More was certainly surprised by the beauty of little Rosina, whose large dark eyes met his with so much natural kindness of expression, that he soon came upon familiar terms with her and her pet dog the poodle. During supper, the whole party became quite like one family. Magnus told Madame Dupré that, very probably, he owed his liberation from the prison of Nantes to the attack of the Royalists under her brother, the Count d'Ouden. Madame Dupré was quite rejoiced to hear that he was alive and well, but sighed to think what a perilous life he was leading; and hoped that, finding the inutility of further resistance to the Republican forces, he would try and escape across the Loire to Nourmontier, and thence to England. She herself was deeply anxious to quit France. She and Janette were in the Château d'Ouden at the time it was attacked and pillaged by the ferocious soldiers of General Moine. The countess, her daughter, and young son, had sailed in a small vessel a fortnight before for England, taking her jewels with her and all the funds she could gather. Madame Dupré was ill, and unable to leave her bed at that time, having heard the news of her husband's death in Paris — he having fallen, like many others, in an attempt to restore the queen and dauphin. On the night of the attack, she and Janette slept in the outer room; at the first assault they both rushed, with whatever garments and bedclothes they could collect, through the secret panel, and remained hid there whilst the château was pillaged and set fire to, and then left. Fortunately, numbers of the peasantry assembled after the departure of the revolutionary soldiers, and extinguished the flames before it reached their hiding-place, and thus they were saved.

Madame Dupré remained concealed from that time, supplied with every necessary through the kindness of Janette's brother, who was formerly the bailiff of the Count d'Ouden; she was also visited by the good priest, Monsieur de St. Amand, who advised Dame Margaret of the Mill to take her *protéges* to the same place; for, so determined was the vengeance of the jailer of Nantes, that he would be sure to find the two lads if they remained in the caves.

Madame Dupré insisted on sharing the quilt and blankets they possessed with Magnus and his attendant — the two cousins had a supply. In vain Magnus insisted he could sleep just as well on the floor, before the fire, without any covering; Rosina added her pretty and pleasing voice to madame's request, saying they had too much for their use; so Magnus was forced to accept a couple of quilts. Bidding madame and Rosina good-night, the young lads retired to the outer room, and having a plentiful supply of firewood, from broken rafters and beams, a good fire was kept up. As they sat round the fire, Alfred and Henry made Magnus O'More fully acquainted with their adventures since they parted; Magnus also told his, and then, with their quilts thrown over them, the hardy lads slept the sleep of youth and hope.

The next day Dame Moulin arrived; she was amazed at seeing Magnus and Phelim. "Why," said the good dame, with a smile, " we shall have quite a little colony of English here by and by."

Rosina laughed her merry laugh; the little girl's spirits were revived. She now thought, with such additional help, they would surely get a vessel and cross the sea to England. Dame Moulin told them that they must keep very close, and not stir abroad; for, as long as the horrid jailer of Nantes remained in the country, they could do nothing towards a final escape; but in the end, finding himself baffled, he would surely depart. She heard that morning that he was gone to La Roche Bernard. In a day or two the good priest would visit them.

In this manner two or three days passed, all doing what they could to relieve the tedium of confinement to Madame Dupré and Rosina. The second day after Dame Moulin's visit, Janette's brother, a highly respectable farmer, visited Madame Dupré; he informed her that the Count d'Ouden was supposed to be concealed in the salt marshes of Guerande, and that a strong force from Vaunes was sent to join the dragoons to drive him out; but it appeared he had retraced his steps, and, no doubt, would manage to cross the Loire; that the worthy ex-priest, Monsieur de St. Amaud, was summoned to La Roche Bernard by the Maire de Arrondissement, for what purpose he could not say; but there was a report spread abroad that there were English spies in the country, so that they must keep very close.

This intelligence alarmed both Madame Dupré and Rosina. Henry, Magnus, and Alfred, talked of going on an exploring expedition along the banks of the Villaine, in order to see if it were possible to seize any boat. But Madame Dupré said that there was a very strong fort near the mouth of the river, and guard-boats would render the passage dangerous.

The following evening Henry Barlow and Magnus were standing at one of the windows of the château, gazing out at the broad, muddy waters of the Villaine; it was just high water, when they observed a chasse-mare coming down the stream under her foresail only; the weather was cloudy, the wind fresh, and blowing right down the stream. The two young midshipmen gazed earnestly at this vessel, till at length Magnus observed to Henry, "I wish we had that craft! She would be a nice thing to run across channel in."

"Ah! that she would," returned his companion. "See! they are coming to off this place, and there are eight or nine men in her, an unusual number for a craft of sixteen or seventeen tons."

The chasse-mare, as she came opposite the château, luffed up in the wind, lowered her foresail, and let go her anchor.

"What does she want here?" said Henry; "it looks very suspicious! Let us watch their movements."

The chasse-mare having anchored, one of the crew hauled up the boat that was towing astern, six or seven men got into it — leaving only what appeared a boy aboard — and then pulled in under the high bank on which the Château d'Ouden was built.

"I do positively think," said Magnus, "that these men mean mischief. At all events, it's well to be prepared;" and calling Phelim from the hall, where he was collecting wood, he and Alfred commenced clearing away every thing in the outer room into a large closet the chamber contained, and putting out the fire, and thus removing every trace of habitation. During these proceedings, Henry Barlow and Magnus kept watch; for, to reach the château, the men must ascend the cliff, and then come very close under their window in order to gain the front. Madame Dupré and Rosina were rather startled by these proceedings; but, knowing the necessity of precaution, they cheerfully helped the youths.

"Here they come up the cliff!" said Henry, as a head showed itself and then the body, until seven men came up and walked towards the château. Henry grasped Magnus's arm, saying, "Look! that is the jailer of Nantes! I remember him well; the others are what we call coast-guards, armed with pistols and cutlasses."

"It is him!" said Magnus, gazing cautiously forth. "See!" his head is bound up, and covered with a red cap. The rascal has either tracked us, or suspicion is excited. Ah! if madame and Rosina suffer for our coming here, I shall never forgive myself; but they are but seven, we are four resolute youths — why not attack them, seize the boat, and then the chasse-mare?"

"Glorious idea!" said Henry with a glowing cheek; "but, alas! we have no arms!"

"I have it!" said Magnus, "but we must be quick. As to the secret hiding-place saving us, it is out of the question. Do you get Madame Dupré and Rosina to go into the two rooms beyond this, leave a little of the panel open, so as to attract their attention — we can be concealed in this large closet — and, the moment they go in, which they surely will, we will close it. It will take them some time to break through, for the panels are strong oak, and in the mean time, we can seize the boat."

"Admirably planned!" almost shouted Henry in his joy.

Madame Dupré and Rosina when they heard the proposal, though their cheeks were pale, were of opinion that Magnus's plans were feasible; for madame also felt persuaded, if once the men entered the château, they would not leave it without finding their hiding-place. It was a good step round from the bank to the front of the château, and, before the sound of the men's voices reached their ears, all were at their allotted posts. Henry, as an inducement and a lure, left a handkerchief hanging out through the partly open panel.

Phelim, before he enconsced himself in the closet, put a dinner-knife in the breast of his jacket, and took up a stout piece of rafter for a weapon. The dog Rosina carried with her; and the animal being singularly sagacious, as all French poodles are, made no attempt whatever to bark, or even growl. A dead silence then ensued, whilst Henry, on the stool they had carried into the closet, kept watching through the panes of glass over the door.

CHAPTER XXXI.

THE silence was at length broken by the sound of a rough voice saying, " This way, this way, comrades ! Here is a staircase, and I dare say there are hiding holes in this old château," said the voice of the jailer, " for all old· châteaus have them ; and, as we know they *are* here, the reptiles ! we shall soon ferret them out."

Magnus O'More pressed Henry's hand, but all almost refrained from breathing. They heard the men's footsteps in the corridor, and then a voice said, " Ah ! here are marks enough on the floor — come here, the marks lead into this room."

" Oh ! " said the jailer's voice, uttering a vile oath, " if I only had my hand on the aristocrat's throat ! "

In a moment more they were all in the saloon, and one of the men with a shout cried out, " We have them. See ! the lads have left the panel leading to their secret hiding-place open, and here's a handkerchief ! "

" Ah ! all's right, then, said the jailer exultingly. " Now, cock your pistols, for the young dog bites and hits hard ; don't spare him or his comrade. Cut him down, but do not kill him. I will brand him, the reptile ! "

" Do you stay on guard at this entrance," said one of the men to the jailer ; " we are quite enough for two ; it's dark inside, and it's a long passage."

The young midshipman heard every word, and Henry Barlow saw what passed in the room. "Now," said he in a low whisper to Magnus, "that ruffian is on guard with a cocked pistol; let me deal with him."

"No, no!" said Magnus, seizing the stout piece of timber Phelim held, and, dashing open the door of the closet, rushed out.

The jailer turned round with a savage oath, instantly saw Magnus, and, levelling his pistol, fired; the ball grazed his cheek; the next instant the blow from Magnus's staff fell across his face, and stretched him bleeding on the floor. As he fell, a shout arose within the secret passage, but Alfred quickly closed the panel, and the secret spring shot into its place. Phelim seized the jailer by the leg, and was proceeding very deliberately to throw him out of the window; but Magnus called out, "No, no! take his pistols and cutlass, and come along." Madame Dupré and Rosina in the mean time were trembling exceedingly; it was getting rapidly dusk, violent blows were heard within the passage, as if, in the darkness, those shut in were hunting for the panel of entrance.

The door of the saloon had a famous lock to it, which, a day or two before, Henry had oiled and repaired; they now locked it, as that would create greater delay. A most violent shower of blows and fierce shouts were heard within the secret passage, but the oak panels and the walls were strong. Henry, supporting the trembling Rosina, and Magnus helping Madame Dupré, hurried across the hall and out into the open air.

"It was getting dusk," said Madame Dupré to Magnus; "what a blessing no one was hit by the shot we heard."

"It is providential, madame," said Magnus O'More; "and it is quite as well also it is getting dusk."

They soon reached the shore, and found the chasse-mare's

boat high and dry — the tide running down rapidly — but the four lads soon had the boat in the water; it was blowing fresh, but a fine and favorable wind. Placing the two females in the stern-sheets, the youths in high glee — Phelim only regretting he had not pitched the jailer out of the window — took the oars, and pulled for the chasse-mare. Magnus was standing up in the bows, with a cocked pistol in his hand, thinking there might be one or two hands still in the vessel. As the boat approached the chasse-mare a loud hail came from the shore; it was now too dusk to distinguish any thing at that distance, but several dark figures on the beach.

"By the powers, you're too late, my beauties!" said Phelim, as he laid by his oar ready to jump aboard.

As the boat ran alongside, a boy came up the hatch and ran to the side; but when he saw those in the boat, he screamed out, " Father, father ! Come up ! here's a boatful of robbers ! "

Magnus sprang aboard, and caught the lad by the arm, saying, " Make no noise — you will not be hurt ! " As he spoke, the head and shoulders of a man appeared above the fore hatch, uttering a volley of imprecations in a jargon of patois. Before he could extricate himself from the hatch, Phelim and Magnus took a fast hold of him, and shoved him back; his rage was almost ludicrous, but down he went, and then the hatch was put on and the bar over it, the prisoner below bellowing like a bull, and uttering no end of threats, whilst from the shore a hurricane of shouts and imprecations were sent across the water. Henry and Alfred, in the mean time, got the females aboard, made fast the boat, and then shipped the huge tiller lying on the deck.

"Cut the cable, Phelim," said Magnus; "you have a knife."

"Ay, ay, sir!" returned the active sailor. The cable was cut, and then both, aided by Alfred, took a pull at the fore halliards, hoisting the foresail, and getting the boat's head round before the wind — the poor boy wringing his hands, and praying them not to murder his father, who, to judge by the row he was making down below, was endeavoring to break through the hatch.

"Now, my lad," said Henry to the young French boy, " if you will put us up to the safe way of steering down the river, I will let your father and you go ashore in the boat; if you will not, it will be a bad job for your father;" he had scarcely said the word before bang went the timber of the hatch, and out came a stout old fellow brandishing a handspike, and vowing vengeance on the pirates who had boarded his craft. The first one he came across was Phelim, just making fast the fore-halliards. Whirling his handspike in the air, he made a furious blow at him; Phelim ducked, and, catching the Frenchman by the legs, he pulled him down on the deck, laughing heartily. Alfred and Magnus, running up, seized the furious old man, and, despite his struggles, bound him hand and foot, and lowered him down again into the fore hatch, his poor boy crying bitterly the whole time, though Alfred said and did all he could to pacify him. The chasse-mare then ran rapidly down the river with wind and tide, Magnus steering.

"Now, tell me, boy," said Henry, "how far down is the fort, and how far is the fort from the sea?"

"Who are you?" sobbed the boy; "why do you steal father's boat — are you robbers?"

"No, my poor boy!" said Madame Dupré, soothingly; "we are only trying to save our lives from wicked people. What is your father's name? for I know most people about Château d'Ouden and La Roche Bernard."

"Eh! are you the lady that was hiding in the Château d'Ouden?"

"Yes, boy, I am!" said Madame Dupré; "I am the Count d'Ouden's sister!"

The boy clapped his hands joyfully, saying, "Then let father up — he wouldn't hurt a hair of your head; but keep away — right away for the right bank," continued the lad, turning to Magnus, "or else you will be on the Tallet Sands!" Magnus at once kept away for the other side, whilst Henry and Alfred went to the hatch.

"My good fellow," said Henry, swinging himself down, amid a torrent of invectives, "do not put yourself in a rage — we are not robbers!"

"What brought you aboard my craft, then — who are you? you're not French."

"No!" said Henry, "we are English."

"Oh!" said the old man, "why did you not say so? I was in an English prison four years. I speak much English."

"Now we shall become friends," said Henry.

"Ay, ay! you untie my legs: we can talk better; besides you will run my craft on the spit, and carry away my masts with this strong springtide and wind aft."

Henry, without any hesitation, released the old man, saying as he did so, "There is the sister of the Count d'Ouden aboard."

"Why did you not say so? let me up, or you will be fired into as you pass the guard-boat. I would die for any of the family of Ouden!" so saying, the energetic old man got on deck and hurried aft, saying to Magnus as he took the helm — "Haul aft the sheet, my lads, you will be on the spit!" and he put the helm down.

Phelim and Magnus hauled the sheet in, and then the old

man kept the craft close in for the eastern shore. Magnus stood watching, for at first he thought he might run the boat ashore to escape, but he had no such intention.

"So you are Madame Dupré!" said the old man, turning to the count's sister. "Surely you remember old François Goheir, of La Roche Bernard?"

"Dear me! is it possible — so it is you, François?"

"Hush!" said the old skipper; "we shall be hailed by the guard-boat, off the fort. All keep silence — I will answer!"

The young people looked before them; it was far from a dark night, and just then the moon was beginning to raise herself over the eastern bank of the river. The party aboard could see about two hundred yards from them, lying next the western shore, a lugger-rigged craft of about fifty tons; and half a mile inshore of her the white walls of a battery.

"Why do you pass so close to the guard-boat?" said Henry to the old man.

"Because," said he, "the channel is not fifty yards broad here, though the river is a league. The flats lie here; you could never have taken the craft past this — you would have grounded."

"Boat ahoy!" shouted a voice from the lugger.

"Ahoy, ahoy!" answered the old man.

"What craft's that?" again sung out the voice.

"The *Clemence*, Captain François Goheir, for Bellisle."

"All right!" answered the voice.

"Now, hoist away, my lads, at the mainsail," said the skipper, "and then we will have a talk. I thought you were pirates! we're past the flats — it's plain sailing now. So, the saints preserve us! You are Madame Dupré," he continued, "and I wanting to kill these fine lads — but they

were too much for old François now; and where do you
want to go, madame?"

"Indeed, François, we have not made up our minds what
to do as yet; but, now I have time to think, would it not
be a good plan to run for the Isle Nourmontier? these young
gentlemen are in the English navy."

"*Ah, ça!* is that the case? then perhaps we may fall in
with a British cruiser off Bellisle." As the old man
spoke, there came the loud boom of a heavy gun astern of
them. François Goheir started, saying. "That's from the
Sans-Culotte lugger; has the alarm spread, I wonder?"

"I fear it has," said Madame Dupré.

"I know that they can telegraph the forts by a light
from Poulet; but those fellows, who went ashore to take
some spies hid in Château d'Ouden — I suppose they called
these lads spies — must have run fast to get to Poulet, for it
is nearly a league from Ouden."

"How came you to have them aboard, François!" said
Madame Dupré.

"Ah! the rascals gave me no choice. I was at La
Roche Bernard, just going to drop down the river for Bellisle. When they came aboard with an order from the
Maire to take my craft as far as Ouden, they scarcely asked
me if I was willing, but drew up the anchor, and away I
was forced to go."

"How fortunate," said Henry, addressing Madame Dupré,
"that you knew this good-natured skipper!"

"Ah! I have known him many years; his family all
live, or did live, on the Count d'Ouden's property. François
is an old man-of-war man, and was a prisoner in England.
When he came back, the count enabled him to purchase a
boat, this one I dare say. He has a wife and large family;

and, with this little craft, he trades with Bellisle, and the other islands off our coast, in provisions, wine, &c."

"Yes, yes!" said the old man listening, "it's all true; I would risk my life for the family! The rascals aboard my boat wanted me to go with them to the château, to show them any hiding-place there, as they said I must know them; but I told them to go hunt themselves?"

"There's a craft coming after us, sir;" said Phelim. All looked astern; they could see the sails, on which the moon-beams fell brightly.

"It's the *Sans-Culotte* lugger," said the old man; "she's a fast craft, but I can baffle her here."

"You, madame," said Magnus, " and Rosina, had better go into the cuddy; it is comfortable, and has a stove; it is too cold here with this biting wind. I told Phelim to settle and arrange it."

"I think it is best," said Madame Dupré somewhat sadly, for she feared the pursuit of the *Sans-Culotte*, but she would not say so, not wishing to make the young lads more uneasy than necessary. Poor Rosina was perishing with cold, and the change, as she sat warming herself at the stove, raised her spirits.

"We shall just fetch clear of the Four Sands with the wind as it is now," said the old skipper, lighting his pipe and buttoning up his great pilot coat; "but we must tack when we come abreast of the Cardinal Rocks; and then, you see, we will run in between the grand reef and the ledge off the main land — there is only seven feet water at low tide, and the *Sans-Culotte* draws ten, so that she will have to work back and go round the Cardinals — we will gain a league and more of her in distance, and two hours as to time. Why, my lads, you could never have worked out of this bay as the wind now is."

" Perhaps not," said Magnus; " but we should have gone to work cautiously. I know the Cardinal Rocks lie outside us — see, they are plain enough; and, with a flood tide, and the water so smooth as this, if we touched a bank we should touch and go."

" Well, you are not far wrong, my lad. Will you have a bottle of good wine to drink, and a jacket or two, for it's cold? "

" Well, I will thank you for the wine," said Magnus; " it will do us no harm — as to the cold, we are well enough."

" Run to the locker, boy," said François Goheir to his son, " and bring a couple of bottles of the best Nantes, and a cup. Stir your legs! Stand by for a tack now," said the old man; " that lugger gains fast on us, and I want to lead him well inside the Cardinals." The chasse-mare went about in style; as she did so, the *Sans-Culotte* fired a gun, and tacked also.

" Oh! fire away, my darling!" said Phelim; " it would take a long eighteen to reach us."

" Now then, my lads," said the French skipper, after they had exhausted all the wine — Henry having also persuaded Madame Dupré and Rosina to take a little glassful and then lie down, assuring them they were quite safe from the *Sans-Culotte* — " Now then, my lads, slack the sheets, and we will make a run of it over the flat; that fellow is very nigh in shot!" In fact, as he spoke, a wreath of smoke curled out from the lugger's bows, and the ball came ricochetting along the water, right alongside.

" Not a bad shot! " said Henry Barlow, as he eased off the fore sheet. It blew very fresh, and away went the *Clemence* at a dashing rate; as she advanced, a huge dark mass of rock appeared on their larboard quarter; but to the right, a long range of sunken rock — so they judged by the white foam of the sea over it.

"You are shaving the rock close, skipper," said Magnus O'More, eyeing the heaps of scattered rocks lying around the great rock itself.

"Ay, ay, master! the closer the better!" in ten minutes the *Clemence* had cleared the narrow passage. The *Sans-Culotte* dared not attempt it; they just caught sight of her dipping her fore lug as she went in stays, and then the *Clemence* was in the open sea. "We should have sailed better," said the old man, ' if we had cast off the boat; but, you see, it won't do to lose my boat, she cost me two hundred francs."

"No!" said Henry, "I even regret our putting you to this trouble and loss of time, and I fear you will or may be called to account for aiding us."

"Bah!" said the skipper, "not they! I can say that you made me do as you pleased — four against one, though you are lads, is too much odds for an old fellow near seventy."

CHAPTER XXXII.

The *Clemence*, having now gained the open sea, hauled aft her sheets and stood for Bellisle. In a couple of hours it would be daylight. The young friends sat down under the weather bulwarks, conversing on their situation, and what was best to be done. The *Sans-Culotte* lugger was between them and the Isle Nourmontier, and would, doubtless, when the dawn made and they doubled the Cardinals, again give chase, and of course capture them.

"Perhaps," said Alfred, " we can — or at least madame can — persuade the old man to make a run across channel; he has lots of provisions aboard."

"Yes! if we could baffle the *Sans-Culotte*," said Henry; "but I trust we shall see a British cruiser."

"Well, I hope we shall, Henry," said Magnus; "for in truth, we have undergone considerable changes of fortune, but providentially escaped so far."

Whilst the friends were conversing, the dawn made, and as the sun rose the old man called out — " A large ship inside Bellisle!" All started up, and, true enough, within three miles of them was a frigate — under her three topsails, her courses hailed — standing leisurely in towards the anchorage of Palais, a strong town and fort in Bellisle.

"Ah!" said Alfred, " and here is the *Sans-Culotte* within two miles of us."

The old skipper rubbed his head; he was perplexed. The

Sans-Culotte had evidently run between some of the Cardinal Rocks. The lugger saw them, and instantly fired a gun. This attracted the frigate's attention, for she instantly threw her fore-topsail aback.

"I feel satisfied, sir," said Phelim, "that that ere ship is a French frigate. I know by the cut of her sails."

"She has no ensign flying, but she's French," said both Henry and Magnus. Alfred sighed, and went to the hatch to inquire how madame and Rosina were.

They were now close to the frigate, and their doubts were soon brought to a certainty, for an officer at once hailed them, desiring them to come alongside. "Well!" said Magnus O'More, "there is no help for it; far better surrender to a vessel of war than to the rascals in the *Sans-Culotte*."

"I agree with you there," said Henry; and then, resigned to this fresh freak of fortune, they lowered their mainsail, gib, and mizzen; and, under their foresail, dropped down quietly alongside the French frigate, whose decks were crowded with gazers. Then it was they understood why the frigate hailed them — the *Sans-Culotte* had signalized them.

Madame Dupré and Rosina, deeply chagrined, wrapped in their mantles, had come out of the fore cabin; Rosina gazing with wonder and awe at the, to her, monstrous fabric, her numerous port-holes, and her towering masts. But Madame Dupré, as she looked up, with a feeling of relief perceived two or three female heads looking over the quarter-deck bulwarks at them.

When the chasse-mare was made fast alongside, an officer slung down the side, and, looking at the young midshipmen, said, "I perceive you are English naval officers — midshipmen — escaping, I suppose!"

"Such is the case," said Henry; "this lady and young girl are French." The officer bowed politely.

"How is this, skipper!" continued the Frenchman sternly, "that you are found assisting at the escape of prisoners?"

"Ha!" said the old man with a laugh, "if you were seventy years of age, you would not find it an easy matter to resist four stout youngsters like these. I had no choice in the matter."

"The old man speaks truth," said Magnus O'More; "we seized his boat!"

"Well!" said the officer, "he could not help it, at that rate. Now, madame and mademoiselle, permit me to assist you aboard; you will find some of your own sex there to receive you, and you may all depend on receiving kind attention from Captain Lenois Durand. And you, skipper, may put back."

"Well, I am bound for Palais," said François Goheir, with a very chagrined expression of countenance, and afraid to show any interest in the prisoners.

In a few minutes they were all aboard the *Unité*, thirty-six-gun frigate, commanded by as gallant and generous an officer as any in the service of France or England. The chasse-mare was cast off, and the three friends beheld the poor skipper and his son hoist their foresail and run in for Palais. The *Sans-Culotte*, also, to their great surprise, put about and stood in for the land.

As Madame Dupré and Rosina gained the quarter-deck of the frigate, Captain Lenois Durand approached, and, with a great deal of kindness of manner, expressed his regret at being obliged to fulfil his duty; he then introduced them both to Madame le Large, wife of the Governor of Rochefort, who, with her three daughters and domestics, were on their way to that port. Madame le Large's son it was who boarded the chasse-mare.

In the mean time, whilst this scene was taking place on the quarter-deck, the three youths were objects of curiosity to the officers of the *Unité*. The first lieutenant questioned them as to what ship they belonged—Magnus still wore the somewhat tarnished uniform of a midshipman. Magnus replied that he belonged to the *Thames*, captured by the *Carmagnole*, and that his two companions were young gentlemen — one the son of a captain in the navy, driven out to sea in a boat, and taken aboard a privateer, which was lost on the coast of France; "but our story is rather too long a one to keep you listening to now, monsieur; we endeavored to escape — as you, doubtless, would do, but fortune is against us."

"You interest me very much," said the lieutenant; "you are prisoners certainly, but I can assure you of good treatment; and, no doubt, you will be exchanged very shortly after we arrive at Rochefort; we are waiting for our boat we sent in to Palais."

Nothing could be more fortunate for our fugitives than their stumbling on the *Unité* frigate — they were left perfectly at liberty, treated with great kindness, and messed with the officers, who appeared greatly taken with their appearance and manners.

Madame le Large showed every attention to Madame Dupré and Rosina; one of her daughters being of the same age, soon became familiar with her, but Rosina fretted at the misfortunes of Henry and his friends, and at her own disappointment in not getting to England to rejoin her dear mother. The little girl, however, was blessed with a wonderful power of mind for her early age; and her beauty and sweet engaging manner rendered her at once an object of attraction; and, when Captain Lenois Durand heard her story, and that her parents were in England, he secretly resolved to get her and Madame Dupré a passage to that country, by some means or another.

The *Unité* remained all that day and night lying to off Palais — a town and citadel that surrendered to the English after a long siege, about forty-six years previous to our story. During the evening Captain Lenois Durand sent for the three friends to his cabin ; and, after some conversation, requested to know their adventures, as Madame Dupré had greatly interested him concerning them. Henry and Alfred told them briefly, and Magnus O'More merely confined his story to the period of his escape from the *Thames* to his joining his two fellow-captives at Nantes.

"Upon my word," said Captain Durand, "you have really had some severe trials, and you have borne them with energy and courage. I regret I cannot restore you to liberty ; but, on our arrival at Rochefort, I will exert myself to procure your exchange. I consider the conduct of your jailers at Nantes abominable, and I am certain if Colonel Moreau can, he will punish the governor of that prison ; I will write to him on the subject."

That evening there was no constraint or hinderance to our young friends conversing and remaining with Madame Dupré and Rosina. Madame le Large took quite a fancy to the little girl, and was also greatly struck with the fine handsome persons of the three young lads.

The next morning the frigate was under way for Rochefort, with a fresh breeze from the north-east. Our three friends were on deck. Phelim, having found one or two of the French crew who could talk English, made himself quite at home, and they seemed much pleased with him. No sooner, however, had the frigate stood out clear of the Island of Bellisle, and opened the broad expanse of ocean, than a large ship was seen standing to the south-east. Henry Barlow immediately called Alfred and Magnus to look at her. "That," said he, "is an English cruiser, as sure as fate!"

The first lieutenant of the *Unité* was regarding the stranger earnestly, and then went below and spoke to the captain, for they both came on deck immediately, and the captain also had a look through his glass at the stranger. The *Unité* was now evidently seen by the stranger, for she at once tacked, and then the topsails of another large ship came into sight.

Captain Durand now ordered every stitch of canvas to be packed on the *Unité*, declaring that the stranger was the leading ship of an English squadron — and the frigate's course shaped for the Island of Nourmontier. The stranger followed, under a cloud of canvas; but, just as the *Unité* got abreast of Nourmontier, the wind shifted several points, and blew out a topsail breeze from the land.

The stranger came rapidly up with the same breeze. Captain Lenois Durand would have run in for Rochelle, but the land breeze came out so strong as to force him to take in his topgallant sails. In the mean time, the stranger, with the English colors plainly visible, came rapidly up, also reducing her canvas. It was now very evident to Captain Durand that the English frigate would soon close with him; and it was also seen by every one aboard, that she was far too powerful an antagonist for the *Unité* to contend against with the slightest certainty of success.

The three lads kept their eyes steadily fixed upon the advancing frigate; Alfred pressed Henry's hand when he clearly made out the English ensign.

"Oh, dear Henry!" he whispered, "there is now a chance of seeing dear England and our parents again. What a noble ship!"

"I rejoice," said Henry, "of course; but, after the kindness we have received, I feel poor Captain Durand's disappointment, for this fine frigate is greatly his superior; but run down and tell Rosina not to be frightened supposing they do fire, but I scarcely think Captain Durand will uselessly sacrifice his men."

"Oh, yes!" said Magnus, coming up and hearing the last words; "yes, he will fight; there is no knowing the chances of war. I would fight if in his situation."

Captain Durand preferred to fight his ship; it was contrary to the express orders of the revolutionary government to lower the tricolor without a struggle. Alfred was gone below; Henry and Magnus were leaning over the bulwarks gazing at the frigate, then nearly within musket-shot, when Captain Durand laid his hand on Magnus O'More's shoulder, saying very kindly — "You are very likely, my lads, to experience a change of fortune. You had better go below."

"Pray, monsieur," said Henry, "permit us to remain; we have always been accustomed to face fire, not to retire from it."

"You are brave lads, I know," returned the commander of the *Unité*, "when in the face of an enemy; but to be knocked down by one's friends is disagreeable."

"Still, Captain Durand, with your permission we will remain," said Magnus. The captain smiled, and turned away.

The frigate, which was now known to be the *Revolutionaire*, soon ran within speaking-distance, when her commander very gallantly and humanely stood upon a gun-carriage and hailed; requesting to know if the French commander would surrender, as the force against him was overwhelming, another frigate coming rapidly up.

No sooner did Henry Barlow get a clear view of the captain of the *Revolutionaire*, and heard his voice, than, with an exclamation of intense joy, he caught Magnus by the arm, saying, "God be praised! I have seen and heard my dear father. He commands the *Revolutionaire*, no doubt."

"Your father!" returned Magnus, equally amazed; "how singular!" At that moment Captain Durand waved his hat in reply, and then the English ship opened fire.

Alfred joined them — "Dear friend," said Henry to his cousin, "do go below!"

"What!" said Alfred in a tone of reproach, his cheek flushing and his eye kindling; "what! after the examples I have received — oh, no! my weakness and timidity are gone for ever!" As he spoke, one of the shots of the *Revolutionaire* tore up the bulwark where they stood, scattering the fragments into the air, dismounting a gun, and killing two gunners. At the same time Henry looked into his cousin's face — the eye never quailed, neither did his color change.

"It's all up with the *Unité*, and this is a useless waste of life," said Henry, as a terrible broadside from the forty-four-gun frigate tore over the decks of the French ship, stretching numbers dead and wounded on her blood-stained planks.

"We have done enough for the honor of the flag," said Captain Durand with a sigh. "Haul down our colors!" and then the firing ceased.

Henry pressed Alfred's hand with a joyful pressure; he would not show his joy before the officers of the French frigate, who looked, with their commander, deeply chagrined. With intense anxiety Henry remained upon the quarter-deck, whilst Captain Durand paced the sacred precincts with a disturbed and serious air. The crew were removing the killed and wounded, and clearing the decks; some, leaning with vexed looks over the bulwark, regarding the *Revolutionaire*. She was lying to, close beside them. Alfred went below to see Madame Dupré and Rosina, and tell them of their change of destiny.

Approaching Captain Durand, Henry said — speaking with the greatest respect —

" Sir, the commander of yonder frigate is my father ! "

" Indeed ! " said the captain, with an air of surprise. " You are fortunate, my good lad, and I hope you will find your father unhurt. We have surrendered, but," casting his eyes over the waters, and directing Henry's attention to another frigate coming rapidly up — " but there is no disgrace in yielding to a vastly superior force ; the *Revolution-aire* alone is a forty-four-gun frigate ! "

" No, monsieur ! " returned Henry, " it would have been a waste of life ; but I am sure my father will be most grateful for the generosity and kindness you have shown us."

" I feel satisfied of that, my brave youth," returned the captain, pressing Henry's shoulder kindly. " A gallant son is sure to spring from a brave sire ! For myself, I have nothing to ask ; but I should wish Madame le Large to be restored to her husband, for they are exceedingly attached."

" Oh ! I am so rejoiced," said Henry, with a pleased look, " that it may be in my father's power to return the kindness I have received." He could say no more, for the boats of the *Revolutionaire* came to take possession of their prize.

22

Two hours after the surrender of the *Unité*, the two vessels were under way for England. Need we paint the
surprise, the wonder, and joy of the father, when he clasped
his beloved and only son in his arms? He could scarcely
believe the evidence of his senses — it appeared a dream.
The following day, Madame le Large, her family and domestics, were put aboard a neutral vessel bound for Rochelle,
from whence she could easily rejoin her husband. Madame
le Large took an affectionate leave of Rosina, and expressed
her deep gratitude to Captain Barlow for his generosity and
kindness in restoring her to liberty and to her husband.

Captain Durand, his officers and men, received every
attention; they were neither stripped of their clothes nor
valuables, all were restored to them — indeed, so overjoyed
was Captain Barlow, that if he could, without infringing on
the rules of the service, he would have restored them all to
their liberties. With Magnus O'More, Captain Barlow was
highly pleased, and showed him every kindness as the friend
of his son. The now happy Rosina and Madame Dupré had
a state cabin to themselves.

During the voyage to Plymouth, Captain Barlow listened
to Henry's and Alfred's adventures with amused and delighted surprise; but when he heard the name of Driver he
started, and when Henry had finished, he said, " So that was
the name of your privateer skipper — Driver! Well, now I

think I can account for that man's ferocity to you both. He must be the same man, from his expressions and language to you, Henry. Some fourteen years ago, I commanded the *Sheldrake* — we were on the West-Indian station — we had lost a great many men by fever, the yellow-fever, and we were glad to pick up a few able seamen to replace them. I took aboard, at Jamaica, a man who gave his name as John Wild; he was then about thirty; there was no mistake about his being a sailor, and a good one, and of a superior class; though a violent, vindictive, rough customer. When at sea a few days, some of our men below, sick, recovered and came on deck — ' Hallo, messmate !' said one of them, stopping and addressing John Wild, ' you here — John Driver !' Dozens of the men heard him, and they laughed. ' No, no !' said they, ' this is not John Driver, but John Wild !' John Wild tried to bully and outswear the other, but he was not to be put down; I heard of the affair, and sent for Richard Dixon, the same man that recognized Driver. ' Where did you know this man ?' I questioned. ' Known him for the last five years, sir; and lost sight of him just before I shipped aboard the *Sheldrake* — he was then first mate of a Liverpool bark.'

" I called up the man, but he was almost insolent; he stuck to his name being Wild, and there I left it. This fellow, from his violent, brutal temper, was in perpetual scrapes. I let him off a dozen times, till at last he beat the man Dixon so severely, and used such outrageous language to one of the officers, that I had him up and gave him three dozen. I rarely flogged, very rarely, indeed — not three times in my life. This man's face was livid with rage when cast off; he seemed inclined to speak, but I turned away, and the very first opportunity I dismissed him the ship. Touching at Jamaica some months after, I learned that this same Driver — for that was his name — had stabbed a black in a quarrel; he did not die, luckily, but Driver fled his ship and entered as a seaman aboard the *Sheldrake*. Now, when you, Henry, said your name was Barlow, and the son of Captain Barlow, he remembered me, and showed his malice to you. I will make inquiries; perhaps he escaped from the wreck of the privateer."

"No," said Henry; "not one in the boat was picked up by those in the other boat."

"You see, my dear nephew," said Captain Barlow, laying his hand on Alfred's shoulder, "how with energy, perseverance, courage, and faith, misfortunes may not only be endured, but even conquered. With all your kindness of heart, you were giving way to an inertness and indolence of disposition, which it is natural to suppose would have increased to a baneful degree; so that, if your future life did not become miserable, it would, at all events, have rendered you but a useless member of society. Example and affection, and a naturally good heart, has, I trust, conquered the defect of your temper and disposition; and, with a sensible mind, you may yet live to remember the cruise of the *Fury*, and with a feeling of gladness that you were put to such trials, and out of which you have come safe, and, I am sure, benefited."

"Indeed, uncle," returned Alfred, with a glow upon his cheek, "but for the bright example of Henry, and his patient endurance of all we had to undergo, his unceasing love, and consoling advice, I had sunk under my sufferings. You may depend I shall never again give way to the slothful indolence I before so indulged in."

"But tell me, dear father," said Henry, "how you came to command this ship, and what you thought at the time of our strange disappearance — Ah! my poor mother! how she must have fretted."

"Yes," returned the captain, "she did so. As to Alfred's parents, they were distracted; but I positively insisted that you would yet turn up. When the fog came on that evening, Mr. Pearson and I were on a ramble to examine a druidical remnant of antiquity. When we came back the fog had set in, and I heard that you were not returned from St. Agnes; half an hour after, the light-house boat arrived at St. Mary's to say that you were out in the fog, and that it was impossible to find you, for they lost their own way. I was not alarmed, for the water was smooth, and the wind light; however, I got the yacht under way, took two pilots aboard, and stood out, firing guns, as you heard; but, as you were picked up by that rascally privateer, of course I could not find you, though I remained out all the next day. Still I flattered myself you were picked up, perhaps by some vessel bound foreign. When I returned to Penzance, I had a terrible task to communicate with Alfred's parents; finally, being solicited by the government and by Lord B——, an old friend, and one of the lords of the Admiralty, I accepted the command of this ship, and sailed for the coast of France; and thus, providentially, I rescued you all from perhaps a long imprisonment."

After a rapid passage, the *Revolutionaire* anchored with her prize in Plymouth Sound, whence a messenger was sent on at once to Deer Park, the residence of Mr. and Mrs. Hammond, so that Alfred might not take them by surprise; also a letter to Mrs. Barlow. Captain Barlow insisted on Madame Dupré and Rosina taking up their residence at Myrtle Hill with Mrs. Barlow, till inquiries were made for the Count and Countess Delancy and the Countess d'Ouden.

Magnus and Phelim were now upon British soil. Captain Barlow pressed the young midshipman to pass some time with Henry before he went to sea again, Henry and Alfred warmly seconding Captain Barlow's wishes. Magnus most willingly assented, but wished first to visit Captain Broomsley — gratitude to his early benefactor was his first thought, his next, to be again appointed to a ship. The young midshipman had but one great object in life, and that perpetually occupied his mind. He thirsted to become a man, and to rise in his profession — he never for a moment forgot that a slur rested on his own and his mother's name; to clear that away was his aim through life. Taking an affectionate leave of his friends, Henry and his faithful follower set out for Torquay. Before departure, Captain Barlow gave him a letter to a very old friend, Lord C——, then one of the lords of the Admiralty. "When you go up to London," said Captain Barlow, "deliver that in person; depend upon it, when you pass your examination, you will receive your appointment as lieutenant."

Captain Broomsley, his wife, and son, received Magnus with the warmth and affection of relations, whilst Magnus himself felt all the love of a child for his parent. Charles Broomsley was grown into a fine lad. All listened with delight and wonder to his adventures. Phelim, anxious to see his parents, left for Ireland; and Magnus, as it was his duty, proceeded to report himself and present his letter to Lord C——. Phelim was to return after a few days' stay with his parents, and meet Magnus at Broomsley Lodge. Magnus O'More was supplied with funds by Captain Broomsley, but he was entitled to a considerable sum in prize-money.

After making sundry additions to his wardrobe, Magnus O'More set out on his visit to Lord C——; who resided in —— Square. It happened, very fortunately, that Lord

C—— was one of those men, of the aristocratic class, who do receive visitors having no pretentions either to rank or station; he was also a nobleman who, in early life, served his country well, and had a great pride in the well-being and honor of the navy. Lord C—— seemed struck with the graceful and handsome person of the young midshipman.

"Take a chair, Mr. O'More," said his lordship. Lord C—— then asked him several questions respecting the different ships he had served in, and was very particular in his inquiries concerning the capture of the *Thames*, of which he required a minute account, and seemed greatly pleased with Magnus's narrative of her captain and his escape. "Captain Barlow mentions, after your escape from the *Thames*, that you had a severe imprisonment in the prison of Nantes; how did you escape?"

Magnus was thus drawn on, by degrees, till he related all his and young Henry Barlow's adventures in Brittany, which greatly amused his lordship. "Well, young gentleman, you certainly, for your age, have had your share of perilous adventures, out of which you have managed to get extremely well; and, no doubt, your family will be greatly rejoiced at your safe return. I suppose you are most anxious to visit your parents before you seek further employment?"

Magnus's ingenuous features betrayed his feelings at these words. He had no parents — no ties — save those of gratitude! Lord C—— perceived the change in the features of Magnus O'More, and the look of dejection that followed his words.

"I fear," said his lordship kindly — for he was an extremely generous and kind-hearted nobleman — "that I have pained you; pardon me if I have. You are perhaps an orphan?"

" I am, my lord ! "

His lordship paused a moment ; and, taking up Captain Barlow's letter, he read a few lines, laid it down, and, looking attentively into his visitor's features, said, —

" Your's is a very old Irish name — the title of Courtown is, I believe, in your family ; the present Lord Courtown of Courtown and I travelled for some months in Germany ; he was a very eccentric man, but still a very clever and agreeable travelling companion.   He has lately married, I understand — a somewhat late period of life for encountering the perils of matrimony ; for I think I am not more than two or three years his senior.   From what part of Ireland are you, Mr. O'More ? "

" The county of Galway, my lord.   My father's "— and Magnus's cheek flushed — " My lamented father's mansion is on the banks of Lough Corrib."

" Dear me ! " exclaimed Lord C——, with considerable animation ; " then you, possibly, are the son of the Mr. Roderick O'More, who was a great friend of the Marquis of Buckingham's, and who was most lamentably and unfortunately killed by a fall from his horse in the castle-yard ; he was riding a very high-spirited horse at the time, and just "— his lordship paused, saying — " but, no doubt, you heard all the particulars at the time, though you, of course, were very young."

" No, my lord," said Magnus, in a tone of bitterness that at once struck Lord C—— ; " they took care I should hear as little as possible."

" How is this, young gentleman ? " said Lord C—— ; " Captain Barlow hints in his letter that your's is a strange history," — a clock over the mantelpiece struck one — " Ha ! " said his lordship, rising, " I was forgetting.   There is important news in this letter.   I feel interested in you,

Mr. O'More; you must serve another year, and, as I have no doubt whatever of your passing your examination, you shall, provided we both live, immediately receive your appointment as lieutenant aboard a ship where you will have an opportunity of distinguishing yourself if this war lasts. Now, let me see you at seven o'clock this evening, to dinner; there are only two or three members of my family in town: I wish to hear your own story, for I was in Dublin at the period of your father's death, which created a great deal of talk at the time, and much affected the viceroy."

Magnus was greatly surprised, and much moved by Lord C——'s kindness. The young midshipman had an easy and naturally graceful manner in expressing himself, which greatly pleased, and never failed in creating an interest. His reply, therefore, pleased his lordship; and he left the mansion of Lord C——, greatly elated at the kind and unexpected reception he had met, and fully determined in his own mind, should his lordship request it, to relate without any reserve the full particulars of his early days.

Passing along Piccadilly he turned down St. James's Street, proceeding to his hotel, *The Golden Cross*, in the Strand. As he came opposite St. James's palace, he took it into his head to have a turn in the park, in order to digest and arrange the confusion of thoughts that troubled his brain. At the period of our story, St. James's Park was a very fashionable place of resort at a certain hour of the day. As Magnus O'More passed up the fashionable avenue, he was soon diverted from his thoughts by the groups of elegant and aristocratic-looking persons that he passed. Wishing to be alone, however, he turned down a shady avenue, seemingly deserted; but, after a few paces along its path, he came suddenly face to face with two remarkably beautiful girls. One, in particular, so struck him by her youth and exquisite loveliness, that, without reflecting, he paused in his walk. As he did so, the two young girls, who were followed at a little distance by a lady and two gentlemen, and who were earnestly conversing, looked up, and the dark, brilliant eyes of the youngest, who could not be more than fifteen, rested for an instant on the expressive and equally dark eyes of Magnus. As their eyes met, the young girl looked bewildered, and started back, changing color. Thinking his unintentional rudeness in pausing in their path caused this start and change of color, Magnus's features were also heightened in color, as, instinctively lifting his hat from his head, he passed on ; but scarcely had he made ten paces, and confronted the lady and two gentlemen, than he again paused, with a feeling of indignation and passion on his youthful features. Both gentlemen halted in their walk, facing Magnus, who remained right in their path. One was a young man, about one or two and twenty, over-dressed, and covered with jewelry ; the other, about forty, also elaborately dressed, but with the air, manner, and look of a *roué ;* the lady was very elegantly attired, but rather showily, and was in years about forty or so. The eldest of the two gentlemen looked up, and regarded Magnus at first with a look as much as to say — " Why do you block up our path ? " but the moment he clearly saw the midshipman's features, which bore still a vivid and striking resemblance to his boyhood, and contrasted remarkably, from their youthfulness, with his tall, graceful figure — than he staggered back, turning deadly pale, and grasping the arm of his companion forcibly.

"I see, Mr. Hamilton," said Magnus, bitterly, "that I have not outgrown your remembrance ; it is more than seven years since we met."

" Sir, I know you not ! " exclaimed Mr. Hamilton, making an effort to recover himself, though his voice trembled from agitation.

The lady and the two young girls, who had retraced their steps, stood bewildered and rather startled; but the young girl with the hazel eyes, and the dark brown curls that half-shaded her sweet features, stood with breathless anxiety gazing upon Magnus.

"Who is this person?" said the younger gentleman fiercely. "Who are you, sir?" he added, turning to Magnus, with a contemptuous curl of his lip, "that so rudely bars our path."

"Sir!" calmly returned Magnus, and, raising his hat, he bowed to the ladies — "You ask me who I am — that person by your side could tell you — my name is Roderick Magnus O'More!"

"You are an impostor!" fiercely exclaimed the young man, his face flushing with passion — whilst the young girl before noticed, said in a low clear voice, "Ah! I thought so."

"You are an impostor! there is no such person now living as Roderick Magnus O'More — leave our path, or I will summon the keepers of the park!"

"Were you not in company of these ladies," said Magnus O'More, still calmly, "I would break this stick across your back; as it is, I entreat their pardon, and leave you."

"And take that with you, as a remembrance of me," furiously exclaimed the young man; and, lifting his walking-stick, he aimed a desperate blow at the midshipman's face; but the cane was caught by Magnus in his right hand, and, with a powerful jerk, wrenched from the striker.

A faint cry from the ladies made Magnus pause; the elder lady threw herself before the young man, saying, "Wretch that you are — dare to strike my son!"

This scene had now attracted attention, and several persons were coming quickly along the avenue. Magnus perceived that the young lady that had so attracted his gaze looked pale and agitated; therefore, breaking the cane in bits, he cast it on the path, and with the recollection of the cruel wrongs he had endured, and the misery he had suffered through the instrumentality of Mr. Hamilton, he quitted the park; and troubled and disturbed, yet still retaining the words uttered by the young girl in his memory — words strange enough to him, simple as they were — he hastened to his hotel.

CHAPTER XXXIV.

"So, then," thought Magnus O'More as he threw himself into a chair in his chamber in the hotel — "after seven years I have come face to face with the heartless wretch that tore me from my home, and consigned me, as he thought, to misery and degradation; seeking even to crush my memory of the past, by forcing me into a life of toil and infamy; hoping, perhaps, that I should perish under such an infliction; but Providence shielded and preserved me, and I may yet live to hurl back my wrongs on the heads of those who plotted my destruction! But who was that young girl?" soliloquized Magnus, as he jumped up and paced the room. "That sweet, lovely face, floats before me, and the words — 'Ah, I thought so!' did she mean she knew my name was O'More, or what?" For more than an hour Magnus sat communing with his thoughts, till at last he roused himself, took paper and pen, and wrote a long letter to his patron, Captain Broomsley, stating, among other matters, his very satisfactory interview with Lord C——, and ending by saying he hoped to see him and his generous-hearted wife in a day or two.

Magnus then proceeded in a hackney-coach, as it rained a little, to Lord C——'s residence. His lordship had not returned from the House when Magnus arrived (a quarter before seven o'clock); there was a lively debate that evening, and Lord C—— remained to hear the end of Mr.

P——'s speech on the proposal of peace with France. Magnus was shown up into the drawing-room, where he was received by Lady C—— with considerable cordiality, saying, she was aware he was expected, and hoped his lordship would not be detained, as he was the previous evening, till near eleven o'clock.

Magnus O'More, though very young and with very little knowledge of society, was still quite free from bashfulness or timidity in meeting total strangers: he therefore answered Lady C——, who was a remarkably fine and pleasing woman, though near fifty-six, with ease, and yet with strict attention to their respective ranks and age.

Lady C—— had heard from her lord that he had invited to join their family party a young midshipman, who had recently returned from France after meeting some rather romantic adventures there. She therefore felt naturally curious and interested; both feelings increased by the very prepossessing appearance of the young midshipman.

The conversation she purposely turned upon France, where she herself had spent some time before the breaking-out of the war. In the midst of a very animating conversation the drawing-room door opened, and two ladies entered the room. Magnus rose up as Lady C—— introduced her youngest daughter and niece; but, as Magnus bowed and raised his eyes, he started, and looked a little dismayed, whilst Lady C——'s niece — whom she introduced as the Honorable Miss Germain — stood actually confounded, looking pale and disconcerted.

It was impossible for Lady C—— or her daughter — a very elegant girl of eighteen — not to perceive the embarrassment of both parties; her ladyship looked seriously from one to the other, as if for explanation, when Magnus, perceiving that Miss Germain really suffered, said —

"Your ladyship is surprised, no doubt, at my embarrassment and Miss Germain's confusion ; she was witness to-day, in St. James's Park, of a most unpleasant occurrence, in which, unfortunately, I acted a principal part."

"But undoubtedly, not your fault, sir," said Miss Germain, making an effort and speaking eagerly, and her cheek no longer pale ; "if you will permit me, another time I will explain this matter to my aunt."

Magnus bowed.

"Well, upon my word!" said Lady C—— with a smile. "Mr. O'More, it appears that you are keeping up your adventures in this country as well as in France. Really, Emily, you must not keep my curiosity on the stretch— you will spoil my appetite for dinner ; so unburden your conscience at once, or permit Mr. O'More to do so."

"Oh, no, indeed!" said the young lady very eagerly: "there are ladies concerned in this, and, — and indeed, aunt," she added, trying to laugh, "it's a very simple affair, and the ladies do not wish their names mentioned."

Magnus was just hoping that the ladies' names would be mentioned ; however, determined to make some explanation, he said, "I should be very sorry, Miss Germain, to urge you to say any thing about this unpleasant affair ; the fact is, your ladyship," he added, turning to the mystified Lady C——, "the fact is, I encountered this morning, in St. James's Park, a gentleman who once did me a grievous wrong ; I spoke to him as I felt, and a young man in his company lifted his cane to strike me ; I merely took his stick from him, broke it, and quitted the park, regretting disturbing the ladies present — Miss Germain was one."

"Lady C—— remained a moment very thoughtful ; but, suddenly looking up, said with a smile, "Well, we must not let this little incident disturb our harmony. I know the party now, Emily, so my curiosity is partly satisfied; but here is Lord C——" (as she spoke, a carriage stopped at the door, and the loud aristocratic summons of the footman announced the importance of his office).

Shortly after, just as Magnus was getting into conversation with the ladies, whose embarrassment was wearing off, his lordship entered the room.

"Ah! Mr. O'More," said Lord C——, holding out his hand very cordially, "I am glad to see you; I have very good news for you. You must proceed to Portsmouth at once and pass your examination; you will then be appointed third lieutenant of the *Terpsichore*, Captain Richard Bowen, as brave an officer as ever lived. I find you are the midshipman who behaved so gallantly aboard the ——, and saved the ship being blown up by what might have been a sacrifice of your life. You have only a few months to complete your time, and as the period passed in France, and what you went through there, &c., will be included, you are all right; before this day week I hope to salute you as Lieutenant O'More, and before long hear more of your exploits, for the *Terpsichore* sails in ten days."

Magnus O'More was indeed astonished; but at once returned his lordship his most grateful acknowledgments, saying it was an appointment his most sanguine hopes could little anticipate for several years.

"O my young friend!" said his lordship, "I hope to see you a commander by that time; so now let us to dinner, for I assure you Mr. P——'s speech would give any one a most furious appetite, not only for dinner, but for war; as to peace after that speech, it's out of the question — so, *Allons!*" The domestic, throwing open the doors, his lordship with a smile said, "I leave my daughter and niece to your care, Mr. O'More;" and, taking his smiling lady on his arm, they proceeded to the dining-room.

Lord C—— was one of the most domestic noblemen in England; he married early in life from love. Lady C—— was the daughter of the rector of D——. Lord C—— was then a commander, and a very gallant, high-spirited officer; he became a rear-admiral, and afterwards succeeded a cousin in his title and property, which was very considerable. Lord C—— had no son, but two grandsons; his eldest daughter married Lord Fitzormond, an Irish nobleman of large estates; his second daughter was married to Sir Edgar Tempest, a baronet of good family, high Tory principles, and an M.P.; his youngest daughter was just eighteen. and a most amiable young lady. The Honorable Emily Germain was the orphan daughter of his sister, who married Lord Germain. At the age of seven years Emily lost both parents, and was left under the guardianship of her uncle; she had just returned from a visit at Courtown Castle. Lady Courtown, residing in London during some months, became extremely intimate with Lady C——, and prevailed upon her to permit Emily to pass the summer months with her at Courtown.

The dinner passed off exceedingly well and pleasantly. The young ladies were most agreeable; Miss Germain plainly showed, as she freely conversed with Magnus O'More, that no impression was left on her mind to his disadvantage, owing to the meeting on the park. Magnus longed to ask her who the beautiful girl was that had then so forcibly attracted his attention; but he refrained from delicacy, having heard Miss Germain say that the ladies did not wish their names mentioned. After the ladies had retired, Lord C—— and his guest sat sipping their wine.

At first the conversation turned upon nautical affairs. "You

23

will have better class frigates in future," said Lord C——.
" We have resolved to give the ships greater length, in pro-
portion to their breadth ; for I perceive the complaint against
all English men-of-war is, their bad sailing qualities."

" We do not, certainly, my lord," said Magnus, " as far
as my experience goes, sail well in comparison with the French
frigates, but we outcarry them in heavy weather. There's
the *Unité*" continued Magnus, " she was formerly the French
frigate *Imperieuse*. She outsails, an officer told me, every
ship she competes with ; and that under her topsails only.

" Yes," said Lord C——, " so I have heard. She was
cut out of Spezzia by the boats of the *Captain*, seventy-four.
Still," continued his lordship, " with all our disparity in sailing, we have captured nearly one hundred and fifty armed
vessels since the war — fifty of these belong to the national
navy — and we have not lost a ship of greater force than the
Thames you were aboard of; but this is a dry subject for one
so young as you. Talking of the *Thames* puts me in mind
of a request I have to make, and that is, if not disagreeable
to you, to let me hear your private history. If you are the
son of Mr. O'More of Ashgrove, county Galway, it is a
most incomprehensible thing how your uncle, Mr. Gorman
O'More, holds the estates."

Magnus replied — " My lord, I shall state to you without
any reserve all that is known to me of the past. My recollections of an early period are very vivid, because — from the
time of my being taken from my home, just after my lamented father's death — I have been in the daily habit of
recalling to my mind every circumstance that has occurred ;
but I will let your lordship judge for yourself." Magnus
O'More, therefore, made his lordship fully acquainted with
his early history up to the period of the capture of the *Thames* ;
his lordship seemed greatly struck, and remained for some
moments in deep thought.

"You have certainly," said his lordship, looking up, "been treated with great cruelty and neglect, even admitting you were not entitled to the heirship of the O'More Estates. But if it is any relief to your mind, I assure you it is my belief that you are. Your father was too honorable a man to have acted as your uncle wishes it to be supposed he did; that he found some terrible difficulty in procuring proofs of his marriage with your mother, there is no doubt. At present I see no earthly possibility for you to make good your claims. Therefore my advice is — Have patience; you are very young; Providence, in its own good time and way, brings things, when little thought of, to light. I shall, I assure you, feel interested in your welfare; and I now advise you to banish from your mind for the present all memory of the past; give your mind and heart to your profession, and let no vain regrets disturb your self-possession : and, depend on it, if it pleases God to spare your life, a bright career is before you. You will make a name for yourself!"

Magnus O'More was deeply sensible of his lordship's kindness and condescension; they were not mere words, for there was a hearty cordiality in his tone and manner that made a deep impression on him; and he showed it in his manner and his reply to his lordship's advice.

"Now, my young friend, let us join the ladies," said his lordship. "I am a very domesticated man, and, except on certain unavoidable occasions, we see little company. In a few days we go into Dorsetshire."

On entering the drawing-room, Magnus perceived the two young ladies at the pianoforte. Magnus was a natural musician, but too young to have had a fair opportunity of testing his talents; but he loved music dearly, and often regretted how few opportunities he enjoyed of listening to it. Lord C——'s daughter was playing when he entered the room and approached the piano.   Without pausing, she looked up, and, with a lively undisturbed air, said, " Are you fond of music, Mr. O'More? though, indeed, as you are an Irishman, I need scarcely have asked that question."

" Then do you suppose, Miss C——, that all my country-men are born musical?"

" I really never met one," said Miss C——, " that was not; and my Cousin Emily here — who has just returned from spending eight months in the Emerald Isle — tells me that all the peasantry, especially the female portion of them, have great taste for music, and sing such beautiful melodies that they quite captivated her."

" What part of Ireland," said Magnus, looking into the beautiful face of the Honorable Miss Germain, " have you visited? "

" A very romantic and picturesque part of Galway," said the young lady. " I was on a visit at Courtown Castle, on the banks of Lough Corrib — do you know that part of Ireland? " and Magnus thought the beautiful eyes of the speaker rested on his with a meaning look.

" Yes ! " returned the midshipman, though not without betraying emotion in his voice and manner — " I was born on the borders of Lough Corrib, and nearly within sight of the place you mention."

" But you must have left your home very, very young," said Lord C——'s daughter; " for I think you said four or five years of your life were spent in the East and West Indies. You must indeed have gone to sea quite a boy."

" Not younger, Miss C——, than boys generally go who become midshipmen. I was, I suppose, at least thirteen."

" Dear me ! what an age," said Miss Germain, " to be tossed about upon the ocean, and thrust amid the horrors of war; but let us join my aunt at the tea-table, we take it here in the old-fashioned way, you may perceive."

"Emily," said Miss C——, laying her hand on Miss Germain's arm, "just play Mr. O'More that little melody you picked up from the pretty Irish girl, Bessy M'Farlane."

At that name Magnus O'More's face glowed with the rush of blood to his cheeks. Bessy M'Farlane was the sister of Phelim — how did Miss Germain meet with her? But neither of the young ladies appeared to notice his change of color, or the start he gave. Miss Germain played with exquisite taste, adding her voice to one of those common airs, since rendered so popular and fascinating by the poet Moore. Magnus listened till he felt he could almost shed tears; his early childhood rose before him with such intense vividness, that he trembled with emotion.

"Come, Mr. O'More," said Miss Germain, suddenly pausing and looking with a world of kindly expression into his serious features, "it will not always do to revive the past."

At the tea-table the conversation became general. Magnus shook off the feelings that bewildered him, and, when he rose to take his leave, he left them all deeply interested in himself and his future welfare. The two fair girls very frankly and kindly took leave of him, and Magnus — he could not well account for it — felt a feeling of depression steal over him as the door closed upon their graceful forms. Entering the study, where Lord C—— sent for him, he found his lordship sealing a letter.

"Well, Mr. O'More, we are going to part; but believe me, as I told you before, I shall keep you in view. This letter," handing the midshipman one, "you will give to Captain the Honorable D'Arcy Winton as soon after you reach Portsmouth as you possibly can." His lordship then bade him farewell with an exceeding kindness of manner, telling him the sooner he reached Portsmouth the better.

Magnus O'More left London the following morning, and reached Portsmouth the same day. He then wrote long letters to his dear friends Henry and Alfred, and paid a short visit to Captain Broomsley, who was delighted with his prospects. He also wrote to Phelim M'Farlane's father, and to Phelim, to join him in ten days at Plymouth.

Magnus O'More passed his examination with considerable éclat, was taken by the hand by the Honorable D'Arcy Winton, and finally proceeded to join the *Terpsichore*, Captain Richard Bowen. Phelim arrived in time, and shipped as able seaman; and, a few days afterwards, the frigate sailed for the Mediterranean.

The further fortunes, exploits, and adventures of Roderick Magnus O'More — should our young readers feel interested in his fate — will form the subject of another volume.

In our next chapter we close the fortunes of our young adventurers — Henry and Alfred.

CHAPTER XXXV.

In the quiet and beautiful residence of Myrtle Hill, Rosina Delancy rapidly recovered from the effects of all she had gone through at such an early age. Inquiries were at once set on foot in order to trace the residence, if she had reached England, of the Countess Delancy; and, as Madame Dupré was also very anxious to gain tidings of the Ouden family, endeavors were made also to trace them. After some time the Countess Delancy and her husband were found; they were residing in a very pretty villa residence in Sussex. The joy and rapture of the mother and daughter, when at length they met, is beyond our power of description; the countess was so overcome that she had scarcely the power to express the rapture she felt. The count was a tall and very handsome man, and felt proud of the beautiful child restored to him through the courage and energy of Henry Barlow and Alfred Hammond; he knew not how to express to them, and to Captain Barlow, his deep sense of gratitude.

The Count Delancy was one of those fortunate emigrants that possessed sufficient means to reside in England in great comfort, if not elegance, waiting and hoping for better times. After a delightful week spent at Myrtle Hill, the Count and Countess Delancy and Rosina, and also Madame Dupré — to whom they offered an asylum till some intelligence of the Countess d'Ouden and daughters was obtained — prepared to set out for their residence in Sussex.

"And now, dear Henry," said Rosina, the evening before departure — "now, that all our troubles are over, surely you will not, as you say, persist in again going to sea. Oh! think of all you suffered aboard that horrid privateer!"

"And yet, my dear little friend, without that same privateer, the *Fury* — a fury her ill-starred commander certainly was — I should never have had the pleasure of seeing you, and of being the means of restoring you to your dear mother; so that, after all, we must allow some merit to the privateer."

"Yes, all that is true," said Rosina; " still I do not see, now that you have escaped all kinds of perils, why you wish to tempt fate again. Come, you will promise not to go to sea?"

Henry laughed gayly; and yet there was so much love and affection in the beautiful eyes of that young girl, that Henry said in a soothing tone, "You would not wish, surely, dear Rosina, that I should draw back whilst England requires the assistance of her sons! You would not have me stay ashore, and my dear father perilling his life for his king and country! Look at our dear friend, Magnus; he is already away — and just eighteen — already a lieutenant! I long to imitate him!" Rosina said no more; she petted Mignon the poodle, kissed his glossy head, and the dog looked at her as much as to say — "I will not leave you!"

From the Countess Delancy they learned what occurred to her, after her separation from her daughter, on the terrible night when the revolutionary troops entered Quiberon. The tremendous rush of the crowd tore the daughter from the mother's grasp, and, impelled along by the terrified fugitives, she had no power to resist. What with fatigue, her agony of mind, and the terrible bruises she received, she fainted; and would, no doubt, have been severely hurt, if not killed, had not a French gentleman, one of the fugitives, lifted her up and placed her in one of the men-of-war boats. A little water restored her to consciousness. The mother, in her distraction, wished to return; but Monsieur Dupré — the gentleman who had so kindly assisted her, and who had a wife and sister also in charge — showed her the impossibility and the inutility of her doing so; he also endeavored to convince her that her daughter would be taken care of by some kind persons, who would soon discover who she was. The bereaved mother could but weep. They were taken aboard a British man-of-war, and were treated with great kindness and humanity. Broken-hearted and sick, the Countess Delancy was landed at Plymouth, and at once took to her bed, ill and unable to exert herself. But Monsieur Dupré, who knew her husband was in England, exerted himself to find him, and succeeded; and thus some consolation in the meeting with her husband was afforded to the disconsolate mother.

Taking a most affectionate leave of Captain Barlow and his kind family, the Delancys departed — Rosina with tears in her eyes; but Henry promised never to forget his young and beautiful friend, and, whenever the war should cease, he would seek their residence. Captain Barlow and his son Henry then went to spend a few days at Deer Park with the now happy Mr. and Mrs. Hammond, previous to embarking aboard the *Revolutionaire;* aboard this noble frigate Henry was to finish his term of midshipman.

Alfred, as good as his word, sent a confidential person, with the consent of his father, to inquire after the children of poor Lieutenant Ross. They were found in sad affliction at the loss of a kind and affectionate father, and with very small means to subsist upon. The two boys were placed in first-rate schools, and the two girls were to become inmates of Deer Park, previous to going also to school; the youngest, Ellen, was a most engaging and lovely girl of fourteen. There was no fear of Alfred's return to a life of indolence; his better nature was completely roused, his inertness shaken off. Having great wealth, he resolved that others should benefit by it, and his plans, aided by his father, were well calculated to insure the happiness of many besides his own.

Six years of war followed, and then the peace of 1802 was proclaimed between Great Britain and France. Rear-admiral Barlow retired from the service, to seek the repose he so well merited. Henry was, at the conclusion of the war, one of the youngest commanders in the British service — having distinguished himself in several brilliant and fortunate actions.

If, during these long and eventful years, Rosina Delancy treasured the memory of her young protector in her heart, so did the young commander retain a vivid and intense remembrance of the innocent and beautiful girl he had rescued from so many perils. Oftentimes the prophecy of good Dame Moulin rose to his memory — "In Rosina Delancy you see your future bride!" — did Rosina remember him? was a question often asked — now the question was to be solved.

The Count and Countess Delancy were still residing in their little villa in Sussex; thither the young commander bent his steps. Rosina Delancy had grown up into one of the loveliest young women England could boast of containing within her boundaries. She was just turned eighteen. Every attention a fond and accomplished mother could bestow, assisted by the best masters, was lavishly conferred upon the fair French girl, and she amply repaid care and tuition.

The young couple met, as they had parted, with unshaken fondness and devotion. Years had neither weakened nor obliterated the memory of the past. Rosina no longer beheld the ardent, enthusiastic boy — in his place stood the young and gallant commander in many a glorious fight. Still Rosina beheld but Henry Barlow, and he Rosina.

The Count and Countess Delancy were about to return to France to accept the very liberal offers of the French Government to emigrants — the count being willing to acknowledge the wise and consistent rule of the first consul.

Before the departure of the count and countess, Rosina became the happy bride of the young commander, who, in receiving the hand of one whose image he treasured in his heart through six years of a turbulent life, obtained the greatest reward his ambition could desire. Alfred Hammond, himself a benedict, was present with his young and interesting bride — no other than Ellen Ross, to whom he had become fondly attached. No doubt that affection was first awakened by the memory of her poor father's kindness to him aboard the *Fury*.

After the ceremony, witnessed by the united families of the bride and bridegroom, the Count and Countess Delancy, the Countess d'Ouden, and Madame Dupré set out for Paris, — the Countess d'Ouden having received letters from her husband, who, after all, escaped the perils that beset him.

Some months after his marriage, Captain and Mrs. Barlow set out for Paris to stay a short time with the Count and Countess Delancy, and then, as his fair bride ardently desired, to visit Brittany, and reward all those who might be living, and who had acted so conspicuous a part in aiding their escape. Accordingly they proceeded to Paris, and remained a week with Rosina's parents.

A mighty change had come over the fortunes of the Republic. The miserable squalor of the Jacobin era, the frivolities and licentiousness of the Directory, was succeeded by a courtly splendor (mingled by a chasteness and elegance of manners remarkable. The mind of the first consul was imbued with a sincere love of order and propriety, and he took very good care to enforce this upon the brilliant circle that surrounded him and his amiable Josephine).

The residence of the first consul was in the palace of the Tuileries, the palace of the kings of France, which he thoroughly purified of its republican insigna — for it was fitted up with a gorgeous magnificence befitting the state of a great monarch. In this palace he held brilliant levees, and gave sumptuous entertainments.

Paris was thronged with strangers from every part of the world, but the military predominated. To Captain Barlow's intense satisfaction, he again met the Count d'Ouden and General Moreau. Their meeting was a source of mutual pleasure. General Moreau heard his young friend's adventures with surprise and great interest; when introduced to his fair and beautiful bride — whom he was led to understand was the grand-daughter of the brave old Marquis Delancy — he was much moved, for well he remembered the cruel slaughter of him and the gallant de Sombreul.

The general stated that, finding they did not arrive in Paris, he made most diligent inquiries after him and Alfred. The governor of the prison at Nantes declared that they had left that prison under the charge of two men; that they were set upon by a band of brigands, who murdered the two jailers, but what became of the two lads it was impossible to say.

"I was ordered to join the army of the Rhine," continued the general, " and, though grieved at your uncertain fate, I could but obey my orders." The Count d'Ouden — we call him count, though titles were not then recognized in France, albeit the day was rapidly approaching for their restoration — the count stated that, after their flight into the salt marshes of Guerande, his followers got quite dispirited and longed to recross the Loire. After incredible sufferings and marvellous escapes, he succeeded in crossing the Loire above Nazaire, and found La Rochejaqueline — he being slain, the war in the Vendée ceased; he then joined Charette, who, however, was taken prisoner, conveyed to Nantes, and shot. The count then remained in obscurity, suffering great privations, and finding an escape to England impossible; finally, he accepted the liberal terms of Napoleon to restore peace to the Vendée, and came up to Paris; his estate of Ouden was restored, but his possessions in Poictu were sold; but he was quite content, for the Ouden property was extensive, and the château was to be restored.

The Count and Countess Delancy, having settled all their affairs in Paris, set out to visit their restored estates in company with Captain and Mrs. Barlow. Very different indeed was the state of the French provinces they passed through on their way to La Roche Bernard. No brigands haunted the roads, or wild bands roved the country, plundering châteaus, and rendering a residence without a walled town a piece of temerity. Agricultural labor was restored — alas! through what seas of blood did the regenerators of France wade to obtain this end! On reaching La Roche Bernard, Captain Barlow's first inquiry was for honest François Goheir, the skipper of the chasse-marée *Clemence*. The old man was alive and hearty, but had resigned the command of his craft to his son, and was living with his old dame in a neat cottage on the banks of the Villaine. The skipper was vastly proud of the visit paid him, and looked with surprise and admiration at the handsome couple who shook him so heartily and warmly by the hand.

"And what did they say to you, François," said Rosina, "when you came back, after putting us aboard the French ship?"

"Ah, madame"—and the old man's eyes twinkled with a very knowing expression—"the good people aboard the *Sars-Culotte* thought I had regained possession of my craft, and put you all prisoners aboard the frigate, and gave me great praise. I took it, and the sum they gave me for the use of my boat, and said nothing. But that rascally jailer came to a bad end!"

"How so, François?" demanded Captain Barlow.

"Why, monsieur, he went with a party into the salt marsh to catch our good Count d'Ouden; and, getting separated from those who knew the paths through the marsh, he got into a hole, and, before any one could get to his assistance, down he went—but he deserved no better!"

Captain and Mrs. Barlow then took leave of the worthy skipper, leaving him a substantial remembrance of their visit. Their next visit was to Château d Ouden, and to the farm of Janette—then a married woman, and the mother of two fine children. An hour or two was spent in rambling over its ruined chambers; Henry recalling to Rosina every little incident that had occurred there—and then they gazed out from the window upon the broad waters of the Villaine, their hearts full of happiness and thankfulness.

Janette received them with a delighted and surprised manner; she gazed at the handsome couple. saying, "Madame! can six years have made this change?" Henry smiled, as he kissed her pretty little girl of three years of age and put a costly necklace on her neck; "here is one that will remind you, Janette, of how time passes—but where is your husband?"

"At Blavet, monsieur, to purchase sheep; he will be so vexed!"

Here again the grateful couple left tokens of their gratitude, and then entered their carriage to proceed to Pont Château, to visit Monsieur St. Amand and good Dame Moulin. Rosina longed to show the good priest his once favorite poodle, Mignon; though years had robbed her of many of her playful tricks, she was yet sleek and handsome, and wonderfully sagacious.

The worthy priest was now happy. The Almighty was again worshipped throughout France. The chapels were again crowded with devout and sincere Christians. The dying received the rites of the church, and he himself was once more the pastor of his flock.

Monsieur St. Amand received Henry and his partner with tears of pleasure and emotion; as he gave them his blessing, he said, " My dear children ! God was pleased to try you by persecution and suffering, but you have passed through the fire unscathed; great is his mercy ! "

That night Henry and Rosina, as we love still to call our hero and heroine, passed at Monsieur St. Amand's cottage, for good Dame Moulin was to arrive in the morning. Margaret of the Mill came, still in looks hale, active, and hearty. It was not without deep emotion she beheld the two she loved, and now united. For some moments, after embracing Rosina, she could do nothing but gaze into her sweet, interesting features; then, brushing away a tear, she turned to Henry, saying with a smile, " And this is the disbelieving boy who laughed at our traditions — who thought the vision of poor Madeleine and the chariot of death the remnants of a barbarous age and rank superstitions; and yet," she added sadly, " the noble Delancy, the gallant de Sombreul, and the Bishop of Dol — seen in the *Karraquel-an ancow* by Madelcinc — all perished! the saints preserve us! Ah! well," she added, with her old smile, "if you laughed at our traditions, you, at all events, believed in Margaret of the Mill's prophecy!"

"Yes, dame," said Henry, looking with fond devotion into the expressive features of Rosina; "yes! and for this true happiness, the glory of my life, I have to thank you, after Providence!"

And thus we end our story of the young adventurers. If their cruise aboard the privateer *Fury*, caused Henry and Alfred to endure much suffering and privation, it yet had most beneficial effects. It brought out the bright, noble, and enduring character of Henry in a most prominent manner, whilst to Alfred its effects were invaluable. He certainly possessed within his breast the seeds of much good, but they lay as if upon a barren soil. Adversity, and the severe trials he endured, added to the bright example of a cousin he dearly loved, caused them to take root, and ever after to flourish.

THE END.